The
Alchemist
Who Survived
Now Dreams of a Quiet City Life

Usata Nonohara

Illustration by **OX**

YEN ON

New York

Usata Nonohara

Cover art by **OX**   Translation by Erin Husson

IKINOKORI RENKINJUTSUSHI HA MACHI DE SHIZUKANI KURASHITAI
Volume 1
©Usata Nonohara 2017
First published in Japan in 2017 by KADOKAWA CORPORATION, Tokyo.
English translation rights arranged with KADOKAWA CORPORATION, Tokyo through TUTTLE-MORI AGENCY, INC., Tokyo.

English translation © 2019 by Yen Press, LLC

Yen On
150 West 30th Street, 19th Floor
New York, NY 10001

Visit us at yenpress.com ★ facebook.com/yenpress ★ twitter.com/yenpress
★ yenpress.tumblr.com ★ instagram.com/yenpress

First Yen On Edition: September 2019

Yen On is an imprint of Yen Press, LLC.
The Yen On name and logo are trademarks of Yen Press, LLC.

Library of Congress Cataloging-in-Publication Data
Names: Nonohara, Usata, author. | ox (Illustrator), illustrator. | Husson, Erin, translator.
Title: The alchemist who survived now dreams of a quiet city life / Usata Nonohara ; illustration by ox ; translation by Erin Husson.
Other titles: Ikinokori renkinjutsushi ha machi de shizukani kurashitai. English
Description: First Yen On edition. | New York : Yen On, 2019-
Identifiers: LCCN 2019020720 | ISBN 9781975385514 (v. 1 : pbk.)
Subjects: | CYAC: Fantasy. | Magic—Fiction. | Alchemists—Fiction.
Classification: LCC PZ7.1.N639 Al 2019 | DDC [Fic]—dc23
LC record available at https://lccn.loc.gov/2019020720

ISBNs: 978-1-9753-8551-4 (paperback)
978-1-9753-3160-3 (ebook)

10 9 8 7 6 5 4 3

LSC-C

Printed in the United States of America

The Alchemist Who Survived Now Dreams of a Quiet City Life

01

Hey!
The Japanese edition of this novel begins with a manga section. To preserve the right-to-left reading orientation of the material, we've moved that section to the back of the book, so flip to the end, read that first, then come back here to enjoy the rest of the story!

The Alchemist Who Survived Now Dreams of a Quiet City Life

OI Contents

und schwarzer Erden

und weißer Erden

Rotte

△ uro

△ Far

♄ Z ♂ ☉

Schwarz   graw   Rot

Rott

AQVA·PIETAS

HVMILITAS

sanctus   MA   SPIRIT   San

ANI

Lapis philosophor

CORPVS

IGNIS·PVRITAS

PROLOGUE

Destruction and Awakening

01

That day, in a dark, cramped cellar that eerily resembled a grave, a lone girl awoke.

Ba-dum.

Her stopped heart sprang to life.

Her congealed blood began to circulate again; her lungs sought oxygen.

When she inhaled with a wheeze, a massive cloud of dust flew into her mouth.

"Hack, cough, cough, gack."

Can't...breathe... Air, fresh air...

Her head pounded from the lack of oxygen, and the first thing she noticed was how painful it was to breathe.

"Ventilate."

Between her parched throat and stinging lips and tongue, she couldn't manage to speak, but as long as she knew the incantation by heart, she could still cast the spell silently. Slowly but surely, the dust and stagnant air in the room were replaced with lifestyle magic, and she could finally breathe normally again.

Now, how did I end up here again...?

The girl pondered, her mind still foggy from the lack of oxygen. Although she wanted to scope out her surroundings, her eyes refused to focus, and she could only faintly feel the light shining through the ceiling from the back of the room.

It seemed she'd been asleep for a very long time. Her stiffened joints screamed in pain as she tried to get up, making awful cracking noises with her every movement. She managed to sit upright, her face contorting in pain from a splitting headache as she cupped her weakened hands together in the shape of a bowl.

"Drops of Life."

Droplets of water glowing white filled the palms of her hands. The portion that spilled through the gaps in her fingers ran along her arms and dripped from her elbows, but it dissolved into thin air before it could wet her clothes. This was Drops of Life, an earthly blessing sourced from the soil's ley lines.

Although most of it had already spilled from her hands, when she brought the rest to her lips, it proceeded to spread throughout her withered body. The water moistened her cracked throat, lubricated her joints, boosted her circulation, and made her headache melt away. Every cell in her body was invigorated. Had any onlookers been present, they surely would have gawked at this miracle liquid.

Only the alchemists with alchemic skills could use Drops of Life, and it was thanks to this liquid that the girl, Mariela, at last remembered why she was here.

"The Stampede."

02

The Kingdom of Endalsia, where Mariela lived, was a small country bordered by the Fell Forest and a steep mountain range. The kingdom had to be wary of the monsters that lived in the forest, but the mountain range acted as a natural fortification that both protected the kingdom's people and provided an abundance of minerals. Endalsia was small, and there wasn't much space for cultivation, but the land blessed the people with an abundance of bountiful harvests.

The multitude of blessings more than made up for the danger of the monsters in the forest, and Endalsia prospered as a small but powerful nation.

People from all walks of life gathered here, from the lowest-ranking nobleman looking to make a name for himself, or even a penniless villager, all the way to the most experienced adventurers and the merchants who served them all. The kingdom was always in need of adventurers to cull the monsters in the Fell Forest, and it was rich enough to provide for them.

Those who struggled to make ends meet were told to go to Endalsia.

In the blink of an eye, it had become a nation consisting of two main groups: the subjects who coveted the peace and tranquility found within its walls and the adventurers who battled the monsters near the forest.

Although some might call them adventurers, they were essentially just refugees who lacked adequate support. Many perished without ever managing to escape their day-to-day struggles, but some stubborn few were able to rise among the ranks and build themselves a small fortune. A vibrant food culture blossomed within Endalsia thanks to the earth's bounty and the region's multicultural cuisine, while the improvements in armor smithing developed to combat monsters were further boosted by the rare materials found in the Fell Forest. The marketplace was bursting with a wide variety of goods, and along the wall's exterior were bars, gambling parlors, and bordellos that served adventurers who were just passing through. At some point this region became known as the Citadel City. The place was full of people and goods and was brimming with enthusiasm and ripe opportunities.

Mariela was an orphan within the Citadel City.

She had no recollection of her parents. As with most orphans, she was probably the result of an encounter between an adventurer and one of the bordello women, immediately cast into an orphanage the moment she was born.

Yet, she never considered herself unfortunate.

There were many children just like her, and most of all, her mother had written the name Mariela on her swaddling clothes. This was her *True Name*, one given to her by a blood relative, something necessary to harness the world's powers and utilize skills. Possessing this True Name was what led Mariela to be taken in by an alchemy master before eventually becoming a successful alchemist herself.

Alchemic skills weren't uncommon, and potions weren't as easy to use as healing magic. Alchemy wasn't a particularly profitable trade, but she was able to eke out a living in the small cottage her teacher had left her on the edge of the Fell Forest. Though she wasn't wealthy, she enjoyed crafting a variety of potions, and living on the edge of a forest suited someone like her who was lacking in social graces.

She thought her modest way of life would continue forever—until the day it met an abrupt end.

Why the Stampede happened was beyond the comprehension of a humble alchemist like Mariela.

Once the desperate screams of those trying to escape alerted everyone to the Stampede, the Kingdom of Endalsia shut its outer gate tight. The swarm of monsters came crashing down like a tidal wave and threw the Citadel City into utter chaos.

Adventurers young and old took up arms with a rallying cry: "Protect our town! Now is the time for glory!"

Some of those unable to fight packed the narrow roads like sardines and evacuated to the mountains, while others who hoped to ride it out barricaded themselves in their homes.

Mariela hurried to the cottage her master had left her. She didn't think she'd make it in time to evacuate, and there was nowhere in town to take shelter. The thin wooden walls of her house would be as fragile as scraps of paper in the face of the horde.

Monsters reacted to human magic.

Long ago, her master taught her that rampaging monsters were very perceptive of human magic, and in such situations, even wards wouldn't be effective.

So if the creatures from the Fell Forest ever grew out of control…

Just as her master had instructed, she rushed to her cellar and locked the heavy iron door securely shut.

To minimize the chance of being detected, she chose not to use illumination magic. Instead, she lit an oil lantern with a substantial supply of fuel and took out a large piece of parchment from a box in the corner of the room. In the dim light, she spread the huge three-foot-square sheet on the floor and checked the magic circle inscribed on it for any defects.

This was a last resort, her master had said, and she'd reluctantly prepared it.

Stolen from the monsters, this parchment was worth a month of Mariela's earnings, and the ink used to inscribe the magic circle was even more expensive; it was specially crafted from dissolved magical gems. Even the magic circle itself was dense and difficult to create, and she had drawn it over a period of several months so as to not waste the expensive materials.

When her master told her that creating this circle would serve as her final certification exam, Mariela had thought, *What a waste!* but thank goodness she'd done it.

The cellar was so small that the petite young woman felt her head might touch the ceiling merely by standing. If she sprawled out on the floor, she and the parchment would be enough to completely cover it. But unlike the house, it was sturdy, built from stone, and the iron door wouldn't break even if it was trampled by monsters. If they sensed that someone was inside, however, they would dig her out in an instant.

Unless every last monster was killed, the Stampede wouldn't stop until all the humans were dead.

She could hear the earth trembling. The swarm was coming.

Mariela lay down on top of the magic circle.

I'm scared.

In the cramped, dark cellar, the flame in the oil lantern trembled.

I'm so scared.

How many monsters were coming? The rumbling was getting closer.

I'm really, really scared. Somebody, anybody...!

Mariela's extremities were colder than the stone floor, and her thoughts became overtaken by fear.

If I don't trigger the magic circle correctly... If this cellar can't withstand the weight of the monsters, then I'll...

Her breathing grew shallow and quick, and her heart hammered so loudly, she was sure the swarm could hear it. As the tremors grew, both the cellar and the lantern shook, making the flame flicker and dance.

I'm scared. I'm so, so scared. I don't want to die here all alone.

Just as she felt as if she would be swallowed by fear, Mariela activated the Magic Circle of Suspended Animation.

03

Ah, right, she had fled to her cellar and activated the Magic Circle of Suspended Animation.

"I survived."

The spell was meant to revive her once the danger had passed. Thanks to the Drops of Life, her sight had mostly recovered, and she could tell that the sunbeams at her feet were coming from the entrance in the ceiling. It looked as if the door had collapsed.

There was no sign of any wind or rain inside the cellar, so perhaps it happened fairly recently.

When she went to exit, she found the wooden ladder had rotted away; maybe the tremors from the Stampede had weakened it. Using gaps and protrusions in the wall's stone framework as footholds, she managed to clamber out of the cellar.

"Hmm."

Mariela was caught by surprise upon emerging aboveground. The spot where her house should have been was now overgrown with trees and vegetation.

"Guess it's safe to say there's no trace left of my cottage. Must've been swallowed by the Stampede," she muttered as she pulled up a bundle of herbs growing at her feet. "This is a medicinal herb I grew in my garden… Why's the entire ground covered in it?!"

The total disappearance of her house suggested she'd been gone for at least a few decades at the absolute best. Mariela held her head. She'd felt something was strange since the moment she awoke. Her body had been extremely stiff, and both the ladder and the iron door were in ruins.

"Did the Magic Circle of Suspended Animation fail somehow?"

It shouldn't have. She'd checked everything before activating it.

The flickering lantern light may have been faint, but she must have examined every inch of the parchment. She remembered the lantern's flame as if it were just yesterday.

"Hmm? The lantern's…flame?

"Ohhh…" With a miserable groan, Mariela sank into a crouch.

She normally used illumination magic, so she forgot—lighting a fire in a locked room would just deplete all the oxygen. Even when the Stampede was over, she must have continued to sleep indefinitely until the entrance door rotted away.

"How long was I asleep...?!"

Mariela's grief echoed fruitlessly through the forest.

Her misery lasted about ten minutes. She finally stopped holding her head and began plucking herbs.

"Dehydrate! Dehydrate! Deeehyyydraaate!"

"Aaargh, without a bag, this is such a pain. I'll have to hang these all from my waist to keep both hands free. And the place is overgrown with nothing but cheap plants. All I can make with these are monster wards and low-grade salves."

Mariela complained as she harvested herbs, dried them with alchemy, and then hung them from her waist. In no time, the dried plants completely encircled her hips like a grass skirt, lending her an indigenous sort of look. Before, her style had been kinda plain, but at least it was...wholesome? Now the grass skirt just made her uncool. She looked nothing like a sixteen-year-old girl.

"Hee-hee-hee... If I wrap myself in this many monster-warding herbs, the weak ones won't come after me. Whee, an anti-monster skiiirt!"

As she playfully shook her hips and rummaged around in the herbs to make a few more bundles, she produced five small empty bottles from her waist pouch.

"Dehydrate, Pulverize, Drops of Life, Extract Essence, Separate Dregs, Condense, Anchor Essence, Enclose."

Using her alchemic skills in quick succession, she finished a potion in moments. She then crafted a monster-warding potion with the same process and stored it in her pouch. Even if she ran into a bit of trouble on the way, she could probably make it to town just with these.

A potion, to put it simply, was a magical medicine that used Drops of Life to boost an herb's efficacy to its maximum potential.

For example, there was the herb curique, which was used in low-grade heal potions. If you simply ground it up and applied the paste directly to the affected area, it could sterilize the wound, stop any bleeding, and encourage healing, among other things. Some injuries would heal within a few days; however, taking it orally had no effect.

Dissolving it with Drops of Life, though, turned the paste into a magical medicine that immediately closed a wound when applied directly, and ingesting it not only healed external injuries but restored one's strength as well.

Immediate recovery was also possible with healing magic. However, because that kind of magic simply increased the patient's own ability to recover, using it to treat large wounds would cause a proportional rebound effect once the healing was complete. And for patients who were in poor physical shape, the restorative effect would likewise be weak.

Conversely, potions had no associated rebound effect because they used the power of Drops of Life. They were even effective on near-fatal wounds.

Drops of Life was an intangible form of energy originating from ley lines; it nurtured plants, gave strength to animals, and eventually dissolved into the atmosphere before returning to its original ley line. Said to be the source of all life, this power dwelled within the soil and was given form by alchemy. Therefore, even if it was fixed in place with *Anchor Essence*, it would fade in less than a year and turn into plain medicinal water.

Furthermore, any Drops of Life taken too far from the ley line it was drawn from would be lost.

Alchemy involved many processes that expended a proportionate amount of magical energy. Healing magic used less magical energy and fewer resources than creating a low-grade heal potion, so medical treatment was inexpensive. Many people earned pocket change on the streets of the Citadel City with healing magic, and as a consequence, low-grade heal potions sold for cheap there as well.

Specialist shops sold all kinds of expensive high-grade potions with unique effects. However, only people of certain occupations bought them, and these shops were managed by skilled master alchemists and their apprentices, so they had no room for someone like Mariela who lacked any connections.

Alchemic skills themselves weren't rare. In the Citadel City, there were more alchemy users than there were bakeries.

For Mariela, who had no combat skills to speak of, just being able to earn her daily bread with alchemy alone was something to be thankful for.

"Oh, skipira herbs."

One important source of her income had survived.

Mariela's custom potions combined a base of skipira herbs with several other kinds of plants for use by the bordellos' streetwalkers. Citadel specialty potion shops wouldn't display products made by a sixteen-year-old girl who wasn't even an apprentice, and even though curio shops also dealt in goods from the potion shops, they wouldn't buy them from a stranger like Mariela.

Mariela earned her meager daily income by opening a stall in the plaza and selling potions in addition to making deliveries to several small shops she'd become personally acquainted with.

Of course, the selling price was less than the market price, so she could make a profit only by growing the ingredients in her garden. A certain bordello caretaker zeroed in on her and offered a business proposal. He was most likely trying to replenish his stock with cheap potions and pocket the difference, even if they were low quality.

Contrary to the man's expectations, Mariela's potions were quite good and cheaper than anyone else's. Unbeknownst to Mariela herself, he made a killing selling the massive number he'd bought from her to bordellos all over the Citadel City. She was grateful to him for allowing her to remain self-sufficient once she was on her own.

Even if she'd known the truth and tried to negotiate a markup, the caretaker wasn't the kind of man who would let her. In fact, attempting as much would have most likely put her in danger. Mariela lived independently despite her limited means, but it was fair to say that it was because she was content with smaller profits and blissfully unaware that she was being exploited.

As she took a good look at her herb garden, she spotted other rare plants with unique effects that had survived.

"With these, maybe I can rebuild."

First, she needed to gather information in town. If she bought some vials and turned the herbs at her waist into potions, that would probably earn her enough to cover a night at an inn. She'd been sleeping on the stone floor of that cellar for ages. She wanted to clean herself off and, if possible, sleep in a nice, soft bed.

"Hopefully, the price of potions hasn't gone down."

Mariela set out toward the Citadel City, dried-herb skirt and all.

CHAPTER 1
The Ruined Capital

01

Daigis is an ivy-like plant that grows in the Fell Forest by absorbing magical energy drifting from the air. Bromominthra is well-known for its use as a monster repellent; it emits an odor that is undetectable to humans but unbearable for monsters.

Since monsters react to human magic, a warding potion made with these two ingredients would effectively conceal its user's presence. The only thing monsters would pick up would be the unpleasant smell.

Mariela's master had taught her that if she covered her roof and fence with daigis and planted bromominthra around her fence, she could even live within the Fell Forest itself. The cottage she'd inherited from her master was set up this way, and until the Stampede, she was able to live a peaceful life without trouble from monsters. When the Stampede occurred, however, the creatures were worked up into such a frenzy that they paid no mind to things like the stench of bromominthra. Since Mariela's cottage stood between the forest and the Citadel City, where the monsters could sense a human presence, the whole building had been razed to the ground.

Mariela sprinkled the newly created monster-warding potion over herself and headed out.

With this potion alone, monsters would avoid her, although the effectiveness varied depending on the species. That meant she could travel through the sparse parts of the Fell Forest without encountering any such beasts as long as she didn't make much noise. She guessed it was around noontime, as the sun was still high in the sky, but she wanted to reach town as quickly as possible. Judging from the ripened fruit on the trees and the state of flowering plants in the forest, it was probably around the end of summer. She didn't sense a high chance of rain from the bits of sky she could see through the gaps in the trees, but currently, she had no house to protect her from the elements, and what little savings she'd had were lost with her old home. The only valuables she had on hand were the low-grade potion she'd just created and the herbs at her waist. How much of a living could she expect to make with these?

After just a short while in the forest, she emerged onto a road used for carriage travel. The forest had changed; the animal trails she'd always used were gone, and the rows of trees were different. Even so, she had made it this far from memory.

Because the Kingdom of Endalsia was surrounded by steep mountains and the Fell Forest, the only way in or out was to pass through the mountain range or use the roads that wove through a gap between the foothills and the woods.

This was one of those roads, and it should have led to an expansive, abundant grain-producing region on the other side of the Fell Forest.

"The forest has taken over..."

However, there was no such area ahead; instead, the same gloomy woods continued onward.

What had happened to the Kingdom of Endalsia?

Though the region had vanished, the road still remained. It was narrower than Mariela remembered but appeared to see periodic human traffic; wagon tracks in the road told her it was still in use. If there were carriages, then human dwellings probably hadn't disappeared, either.

At any rate, Mariela was about to continue along the road toward the Citadel City when she heard animal cries, possibly wolves, as well as sounds of fighting.

Mariela couldn't fight. She had no combat skills, and she'd always been clumsy.

Normally, she would have run away at once, but she'd been on her feet since she woke up, and her senses were dulled. There was too much going on that she didn't understand; curiosity born from the desire to comprehend the situation before her led Mariela to turn toward the direction of the noise. She hid herself in the trees along the edge of the road as she crept forward, keeping an eye on things from the shadows.

Forest wolves and... Are those carriages?

The drivers of three ironclad carriages were under attack.

Each vehicle was covered with crude iron plates and had only a small window at the front for visibility and holes for shooting bow guns. Upon further inspection, she saw that the iron plates had been pieced back together many times; scars from monsters' claws and teeth remained along the exterior. She could tell this crowd had frequent brushes with death.

Two bipedal carnivores called raptors were tied to the armored carriages. These ferocious creatures had tough skin, and they shrugged off the likes of low-grade monsters, but they were difficult to train and rarely seen within the Citadel City. Mariela had never seen any carriages this heavily armored, period.

But more than anything, it was the sheer number of forest

wolves swarming the carriages that made Mariela gasp. They had surrounded the armored vehicles from the rear as they made for the Citadel City. There must have been around a hundred of them.

Forest wolves were twice the size of a normal wolf. They were a comparatively weak type of monster within the Fell Forest, closer to regular beasts, but they moved in packs and followed a designated leader. Once they'd chosen something as their prey, they would chase it down for miles upon miles, even teaming up with other packs of forest wolves if they were unable to take down their target alone.

Perhaps the situation here was the same. How long had these carriages been traveling along while enduring these forest wolves' attacks? Their iron exterior showed numerous scratches, and some of the plates had fallen off.

The raptors' riders were fighting back—one with a black spear and one with a sword—but their heavy armor impeded their movement. Though protected from the fangs of the beasts, they seemed to be having a difficult time against the rapid succession of incoming attacks.

The wind began spiraling into a vortex around the spear (a spear technique, perhaps?), and a moment later, a sharp blow to one of the frontline forest wolves turned it into a piece of meat. However, it was all for nothing as another of the beasts rushed in to fill the gap.

Crossbow arrows flew out of the holes in the armored carriages at the forest wolves trying to tear off the wheels. The arrows struck them in the head and sent them tumbling to the ground. Just before their fangs and claws could strike the rear carriage, the beasts appeared to crash into an invisible wall. Any skilled combatant would have recognized this as an extremely safe and reliable extermination tactic. The group of armored carriages had rushed through the Fell Forest while avoiding monsters, and now the forest wolves that had followed them this close to town were being herded for collective slaughter.

However, Mariela, who'd never witnessed a battle before, didn't know this. All she saw was a massive pack of forest wolves attacking the armored carriages on all sides, depleting their defenses.

They're completely surrounded! And those things are forest wolves, right?

Such a horribly large group of them surrounding the carriages and attacking in waves with sharp fangs and lightning-quick movement!

This looks bad! I've gotta help. After all, they're in just as much trouble as I am.

Mariella opened the monster-warding potion and tossed it toward the center of the pack with a "Hiii-ya!" Due to her poor control, the throw sent the bottle hurtling through the air and scattered the contents of the potion all over the place.

"GRARARRR!"

All at once, every single forest wolf turned and fled.

These were wolves, after all. They had a sharp sense of smell, sharp enough to be repelled by the stench of this particular potion.

That's why sprinkling one of those potions on yourself would ensure you'd never encounter the beasts—or at the very least, you could easily drive them away.

Mariela's monster-warding potion must have been strong. To a human, it was nothing more than plain, odorless water, but it would be an especially pungent stench to a forest wolf. That foul-smelling concoction had fallen from the sky and landed on the pack. Their tight formation ended up backfiring as every last drop of potion spilled onto them. Those it landed on desperately chased after their pack mates, who in turn fled from the stench. All par for the course for close-knit monsters like forest wolves. This was a perfect demonstration of their preference for traveling in packs as well as their energy to chase enemies to the ends of the earth, and now they'd begun a fierce game of tag with one another.

It used to be customary to purchase monster-warding potions when preparing to travel along the main road, and you could do so cheaply even at the border between the kingdom and the forest. Just five coppers could allow you to travel through the sparse areas of the forest—let alone the main road—without encountering any monsters.

I mean, even a little kid would know that, right? Maybe they forgot to buy one. Or maybe they lost it along the way? There's no way they don't know, right?

Once she'd confirmed that the forest wolves had dispersed, Mariela approached the main road. The two iron-carriage cavalrymen who'd been fighting the wolves appeared dumbfounded as their eyes traveled from the direction in which the wolves had disappeared to the potion bottle on the ground. One of them turned and addressed Mariela.

"Was that a monster-warding potion just now?"

Aha, they do *know.*

She felt a bit awkward, but in any case, these were the first humans she'd run into since waking up. Surely they'd be able to give her some information.

It'd be real nice if I got a reward for saving their necks...

With not even a single copper coin in her purse, Mariela summoned her friendliest smile as she answered.

"Yes. I wasn't sure if you needed it, but I wanted to help however I could."

The taller cavalryman dismounted his raptor, removed his helmet, and took several steps in her direction. As he got closer, he was so overwhelmingly large that he seemed to tower over her.

His lean features gave the impression of a seasoned adventurer, and he looked to be around thirty years old. His watchful eyes, common for skilled adventurers, gazed down from under thick dark-brown eyebrows. This man appeared to be the leader of the iron carriages. Along with his strong build, he carried an air of dignity about him.

"No, you really did us a service there. Bringing those forest wolves all the way to town would have put the people in danger, and we weren't having an easy time of things. My name is Dick, captain of the Black Iron Freight Corps. Might you be a forest spirit?"

His speech was very courteous, but he was bizarrely mistaken about her.

"F-forest spirit?"

Mariela tilted her head to the side ever so slightly, her most practiced smile still plastered across her face. Certainly, there were spirits who took on the form of humans, but she was an actual, physical person, and she didn't glow like a spirit, either. How strange it would be if she did.

"Th-these are just to keep monsters away!" she hastened to explain, thinking he'd gotten that impression from her grass skirt. It was bad enough to be mistaken for a forest spirit, but she had no intention of having this guy think she was part of some tribe of grass skirt–wearing natives.

"Oh, no, that's not it. It's just, forest spirits don't attack people like monsters do; in fact, I hear they actually help. There are stories of spirits giving herbs to a child gathering them for her sick mother and then showing her the way out, or leading an injured hunter to a spring. You often hear those kinds of tales about the Fell Forest, too. I was just speaking hypothetically."

The giant of a man introducing himself as Dick scratched his cheek, somewhat embarrassed. Forest spirits, unlike those of fire or water or the other Four Great Elementals, didn't lend their powers to people who performed certain skills or magic spells, nor was there any known way to summon these beings. They were inherently friendly toward people and considered to be symbols of good fortune, so perhaps he was hoping to meet one.

"Aw c'mooon, Captain. Obviously, she's not a forest spirit. She's clearly a girl no matter how ya look at her."

Just when Mariela had been wondering how to respond, a calm voice interjected.

A young man with hair the color of straw stepped down from one of the hunks of iron. He appeared to be around sixteen or seventeen years old, roughly Mariela's age. The young man's sharp eyes almost disappeared into a broad, affable smile.

"No, it's just, she looks different."

"This is a monster-warding skirt." Mariela tried to draw attention to her herb dress's functionality as opposed to its appearance.

"Anyway, are you from the Labyrinth City?" Captain Dick quickly brushed aside her attempt at an explanation. It didn't seem to make any difference to him what the grass skirt was. Perhaps because he now knew he was speaking to a human, he immediately dropped into a more blunt manner of speech.

He was just a short distance away from Mariela now. This

large, stern man clad in heavy armor over his muscular frame was rather daunting, and Mariela instinctively took a step back.

"Hey, hey, that was a monster-warding potion you used just now, yeah? Got any more of 'em?" The smiley youth cut in on Captain Dick before Mariela could reply.

Whoa, this guy is way too chummy! Interrupting his captain like that, really? And what's this Labyrinth City?

When she glanced at Dick, she noticed he was examining her closely.

Between this and the smiley youth's overly friendly attitude, Mariela felt rather uncomfortable. The heck was with the reaction to her cheap potion? This transportation crew had been traveling in armored carriages through the main road of the Fell Forest without any monster repellant. And then there was a place called the Labyrinth City she'd never even heard of. What had happened while she was asleep?

"I only have these potions left. I need money, so I was on my way to sell them," she answered cautiously. She felt a slight twinge of regret at having rushed into things out of sheer loneliness, but she nevertheless opened her pouch and showed them its contents. It wasn't a lie, nor was she telling them any more than they needed to know.

"Whoa, three monster-warding potions and five low-grade heal potions? That really was a hot commodity you used there."

Although the young man was still some distance from her, he recognized the contents of the pouch.

He's gotta be more than ten steps away from me...but his eyes widened in an instant. Seriously, they're practically glowing!

At the words *hot commodity*, Captain Dick glanced at the young man and then took a step toward Mariela while continuing the conversation. Yet again, she felt uncomfortable as the gap she'd created between them closed once more. The captain's armor and their proximity to town didn't suggest him to be a thief, but if she was mistaken, he could be about to demand she hand over all her potions. Mariela clamped her mouth shut and steeled herself for what he might say next.

"Hrm. We could have managed, but the fact is that you helped us. What do you say we purchase those potions from you, including the one you used?"

"Huh? You'll buy my potions?"

Why had he been acting all intimidating just moments before? If he wanted to buy them, he should've come out and said it. Mariela cocked her head once more.

Score one customer! And I didn't even have to haggle with the guy.

When Mariela agreed to sell her potions, the captain responded with "I see; thank you," followed by a small sigh of relief.

Huh? Was Captain Dick relieved just now? I wonder if there's an herb shortage that's making potions hard to get. If that's the case, maybe he'd buy them at a good price. I'd love a hot meal and a bed to sleep in, even at a cheap inn. And since I'm fuzzy on a lot of things, maybe they could tell me what happened after the Stampede, too.

The sudden business negotiation had Mariela daydreaming about dinner.

"As for the payment... Let's see."

The other cavalryman, who'd been watching in silence this whole time, walked over to Captain Dick and whispered something in his ear.

Cut it out; this is bad for my heart. I don't need it stopping again.

What could they be talking about? Were they going to confiscate her potions after all? It wasn't as if they were terribly expensive, but she was trying as much as possible to avoid having Fell Forest mushrooms for dinner and then curling up to sleep under the eaves of some person's house. She'd be fine with foregoing meat as long as she had some warm soup. As Mariela's stress grew, Captain Dick finally named a price.

"How about five large silver coins for the nine potions?"

"......Huh?"

Mariela froze in shock.

Okay, calm down, Mariela. I swear I felt like my heart was gonna stop. But I'm fine; that's not going to happen. It still works. In fact, it's pounding like mad.

Back in the Citadel City, the market price of both monster-warding and low-grade heal potions was around five copper coins. In the forest, ten copper coins would be considered a good price, though it was a rip-off for the buyer.

Even as a reward, just a single silver coin—worth one hundred copper ones—for nine potions would have been a lucky sale.

He said large *silver coins, right? And five of them to boot. A large one equals ten regular silver coins, so that's...a fiftyfold increase? Has hyperinflation driven up the cost of goods? Like, does a loaf of bread cost fifty copper coins now?*

Mariela didn't know how Captain Dick would take her shocked reaction, but he looked a little flustered and corrected himself.

"Well, actually, we already saw the effects on the forest wolves earlier. The potion seemed freshly made. Hrm, how about one gold coin?"

Her shock had made the price go even higher.

Suddenly offering double? Which is two hundred times the normal price? Ummm, what's going on here?!

She had no idea why she'd ended up with an offer two hundred times what her potions were worth, but if prices in general hadn't gone up as much as potions had, she just might be able to enjoy a little meat in her soup that evening. Maybe she could even stay in a decent inn and have a bath.

In the end, Mariela sold Captain Dick the nine potions, including the one used on the forest wolves, for one gold coin. After she handed over the three monster-warding potions and five low-grade heal potions, he placed them in a special box inscribed with a magic circle for long-term storage and securely closed it.

Oh, that's one of those things you use to store high-grade potions. It's a magical apparatus that preserves Drops of Life's effects. I'm an alchemist, and I don't even have one. They're expensive and use magical gems for preservation.

If you took a potion too far away from the region it was created in or, more precisely, out of range of the ley line the Drops of Life was drawn from, the power would escape in an instant and render the potion into ordinary medicinal water. Putting the potion in a special storage box curbed degradation no matter where you took it, so it wouldn't be strange for a group that passed through multiple regions like the Black Iron Freight Corps to have one. Mariela had also heard of wealthy families who stored mid- and high-grade potions in this way as a substitute for household medicine.

Considering the cost of the magical gems required for storage, it wasn't worth it for low-grade potions that were originally inexpensive. But then, it was a different story for ones worth a large silver coin each.

The man who'd whispered to Captain Dick during the price negotiation provided the payment.

In contrast to the stern captain, he was slender and elegant. He had wavy, dusty-blond hair pulled back in a ponytail and emerald-green eyes. From his refined manners, he seemed like something of an aristocrat.

"Thank you for your help earlier, miss. I'm Malraux, lieutenant of the Black Iron Freight Corps."

"My name is Mariela. I'm sorry I didn't mention it sooner."

Having forgotten to introduce herself, Mariela took the opportunity to formally do so as she accepted Lieutenant Malraux's payment.

"Oh, nice! Gee, that's a great name. Really suits your style. I'm Lynx, nice to meetcha."

The smiley youth introduced himself in turn. It embarrassed Mariela a little to be praised to her face like this. Lieutenant Malraux resumed their conversation.

"Mariela, is it? Incidentally, do you have plans to sell other potions?"

Naturally, there was no smile in his eyes. He seemed to be saying that if she did have such plans, she should sell the potions to his group. Mariela wasn't great at conversations where the participants were feeling each other out.

"If there's anything you need, by all means ask" was her ambiguous reply. She was grateful they'd bought the potions at such a high price, but without being able to get a read on the situation, her sense of caution prevented her from giving an easy answer. *Man, that was rough*, she thought.

With the transaction completed, the Black Iron Freight Corps offered Mariela a ride to the Labyrinth City.

They recommended she sit in the coach box, but the inside of the nearly windowless iron carriage was terrifying, and she wanted to see how the outside world had changed after the Stampede. She'd reasoned that it wouldn't be long until they got to town, so they seated her in the back of the carriage on the ramp used for boarding and disembarking. She removed her grass skirt and hung it on the carriage so she wouldn't sit on it and crush it.

"Then I'll sit with ya," said Lynx as he settled beside her. Though the ramp was wide, two people were a tight fit.

Not that she didn't feel trapped, but the nonchalant way in which Lynx sidled up to her somehow didn't make her uncomfortable. Maybe because his body heat warmed her just a little after she'd been chilled to the bone on the stone cellar floor. At last, the reality sank in: She'd survived the Stampede.

02

The ironclad carriage continued along the main road. It wasn't moving very fast, and yet, it clattered and shook quite a bit. This was Mariela's first time in a carriage, and her backside had started to hurt from the long ride.

"Carriages really shake, huh? If it's this bad when we're going slowly, any faster and I'd get dizzy and fall right off the ramp."

"For sure. If we went full speed, your ass would break into four pieces."

"Liar."

"No lie. I'm tellin' you, it'd tear your belly into six pieces."

"! Carriages are nuts."

"Uh, I was just kiddin'."

This was the sort of conversation the two of them had. They were unlikely to encounter monsters this close to town, and the sun was still high in the sky. Lynx laughed as he told her she'd be fine, since they were continuing at this leisurely pace. Forest wolves didn't show up in this area at all—in fact, they even seemed to have run off deeper into the woods, so they weren't going to follow anyone into town.

"Anyway, where do you live, Mariela?"

"Well, I was living in the forest, but I guess I can't really do that anymore…"

Lynx seemed to be probing into her personal history, and she dodged the question with a flustered answer as she surveyed their surroundings.

The Citadel City should be very close. She wondered what on earth it was like now.

As they got closer, Mariela began to noticeably fidget, so Lynx spoke up.

"I toldja—we'll be fine. It's still daytime, and you won't see any zombies or wraiths in these parts. Heh, I never get used to it no matter how many times I come here, though. I mean, it's not exactly the kinda place that'll give you the warm fuzzies."

Right as Lynx said "warm fuzzies," the iron carriage entered the area where the Citadel City used to be.

She thought it might be like this. After all, Captain Dick had called it the "Labyrinth City."

But to Mariela, the Stampede felt as if it had happened just the day before, as if the Magic Circle of Suspended Animation had been activated mere hours ago.

Mariela remembered it all: the crowded buildings that stood in the Citadel City, the shops overflowing with goods and the mouth-watering aromas of street food wafting from the carts, the hustle and bustle of cheerful adventurers weaving through the crowds. She even remembered people's conversations and the expressions on their faces.

And yet.

There were no traces of the rows of buildings that leaned up against one another after being rebuilt and expanded time and again, and only a little stonework remained of the large stores that had once peddled every kind of item imaginable.

The irresistible smell of sweets and foreign cuisine from the street stalls had been replaced by the scent of trees, and she could hear no feverish hubbub.

"It's crazy how a city more prosperous than the imperial capital vanished in one night. Hey, you okay? You're white as a sheet."

The Corps men may have been lacking in social skills, but they still had some kind people in their ranks.

"I wonder if there were any survivors... If they were able to escape..."

Mariela knew her speech was strained, but she couldn't help it.

"Eh? They're livin' in the Labyrinth City, aren't they? Not the survivors per se but their offspring."

Thank goodness. I'm glad some of them made it.

Mariela almost breathed a sigh of relief, but she swallowed it instead.

"I mean, this is two hundred years ago we're talkin' about. It's practically like a fairy tale nowadays."

Two hundred years.

She'd been asleep for that long?

Mariela remained in stunned silence for an extraordinarily long time.

Lynx continued to talk, but Mariela didn't hear a word he said.

03

She remembered that day.

Although winter had finally passed, clouds still blanketed the sky all day long, and her room was very dark early that morning. The cottage her master had left behind was quite small and had only two rooms: one for sleeping and one for not sleeping. The former, of course, was the bedroom. The incredibly cramped little space had two beds and a small dresser between them.

After she was taken in at the age of eight, Mariela slept in the same bed as her master until she reached ten years old. She stopped only because she had complained that it was too hot that summer and was subsequently given her own bed. Her master took the opportunity to separate the two beds in the already-small room with a dresser, declaring with a laugh, "Now we've got private rooms. You need to be independent, too!" The top of the short dresser was constantly overflowing with all sorts of items belonging to her master: clothes tossed to the side, various cups or books that had been brought into bed. Or rather, they were overflowing onto Mariela's side of the room. Every day, she cleaned and wished her master would recognize the hypocrisy and be more self-sufficient, too.

Mariela had left the bedroom furniture as it was even after she had suddenly found herself alone. She had seen enough by then to know she should expect her master's return at any time. Mariela felt that way even after three years on her own there, despite enjoying how easy the cleaning had become. The top of the dresser was always tidy now.

The "not sleeping room" had a table and chairs, a washing basin on a kitchen range, and a shelf stacked with sundries. Any activity that wasn't sleeping happened here, from cooking and eating to potion-making, from reading and writing arithmetic to alchemy and even lessons.

Her master was disastrously bad at housework—cooking, cleaning, laundry—but extremely knowledgeable. In exchange for studying and doing chores, Mariela learned a great many things, some she might find useful, others perfectly pointless. For this reason, the room was always so lively that when she first started living there, she worried the monsters from the Fell Forest might notice them and attack.

Now it was entirely silent and dim. Without even turning on the light, Mariela had washed down yesterday's stale bread with some unappetizing soup made from mushrooms and herbs gathered in the forest.

A variety of herbs grew in the garden surrounding the house, and she picked the ones she needed, dried them, and tied them in a bundle. As always, she was going to the Citadel City to sell potions.

Among the fifty she'd prepared the day before, she placed twenty in a basket, hid the other thirty in the bundle of dried herbs, and packed them into her wooden rack, which she then hoisted onto her shoulders. With her meager strength, carrying fifty was the most she could manage, but such a small number didn't earn her a lot of money.

As always, she doused herself in a monster-warding potion and set out for the Citadel City.

And as always, a guard stopped her at the Citadel City checkpoint and demanded 20 percent as an entry fee, to which she pulled out four or five potions. Unlike the entrance to the kingdom, a fee shouldn't have been necessary for entering an adventurers' hub like the Citadel City. Though he said 20 percent, he would take away the most expensive potions, so that's why she put the cheap ones in her basket and hid the higher-priced ones in her bundle of dried herbs. It seemed she had successfully hidden them yet again.

After entering the Citadel City, she visited her most familiar patrons to sell potions and herbs. The very last one was the bordello. Since that area wasn't particularly safe, she had to be as nimble as possible. There were empty bottles of potions that had been drunk and discarded on the ground nearby, so she placed any she found in her waist pouch. That day, Mariela had collected around ten. Finding this many was nothing to sneeze at. As always, she went to the bordello's rear entrance and handed potions over to the male caretaker, and in return, she received 30 percent of the sale money. As always, small profits. If she couldn't grow the materials she needed in her garden for free, she'd make no profit at all and would be forced to haggle. However, this man was the only customer who would buy in bulk, so in Mariela's eyes, it was a good deal.

Had this day continued just like all the others, she would have visited a bakery called Copper Bread. The bread there was hard and dry, and the owner hardly ever used eggs or butter, but she would buy a large loaf for one copper coin—hence the name. Then, after purchasing a small number of necessary food items and potion bottles, she would have returned to her cottage in the Fell Forest.

But unlike all the other days, the toll of bells signaling a monster invasion reverberated through the Citadel City just as she received her payment from the caretaker.

The man immediately shut the door to his bordello and urged Mariela to go. The large white gate to the Kingdom of Endalsia in the outer wall had already been closed, and people crowded around it crying "Open the gate! Let us in!" Adventurers were gathering in the plaza as they planned their counterattack, and those who couldn't fight had long since fled or shut themselves in their homes with barred windows and doors.

Mariela dashed toward the entrance to the Citadel City. Countless times she bumped into people and fell down, and in the chaos, she somehow lost both the day's earnings and her wooden carrying rack with the herbs inside. Not a single soul stopped this girl, now completely empty-handed, from rushing headlong into the Fell Forest all alone, nor did anyone offer to take her into their home.

But Mariela knew—even those who shut themselves in the Citadel City had no hope of being saved. She knew that both the people who took shelter in their homes and the adventurers preparing for battle understood they couldn't be saved. And Mariela knew that was precisely why none of them had stopped her.

At the entrance to the Citadel City, the guard who always confiscated her potions had said to her, "I'm shutting the gate. Get out of here now!" and tossed something to her before kicking her out. It turned out to be a monster-warding potion. She hadn't brought any that day, so it was probably something he had been rationing.

Mariela remembered the guard's trembling hands as he closed the gate. Even though he was afraid of the monsters, he'd given her his own potion.

It really did feel like yesterday.

Two hundred years…

Mariela knew no way to find out what had happened to them.

Even if they'd survived the Stampede, this knowledge would be lost in the centuries since, and she'd never see them again.

Now there was nobody in this "Labyrinth City" who knew Mariela, nor did she know anyone here herself.

Back in the Citadel City, people treated her quite harshly, and she didn't have an easy life. Yet, although she could only make potions, she'd begun to feel that maybe, just maybe, she did belong there. That had certainly been the case on that day.

But now that she'd survived the Stampede and awoken from

her slumber, neither the cottage her master left her nor the tiny niche she'd carved out for herself remained.

04

"Heeey, Mariela!"

The reality of being asleep for two hundred years and the complete transformation of the Citadel City had sent Mariela into a daze. As Lynx shook her shoulder, she finally returned to the present.

"S-sorry. Guess I'm just tired."

"You *were* walking all by your lonesome in the Fell Forest, after all. That's gotta be tiring. But look, it's the Labyrinth City. We're here."

Before she'd even realized it, the iron carriage had stopped. It looked like Lieutenant Malraux was requesting the gate be opened.

When she got down from the ramp and looked around, she saw the same outer wall she remembered so well.

There was no doubt that the place known as the Labyrinth City used to be the Kingdom of Endalsia.

This familiar white exterior had once surrounded the kingdom's capital.

It must have been breached by the Stampede.

The wall had retained its white facade, but it showed signs

of previous devastation and subsequent repairs. Wrapped around its surface was the ivy daigis, which concealed the presence of humans from monsters by absorbing the magical energy escaping into the atmosphere.

A large portion of the forest near the outer wall had been cleared away, and the monster-repelling plant bromominthra now grew there in its place.

Both plants had also grown in Mariela's hut in the Fell Forest; they were necessary for people to live near monsters. But the daigis that twisted and turned resembled blood vessels eating away at the white wall, while the purplish-red bromominthra covering the ground was somewhat unsettling, and neither one flattered the Kingdom of Endalsia's beautiful alabaster facade.

In the past two hundred years, the glory of Endalsia had become a mere fairy tale.

The large front gate of Endalsia's outer wall, which used to remain open except during emergencies, was now firmly shut, and it looked as if a guard was stationed at the back door where only one person at a time could go through. Captain Dick seemed to be acquainted with the guard, and a short while after they exchanged salutations, the gate opened with a colossal noise. The iron carriage Mariela rode on passed through it and into the Labyrinth City.

The interior had completely changed, too.

Unlike in the Citadel City, a town of refugees, all the buildings in the capital of Endalsia were made of sturdy stone. More structures remained there than in the Citadel City, which had transformed from a vacant plot of land into a forest.

Even so, over half the elegant dwellings had collapsed, and

the remaining structures appeared to have been patched up with purely functional wood and dark stones. Compared with Endalsia's ornate architecture, the bland stone and wood of the repaired sections simply looked distorted. It was upsetting, as if someone had smeared mud across a priceless work of art.

The main street was once uniformly paved with stones and flanked by rows of flowers bursting into bloom. Now, it had been stripped of most of the stones, perhaps used for repairs in other places, and the earth underneath was exposed. Fine cracks had developed in the few stones that remained. The occasional tents hawking goods on the street occupied the sections where flowers used to be—they looked as if they were clinging to the buildings.

The people coming and going were all guards or experienced adventurers. Laborers squatted on the ground, perhaps because they had failed to find work in the narrow alleyways or because they were injured.

Witnessing the fall of the beautiful city that had once been at the height of glory would probably bring tears to the average onlooker's eyes, but Mariela didn't feel as shaken as when she'd seen the Citadel City. This place was meant for the citizens of Endalsia, so Mariela and the refugees who lived in the Citadel City didn't belong here.

The front gate had stayed open to show off the city's splendor, not as a welcome to Mariela and the Citadel City residents. She had been inside the gate only once, when her master brought her there for the alchemist certification ceremony.

To Mariela, the changes inside the gate weren't her concern, and she regained her composure.

"Say, Mariela. You haven't decided where you're gonna stay tonight, yeah? In that case, come to our usual lodging. It's pretty sketchy around here; there's all kindsa stuff in the City. We have to unload our cargo first, but it won't take long, so come with us."

Come with us. Lynx's words were what Mariela had wanted to hear since seeing the effects of the Stampede on the Citadel City. The fact that they hadn't sent her on her way even after reaching town meant they were probably after more potions. Understandable that they'd be worried whether they'd be able to readily do business with her again.

But he seems genuinely concerned about me...

They had paid for the potions, and although she'd spent a short while with them in the middle of the forest with no one else around, they had neither threatened nor restrained her. She didn't yet know them well enough to trust them, but going with them was probably much safer than being tossed onto the unfamiliar streets.

"Thank you. That would be a big help."

When she replied with her honest thanks, Lynx grinned widely.

The warmth of his expression soothed Mariela's raw and wounded heart.

CHAPTER 2
The Black Iron Freight Corps

01

In the Endalsian capital of old, there were four main roads that branched out from the royal castle at the center, and smaller streets intersecting those roads had been developed in a pattern of concentric circles. Surrounding the castle walls was a path roughly as broad as the main roads, from which the circular streets fanned out to reach all the way to Endalsia's outermost ramparts. The townscape had changed in two hundred years, but it looked as though the roads were still being used as before.

There was no trace of the royal castle that was once visible from any point within the Endalsian capital; nowadays, it was said to open up into the entrance to the Labyrinth. The castle walls that had once protected the royal family had been repaired and now protected the general population by preventing monsters from flooding out of the Labyrinth.

The breadbasket region to the northwest of the Labyrinth City still boasted plenty of farmland despite having shrunk as a result of the Fell Forest's encroachment, and as such, a large part of the population lived within the City's northwestern district. Incidentally, this region had received the most damage from the Stampede, since the monster horde encountered nothing to block its way as it engulfed the entirety of the grain-producing lands in an instant, and the outer ramparts there were the first to be breached. The buildings here had been completely destroyed when the monsters surged into the capital.

The aristocratic district to the southeast remained unchanged save for a mansion built for the family of Margrave Schutzenwald, who governed the Labyrinth City. This district was the closest to the mountain range; the road through the mountains was precipitous and unsuitable for caravan traffic or large numbers of people, but its proximity to the city itself made it easy to escape to in an emergency—hence why it became the aristocratic quarter, or so it was said.

The Black Iron Freight Corps's carriages entered the southwest side of the city through the former Citadel's large gate. After traveling along a main road to the city center, they turned west onto one of the circling streets near the Labyrinth and eventually reached the northeast district.

This section of the city also commanded a view of the mountain range on the other side of the forest. The mountains had mines that produced an abundance of mineral resources. The highway going through them was treacherous here as well; carriages couldn't traverse it, but this path was safer than the one in the southeast mountains, so people used it mainly to travel to other countries without encountering monsters.

For this very reason, it was a popular spot for merchants who peddled resources from the Labyrinth and the mines, and the Labyrinth City flourished. The partially destroyed Endalsian structures were demolished, and the massive warehouses of mercantile companies lined the city's perimeter near the mountain range. The Labyrinth side of the city center was home to a variety of thriving business establishments that catered to adventurers, such as shops, restaurants, lodging, and an Adventurers Guild.

Every single structure rebuilt after the Stampede had apparently been designed with fortresslike defenses in mind.

The cargo's destination appeared to be in a relatively nice location near the Labyrinth, and they arrived at a rear entrance after entering a side street. The double doors at the back of the building were bigger than those in the front, enough to allow three carriages to enter and unload in the courtyard.

The structure at the front of the courtyard seemed to be some sort of commercial establishment, flanked on either side by sectioned-off animal enclosures, a carriage storehouse, and a place for washing up.

The three iron carriages were guided inside and halted next to one another.

A strapping gentleman who appeared to be the supervisor emerged from the back entrance. He was accompanied by two of his lackeys, along with several servants and male guards. With an account book in one hand, he began to talk business with Captain Dick and Lieutenant Malraux.

Five members of the Black Iron Freight Corps disembarked from the coach boxes and unhooked the raptors from the carriages. A young boy took the bit of the raptor the captain had been riding, whistled sharply, and walked toward the enclosures.

The typically temperamental raptor obediently let the boy lead it on, and the other raptors followed after them in turn.

"Yuric is an animal trainer. Amazing, right? Let's go."

Led by Lynx, Mariela followed the raptors and found that the building was indeed for housing livestock. A man who looked to be the caretaker was waiting there with food and water, and Lynx informed her that this was the man who tended to the raptors exhausted from darting through the Fell Forest without any rest.

"Not a whole lotta places provide food for them. Mr. Reymond is a generous man."

Because the enclosures were for guest use, there were no other mounts inside. In a routine fashion, Yuric secured the raptors and gave them the meat and water Reymond had prepared for them.

In contrast, the caretaker appeared decidedly fearful as he made sure to push the feed trays far away from himself after filling them.

"GYARGYAR!"

"Eek!"

Water spilled onto one of the raptors, and it barked a complaint, causing the caretaker to shriek.

"There, there, why so angry? I'll give ya some more, mkay? I know ya need it."

Yuric spoke with a slight accent, and when he stroked the raptor's snout, it immediately turned docile. He asked the caretaker for more water, and the flustered man held his hands over the bucket.

"Water."

Using lifestyle magic, Reymond filled the bucket to the brim with plain water. He would have been better off pouring it straight into the raptor's trough instead of over on the other end of the enclosure, but perhaps Yuric figured it was pointless to complain to a man staring at the ground to avoid eye contact. Instead, he silently carried the bucket to the raptors and poured it into one of the troughs.

"'Ey, Lynx, couldja give me a hand?"

"No prob."

Yuric was about fifteen or sixteen, and Lynx was no more than a year or two older. The two young men so close in age seemed to be good friends. Lynx delivered meat to the remaining unfed raptors.

"Mariela, you want to try it? They're greedy little rascals, but they ain't gonna bite you."

Lynx offered her the bowl of feed.

"'Course they won't. My trainin' is perfect, y'know?" boasted Yuric as he continued to stroke the raptor. His curt behavior toward the caretaker had completely changed as he now gazed tenderly at the reptilian creature.

Mariela inspected the raptors. Frightening carnivorous beasts though they may be, there was something endearing about the way they single-mindedly devoured their meat. Maybe if she made friends with one, it would let her pet its glossy skin.

The caretaker used lifestyle magic, so I guess it's okay if I use it, too.

She held her hands over the trough of one of the raptors that hadn't been watered yet.

"Water."

The creature drank in a single gulp the water that appeared.

"Were you that thirsty?" she asked, and it grunted in response. "Yeah? You like it? Want some more?"

Mariela's mood had improved a little. As she poured a second helping, the other raptors began to gurgle noisily to get her attention for water.

Once they'd all been attended to, Yuric and Lynx began to wash the raptors.

When Mariela followed suit, her raptor growled and turned away.

"It tickled 'cause you weren't rubbin' hard enough."

Yuric translated to let her know the raptor didn't like that, so she petted its head instead. Its skin was pleasantly silky to the touch, more so than she'd imagined.

She noticed the creatures chattered a lot.

Only Yuric understood what they were saying. Every one of them made a racket no matter what they were trying to communicate: The base of their neck itched; or the feed wasn't fresh; or Yuric's water was the best, but Mariela's was also good. She never knew animals could be so entertaining.

"When we reach the inn, you'll get plenty o' rest, mkay? Just hang in there a bit longer, 'kay?"

The two young men diligently washed the raptors. The caretaker seemed to realize the creatures weren't scary, and following Yuric's and Lynx's instructions, he changed their bathwater and polished their saddles and stirrups.

Having run out of things to do, Mariela casually peered into the courtyard, wondering if the others had finished unloading the cargo.

Huh...?

A large number of people stood in single file next to the iron carriages.

The Black Iron Freight Corps had been carrying *human cargo.* They were lined up between two of the carriages—men on one side and women on the other. The men wore only loincloths, while the women were clad in a single piece of fabric each, and their hands were tied in front of them.

They're slaves...

There had been slaves in the Citadel City, too. All the women working in the bordello that bought Mariela's potions wholesale were either debt laborers or former slaves.

The debt laborers Mariela knew of worked for a period of

time according to how much debt they had, doing anything from shop labor to carrying an adventurer's bags, collecting garbage, or dissecting monsters. Those they worked for were obligated to provide them with the bare minimum needed to survive so they could do their work. Although the amount was basically pocket change, there was even a wage accumulation system for times when they couldn't get work.

This was the way of life for the slaves Mariela knew. These people didn't seem to be getting treated so poorly that it was obvious they were slaves, but still...

The males were scrawny. Their hair and beards had grown out, and their bodies were filthy.

One of the company's manservants used lifestyle magic to douse each of them in turn with water. The slaves were forced to wash themselves up on the spot before they were scrutinized one by one by a clerk carrying an account book, as if he was inspecting livestock.

Not only that, the servant used a pole to prod them, as if they were too filthy to touch with bare hands.

The defiant ones were restrained from behind and mercilessly pulled to the ground by guards.

If a slave showed even a bit of resistance, he was held down by several people and thoroughly scrutinized in a much more humiliating position. Even after it was over, his arms and legs were hogtied behind his back, and he was thrown to the ground. The others who witnessed this quietly submitted themselves to the mercy of the clerk, whether he shoved his pole inside their mouths or examined under their loincloths.

The last man in line may have been injured; he wobbled unsteadily on his feet. The clerk's prodding was enough to knock him to the ground. The guards grabbed his hair and roughly lifted his head, and his entire body was violently jostled back and forth while he was only barely conscious.

"This is awful…," Mariela uttered despite herself.

"First time you've seen penal laborers or lifelong slaves?"

Lynx's question made her jump. She hadn't noticed him approach.

"Once they're sent to the Labyrinth City, they stay there for life. Sometimes they die mid-transport when monsters attack their carriages. There's always a shortage of labor here, but since the human rights of debt laborers are protected, we can't bring proper slaves to the city."

Penal labor was punishment for someone who had committed a serious crime such as murder or robbery, and unless they received amnesty for some sort of meritorious deed as recognized by the general public, it was a lifetime sentence.

Those who committed minor offenses such as petty theft that didn't merit penal labor were ordered to pay a sum of money equivalent to the damages caused. If they were unable to pay, they could sell themselves off as debt laborers to obtain the needed funds. If the amount of debt was deemed too large to be repayable when considering age, ability, gender, or other circumstances, they were sentenced to a lifetime of hard labor as lifelong slaves. In either case, they lacked anything resembling human rights, and Mariela had even heard they were forced into extremely dangerous and cruel labor, such as serving on the front lines of battle as so-called meat shields or working in mines.

There were certain monsters in this world that ordinary people were no match for, and then there were the individuals with the power to oppose them. Nothing was more dangerous than a powerful person lacking in moral values. This world had no resources to spare for rehabilitating such individuals, so binding them to a contract to pay for even a little of the harm done to society was seen as the right thing to do.

That is, if you set aside the psychological revulsion from buying and selling people.

"Are you slave traders?" Mariela asked without thinking, but Lynx didn't seem bothered.

"We transport anything we get a request for. This time it was slaves, but sometimes we carry booze and tobacco or sugar and spices. We've also transported stuff like fabric, books, musical instruments, that sorta thing. There's a lot of stuff the Labyrinth City's lacking 'cause the only ones who can transport it all are the knights on patrol or the yagu caravans that come through the mountains."

"I hate transporting slaves the most, y'know? They stink, so the raptors hate 'em, too."

"'Cause they soil themselves. I can't stand cleanin' up after 'em."

These two were talking about the slaves as if they were mere cattle. It made Mariela a little dizzy.

Penal laborers, lifelong slaves... They're still human beings.

Even in the Citadel City, you'd commonly hear people say things like "I got rid of that thief." In this case, *got rid of* was understood to mean the thief had been killed. It was considered best to subjugate those who threatened your life or property by force. Otherwise, the number of victims would only increase.

Mariela understood as much, yet she couldn't help feeling uncomfortable about treating people like livestock.

Only because they were never a threat to me.

Thieves targeted those with property or people in similar criminal circles. Those seeking fame and fortune who were too big for their britches were easily swayed into crime, and crime often happened around such people.

Though Mariela gave it her all, she had barely enough money to eat, so she tried to avoid dangerous areas as much as possible. She had little in the way of vanity; she just wanted to live quietly in the Fell Forest. An impoverished, tranquil, and safe life had been her daily reality. So when she looked at the slaves before her, she understood in her head, but not in her heart, that it was natural to treat them this way.

Mariela felt it was dangerous not to fully understand.

Potions...

The variety of goods that hawkers were selling in the Labyrinth City seemed expensive compared with those in the Citadel City, but even in two hundred years, prices hadn't gone up. More importantly, she hadn't seen any potions for sale at all; "medicines" were now being sold in their place. There was no doubt that potions were valuable. And she had already used and sold them so freely.

I need information. I have to get myself an ally, someone who won't betray me.

These thoughts were based on the current appearance of the town. But she had no proof that was how things were now. After finally coming here, she felt incredibly impatient.

At that moment, the slave inspection ended.

Captain Dick had begun negotiations with the man—probably Reymond—who had taken the inspector's ledger and seemed to be the business's representative.

For some reason, they couldn't reach an agreement, and they moved over to the end of the line of male slaves.

"Two large silver coins won't cut it. If I don't get ten, I won't make a profit."

After secretly chanting *Wind's Whispers*, Mariela picked up on the conversation.

This wind-element magic let you listen to gossip downtown or hear things like the noise beasts made in the forest. However, its scope was limited, and it could be blocked by obstructions such as walls. After all, it was only as effective as lifestyle magic. But she could hear the conversation between Captain Dick and Reymond just fine.

"You say that, sir, but he can't move either his right hand or his left leg. I would be hard-pressed to find a buyer."

They seemed to be arguing about the man who'd been grabbed by the hair and shoved around.

"He'd be good as a meat shield in the Labyrinth or even working in the mines."

"With that leg of his, he won't be able to keep up with an adventurer, and that right hand isn't capable of swinging a pickax, either."

"He's missing an eye, but the man's got some nice features. There's gotta be someone who's into that, right?"

"You mean as a plaything, sir? Certainly, a person with exotic tastes would fancy him, but he is already well beyond twenty years old. I'm afraid he's past his prime."

Meat shield, the mines, a plaything... As even the worst conceivable options were deemed impossible, the man's entire body trembled.

He was the thinnest among the slaves. Wet soil was stuck to

him where he'd fallen, and with his dark-gray hair clinging to his entire face, he looked shabby and pitiful.

"This here's the reference letter for his purchase."

"Of course he has all his limbs as notated, but since some of them don't work, does that not make him defective merchandise? I hesitate to say this, but perhaps the seller deliberately misrepresented his condition in order to make a sale?"

"…Be that as it may, two large silver coins is a no go. At least gimme five…"

"I'm doing my best to compromise because I cannot sell back something you brought all the way here, sir. If I find no buyer, the merchandise may end up counting as a loss."

Geez, Captain Dick, you suck at negotiating!

Although the intimidating Captain Dick was brutal in his negotiation, the slave trader Reymond was in another league entirely. Lieutenant Malraux, apparently used to this, had a look of resignation on his face.

Hey, could this be my chance?

Any slave would obey his master's orders because he was bound by subordination magic.

She'd heard that the strength of such magic was equivalent to the strength of its power to compel its subject to obey, and it varied based on the amount of debt or severity of the crime.

That man is either a penal laborer or a lifelong slave. He'd be my ally for life. For life…

Normally, she would have considered buying an ally to be the idea of a complete sleazebag. She would have most likely given a wide berth to the likes of penal laborers and lifelong slaves, as she thought they were crazy. And there was no doubt that she would have smugly laughed at herself now for pitying this man at his weakest in a hopeless situation.

How would she save this man at death's doorstep? Her own course of action was uncertain, never mind supporting anyone else.

But Mariela remembered the terror of impending death from the Stampede as if it were yesterday. And the disconcerting exchanges she'd had since awakening, as well as the town's complete transformation, were keeping her from thinking with a level head. Most of all, the soaring prices of potions had made her extremely impatient.

Even if she had information, even if things were exactly as she imagined, what could she do by herself? She wasn't in the Kingdom of Endalsia or the Citadel City now but a place wholly unfamiliar to her. She knew nobody, and nobody knew her. Nothing remained of the cottage her master had left behind in the Fell Forest. That warm room became a mere phantom two hundred years ago and existed only in her memories now.

Before her long sleep, seemingly just a little while ago, she'd had a place to belong—and now it was gone.

So cold...

Had the deathlike slumber been a dream? Was she still unconscious in that small, dim cellar? She could still feel the chill in her hands, her feet, her very core.

Mariela had a powerful recollection of the profound loneliness and fear she'd felt before activating the magic circle.

That's why she had to do it.

"Sell him to me!" she shouted before she realized it. Everyone—Captain Dick, Lieutenant Malraux, Reymond, his employees, even the slaves—looked toward her in astonishment. Her face flushed red-hot under their stares.

Crap, what should I do?

The thought raced around and around in her head, but Mariela noticed that the gray-haired man on the other side of Captain Dick was looking her way. Though the right side of his face was hidden by hair, she saw his left eye was deep blue.

"I need another set of hands. I don't have much, but I can offer five large silver coins!"

Mariela had nothing if not enthusiasm. She couldn't negotiate worth a darn, either.

Up until just a little while ago, she'd shared her cottage from two hundred years back with her master. But she'd been left all alone. She'd left her master's room untouched, waiting for the day it would be needed again, but two hundred years had gone by. The house was now entirely gone and waited no more.

Although it was harsh and relentless, the Citadel City had been her home, too, until that day two hundred years ago. Everyone in the city had let her escape, but nobody came with her.

Bonds form between people, whether through compassion, pity, or contracts.

Mariela wanted to have someone around, and at that moment, she thought maybe this persecuted man would stay with her forever.

"Pfft."

A snort from Lieutenant Malraux shattered Mariela's all-out seriousness.

Huh? Did he laugh at me? Why?

"In that case, we shall sell him to Miss Mariela for two large silver coins."

"What...?" Captain Dick shouted in surprise.

Mariela's interjection into the negotiations and Lieutenant Malraux's subsequent response left both Dick and the slave trader Reymond in shock. With a sidelong glance at the two dumbfounded men, Malraux made a brazen offer.

"Mr. Reymond, earlier you said the man might be a loss. This young lady has offered to take on that burden. What say you to covering the cost of the contract?"

Coming out of his stupor, Reymond was about to protest about doing his job free of charge for a girl he didn't know when Malraux quietly approached him and whispered, "I daresay you'll likely be doing business with her for a long while."

Upon hearing this, Reymond closed his eyes for a moment, then put on his shrewdest of smiles and addressed Mariela.

"I am terribly sorry you had to see such an unsightly display. We're most grateful for your offer, miss. Per Lieutenant Malraux's wishes, we shall provide you the contract for free."

"Huh? Two large silver coins...?"

Malraux took what appeared to be appraisal papers from Captain Dick, who still hadn't caught up with what was going on, and looked them over.

"After that... Mm, this amount is fine. Captain, this will do, yes?"

With his inspection of the papers complete, Lieutenant Malraux promptly finalized the deal.

Captain Dick, who had snapped out of it at last, signed the papers prepared by the person in charge of accounting and began discussing the payment. Even though Malraux had barged into the conversation and closed the deal of his own accord, the captain didn't appear to be angry with him.

After Mariela paid the two large silver coins to Lieutenant Malraux, she heard someone say, "The contract is ready." A desk and a brazier with items resembling fire pokers inside it had been brought out when she wasn't paying attention. The slaves whose transactions had been finalized were lined up in view of the brazier.

Reymond turned the pages of the account book and read aloud its contents.

"Now, this man's name is Siegmund, is it? During his time as a debt laborer, he injured his master's son and became a penal laborer."

Siegmund, the gray-haired man who'd been hauled in front of the brazier, jerked in surprise and at last uttered, "Th-that's not—"

"It's what everyone says happened. And no one will question it if they see *this*."

One of his staff clerks, who'd been waiting in front of the brazier, lifted a white-hot poker.

It wasn't a poker at all but a branding iron as big as Mariela's palm with a delicate pattern carved into it.

"Ah...!"

Siegmund gasped, and the clerk slowly brandished the iron before him—no, before the other slaves, too.

"A mark as large as this wouldn't be necessary for an obedient slave... You, who failed to repay your debt! During your servitude, you inflicted harm! On the cherished son of your master! The one whom you were supposed to obey!"

Reymond emphasized each phrase as he spoke, and Siegmund's lips tightened.

"It is impossible for a man with such a heart to adequately

serve the kind young lady. We will increase the contract's strength so that he may at last be a worthy servant. I think it's the least we can do."

Sorry to interrupt your brainwashing session, but...

Mariela trotted up to the brazier from behind the slave trader and pointed to the smallest branding iron, saying, "This one is fine." It was roughly the size of the circle formed with a thumb and index finger, very similar to a large silver coin.

Reymond abruptly looked over his shoulder. Not even a forced smile crossed his face.

Yikes, he looks freaky! It's like he's saying, "I'm doing this for free, so you'd better cooperate at least this much."

Mariela faltered a bit under his stern gaze but soon plucked up her courage and persisted.

"He's missing an eye, and his hand and leg are impaired, so I think this is enough."

Siegmund was already weakened. If he was stamped with a branding iron that large in his condition, he might die from the shock alone. All she wanted was for him to explain the status quo and then to keep her secret. She had no intention of giving orders he would hate so much that she needed a contract of that size and power.

Siegmund was gazing neither at Reymond nor at the branding iron but at Mariela. There was nothing to hate within that deep-blue eye of his. She couldn't imagine anyone with such purity in their gaze to be a terrible person. Mariela returned Reymond's gaze as if to tell him, "There's no way in hell I'm gonna let you use that huge brand on him."

"Ohhh, such benevolence!"

Reymond turned to face Siegmund and the other slaves and continued his speech. He knew arguing was pointless.

"Always express gratitude to merciful masters! Be joyful in obeying their commands! Know that even giving every last ounce of your flesh and blood will never be enough to repay their kindness!"

Reymond raised his voice as he began to chant.

"Your body is worth no more than dirt!"

The branding iron Mariela chose glowed dimly from the earth-element magic within it.

"Your blood runs for your master's sake!"

The element of water gathered in a cup up to the brim before overflowing and trickling down the desk it sat upon.

"Let your feelings of devotion toward your master sweep over you!"

Wind-element magic gathered around the brazier in a spiral.

"Know that your life burns for your master!"

The brazier surged with fire-element magic, and all at once, a pillar of flame erupted.

Although the magic wasn't as powerful as it would be if he borrowed the strength of the spirits, incorporating dramatic expressions into his chanting along with the visual effects created a truly impressive ambience. It was also a psychological technique that guided the subject's thoughts into a shape that made them easy to bind, heightening the effect of the magic rite.

Reymond seemed to be a wily, highly capable person who understood both human nature and magic rites.

The slave trader swiftly seized the red-hot branding iron and stood before Siegmund.

It seemed like part of a religious ceremony.

The company's servants gripped both of Siegmund's arms and pushed him into a kneeling position.

The slave did not resist as he looked up at the branding iron.

"Hear ye, Siegmund! Resign yourself from your very soul!"

With a *ffshhh*, the branding iron pressed into his chest above the rib cage and released an unpleasant smell of burnt flesh into the air.

Siegmund clenched his teeth but made not a single sound.

Urged by the employees standing by, Mariela sprinkled her own blood into the cup on the desk. A water-like liquid had gushed forth into the cup from the chant a short while ago, and the blood quickly mixed with it. After Reymond picked up the cup, one of the servants restraining Siegmund opened his mouth.

"Etch your master into your very flesh!"

He emptied the contents of the cup into the slave's mouth, then seized the man's jaw to ensure not a drop would spill out before forcing him to swallow it.

The four magic elements united inside Siegmund's body and bound the rite. The magic circle within the branding iron glowed faintly, and the subordination magic was etched into his entire body.

"The contract is now sealed!"

With the chanting over, the Contract of Servitude was complete. Mariela stared at Siegmund's blue eye; he looked as if he was in a trance, maybe due to the effects of the magic.

"All right, let's head to the inn."

During the rite, Lynx and Yuric had brought the raptors and were now waiting.

The six raptors were already tied to the iron carriages, and Yuric passed one bridle each to Captain Dick and Lieutenant Malraux, then climbed into the coach box of the lead carriage.

"We'll load him into the cargo hold. C'mon, get in."

The other Corps members lifted Siegmund into the cargo hold of the lead carriage and closed the door.

After apologizing to Reymond for barging in on the negotiations and thanking him for the Contract of Servitude, Mariela hopped onto the ramp of the iron carriage Siegmund was riding in.

"Not at all, miss; in fact, it was good timing. I'm sure the other slaves who observed the contract ceremony will now do their best to serve good masters. We'll be awaiting your next visit," Reymond said as he saw them off. He seemed to be in a slightly good mood.

The Black Iron Freight Corps had traveled through the Fell Forest for three days straight. The slaves spent the entire time tightly packed into the dark cargo hold with nothing but a small window for ventilation. They weren't given enough food and couldn't lie down. Monsters had attacked the iron carriages en route many times. In the darkness of the cargo hold, they could constantly hear the roar of distant monsters. The carriages were shaken around in the attacks, and fangs and claws scratched the armor with excruciating noises.

Between their fear of death and the turbulent jostling they experienced in the cargo hold, the slaves' minds and bodies alike were at their limit. After finally reaching the trading company and finding relief from their terror, as well as relief from the extreme sleep deprivation and malnutrition, watching that ceremony probably instilled obedience deep into their consciousness.

The value of penal laborers and lifelong slaves was low. Their fate was to live in substandard conditions where even their life wasn't guaranteed. All of them were deeply pessimistic about their life and had no energy or passion. They did only the bare minimum to obey commands for their master's benefit. From a buyer's point of view, their only purpose was to be used up.

If they saw that ceremony and became more or less obedient toward their masters, they'd benefit not only Reymond as good products but themselves as well.

Lord Malraux is a shrewd man. Although I don't understand what he meant when he said I'll have a long-term business relationship with that girl...

After directing his subordinates to inform him of the state of the newly arrived products at a later time, Reymond began to walk toward his store.

02

The Black Iron Freight Corps's usual inn was located along the side of the mountain range, just a short way past the main street and the slave trading company.

The sign displayed at the inn read Yagu Drawbridge Pavilion.

A yagu was a goat roughly the size of a donkey that inhabited this part of the mountains. These animals were essential for traversing the narrow mountain paths, which were too narrow for carriages to pass through. Tens of yagus at a time were loaded with cargo and led in a line through the range. Yagus could receive infrequent feedings, had a gentle disposition, and provided milk and meat, so many were bred even in the Citadel City.

Just like mountain goats, yagus were naturally inclined to scale steep cliff faces.

The nonchalant manner in which they descended cliffs, jumping from one precipitous mountain rock to another, would shock any onlooker.

The way they bounded over these cliffs was described as a "yagu drawbridge," a phrase often used in the Citadel City as an expression that meant making it through a desperate situation.

Like others in the district, Yagu Drawbridge Pavilion was a sturdy stonework building, but its front was wider than the others, and the double doors stood open to welcome guests.

Captain Dick and Lieutenant Malraux dismounted their raptors and headed toward the entrance, followed by Mariela and Lynx.

"I want to get Siegmund out of here quickly," said Mariela, and Lynx replied, "Once he washes up in the back." Sieg remained in the cargo hold as the iron carriage drove behind the building.

Through the front doors was a combined restaurant and tavern, and stairs in the back right corner led up to the second floor.

It was well past lunchtime but still early evening, so the place was deserted. Mariela saw a woman with fiery-red hair working behind the counter.

"Dick! You're early today!" the redhead called out, and she ran up to him. They seemed to be close friends.

She appeared to be a strong-willed woman—and a very well-endowed one, at that.

"Hey, we managed to dispose of the whelps quickly." For some reason, Captain Dick puffed out his chest and looked pleased as he answered.

"Your usual room is available. Now, take off that armor; I've already prepared your meal. Oh, I don't believe I've ever seen this young lady before, have I?"

"Nice to meet you. My name is Mariela. I'd like two rooms, please."

The beautiful redhead's gaze turned to Lieutenant Malraux.

"We met her along the way. We'll vouch for her reliability. Miss Mariela, slaves cannot book a room at an inn even in the Labyrinth City. There's a sleeping quarters for slaves in the shed out back. Having said that, I suppose there's no harm in bringing your personal property into your own room. Miss Amber, would it be acceptable to bring dirty luggage into a room at the back of the second floor?"

To prevent slaves from escaping or committing crimes, any honest establishment wouldn't rent rooms to them. This didn't apply just to the Labyrinth City; it was a universal truth. Although it was common sense that hadn't changed in two hundred years, it made Mariela a little sad. They wouldn't give Sieg a room even though he was practically at death's door. Nevertheless, she was deeply grateful to Malraux for trying to arrange a bed for the man.

"We do have a room that would fit the bill. The *extra* bed might get in your way, but it's no problem. Welcome to the Yagu Drawbridge Pavilion! I'm Amber. If you have any questions, I'm here for you." Amber greeted Mariela warmly upon her introduction from Lieutenant Malraux. Mariela paid for three nights just for the time being and received her room key. The rate for two people was thirty copper coins per night, and breakfast was five copper coins a head. She requested two servings.

It was a steal. The Yagu Drawbridge Pavilion was a prominent building in a good location, and it even had a restaurant. It was better than a mid-grade inn, but the cost per room was just way too low.

"Whoa… That's chea—," she started to say without thinking.

"Ah, it's because the Labyrinth City's inns receive subsidies. Besides, this is practically the sticks out here, right? We've got the Labyrinth, but it's tough to make it all this way, so it's pretty deserted. We can live so cheaply thanks to the margrave, you see. Take a load off, Mariela."

She still didn't have a grasp on the cost of living in the Labyrinth City, but she had more than six large silver coins left from selling her potions.

It looked as if she'd be able to survive for a while.

In any case…

Mariela secretly put her hand to her chest.

…Amber's boobs are huge…

Mariela sighed as she wondered if any potion existed that could make her chest bigger.

Captain Dick and Lieutenant Malraux ascended the stairs to their rooms on the second floor.

Lynx said he was going to give the other Corps members their room keys, so Mariela joined him.

When they went out the back door, she saw a building resembling an outhouse and a watering hole, and farther back were a carriage house and a shed for livestock. It looked as though you were free to do your laundry at the watering hole—someone had set aside a loaned washboard and tub. The watering hole also had a space for bathing in the corner, partitioned off with cloth.

"Hey, Yuric! We're gonna go eat!"

When Lynx called out to him, four members of the Black Iron Freight Corps appeared from the carriage house.

"Yuric's coming after he finishes up with the raptors," answered one of them as he received his key.

"That guy reeeally likes his raptors, huh? Here's his key. I'm off."

With that, Lynx walked in the direction of the shed.

Mariela looked around, wondering where Siegmund was, when she spotted him coming out of the bathing area. He seemed flustered. Apparently, he was in a hurry, too; his hair was still wet, and he looked cold. The loincloth he'd put back on was also wet and clinging to him.

He used it to wipe himself up...

Mariela herself had no change of clothes, either.

The cloak she currently wore was woven from daigis fibers, and it had no visible deterioration because it automatically repaired itself by absorbing magical power from the wearer and the atmosphere. However, the clothes under it were probably tattered after two hundred years. Her pouch and the outside of her shoes were cracking everywhere and looked as if they were about to fall apart.

Once I check on Siegmund, the first thing I'll need to do is go shopping.

After drying him with the *Dehydrate* lifestyle magic, Mariela went to her room.

Siegmund obediently followed her when she told him to. His left calf was swollen and discolored, and he practically dragged it along behind him. He carried Mariela's grass skirt—er, bundle of herbs—in his right arm. It wasn't that he couldn't move his arm at all, but he wasn't really carrying the herbs so much as clumsily cradling them, so his limb must have been impaired. Finally, there was his right eye, which his hair always covered. He had a pale complexion, and his breathing came in shallow, short puffs. Seeing him up close, she could tell he was in even worse shape than she'd thought.

Mariela's room on the second floor was adequately spacious, with a bed on each side and a desk and chair in the middle. Between the door and the rest of the room itself was a closet for luggage and armor, and though small, there was also a room with a bath.

It could hardly be called a bath, though. It was a deep tub that barely one person could fit in, with a drainage hole. And it had no water-supply equipment. Water had to be formed and heated with magic or magical tools. Nevertheless, Mariela knew a room with a bath had been a feature limited to high-class inns back in the Citadel City.

A bath! That's great. I'm gonna have myself a long soak later.

She'd assumed she would only be able to splash herself with hot water and wipe it off to get clean, so she was very grateful for the chance to take a real bath.

Though the room was much nicer than she'd anticipated, the sleeping area had a damp, moldy odor. Since there was only a small window, it probably didn't get much sunlight. The sheets were clean, but there might be bugs in the straw mats.

It's a room they were fine letting a grimy slave into, after all. Oh well.

Siegmund seemed to have completely washed himself, but a sour smell emanated from his person, and mud and dust and gosh knows what else were embedded in tangled mats in his hair and beard. She was just thankful they'd even let him in.

After ventilating the room with lifestyle magic, she closed the window, then latched the door shut. Since the inner door to the sleeping area was also closed, no one outside would hear them. She imbued the room's lighting with magic to make it bright enough for a medical examination even with the window closed. Some of the herbs were missing little pieces here and there from being jostled by the carriage, but she hadn't lost a single one. These would be enough for emergency first aid.

"Sit there."

She indicated one of the chairs, but for some reason, Siegmund sat on the floor next to it. He must not have been able to bend his left leg, because he stretched it out behind him while tucking his right leg beneath him in a shaky kneeling position. He didn't look up; his eye was fixated on the floor near Mariela's feet.

Why did he sit on—? Well, whatever.

Mariela shifted a chair to face Siegmund and sat down.

"My name is Mariela. Would it be okay if I call you Sieg? Under the Contract of Servitude, you have to follow my orders. Is that right?"

"Yes. Please call me whatever name you like, Mistress. I will never forget the kindness you've shown in choosing someone unworthy like me. No matter what order you may give, I swear not to disobey. Please command me however you desire." As he spoke, Sieg touched his forehead to the floor and prostrated himself before her.

Whoa...

Mariela recoiled. This large man had just groveled before her without a moment's hesitation. She could hardly believe what he'd said. She even suspected the slave trader had used some kind of mind magic.

A-anyway, treatment! I've gotta heal him!

As an alchemist, Mariela knew it wasn't just his injuries to worry about but the fact that he was near his breaking point physically. The best course of action would be to slowly address some of his mannerisms after she'd taken care of his wounds.

"Call me Mariela. Lift your head so I can get a good look at you."

Sieg raised his head and brushed away some of the hair that clung to his face.

His cheeks were sunken, but he had handsome features. The single deep-blue eye of his was beautiful. If he shaved his beard and spruced up a little, he might make for something of a silver fox.

When Mariela raised her hand to examine his right eye, his body stiffened in surprise. Mariela once knew a child who reacted this way; one of the children in the orphanage's care had been frequently beaten by his parents. Sieg had probably been on the receiving end of violence on a regular basis, too, given the many scars covering his body. If he was immediately groveling in front of a girl younger than he was, who knew what kind of hell he'd been through? Mariela's heart ached.

She slowly moved her hand so as not to frighten him, and she touched his face. It was hot. As she suspected, he had a fever. Three large scratches ran down the right side of his face, probably from monster claws. The wound was old and completely closed up, but it had rendered his right eye useless.

This'll need an elixir or a special-grade potion specifically for the eyes.

An elixir was an incredibly effective medicine. As long as the subject was still alive, it was said to heal any injury and cure any disease and even instantly restore lost body parts.

It would require rare and expensive ingredients and the most skilled alchemist to perform the complicated transmutation, so of course Mariela couldn't make one. Rather, it was treated as a legendary medicine in the Citadel City, and Mariela had never even heard of anyone who knew the recipe, let alone was able to make one.

Instead, there existed "specialized potions" distributed as medicine to restore lost body parts. Using special-grade potions from expert alchemists as a base, specialized potions were made by honing materials corresponding to the body part in question. Mariela didn't know how to make one of those yet, either; top-tier alchemists had researched the ingredients and production, and the original recipe they developed was hidden away.

And anyhow, Mariela's alchemy skill level allowed her to make only high-grade potions, which were one rank below special-grade base potions.

No way I can fix his eye...

Next, she examined his right arm. The forearm was scarred from what she guessed was a monster bite. When she asked him about it, he said a black wolf had attacked him half a month ago.

These creatures were also called miasma wolves, and although they were smaller than forest wolves, their fangs contained poison that slowed the healing of wounds. They weren't particularly powerful on their own, but because they moved in groups, they spilled their prey's blood during the chase, weakened it, and eventually devoured it.

The wound on his arm had never completely healed. The flesh where the bite marks were was discolored and sunken; it was likely improperly treated. The poison in the monster's fangs had entered the wound and delayed the healing process.

Finally, the left leg. Part of the calf had been gnawed on—again, courtesy of a black wolf. It looked to have been cauterized to stop the bleeding. Not only had the resulting burn not healed, but bacteria from human waste had entered the wound when he had been transported in unsanitary conditions. His calf was so massively inflamed that it was plainly obvious.

First, I need to do something about this inflammation. I think I can manage with just a mid-grade potion for the arm, but I really need a high-grade specialized potion for the leg. Even so... He looks so calm, but surely he must be in excruciating pain?

The fresh brand on his chest was reddish brown and similarly inflamed, with the engraving an even darker color than the rest.

She could heal everything in the blink of an eye with a special-grade potion, but she couldn't make one, so that wasn't an option. Healing with a lower-grade potion required several steps.

"First, I'm going to wash your wounds."

With that, Mariela began the treatment.

If you showed intense pain on your face, you were deemed unusable and tossed aside. If you collapsed, you were left in the field to die.

This was how little those two large silver coins were worth.

She didn't want Siegmund to die in this condition, maybe precisely because he *was* in this condition.

Mariela had no way to know this, but Siegmund was feigning calmness through sheer willpower.

After seating him in the chair, she picked up a pitcher and her last remaining vial and headed to the bathroom. She used alchemy to wash, disinfect, and dry both items, then picked up a pail as well and returned to Siegmund.

"Do not reveal to anyone the things I do from here on out. This is an *order*."

"Yes, ma'am," Sieg responded robotically.

His single blue eye had a vacant look, perhaps from the fever. Mariela was able to detect a slight magical reaction in the brand on his chest.

She placed the pail on the desk and had him hold out his right arm so the wound was facing upward.

"Clean Water, Drops of Life, Anchor."

Cleansing water materialized in the pitcher.

Mariela's master believed inflammation was better treated using clean water imbued with Drops of Life's power as opposed to water infused with antibacterial herbs. Per this method, she first used a liberal amount of the cleansing water to wash the scars. The black wolf's miasma wafted up from the cuts like smoke from a pipe; she could tell the Drops of Life was drawing it out of the wound.

Next, his leg. She had him kneel on the chair so the wound on his calf was facing upward, and she made sure to clean it with the utmost care.

After repeating this process many times, she dumped out the water from the pail she was using for washing.

Since Mariela lacked a cloth to wipe up with, she tore a piece from one of the sheets and dried off his skin except where the scars remained. She left the Drops of Life on those. Since it disappeared quickly if not bound to water or herbs, only skilled alchemists could absorb it in that form. Mariela considered it convenient because it would leave the wounds dry after vanishing. This was much more hygienic than drying them with the room's unsterilized sheets or a blast of the moldy-smelling air.

Finally, the brand on his chest. She seated him on the chair so he could lean back and washed the area under the brand with the sheet. This would have been no sweat with just a low-grade potion, but it was always best practice to cool the burn first. A potion would be more effective once the area had been cleaned. She washed it several times after wringing out the sheet again.

And now for the potion.

From the bundle of dried herbs, Mariela took out some curique; a root called calgoran, which had a strong nourishing effect; and some peshrinion, the round blue seeds of the curique plant.

Peshrinion, though rare, could occasionally be cultivated from curique plants growing in damp, shady areas. It was effective treatment for wounds that had festered from unsanitary conditions as well as for long-lasting fevers. Since curique plants liked areas with a lot of sun, peshrinion tended to be scarce in the wild unless they were deliberately planted there.

Mariela had once absentmindedly left a flowerpot for curique seeds in the shade, which then produced peshrinion. Furthermore, when she grew more curique from that peshrinion, it grew even in the shade, leading to a variety of seed from which she could easily raise peshrinion. Since then, she'd been able to regularly harvest the seeds from her herb garden. Some remained in the garden even after her long sleep—it was a good thing she'd brought it with her to sell.

She transmuted a potion in her one remaining vial with the curique, the calgoran, and a pinch of peshrinion. It was a simple heal potion that could be classified as low-grade but also as a specialized type. It ought to have about an intermediate-grade effect on Sieg's symptoms. Mariela included as much Drops of Life into the concoction as she could since he was basically hanging by a thread. It had to help—she was sure it would.

"Drink this."

Sieg's jaw dropped in amazement as she handed him the potion.

He remained frozen in place, so she thrust the potion into his mouth, and he drank it down spluttering.

"You're...an alchemist?"

It was the first time he'd said anything other than a response. He'd been incredulous when Mariela first produced the cleansing water, but after she made the potion, he appeared convinced.

"Yeah. Are there no more alchemists—no more Endalsian Pact-Bearers in this town?" she asked as she took the empty vial from Sieg. She wanted to know the answer to this question more than anything.

"There are no pact-bearing alchemists. It's been that way for a long time...because this is the monsters' territory."

Mariela had expected as much.

Huh. I see. They call this place the Labyrinth City, after all. Of course that would happen after two hundred years.

"So this is an *order*. Don't ever reveal to anyone that I'm a Pact-Bearer."

She once again compelled Sieg to do as she said. The order's effect was palpable.

"You can sleep in that bed. When you wake up, your fever will have gone down and you'll feel much better. I'm gonna go do some shopping, so even if you wake up, just stay in bed, okay?"

She urged Sieg to lie down on the inner bed that no longer had sheets. She put the damp sheets and the vial in the pail and carried it into the bathroom.

Once she'd briefly washed them in the bathtub, she dried them with the lifestyle magic *Dehydrate*.

When she came back, Sieg had already fallen asleep—he must have reached the end of his rope.

Oh, there might be bugs in the bed.

She transmuted an insecticide potion and placed the vial in a corner with its lid off.

She'd also mixed in some bendan, a flower that promotes restful sleep. It replaced the moldy stench in the air with a faint, pleasant fragrance.

Hope he sleeps well.

Mariela put clean water in the pitcher and placed it on the desk along with a cup. Then she extinguished all but one of the lights in the room and quietly left.

Lieutenant Malraux was waiting in front of his room.

Mariela's room was at the very back of the second floor, behind the Black Iron Freight Corps's quarters.

"Were you able to get the information you wanted?" Malraux asked quietly.

"Were you listening to us?"

Mariela responded with a question of her own, and Malraux

shrugged as if to ask, "Would I do such a thing?" He really was a cunning man.

He probably realized it from the beginning.

At Malraux's urging, she entered his room.

The overall layout and size were the same as Mariela's room, but this one had only one bed and a couch and table where the other bed would have been. A partition had been placed between the bed and lounge suite for simple meetings.

She sat on the couch at Malraux's suggestion, and he sat across from her.

"I wanted to discuss business with you, Mariela."

"You mean potions, right?"

Malraux answered with a smile that said he appreciated getting to the heart of the matter.

Two hundred years ago, the Stampede occurred, and the Labyrinth appeared where the royal castle once stood.

The Kingdom of Endalsia, which had belonged to the humans, was destroyed and became the domain of monsters.

People lived in the Labyrinth City, but just like the Fell Forest in which Mariela had once made her home, the Labyrinth City belonged not to people but to monsters.

Drops of Life, which was used to create magical potions, was drawn from ley lines by a *Nexus*. This Nexus bound the ley line and the alchemist together through the spirits of a particular region. Alchemic skills themselves were once said to be even more commonplace than bakeries, but not all alchemic skill holders could form a pact with a ley line and become true alchemists. Only those who trained under a master and connected to a ley line through a Nexus could claim that title. Alchemic skills drew on Drops of Life, and if you didn't use it, you wouldn't gain enough experience to do things like adjust temperature or pressure or form a *Transmutation Vessel*, let alone craft potions.

Forming a pact with a ley line was absolutely essential to becoming a full-fledged alchemist, hence why those who possessed a Nexus were also called *Pact-Bearers*.

The ceremony for making a pact was of great significance. The alchemist, guided by their master and the spirits, exchanged True Names with a ley line. However, the spirits spoke the language of whatever entity ruled over the region.

The former Kingdom of Endalsia was a territory ruled for many generations by the Endalsian royal family, who received the spirits' divine protection. All the kingdom's spirits spoke the human tongue; however, those that inhabited the Fell Forest were unintelligible, even though they were born from the same ley line.

They could not be communicated with.

The sole time Mariela had entered the Kingdom of Endalsia's walls was to make a pact with its ley line.

Spirits don't participate in the alchemic process itself once a Nexus has been established. As long as an alchemist is within range of the ley line they've formed a pact with, they can draw Drops of Life without issue, even in a region controlled by monsters. Once they become an Alchemist Pact-Bearer, they can use Drops of Life to create potions.

However, suppose there were no new Pact-Bearers over a span of two hundred years.

Those who could incorporate Drops of Life directly into their bodies generally aged slower than most and lived a long time, but not as long as two hundred years. Eighty years was considered a long life for ordinary people, and it was rare to see anyone live to a hundred and twenty.

In the two hundred years Mariela had been asleep, the alchemists who survived the Stampede had all died out without creating any new ones.

In the Labyrinth City—no, in the entire scope of the local ley line—no potions existed except those securely stored away.

"We had an intermediary merchant appraise the potions you sold us. He said they were so well-preserved that they appeared to have been freshly made. They were as effective as the mid-grade potions that rarely appear on the market. He insisted on finding out where we had obtained them. Ah, of course, we didn't tell him. Everyone in town wants these sorts of potions, you see. If anyone discovered they were in the possession of an innocent young lady such as yourself, they would go to extreme lengths to get their hands on them."

Lieutenant Malraux spoke slowly and quietly. He seemed to be asking if she was understanding him correctly.

"Could I safely sell them in bulk to your crew?" she asked, to which Malraux smiled in satisfaction and answered, "Of course."

Hey, I gotta sell my potions somewhere. Whether or not I cut out the middleman, it'd be great if I could get better prices than in the Citadel City.

Mariela had no means of survival other than making potions.

It was only natural that those who had no way to compete and lacked the support would end up being exploited. Cutting out the middleman was a given even when selling potions in the Citadel City. Mariela knew she could scrape by with the minimum profit if she accepted this injustice.

Nevertheless, there were some things she wouldn't budge on. Mariela gave Malraux her terms of service.

"First, I cannot sell potions that are special-grade and above or poisons used to harm people. Additionally, there are certain specialized potions I can't sell, even if they're high-grade or lower. So I'd like to have the right to decide the available items for sale."

Mariela couldn't sell potions she couldn't make, and she refused to take part in any criminal involvement. She absolutely wanted to avoid people dying from the potions she made.

"Next, this depends on the potion, but there may be occasions where I will require an advance."

She couldn't make anything without ingredients, so he would need to accept this, too. Mariela's herb garden was partially destroyed. She didn't know what products the Labyrinth City had to offer, but she wanted them to obtain what she couldn't.

"Lastly, I ask for strict confidentiality. Do not reveal in any way that I'm the supplier. This secret must be maintained even in emergencies. If you'll accept my conditions via a magic contract, I will sell you my potions."

Mariela, having set out her terms, fretted internally.

I wonder if adding the magic contract part was going too far...

She wasn't willing to budge on any of her terms, but perhaps she could've worded things a bit better.

Lieutenant Malraux repeated the conditions back to her as if digesting them one by one.

"It's a shame you cannot sell special-grade potions, but I acknowledge your conditions. As far as payment is concerned, would forty...no, thirty percent..."

Ugh... I piled on too many conditions, so no wonder he's driving

a hard bargain. But if I have to buy the herbs I need, can I make a profit at thirty percent? I hope the price of herbs hasn't gone up—

"...of the market price be an acceptable commission for us?"

"Pardon?"

Wait, isn't that, like, backward?

"I can decide what kind of potions to sell, right?" she asked in turn.

"Yes. There is available inventory to account for, so that's reasonable."

"And you'll give me items I need in advance?"

"Our company stocks goods as well, and since we're doing business based on mutual trust, we can provide that degree of service."

"And you'll help me out if my secret gets leaked?"

"The deal I've proposed comes with inherent risks. After-sales service is essential."

"Then, isn't a thirty percent commission too low?"

"Eh?"

"Huh?"

They were both equally puzzled.

In the end, they agreed Mariela would initially receive 60 percent of the market price. The magic contract required additional enhancements in order to provide complete confidentiality and any emergency backup procedures should the information ever be leaked.

This was exceptional service all for just a single girl who came to the Labyrinth City by herself with no support whatsoever. Such convenient, honeyed proposals were typically rescinded or flipped on their head at a moment's notice; the likes of a sixteen-year-old girl with no combat skills could be silenced just by loud, angry shouting.

Magic contracts produce binding power through judicial authority, so those who are dishonest in their business dealings hate them. Even if Malraux had put his foot down about one thing or another and twisted the negotiations to his advantage, Mariela would still have been grateful to have a magic contract, but he accepted all her conditions without batting an eye. Confirming the contract with these details meant he considered her a business partner rather than someone to be exploited.

After all, he waited to talk to me until I'd finished up with Sieg first.

If she'd been wheeled and dealed without information or knowing which end was up, he could have formed the contract with conditions beneficial solely to him and his group. However, that wasn't the way of the Black Iron Freight Corps. Partial though they might be to the use of force, their attitude of fairness and politeness made Mariela feel they were well worth her trust.

She was particularly pleased with how honest they were in giving her 60 percent.

They agreed she would deliver the promised goods in three days: ten each of high- and mid-grade heal potions, five each of high- and mid-grade cure potions, and twenty each of low-grade monster-warding and cure potions.

Lieutenant Malraux informed her with a friendly smile that he would prepare the document the next day.

Feels kinda like we were coming at this from two completely different angles, but... Eh, whatever.

Exhausted from her little adventure in the Fell Forest, Mariela wanted nothing more than to take it easy, so she didn't mind if the contract was late.

She answered that she'd check the town's shops for the items she'd need to make the potions.

Incidentally, the market price of low-grade heal and monster-warding potions seemed to be one large silver coin, which was about how much she sold hers for. Malraux told her with a bitter smile that he'd said to Captain Dick, "Start negotiations at five silver coins. The market price is one large silver coin" because the market price had suddenly jumped from the former to the latter.

I suspected as much when he was dealing with the slave trader Reymond, but Captain Dick really isn't cut out for negotiation.

"He puts me in charge of crucial negotiations. He may not look it, but Captain Dick is a man who understands what's important and won't make a mess of it," Malraux cheerfully answered as if reading her mind. She didn't know which of the two was the real captain, but she felt she could rely on them.

04

We had a good talk, but it sure took a long time. I need to go buy some necessities and clothes for Sieg before it gets dark.

Members of the Black Iron Freight Corps were having dinner when Mariela hurried down the stairs into the restaurant-cum-tavern. They were drinking, too, even though the sun was still high in the sky.

Flanked by a large-chested woman on each side, Captain Dick was in good spirits. The rest of the members also had a lady sitting next to them and refilling their drinks.

Every single one of the women looked positively alluring, what with their revealing outfits.

"Ela, there you are. I'll go get you your food."

Amber addressed Mariela, who couldn't figure out where to look. Perhaps Amber had changed into clothes more suitable for serving customers; her red dress went well with her red hair. The shoulder straps holding up her extra-large basket of fruit looked like they were barely managing. Mariela was certain they must be made of some special monster material.

"Heeey, Amber, hurry up and get over here."

Captain Dick appeared to be the very definition of useless. There was no comparison between him and Lieutenant Malraux's honorable speech a short while ago.

This inn seemed to satisfy the three desires of humankind—namely, food, sleep, and barrels upon barrels of beer.

While Lieutenant Malraux was negotiating, this guy was...

Looking at how skillfully Amber handled Captain Dick, Mariela felt a tiny bit of sympathy for Lieutenant Malraux.

Just as Mariela went to leave the inn after telling Amber she was first going to do some shopping, Lynx piped up.

"You're goin' shopping? In that case, I'll show you around!"

He must have taken a bath; he looked refreshed and had changed into more casual attire.

Mariela wanted clothes for both herself and Sieg, so Lynx led her through a back alley onto a street near the northwestern district.

"The northwestern district's main road is full of stuff geared toward adventurers who work in the Labyrinth, so prices are kinda high. On this street, you can find little necessities and clothes for a good price without sacrificing quality."

The Yagu Drawbridge Pavilion was an inn on the lower end of first class, so although it received subsidies for lodging and meals, the alcohol and snacks were expensive. There was an additional cost if a young lady served your alcohol, and you could receive further "service" if you were on good terms with her. For a fee, of course.

Few people lived in the Labyrinth City, and few adventurers visited, either. To encourage people to live there, the costs of the minimum necessities needed to survive were kept to a reasonable level, and policies to attract adventurers had been enacted. Shop owners also decided to offer a variety of items and extra services in the hopes that those with deep pockets would spend as much money as possible.

"Captain Dick's obsessed with Amber," said Lynx. The implication was that he wanted to buy her freedom.

"She's good at handling him, but does he have a chance?" Mariela tilted her head questioningly.

Lynx laughed as he answered with an ambiguous "Well, he *is* the captain!"

The shop he led her to sold only really simple, basic clothes. Didn't look as if any crazy fashion trends had developed over the past two hundred years.

"Don't you think these go with your cloak?"

Both the tunic and the pants the shopgirl had picked out were very short.

"Th-th-th-this shows a lotta leg."

"Yeah, it's cute, right? You should pair it with these leggings underneath. They're thin, but the caterpillar thread makes them plenty strong."

The clothes the staff recommended were much shorter than those from two hundred years ago. The fact that they showed so much perplexed Mariela, but the leggings fit her perfectly, so it wasn't as if her legs were completely bare.

Since I'm wearing shorts over these, it only feels like my legs are exposed.

The clothes were very cute once they'd been arranged on the table to show what they'd look like when worn. The tunic had a lovely hemline decorated in a tricolor pattern, and although the pants were short, the accents along the hem matched the color of her cloak.

"A blue waist cord would make a great accent for these colors," said the lady as she produced a decorative cord for Mariela. The addition to her ensemble instantly made the whole thing more vivid.

I've never worn anything this cute before... But my legs...

The employee, as if surmising why Mariela kept glancing at the leg portion, spoke up.

"These leggings are black, so they'll make your legs look slimmer."

"I'll take them."

Mariela purchased the entire set. This was her Labyrinth City debut.

All riiight. Ack, too much leg! Too much!

Since she was on a roll, she also bought three pairs of underwear and three undershirts. She didn't know what size Sieg wore, so she let Lynx pick out his clothes, ending up with three largish shirts and three pairs of pants. She also found sewing supplies at the edge of the shop, so she bought scissors to cut Sieg's unkempt hair. The cost of the clothes was a bit on the high side at twelve silver coins.

Her next stop was the general store.

One handkerchief, two bars of soap, two toothbrushes, a hairbrush, and a rucksack to carry them in came out to two silver coins. Even though the city was isolated, the prices of these items were the same as in the Citadel City, maybe because they were daily necessities.

Mariela still had plenty of money left, but there were also a lot of things she needed.

First, I need to get ingredients for the potions the Corps ordered. I wonder what the prices of medicinal herbs are like now? Everyday necessities haven't changed, at least. After that, I also need to secure a place to live. Not much I can do about it right now, since Sieg's in bad shape, but it would be awkward to share a room with him forever. Still, I'm not gonna make him sleep in a shed.

Mariela pondered while she counted what she needed on her fingers.

I'll work hard to earn a living. I wanna make sure Sieg can eat as much as he wants.

Although she'd bought him on impulse, Mariela surprisingly found herself taking a liking to Sieg. She wanted him to have lots of food and rest so he could recover all the more quickly. Reymond had said he became a penal laborer during his time as a debt laborer when he'd gotten his former master's son injured. However, the way Sieg recoiled in fear just from her hand near his face showed he'd routinely been a victim of violence. Above all else, she just couldn't think of him as a miscreant.

That single blue eye is beautiful.
Mariela felt Sieg's eye showed his true self.

It was already close to evening when she emerged from the last shop.

She could see the mountain range on the other side of the Labyrinth City's outer wall drenched in the light of the evening sun. It was a familiar view, just like two hundred years ago. The town had gone through huge changes, yet life went on. If some things remained the same, maybe she could find a place to fit in.

After all, I've got Sieg with me. I even survived the Stampede. There's gotta be a way for me to have a quiet sort of life—I'm sure of it.

After admiring the evening landscape for a while, she ran over to Lynx and apologized. "Sorry for the wait."

"I'm staaarving." Lynx rubbed his stomach at the delicious smell wafting through the air, probably from dinner preparations.

"Didn't you just eat?"

"They say there's a separate stomach only for meat. I'm a growin' boy, y'know."

"What? Ah-ha-ha!"

The shadows lengthened in the evening sun.

"Ha-ha, look how long my legs are. I'm as tall as Captain Dick."

Lynx's shadow had spindly legs and walked with enormous strides.

"I wonder if I'm still growing, too."

"Mariela, shouldn't you be more worried about your chest than your height?"

"The heck?! That was mean! I'm gonna get Amber to teach me her secrets later."

The two shadows jovially hurried back side by side.

When they returned to the Yagu Drawbridge Pavilion, Captain Dick was passed out.

He lay on a table holding a cushion and talking in his sleep, his hands massaging it rather indecently as he mumbled "Amberrr," among other things.

He really was the definition of useless.

The other Corps members seemed accustomed to this scenario. They ignored him and enjoyed their meals and chitchat with the young ladies.

Meanwhile, Amber was busy serving a group of adventurers and a number of knights who'd just started eating. Apparently, she was a favorite.

When Mariela and Lynx sat at the counter, they heard a man who appeared to be an adventurer-turned-shopkeeper place an order. Today's menu was orc meat cutlet and hearty yagu milk stew.

"I'll take both. You, Mariela?"

Did his growing stomach have some kind of spatial magic cast on it?

Envious that he didn't have to worry about which one to pick, Mariela replied, "I'll take the hearty yagu milk stew. And could I get something for my companion that's easy to digest?" After she finished ordering, Lynx invited her to the Black Iron Freight Corps's table.

"Mariela, you haven't met the whole crew yet, have you? I'll introduce ya while we're waiting."

Captain Dick and Lieutenant Malraux were the founders of the Black Iron Freight Corps, and their crew included Lynx, the scout, and Yuric, the animal trainer, along with four additional members for eight in total—plus eight raptors.

Donnino, whose forte was maintaining the armored carriages, appeared to be a craftsman in his late thirties and thus the oldest member of the Corps. He was talking passionately about the carriages' armor as he chowed down on his meat, but when the alcohol came around, his true enthusiasm showed through as he went on at length about the types of steel used for armor or welding techniques.

The only one who seemed to understand what Donnino was talking about was Grandel, the shield knight. He was the next tallest after Captain Dick but slimmer than Lieutenant Malraux, and he sported a handlebar mustache. In contrast to Donnino and his carnivorous appetite, Grandel munched on a vegetable kebab.

I wonder if someone this pitiful-looking is fit to be a guard? I doubt he can even manage a shield, let alone armor.

Mariela had her doubts. Next to her sat a man named Franz, a healing magic user. Although they were indoors, he wore a hood low over his eyes and a mask that covered the upper half of his face. He seemed like a foster parent to Yuric; they did a lot together.

Then there was Edgan, a young dual wielder in his midtwenties. For some reason, he was passing envelopes to the young ladies in tow, trying his hardest to look cool. He could have just handed them over normally, but he instead grasped them between his index and middle finger while shooting the ladies a flirtatious sidelong glance. However, every one of the ladies was absorbed with her respective envelope and brushed aside his advances.

As Mariela mulled over each of the men and their distinctive personalities, Edgan tousled his short bangs as he said to her, "Feel free to hit me up if you ever want to send a letter to the imperial capital."

Just as Mariela was wondering what he handed over to the ladies, she was told he transported letters free of charge from the Yagu Drawbridge Pavilion to as far as their regular inn in the imperial capital. According to one of the ladies, the only way to send a letter from the Labyrinth City to the capital was to either ask one of the Merchants Guild's yagu caravans or personally request an adventurer or a private enterprise like the Black Iron Freight Corps to do it. Either way, the shipping charge would be expensive, and it wasn't easy to afford with their allowances. Everyone who had just received a letter was reading theirs attentively, and Mariela could tell they were very grateful.

"Oh yeah, I just deliver them along the way. If you can't come to the inn in the capital to pick it up yourself, there's a shipping fee, y'know."

He was attempting to be nice, but Mariela felt Edgan somehow ruined it by trying so hard to make himself look like a big shot. He was strangely proud about something that was a service from the Corps as a whole rather than something he did himself.

Some of the adventurers Mariela had known would leave a mess after finishing their meals, cause a considerable racket with their banter, and fondle the female staff before getting kicked out. However, the members of the Black Iron Freight Corps were decent, mature adults who enjoyed themselves in moderation.

"Amberrr..."

Geez, this guy's pathetic!

What happened to the dignity he'd shown when they first met?

At a time like this, she didn't see the reliable Lieutenant Malraux anywhere, nor Yuric.

"Hey, Lynx. Is it okay to leave the captain alone? And where are Malraux and Yuric?"

"The captain's always like this," Lynx replied, laughing off her concern. "Yuric can barely sleep a wink in the Fell Forest, so he's already in bed. The lieutenant went home."

It was a surprise to learn that Lieutenant Malraux was a married man with children and a house in the Labyrinth City.

Just then, their food was ready.

A wonderful aroma wafted from the yagu milk stew. It included a heaping amount of chicken and vegetables, both of which had been thoroughly boiled to a melt-in-your-mouth texture. The yagu milk had a gamy smell, but when she gave it a try, she found it had been blended with a lovely mixture of herbs that balanced out any gamy taste. The ingredients had been expertly condensed into a soup that boasted a depth of flavors.

The stew came with a side of fluffy white bread; a salad garnished with a thick, creamy dressing; and crunchy, thinly sliced fried potatoes.

"So good…"

As soon as the warm soup reached her stomach, she suddenly felt ravenous. So much had happened since she woke up, so she'd failed to notice she'd apparently been starving. Mariela devoured her meal in no time flat.

"Say, whatcha gonna do tomorrow?"

Although she'd eaten with gusto, Lynx had finished eating even sooner.

"Whoa, that was fast. Finished already? You had enough for two people, too…," Mariela answered in astonishment. "The plan for tomorrow is to go buy some medicinal herbs."

"If you're lookin' for herbs, I know a great place. I've got tomorrow off, so I'll take ya there. 'Bout what time d'you wanna go?" Lynx asked as he rubbed his belly. Though he'd just consumed two meals' worth of food, his stomach looked as flat as before. There just had to be some spatial magic involved.

Lynx and the rest of the Corps must have been tired from

running through the Fell Forest. And Mariela hadn't slept in a bed for two hundred years—it would be nice if she could sleep in a bit. She and Lynx agreed to head out just before noon.

With impeccable timing, the server came back carrying a tray of yagu milk risotto full of minced vegetables and meat and thick melted cheese. It was just as luscious as the stew had been. She had no doubt something with such excellent presentation was delicious.

"Whoa, that looks amazing…"

"Lynx, you just had two helpings of food…"

Even the server was astonished.

The female staff giggled, and Mariela couldn't help but join in. She'd laughed a lot today thanks to Lynx; tomorrow would surely be lots of fun, too.

"Well, see ya tomorrow!" Lynx headed back to the table with the rest of the Corps, scratching his head in apparent embarrassment. His gaze was fixated not on the ladies nor on the glasses of liquor but on the snacks—surely she wasn't just imagining things.

"Good night!" Mariela said, and everyone replied in kind. She took the tray of steaming, piping-hot risotto and headed for her room, a slight sense of warmth now in her heart.

05

Mariela entered her room carrying the rucksack she'd just bought, along with the tray.

Perhaps Sieg had been woken by the sound of the door opening, as he was trying to get up from the bed. His single blue eye darted restlessly around the room; he may have been slightly disoriented.

"Siegmund."

When she called his name, the deep-blue eye focused on Mariela...and then fixated on the steaming risotto.

You too, huh...?

Lynx hadn't been the only starving one.

"Can you get up?"

When she placed the tray on the table, Sieg got out of bed as if he'd been beckoned. His complexion looked a lot better, so maybe his fever had gone down, but his malnourished, emaciated body trembled, making him look like a newborn yagu.

"A-anyway, how about you wrap yourself in those sheets?"

It hadn't bothered her during his medical treatment, but now it was hard to look at him with the loincloth completely exposing his legs. She wanted to get him wrapped up into the many sheets for now. Seemingly embarrassed, Sieg quickly did as she suggested.

"How about you take a seat in this chair?"

His hesitation made her wonder if he'd always been forced to sit on the floor.

Even when he did sit, he simply swallowed hard as he stared at the risotto and made no move to tuck in.

"You can go ahead and eat. It's hot, so be careful."

On hearing this, Sieg finally reached for the spoon. He didn't seem to have any strength in the fingers of his right hand, so instead he gripped the handle with his left and scooped up some risotto. He brought it close to his face and took the first bite.

Sieg's blue eye opened wide. Another bite, then another.

099

He must have been famished. He cradled the plate in his right arm, which he couldn't move well, got a firm grip on the spoon in his left hand, and began to stuff his face with abandon.

"Here, have some water."

The risotto was well cooked and soft, but even so, he was eating with ravenous gusto. She poured him a cup of water so that he wouldn't choke, and it was when she was placing it on the table that she noticed.

He's crying.

Tears rolled down Siegmund's face as he ate.

Looks like he didn't bite his tongue or burn his mouth or anything. As I thought.

He finished every last grain of the risotto. The plate looked as if he'd licked it clean. As he drank the water, she could hear muffled sobs through his tears.

"Um, use this to dry your face, okay?"

She produced the handkerchief she'd bought and placed it in his left hand. When he looked at the brand-new towel he'd just been given, he let out a sound like a moan and burst into a fresh round of tears.

Yikes, what should I do...?

She didn't know how a hand towel could make someone cry, but the way his tears came flooding out made Sieg seem like a little boy to her.

"It's okay. You're okay."

Softly and slowly so as not to frighten him, Mariela reached out and stroked his head.

"You were scared and hurt; I know. But everything's gonna be okay now. Your swelling's gone down, and by tomorrow, your fever will, too."

As if comforting a small child, she embraced Sieg's head and continued to stroke it.

He'd probably been in constant pain ever since the black wolves had bitten him—no, maybe he'd been suffering long before that. He must have been terrified the entire time he was shut away in the dark, cramped carriage as it passed through the Fell Forest. Even after arriving in the Labyrinth City, there was no mistaking the anxiety he felt, not knowing whether the next moment would be his last.

Mariela believed the taste of the warm food must have brought him relief at last.

The medical treatment and food Mariela provided for Sieg had stirred his heart far more powerfully than she imagined.

Ever since he became a slave, Siegmund had never been treated as a human being. He was treated worse than livestock and even made to believe that it was right. His body and head were in such agony, not only from the arm and leg wounds but from the inflammation, too; he couldn't even think clearly. All this pain and suffering steadily robbed him of his strength, but even though he was dying, he didn't want to succumb. He couldn't help feeling terrified of his approaching doom.

All that pain, all that suffering, went away in an instant thanks to Mariela. She washed his contaminated wounds and gave him medicine and a warm bed. The change was so drastic that he thought he was in the throes of a fever dream. The reality hit him the moment he tasted the warm food.

How long has it been since I've had a hot meal or sat in a chair to eat? I'd even forgotten how to use a spoon.

The warm risotto was full of meat and vegetables, grains and yagu milk. When was the last time he'd eaten a dish with so many ingredients?

As Siegmund ate the risotto, he remembered a time when he sat in chairs and ate cooked food—all things that were natural for a human being to do.

Why, why, why…?

He recalled his own lot in life, the resentment he'd carried all this time, things he'd unknowingly stopped thinking about.

His life had sunk so low. He didn't feel he was blameless, but it was a fact that he'd been denigrated and senselessly robbed of any shred of decency.

And now a girl named Mariela had unconditionally provided him the warmth and dignity he'd lost.

All by herself, she'd healed a filthy, reeking, wretched man worth just two large silver coins, and she'd given him food—as if it was the most natural thing in the world to do.

Then when he'd shamefully burst into tears, she'd offered a brand-new handkerchief.

She treated him just like a human being.

This girl probably had no idea how rare that was for him.

After all, she seemed perplexed as she embraced and comforted him.

He'd lost everything, and she'd given him everything. Siegmund vowed he'd protect Mariela for the rest of his life.

"You still have a slight fever, so you should go right to bed."

Sieg had stopped crying at last. She dried his face with a different hand towel and put him to bed.

He still clutched in his left hand the handkerchief she'd given him.

Come to think of it, there was this one kid in the orphanage who would never let go of her favorite handkerchief. Maybe Sieg's like that, too?

She pushed the desk next to Sieg's bed and filled the pitcher with water in case he got thirsty in the middle of the night.

"I'm gonna take a bath, so I might make a bit of noise, but be sure to get some sleep."

Once she'd finished putting Sieg to bed, Mariela picked up her rucksack and headed for the bathroom.

For the first time in two hundred years! A baaath!

Since Sieg was sleeping, she didn't say it aloud, but Mariela was on cloud nine.

I've still got some magic left, so I'm gonna treat myself!

"Water, Drops of Life, Anchor, Ignite."

Mariela used lifestyle magic to add plenty of Drops of Life to the water in the bathtub and heated it.

Drawing up Drops of Life consumes magical energy, so normally, she couldn't be so indulgent in its use, but somehow her magic hadn't decreased very much today. A Drops of Life bath would relieve fatigue and make her skin soft and supple.

After removing her cloak, she noticed her clothing underneath it was worn out. The stitching was in especially bad shape; more than half of it had come loose. Unlike her cloak, which was woven from daigis fibers and repaired itself automatically, her other clothes were made of ordinary cloth, so it wasn't a shock that they'd deteriorated. But it was a marvel the same hadn't happened to her body.

Well, nobody has a body like this!

That wasn't quite the case here, but Mariela nonetheless flexed her muscles as she struck a defiant pose, then shucked off the rest of her clothes and got in the bath. Since she'd been asleep with suspended animation magic, her body wasn't full of sweat and grime, but she was extremely dusty. After rinsing with the water many times over, she washed herself thoroughly with the soap, taking extra care with her hair. Washing it just with soap alone would make it squeaky clean, but now the Drops of Life really made it shine.

After washing every last inch of her body, she refilled the tub with hot water and slowly immersed herself in it.

Ahhh, I feel alive again. I mean, I was literally just revived today, though.

It had really been a long day.

She'd met all kinds of people.

That reminds me—what Lynx said was really rude.

There was no way to avoid being reminded about it in the bath, since she could clearly see her chest. And here she'd gone to all the trouble of making a Drops of Life bath, too. She offered a prayer to the Goddess of Girth, Amber. *Perhaps I oughta massage 'em a bit; that's what the ladies in the brothels used to say. May the Goddess of Girth be generous in her blessing. Rub, rub.*

Tomorrow she would cut Sieg's hair, pick up some medicinal herbs, and browse the shops in town. She also wanted to buy Sieg shoes.

Mariela got out of the tub and changed into one of the shirts she'd just bought. If she had time, she wanted to get pajamas, too. She dried and combed her hair, and after brushing her teeth, all that was left was hitting the hay.

"G'night, Sieg," she said as she crawled into her own bed. There was no reply, so he must have been asleep.

I wonder when the last time I said "good night" was..., Mariela thought as she gazed absentmindedly at Sieg. She hadn't turned off the lights yet. Even though she was about to go to sleep now, it was still very bright.

She gazed at the walls and ceiling; they were so different from those of the cellar in the Fell Forest. The Stampede was a thing of the distant past. When she closed her eyes, she would wake up tomorrow morning.

You're okay; you're just gonna go to sleep and wake up like normal. You're fine; Sieg will probably say "good morning" when the sun wakes you up. Everything's okay; Sieg and Lynx and all the guys in the Black Iron Freight Corps I met today won't disappear.

Mariela told herself over and over again that things would be fine. Yet, she couldn't put out the lights. It made her remember the lantern's faint, wavering flame back in the cellar. Dim light was terrifying. She vividly remembered the sound of footsteps from the monsters flooding out of the forest and the macabre tremors that reverberated all the way to the cellar.

It's okay; it's fine; I'm okay. I don't hear any sounds like that. I'll be okay—now I'm not alone anymore.

Mariela curled up into a tiny ball on the wide bed and held her knees. Despite her attempts to reassure herself, she still strained her ears for the footsteps of an approaching horde.

What reached her ears instead was the laughter of the drunkards who were still making a racket, the cries of the raptors from outside the window, and Siegmund's slow breathing. At some point while she was listening to the sounds of life from the people and town, Mariela fell asleep.

CHAPTER 3

Bonds of Servitude

01

Creeeak, thud.

The sound of a door closing woke Mariela.

When she looked in the direction of the noise, she saw an unfamiliar half-naked man holding a pitcher. Well, more than half-naked—all he wore was a loincloth, which left most of his body basically out there in the open.

Is this one of those "shady characters" I've heard so much about?

No, it was just Sieg. Siegmund.

"G-good…morning…Lady Mariela."

Wow, he greeted me. He didn't say much yesterday. I wonder if having a good cry calmed him down.

Sieg's impactful "good morning" made the previous night's anxieties disappear once and for all.

"Morning, Sieg. You can just call me Mariela."

"I cannot…do that," he replied as he poured water from the pitcher into a cup and timidly held it out to her. "I f-fetched some… water. If you would like any."

Slightly embarrassed by his awkward good intentions, Mariela accepted the cup and took a sip. She could immediately tell that only a minimal amount of Drops of Life was mixed in.

"Well water? Sieg, you can't use lifestyle magic?"

"I…can use a little. But I heard well water…was better for you."

Groundwater contains Drops of Life, which is imbued with

the power of a ley line. The amount is so small that you can't feel its effects, but it's enough that there's a noticeable difference in those who drink it regularly. "A child raised on well water is a well-raised child," as the saying goes.

So he deliberately went out of his way and drew some water for me. And all while looking like that... I wish I'd given him his new clothes yesterday.

He'd starting crying while eating his risotto, and between comforting him and putting him to bed, she'd regrettably forgotten about the clothes.

"Thank you," she replied, and she drank the rest. Sieg stood at the ready by the door. His tone was very polite, but his appearance was rather unseemly.

Mariela had him leave the room, then quickly changed into the clothes she bought yesterday. She was a bit bothered by how much leg was showing, but the outfit was just as cute as she'd thought. Furthermore, it was comfortable and easy to move around in.

Mariela brought Sieg back into the room and checked on his injuries. The fever was completely broken, and he seemed to be able to properly move his right hand now. The grip strength in his right hand had recovered only about halfway, and his arm felt stiff, but he reassured her it would soon be back to normal as he flexed his hand.

She knew the brand on his chest would still be there, but it had faded enough that it was less noticeable now.

The serious swelling on his leg had subsided as well, and the discolored burn marks were now covered in a thin layer of pink skin. The gnawed-off flesh hadn't grown back, so he couldn't walk normally, but for the time being, she was relieved.

"Soon my leg...will be healed enough for me...to run again."

Sieg was filled with determination, a complete change from yesterday.

Geez, Sieg, you're flying high now that you're on the mend. Well, I'm gonna heal your leg once I make a high-grade potion anyhow. But before that!

She picked up her rucksack, and the two of them headed to the inn's backyard. Ever the attentive person, Sieg took the rucksack and carried it out as if it was second nature.

Mariela borrowed a stool from the livestock shed and had Sieg sit on it. "Today, we'll cut your hair," she declared. "I don't want to get any in your eye, so please keep it shut."

"Understood... Thank you."

Yesterday, merely bringing her hand close to Sieg's face had frightened him, so she was worried about how he might react to the scissors, but he squeezed his eye shut and sat there in docile silence.

Mariela gently touched his hair.

How will this turn out...?

It was stiff, probably caked with soil and dust, and so heavy that it didn't even look like hair—she couldn't get the brush to go through it. His hair was like the matted balls of fur that hung from wild yagus. With no other choice, she snipped the mats off.

There were tons of these mats, and she cut them all. Only once she could actually brush his hair would she tidy it up, so she snipped away with vigor.

Shoot... I cut off too much...

Only about an inch of hair remained.

Mariela couldn't make them, but she'd heard hair-growth potions existed. Apparently, they were specialized special-grade potions that aristocrats with thinning hair bartered for in secret...

Ah well, it'll grow out in no time!

She left the bangs long and trimmed the back to a short, uniform length.

Mariela had thought leaving just the bangs would more or less get the job done, but it was an unexpectedly stylish look.

Next came the beard, but…

I have no idea how to shave a beard! And I don't have a razor or a knife, either!

Just as she was wondering whether she should give him the scissors and have him do it himself, she heard a voice. "What's up? You cuttin' his hair? Whoa, you're pretty good. Hey, cut mine, too." Lynx had appeared. Perfect timing.

"Sure thing. But before that, what do I do with the beard?"

"Eh? C'mon, that's the kinda thing you should let him do. Oh, you got no knife? Here, borrow mine."

That was Lynx for you: sensible.

"I'm done with your hair, Sieg. You should shave with the knife Lynx is lending you. After that, I have soap, a toothbrush, a change of clothes, and a hand towel, so you can take a bath."

She handed Sieg the rucksack as she spoke, to which Lynx laughed. "What're you, his mom?"

"What sort of hairstyle are you interested in today, sir?"

"Somethin' kinda…cool?" Lynx's request was rather vague.

"Whaaa—? Not a chance."

"That's harsh!"

Mariela cut Lynx's hair as they bantered back and forth. He seemed to want it only evened out, so after trimming about an inch total, she was done.

"Here you are! One handsome man, as requested."

"Whoo-hoo!"

"Wind."

Lynx blew off the cut hair with wind magic. Although this type was normally used in battle, he adjusted its potency so it sent only the hair flying off his clothes without blowing any dirt around. He was quite skilled.

"So you know wind magic, Lynx."

"Yup. Everyone in the Black Iron Freight Corps can use magic. But I didn't have much magic left yesterday, so I didn't use it."

She'd heard it was difficult to temper attack magic into lifestyle magic. If someone as young as Lynx had mastered it, the Black Iron Freight Corps must be a highly capable group of individuals. Even so, for Lynx to have almost run out of magic meant traveling through the Fell Forest really was no joke.

As they talked to pass the time while they waited, Sieg returned.

"Huh…? Sieg?"

With a shave, a thorough washing, and a new shirt and pants, Sieg now appeared to be in his midtwenties.

His hair, which had looked gray before, was actually silver and complemented the deep blue of his eye.

Overall, he needed some meat on his bones, but he had a nice, straight nose and full lips, and he was actually quite the looker. The scar over his right eye, now exposed after the haircut, was a gruesome sight, but it made the handsome left side stand out all the more.

The bangs she'd left a little longer than the rest to disguise the too-short haircut were also oddly sexy.

I thought he was middle-aged…

Sieg respectfully thanked Lynx and returned the knife to him. For some reason, Lynx had a look of indifference on his face.

So the half-naked old-timer evolved into a dashing barefoot man.

In Mariela's eyes, it made no difference whether he was an old man or a handsome young one.

"Let's grab breakfast."

More importantly, their stomachs were empty, so the three of them headed inside for some food.

A girl about ten years old whom Mariela hadn't seen before was working in the restaurant.

"Emily, breakfast pleeease!"

"Oh, Lynx, it's you. Gooood morning!" After Mariela had greeted her, too, Emily replied brightly, "This is the first time we've met, isn't it, miss? I'm Emily!"

"She's the owner's only daughter and in charge of breakfast. Well, more like she just warms the dishes the owner makes."

"Lynx, you're so meeean. It's hard to warm food without burning it, y'know! Here you are!"

Emily puffed up her cheeks at Lynx's explanation as she rolled over a tea trolley holding breakfast for three.

Breakfast was a piece of bread about twice the size of her palm, soup, a big sausage with scrambled eggs, and a salad.

It was a lot of food for first thing in the morning.

"Ahhh, man, this looks great!"

Lynx took a plate and began to chow down with gusto.

Mariela indicated the seat next to her, and Sieg sat down without objecting. When she said "Here you go" and handed him a plate, he also started to gobble down his food, though not quite as fast as he did yesterday.

Mariela split her bread into three pieces and put one each on Lynx's and Sieg's plates.

"Fanks."

"Fank you...very muth."

"Swallow first, then talk."

She ended up splitting her sausage among the three of them, and they all happily finished their late breakfast.

"Mariela, you wanted to buy medicinal herbs, right? Wanna go now?"

Everyone in the Black Iron Freight Corps seemed to still be asleep. With nothing else to do, Lynx invited her to go shopping.

"I want to buy shoes for Sieg first. Know any good places?"

"Hmm. Shoes, huh...? What was that place called again?"

"I got these shoes the other day from Elba's Shoe Shop!"

Apparently, Elba's Shoe Shop was Emily's recommendation. She spun round and round in the shoes that had been bought for her before she began to wobble and say, "I'm dizzy..."

"Let's go look at Elba's Shoe Shop, then."

Emily saw the trio off, saying "Have a nice day!" as they departed the Yagu Drawbridge Pavilion.

02

Elba's Shoe Shop sold traditional, relatively inexpensive shoes marketed toward a range of customers, from ordinary citizens to moderately experienced adventurers. The inside was overflowing with stacks upon stacks of all types of footwear.

"Welcome. What kind of shoes are you looking for?"

"Men's shoes, preferably orc leather boots."

Orc meat was a popular food, which meant a large quantity of orc leather was in circulation, too. Since it was supple and easy to work with, apprentice artisans used it in a lot of their products, making it easy to find at a bargain price. However, it wasn't sturdy enough to endure combat, and orcs weren't exactly well liked, so it wasn't considered good leather. It was commoners' everyday wear at best.

Shoes were created with leatherworking skills, but they were individually handmade and didn't run cheap. Orc leather was frequently used in shoes for children, whose feet grew quickly, but adults with money to spare often chose slightly higher quality leather products.

The shop employee—perhaps he was Elba—took one look at Sieg's bare feet and Mariela's tattered shoes and brought out several pairs of boots from the back of the shop without a word.

"If you want orc leather, these should do it."

"What are the soles made of?"

"Orc hide for these two, wood on this one, and creeper on those three pairs. Well, I say 'creeper,' but it's from a sapling. It'll deteriorate quickly."

Creepers were climbing plant monsters that inhabited wetlands. After paralyzing prey with its venomous thorns, it twined around them and sucked their blood. The vines it used to quickly catch prey were several yards long and as thick as a person's arm. Cutting one off with a sharp blade would cause it to leak a gooey, viscous fluid that was used to make creeper rubber, a popular material for high-quality wheels, armor lining, and shoe soles, among other things.

Not only did creepers live in wetlands with poor footing, but their vines were fast and poisonous. This made them difficult to keep under control, so creeper rubber was a luxury material.

Creeper saplings were a cheap alternative to the rubber. They grew in shaded areas of forests and were poisonous as well, but they lacked thorns, and their vines moved extremely slowly. They would wrap around small animals paralyzed from carelessly gnawing on the vines, and they sucked only a little bit of blood.

The vines were roughly the thickness of a human thumb, but they were soft and flabby enough to be torn off by the likes of rabbits. Even children could harvest them with gloves, so the material was cheap and widely distributed. Performance-wise, however, the saplings were inferior to their parent stock, and they consequently tended to be used in disposable items.

"Huh, is something blended with this creeper rubber?"

"That's one of my prototypes, blended with slimes. I wanted to see if I could make a springier rubber from creeper sapling. It's well made and doesn't slip or cause fatigue easily, but the durability isn't nearly up to snuff. It'd be serviceable if we were elsewhere and could just keep using restoration potions on it, but here in the Labyrinth City, it doesn't measure up to the longevity of orc leather."

All the rubber-soled shoes made by Elba were of good craftsmanship and reasonably priced at one large silver coin, so Mariela chose a pair that fit Sieg.

"Thanks for your business. Here's a freebie for ya. If you take good care of the shoes, they should last you four or five years."

Elba even threw in some free wax for maintaining the shoes. He was a kind shoemaker.

I'll buy shoes for myself when the potion payment comes in.

When Mariela finished paying and left the shop, Sieg was holding the shoes very carefully.

"Sieg? You're not gonna wear them?" Mariela asked as he carried the brand-new boots as if they were treasure.

"I-I'm...still limping... If I was to damage the soles, then..."

He seemed to want to say he'd damage the shoes if he wore them while dragging his leg, so he'd wear them as soon as he could walk properly.

"But if you're still limping, does that mean your leg hurts?"

"M-my leg is okay... Um, thank you very much...for the shoes."

Sieg bowed deeply and expressed his thanks, boots still in his arms. His expression was stiff, as if he'd forgotten how to smile, but it cracked just a little. Lynx, who'd been watching and noticed Mariela didn't seem to understand, said to her, "Let's go. I bet it's been a looong time since he had new shoes. Seems like a lotta people don't provide 'em to their slaves. So, like, I guess what I'm sayin' is, I get where he's comin' from."

Lynx seemed to sympathize with Sieg, so she let him carry the shoes as he was, and the three of them headed to a medicinal herb shop next.

*   *   *

They went to a back alley in the northeastern district to buy the herbs.

Many shops in the Labyrinth City offered herbs because they could be gathered in the Labyrinth. There were even major enterprises and specialist shops.

Mariela had heard the environment in the Labyrinth differed among the strata, from snowy mountains, to deserts, to tropics, all of which had various kinds of herbs for harvesting. Of course, they had monsters, too. Since Mariela couldn't fight, she'd be unable to travel through them alone, but some adventurers specialized in collecting herbs.

These adventurers took the collected herbs to the Adventurers Guild or specialty shops. The herbs purchased there were then either sold to customers within the Labyrinth City or dried by specialist shops or businesses to preserve them and then transported out of the city.

Their circulation in this area was the same as for other materials. Most of them were processed in the Labyrinth City and then loaded onto yagus and sent across the mountains.

The Labyrinth City was no longer an independent country but a frontier territory of the Empire, which used to adjoin the Kingdom of Endalsia. No wonder the Empire's currency was now in use.

If the monsters in the Labyrinth and the Fell Forest weren't controlled through culling, another stampede would happen and cause catastrophic damage. This was why a monster subjugation army was stationed in the city and was proactive in attracting adventurers. The associated costs were covered by taxes on materials and treasure obtained in the Labyrinth. The tax rate was the same as for other labyrinths, but no route existed that allowed safe transport of large quantities. Since the route that used yagus had a high shipping cost, purchase prices were cheaper than in other labyrinth cities.

To balance this, the tax rate within the Labyrinth City and the costs of items adventurers needed for exploration were lowered, but one would hesitate to say that it was attractive to either adventurers or merchants. Mariela and the others didn't know this, but managing the Labyrinth City has been a headache-inducing problem for generations of margraves.

Lynx led Mariela to a medicinal herb specialty shop that did business with the Black Iron Freight Corps. Shops like this would purchase herbs and process them through dehydration or other methods to prepare them for transport out of the city. Depending on the shop, the herbs could also be processed into medicine and sold to city residents. While these medicines weren't as effective as potions, people known as chemists created a variety of them from medicinal herbs, and those who possessed alchemic skills would often run an herb shop while serving as chemists.

The medicinal herb specialty shop Lynx showed her to was on the small side, but it sold a wide variety of herbs, all of which seemed to be good quality.

In the shop's dim interior was an eccentric-looking bespectacled old man inspecting herbs.

"Ol' Man Ghark! You alive in there?!"

"Izzat you, Linnie? Y'brought a woman with ye today. Yer really movin' up in the world."

"Shut it. She's your customer today! Show some consideration, wouldja?"

The two were quite close.

The inside of the shop was packed with a large variety of dried herbs lined up next to one another, from familiar items such as curique and calgoran to rare materials used in special-grade and specialized potions.

Unfortunately, though, they were processed poorly. There are proper ways of processing herbs for each kind of medicinal effect, but all of them require taking conditions like temperature and pressure out of the equation little by little. Furthermore, a long time had passed since these had been dried, and the effects of some were completely gone.

Their efficacy's halved.

She lifted an herb she needed and asked if he had any that weren't dried.

"Over there. Dryin' herbs ain't a job for an amateur. I swear, rookies sure are picky about the oddest things."

"These fiorcus petals were dried without removing the pollen. The lunamagia here was dried at too high a temperature. And it's pretty old, too. I don't want them," Mariela replied, a little offended by his curtness. Ghark removed his glasses and peered at her.

"You an appraiser? Or maybe a foreign Pact-Bearer? Whatever y'are, nothin' gets past ye. Ye've got sharp eyes. Wait here."

Ghark headed to the back and brought out some undried medicinal herbs. They were in good shape, as if they'd just been picked.

Appraisal was a skill possessed by around one in ten people and allowed its user to learn about people and objects by accessing the Akashic records. However, despite its name, it mostly targeted things like people, plants, monsters, and weapons, and it was hard to get better at the skill. Information beyond human intellect, such as in the Akashic records, couldn't be used through ordinary effort or talent.

Incidentally, Mariela didn't have the Appraisal skill. Her ability to tell what condition materials were in was due to her alchemic skills.

Like a chef who can determine the ingredients and seasoning used in a dish by tasting it, an experienced alchemist could determine the condition of materials through their alchemic skills. Unlike with Appraisal, which could give you information on items you're not familiar with at all if your level was high enough, subjects were limited to alchemic materials and created items you already knew something about. However, plants weren't the only alchemic materials; there was also a wide range of other types such as minerals, animal materials, and monster materials, so it was very convenient.

However, even if you had alchemic skills in the Labyrinth City, being unable to make a pact with a ley line meant you couldn't make potions, so you couldn't improve. Even if you handled materials daily, you wouldn't be able to assess their condition at a glance like Mariela as long as your alchemic skills remained low. Alchemists who made a pact in the vicinity of the Empire and had sufficient experience could do it, but if they left the area where they made the pact to a place they had no connection to with a Nexus, they couldn't draw Drops of Life to make potions. That would take away their source of income, so it was rare for a Pact-Bearer to move to another region unless there was a special reason.

"I've only got non-astringent apriore seeds. I'm outta lund petioles today. If ye come back tomorrow, y'can get the rest of what you need then."

Ghark apparently ventured into the Labyrinth himself.

The apriore seeds were processed flawlessly, but he didn't have quite enough of them. Considering Lieutenant Malraux's requested delivery date, removing the astringency herself seemed to be the best option, so she requested trona crystals as well for that purpose.

"I thought ye were a novice chemist, but y'can handle processin' materials? Yer a lot different from those fools who can only mix herbs together. Need anythin' else? I'll put it all together for ye." He grinned broadly as he spoke, giving her the feeling she'd made a good impression.

"Do you have nigill buds, ones without open leaves? Frozen ones are fine, too. Also, I'll need leech venom glands. I'd like ones pickled in oil if possible."

"Got 'em. How're these?"

Nigill was a bulb plant that budded under snow, and brand-new buds that hadn't been exposed to the air were used as ingredients in specialized potions that restored muscle tissue. Since there was demand for these potions from adventurers who'd been bitten by monsters, some farmers in the Citadel City specialized in growing nigill. The nigill buds Ghark showed her had been harvested at the ideal time and then frozen. Their quality was just as good as those from nigill farmers.

Parasite leeches are creatures about the size of an adult's thumb that will latch on to any living thing—human, animal, or monster. They produce an analgesic poison from their venom gland, so when they attach to a part of the body the victim can't see, such as the back, they will continue to suck blood without being noticed—hence why they're called parasite leeches. Because the venom itself is hematogenic, the victim won't become anemic. The leeches are so revolting that, if anything, a goblin covered in them would cause an adventurer more mental trauma than physical danger.

Since paralyzing poison dissolves in water and blood-forming components dissolve in oil, extracting the components was an easy task. But since the leeches were so gross looking, Mariela didn't want to touch them if at all possible. These ones had been processed with the utmost precision and pickled in oil; they didn't even register to her as leeches in this form.

"Thank you, Mr. Ghark! These leeches are perfect!" The old man's professional work impressed Mariela.

"Ye just didn't want to touch 'em...," Ghark said in exasperation. He'd seen right through Mariela, who laughed sheepishly as he asked, "Was that all ye needed?"

"Um, besides that..."

Mariela ordered the number of components she needed for Lieutenant Malraux's request and for Sieg's potion.

With these, I can make a potion to heal Sieg's leg!

She looked over her shoulder and smiled at Sieg, who stood at the entrance to the shop with his shoes in his arms. He walked up to her, perhaps interpreting the sudden eye contact to mean he was being summoned.

"Hang on, Sieg."

"U-understood," Sieg replied, unsure of what Mariela wanted, and Ghark handed him the bundle of medicinal herbs.

"Includin' the stuff ye ordered, that'll be twenty-two silver coins."

Though Ghark's work on the herbs was perfect, they cost 20 or 30 percent less than they would have in the Citadel City.

"That's because I can collect all of 'em in the Labyrinth myself, so there's no transport fee, and there're no taxes in the middle of town."

"Taxes are levied when you leave the city limits," added Lynx. "But I think Lieutenant Malraux said the tax rates aren't any different from other places."

Apparently, Mariela had the Citadel City's policies to thank for being able to buy the items cheaply. She could get everything she needed for about half the amount of money she had left.

"Do you have any po—medicine vials?"

"The only things I got that ain't herbs're over there in the corner."

The corner Ghark indicated was filled with a haphazard display of alchemic materials other than herbs, such as medicine vials, halite, crystal fragments, and small magical gems, along with a wooden box packed with odds and ends unceremoniously shoved underneath the display on the floor. When Mariela looked inside, she found items used in alchemy—or rather, items that had no use other than for alchemy—such as odd gadgets, paper, ink, and pens. Bags and vials full of unknown substances had also been tossed in. They were all secondhand and covered in dust.

I guess he wouldn't have potion vials, huh?

Although one might lump potions into a single category, they were often fickle things with disjointed ingredients and effects that had to be managed differently depending on the type of potion. For example, some weakened in sunlight, some deteriorated easily at room temperature, and some lost their efficacy when exposed to air for an extended period.

From an alchemist's point of view, it was a matter of course for potions to deteriorate easily, since they had an immediate effect on wounds after being consumed. However, for the way they were used, it was too much trouble to change the storage method for each individual potion.

This was why potions were stored in vials created with alchemic skills. Vials that mitigated potion deterioration were made of a special glass tempered with magical gems and Drops of Life. Ones for potions that were expensive or deteriorated easily were etched with a magic circle as well as a magic circle–inscribed seal or label.

Because potion vials were easy to reuse, they were bought and sold in every town.

But without potions, there's no reason to sell the vials. Guess I've got no choice but to make 'em myself.

Creating vials was a time-consuming task, so much so that there were alchemists who specialized in it. Mariela's master was strict and trained her in vial-making, so she could do it her-self, but...

What a pain...

She would have to start by gathering the ingredients. Tomor-row was going to be wasted on vial-making.

Although there were no vials, she fished around in the dusty box in case it had anything else that might come in handy. Ghark noticed and called, "If anythin' strikes yer fancy, bring the box over." He offered them for free.

Apparently, alchemists who came to the Labyrinth City from the outside were forced to sell these items when they left countless years ago. Ghark told her it was too much of a bother to throw away these used items he'd already bought, so her taking them was perfect.

The only items left were useless to anyone who couldn't make potions. For someone who couldn't appraise them, throwing away unfamiliar powders and seeds with no label would be worrisome. However, not only did Mariela need some of them, she was also grateful to find items she'd normally have to pay a lot for. Of course, there was obvious junk, too.

Mariela bought the items she needed: medicine vials, halite, magical gems, and spare herbs for three silver coins as thanks for Ghark's generosity. In total, she paid two large silver coins and five silver coins, then left the shop.

"Yer order should be ready tomorrow evenin'. If ye ever need any more medicinal herbs, come back anytime," said Ghark as he saw her off.

"You're awesome, Mariela!" exclaimed Lynx with admiration as soon as she exited the shop. "Ol' Man Ghark's a real crank and only puts out processed herbs he messed up. He says they're enough for people who don't know any better. That was the first time I've seen him judge a person capable on the spot. He said to come back anytime, so he must like you a lot."

Mariela got a box of odds and ends and a large variety of good-quality herbs. She was glad Ghark liked her. It was all thanks to her master's strict guidance, and for that, she was grateful.

It was long past noon now, and despite her late breakfast, Mariela was hungry. Food carts serving adventurers had popped up in the Labyrinth's vicinity, and in one corner alone near Ghark's shop, there were carts selling dried fruit, bread, meat skewers, and other sundries. Mariela ended up purchasing ogre dates, dried apricots, and a small bottle of olives, as well as a skewer to thank Lynx for showing her around. As they ate, the three of them headed back to the Yagu Drawbridge Pavilion.

03

When they returned to the inn, Yuric was waiting for them.

"'Ey, Lynx, skippin' out on cleaning the carriages?"

"I'm not skippin' it, man. But c'mon, can't we do it after lunch?"

"You're gonna find another excuse after lunch, yeah?"

Lynx tried to put off cleaning the cargo holds of the armored carriages, but his resistance was in vain as Yuric dragged him off. Mariela resisted quipping, "Wasn't that skewer you just had lunch?" and instead cheerfully waved good-bye to Lynx.

Mariela needed one last ingredient. She went up to the counter of the restaurant-cum-tavern and asked the owner for a bottle of bolka.

Bolka was a cheap spirit so intense it felt as if your mouth was on fire when you drank it. The owner's expression seemed to be asking what possible use she could have for it, which was why she told him, "I'm using it to sterilize a wound." That reasoning was apparently enough, and he brought out a bottle from the back.

With this, I have all the ingredients! Now I can finally make medicine for Sieg.

Mariela balled her hands into tight fists. After a quick dusting of the hodgepodge box outside the inn, she and Sieg carried it to their room.

Once they were in the room, Mariela took the implements she needed out of the hodgepodge box and asked Sieg to wash them in the bathtub. Since she'd dusted it off, just washing it with water produced through lifestyle magic would be enough. While he was doing that, she began processing the ingredients.

High-grade potions used lunamagia as a base. Lunamagia was a grass that grew along the banks of underground lakes and didn't freeze even in wintertime. It could be used in a high-grade potion only if it was bathed in the light of a moonstone, a faintly glowing magical gem, as it grew.

The first step is to dry the lunamagia at ten to eleven degrees Celsius, the same as the environment in which it grows. Any higher or lower and the potion will lose efficacy.

"Form Transmutation Vessel, Tune Temperature to Ten Degrees, Decompress, Crumble, Dehydrate."

She used her alchemic skills to produce an invisible vessel called a *Transmutation Vessel* and adjusted its temperature to ten degrees. Then, to quickly dry the lunamagia at such a low temperature, she decreased the pressure and further dehydrated the plant, spinning the air around inside before pulverizing it.

Mariela skillfully and efficiently processed the material, but she was handling only five aspects at once: maintaining the Transmutation Vessel and controlling its temperature, pressure, dryness, and circulation speed. If she were more proficient, she could control an even greater number of alchemic skills at once, but managing temperature was a tricky thing. The ability to control it within one degree of difference was limited to a handful of experts. Even if you said "ten degrees," it's not as if there was a thermometer; you had to rely on intuition. Since the flow of air during drying could also cause temperature inconsistency, you ended up having to manage it while keeping an eye on the state of the materials. The craftmanship needed for this process went beyond skills alone.

Such difficult temperature control was Mariela's specialty. She could precisely match the desired temperature, then maintain that temperature and dry materials evenly—all because of her master's training, of course. Mariela's master would buy rainbow flowers, which change color depending on their drying temperature, and make her dry them. The optimum drying temperature for a rainbow flower depended on the number of petals it had. As its name suggests, if dried to perfection, it will turn into a beautiful blossom reflecting all the colors of the rainbow.

If she failed to do it correctly, she'd go without a meal, and if she succeeded, she got to eat an extra helping. Sometimes it was the food that motivated the young Mariela, but the beauty of the finished rainbow flowers enchanted her as well. Day after day until her magical reserves ran out, she dried all sorts of plants, from her garden's medicinal herbs to weeds in the Fell Forest, and before she knew it, she'd acquired a top-notch skill.

Mariela clearly remembered the beautiful sight of the wall in her room completely covered by rainbow-colored flowers.

Since herb-drying by itself wasn't a job in the Citadel City, Mariela herself had no idea just how advanced her skill was.

Sieg handed her the implements she'd had him wash.

"Clean Water, Wash, Drain, Dehydrate, Sterilize."

She put the finishing touches on the prewashed implements with alchemic skills.

Although she had wanted Sieg to wash the other glass implements, too, he was watching her work with great interest, so she had him sit on the bed to observe so he wouldn't be in the way.

Extracting the medicinal components from the lunamagia was the first step. The cylindrical glass vessel was equipped with a metal tripod, allowing it to stand upright. This was a tool often used for lunamagia extraction, and the diameter of the cylinder was about the size of a thumb and pinkie finger put together. It was a small extraction vessel that could distill one to ten portions at a time.

The lower part of the cylindrical vessel was a thin funnel with a stopcock that could be opened and closed to empty the liquid inside. She set a beaker underneath and closed the stopcock. The vessel narrowed at the top as well, with a hole in the very center that could be closed by a valve and a ventilation hole at the top with a stopcock that was currently in the open position. The valve had a nozzle, and it could spray liquid from the top when the tank was connected to a ventilator.

The cylinder and tank seemed to originally come with a magical temperature adjustment tool, but someone else had bought it. It also lacked a ventilator, but Mariela could adjust the temperature and ventilation through her alchemic skills. As long as she had the vessel, that was enough.

Before putting any herbs in, she tested it. The cylindrical vessel was slightly below the freezing point. She set the temperature of the tank and water within it just above the freezing point and sprayed the water. It was important to control the temperature of the nozzle so the inside wouldn't freeze. The mist it spouted froze when it reached the inside of the vessel and turned into minute snow crystals. When she controlled the vapor inside the vessel and created a vortex that swirled from the center to the top and bottom, the snow crystals were caught up in the current and danced around and around.

"That oughta do the trick."

Lunamagia's medicinal components dissolved in below-freezing water. Therefore, to extract them, the lunamagia needed to make contact with either water that'd had salt added to it to keep it from freezing, or ice. Since it needed to come in contact with something solid, the sprayed water should be frozen into tiny pieces of ice to maximize the contact area, and then the lunamagia and ice should be stirred together in the vessel to cause a reaction.

The powdered snow was pretty as it twinkled and turned. Mariela controlled the temperature of the vessel, the spraying water tank, and the nozzle, as well as managing the spraying vapor, the atmosphere in the container, and the airflow all at once. Most alchemists used magical tools for three-point temperature control and spraying vapor management, and they controlled only the vessel's atmosphere and airflow themselves. Considering this, Mariela's alchemic skills were nothing to sneeze at, but she was using the fullest extent of her ability to control all these elements. If she didn't have the extraction vessel, she would've needed to use salt water for the extraction. Since a saltwater extraction weakened the efficacy of the finished product, the vessel was a big help.

She put the finely crushed lunamagia in the vessel and replaced the water in the tank with liquid containing Drops of Life. After she finished spraying one potion's worth, she focused on managing the temperature and airflow in the vessel. This stage was the most crucial part of making a high-grade potion. She was exhausted.

Somehow, she did it, as the white snow crystals emitted the yellow-tinged light of a moonstone.

She ended her control of the vessel's interior, opened the stopcock, and collected the extract in the lower container. After that, she would normally let it return to room temperature, but this was for a specialized potion to restore Sieg's gouged flesh. Next was to peel the still-frozen nigill buds.

When nigill was close to thawing, it sprouted and broke through the snow in a single night. She removed the buds, which were harvested right before they could sprout, and crushed them with her fingertips, then added them to the chilled lunamagia extract. Now, as the liquid returned to room temperature, the medicinal components began to dissolve.

The most difficult part of the process was over, but a troublesome step still remained.

Mid- and high-grade potions were highly potent and brought about rapid recovery. Because of this, certain components were mixed in to regulate the body and suppress any backlash: ogre dates for mid-grade potions, treant fruit for high-grade potions. Ogre dates were commonplace and even sold dried, but treant fruit was rare. Ghark's shop would probably sell it, but it was too well-known as a high-grade potion ingredient, and a chemist wouldn't be likely to buy it even taking the efficacy into account.

So she didn't buy treant fruit this time, instead creating a substitute with ogre dates used for mid-grade potions and medicinal herbs. The recipe called for three roots of mandragora and its subspecies, three leaves, two stalks, one seed, one petal, two mushrooms, and one piece of bark. After drying each of the thirteen materials at the appropriate temperatures, she measured a certain amount of each, mixed them together, pickled them in olive oil, and pressure extracted them for about an hour to speed things up. Normally, this would be a complicated process involving a scale and a pressure vessel, but Mariela skillfully and efficiently proceeded with just her alchemic skills, set on the notion that "going tool-free is fundamental."

While the hour-long extraction took place, Mariela arranged other liquids. She extracted curique, ogre date, and mandragora components, which were materials in low-, mid-, and high-grade potions, to remove the poison from arawne. This plant's roots had analgesic components, while its leaves contained anti-inflammatory ones. After processing other materials as well, she either wrapped them in oiled paper or stored them in medicine vials. They would be good for about a month in these conditions.

The substitute ingredient was ready around the time she finished her other tasks. Mariela slowly reduced the pressure while making sure it didn't drop too far below room temperature. The oil was now an amber color, signaling quality execution. She ladled out a spoonful and dissolved it in a mixture of Drops of Life and alcohol distilled from the bolka.

She carefully mixed the four types of completed extracts together after removing their dregs. Because they had to be mixed in order and there was a large quantity to be mixed all at once, she had to stay vigilant until the very end.

"Anchor Essence."

The specialized high-grade potion was complete at last.

"Alllll doooone! Applause, please!"

"Ohhh...?"

Sieg, who had been watching Mariela's process intently, seemed confused at her sudden pronouncement, but he clapped as instructed.

"Man, I'm beat. I didn't think just one bottle would make me this tired!"

"W-well done."

Under normal circumstances, the time-consuming substitute ingredient would have been prepared in advance so she could process all the ingredients at once. Today, she made everything from scratch, so it was no easy task.

Mariela tested it immediately.

"Here. Sieg, hold out your right arm."

"O-okay."

Sieg still looked perplexed as he held his right arm out with his palm facing up.

"Other way, other way."

Mariela grabbed his arm and turned it so the spot where the black wolves had bit him was facing up, and she poured drops of the newly made potion onto it.

"Good. It works."

The sunken scar from the black wolves emitted a faint light and quickly swelled, then disappeared without a trace in an instant.

"Can you try clenching and unclenching? Is it moving properly? Ah, it is."

Just this morning, his right arm had had no strength and could only move slowly, but now it was moving without a hitch.

"Oh...I can... I can move it..."

"Good, good. Okay, go ahead and kneel— Oh, on the chair, okay? Now turn around and roll up the leg of your pants so I can see your left calf."

Sieg had been attempting to put his feelings into words when Mariela urged him to show the wound on his left leg.

This wound had been cauterized to stop the bleeding after it was inflicted by the black wolves. He'd received the minimal treatment with healing magic, only enough to form a thin layer of skin over the bite wound. Bacteria had then entered it and further aggravated the lesion as he was being transported to the Labyrinth City. Mariela had cured the inflammation yesterday with a potion, but internally, it was still a mess.

She poured an especially generous amount of the potion on his calf, and the gouged flesh immediately began to regenerate. She could tell that the muscular tissue under the thin layer of skin was healing bit by bit.

"Ngh…"

The toes of Sieg's left foot jerked slightly. There shouldn't have been any pain, since the potion contained an analgesic, so the faint noise he made must have been from the discomfort of tissue rapidly regenerating.

In the blink of an eye, the burn marks had vanished, too.

She knew a freshly made potion would be extremely effective.

Although his leg was healed, there was still about a third of the potion left. "Here, Sieg. Drink the rest. All at once, now. Chug! Chug!"

She pushed the potion vessel toward Sieg, who was looking behind him to check his leg.

She'd noticed it this morning while cutting his hair, but Sieg had scars all over his body—possibly whip marks.

Sieg dutifully drained the high-grade potion and shivered.

His whole body shone faintly, and the remaining injuries were instantly healed.

Sieg looked at his right hand, which he could now freely move, and his once gouged left leg. He quietly got off the bed and stood up.

Then he stepped forward with his left leg. One step, then another. He walked without discomfort.

He raised and stretched both hands, and he lightly hopped up and down. He rotated his arms and twisted his waist. He moved around to check how his body was feeling. He had tended to slouch before, but now he stretched his back muscles in a dignified fashion, making himself taller and looking rejuvenated.

"I can…move them… I can move them. My leg, my arm… I couldn't even turn my shoulder, but now I can. And my back… doesn't hurt. My stomach cramps are gone…"

Uh, just how thoroughly injured were you, Sieg…? Also, that high-grade potion was, like, super-effective. Labyrinth materials are really somethin' else!

As she watched the delighted Sieg, who looked ready to burst into tears, Mariela was glad she became an alchemist.

She could think of no greater reward than seeing the joy on someone's face after they'd recovered from an injury or illness.

After Sieg finished checking himself over, he abruptly turned to Mariela and dropped to one knee.

Was he going to start groveling again?! Mariela braced herself for an instant, but this time he was just on the one knee.

It was the kind of pose a knight assumed when taking an oath.

"Lady Mariela, thank you so much. Never… Never in my wildest dreams…did I think the day would come…when I could move like this again. I truly wish I could properly express my gratitude… Since yesterday, you've done nothing but help me, so I…I will serve you with all my heart and soul. For your sake, Lady Mariela, I'll do anything…"

Sieg stitched his words together, overcome with emotion. His single blue eye was wet with tears, and he expressed his gratitude in faltering sentences as if delirious.

To Mariela, his eye was truly beautiful. It was a shame she couldn't heal the other one.

"I'm sorry I can't heal your eye. Just hang in there until I can make special-grade potions, okay?"

"There is no need... This is enough. I thought I was going to die, but now...I'm no longer in any pain. Truly, I will do anything. Anything at all..."

Sieg's intensity had been dialed up to the strangest degree.

"Hey, Sieg, I have a request."

He shouldn't say "I'll do anything" so easily!

"! Ready and waiting!"

"I want you to wash that glass vessel over there!"

"?!"

Mariela left the cleanup to Sieg and took a nap until dinnertime.

As she napped, Sieg washed and dried the glass vessel, tidied up the scattered medicinal herbs on the desk, dusted the contents of the hodgepodge box, and arranged them on the floor so that they were easily identifiable.

And then when Mariela woke up...

"There's trash over there."

"Understood."

"I'm taking these with me tomorrow, so put 'em in the bag."

"Understood."

"Those I'm gonna use again, so put 'em back in the bag and put it in the corner."

"Understood."

…Mariela ordered Sieg around while sprawled on the bed.

Ahhh, this is the life. I bet my stupid master felt the same way.

If only she could eat her meals in this position, that would be fantastic. A knock at the door interrupted Mariela's daydreaming.

"Yeees?"

"It's Malraux. The contract is ready, so could you come to my room?"

A bit of predinner work had surfaced.

04

Captain Dick was waiting for Mariela and Sieg inside Lieutenant Malraux's room when they entered. He seemed surprised when he saw Sieg, who just yesterday looked to be in the direst of straits. Now, although he was underweight, this handsome man appeared to be a different person altogether, a feeling Mariela understood well. After all, she'd been surprised, too. However, Dick was easy to read, as always. She worried whether it was okay for the captain of the Black Iron Freight Corps to be this transparent.

On the other hand, Malraux's expression was neutral. At his suggestion, Mariela sat down on the couch. Sieg remained in the background.

"Considering the confidentiality of this matter, it will not be communicated to anyone other than Captain Dick and myself. Here is the contract; please review it."

Lieutenant Malraux handed over a number of papers. When she looked at the top sheet, she saw all the demands she'd set forth yesterday written on it. The confidentiality was a given, and in the unlikely event information leaked and Mariela was exposed to danger, the Black Iron Freight Corps would take it upon themselves to resolve the problem and, depending on the circumstances, would even aid her in escape.

This was the first proper business deal she'd ever been a part of. Up until now, she'd always exchanged goods and payments on the spot and never had anything like a contract. The one Lieutenant Malraux just gave her had a magical effect on it from the Merchants Guild and seemed to have been created with great precision.

"Um, what do you mean by 'close a contract of sale for each transaction'?" Mariela asked, since nothing was written about payment.

"Market prices often fluctuate, which is something that cannot be incorporated into a magical contract," Lieutenant Malraux replied fluidly. "The price of the goods will change for every transaction. We will execute either a unit price contract or a contract of sale for each negotiation, which will be separate from this basic one. Here is the contract of sale for the current transaction."

He pointed to a document below the one she was looking at. It seemed to be the current contract of sale, and it included the types and number of potions ordered yesterday as well as the unit price to be paid to Mariela.

The written prices were six silver coins for each low-grade heal potion, low-grade cure potion, and monster-warding potion and six large silver coins for each mid-grade heal potion and mid-grade cure potion. She was astonished by these amounts, but there was nothing written for high-grade heal potions and high-grade cure potions, and the sum total was also blank.

"Um, the spot for high-grade items is blank."

"That's correct..." Captain Dick, who'd been silent until now, finally piped up. "High-grade items haven't been sold on the market for over ten years."

Apparently, it was unknown how much they sold for because they weren't in circulation.

Dick candidly explained the situation. "Potions in the Labyrinth City are distributed solely by the Aguinas family except for items managed by the margrave and each respective house. The Labyrinth Suppression Forces are provided with a fixed supply in accordance with an agreement with the margrave, but things like transaction prices haven't been disclosed."

Mariela had heard the family name Aguinas before. Two hundred years ago, the Aguinases were the head alchemists in the Kingdom of Endalsia. That meant the family must have survived the Stampede. For them to still have power over potion sales two hundred years after the kingdom's destruction showed just how formidable they were.

"We would like to determine the price based on the market value, but since we don't know that, it's possible the price will be negotiated down. You can set the minimum price you're willing to sell them for, or if you don't trust us, you could also attend the negotiations yourself. What do you think?"

Captain Dick folded his arms and plopped down on a chair with an imposing flourish, but the position of his thick eyebrows showed how languid he really was. He was the kind of man whose outward appearance stood in stark contrast to how he actually felt. She knew from their interactions so far that Captain Dick wasn't a bad person, but he seemed like the type who'd get the short end of the stick in a business interaction. Although she supposed Lieutenant Malraux would step in if that happened.

"There's something I'd like you to tell me if possible."

"Mm? What is it?"

"Who will you be selling the potions to?"

"The Labyrinth Suppression Forces. They'll be heading out on a routine expedition soon. We'll also buy some of the monster-warding and low-grade potions ourselves."

She hadn't thought he'd say who their customers were. Was it really okay for him to tell her that so readily? She glanced at Lieutenant Malraux, who looked dignified as always, but his eyes were smiling as if he was somehow enjoying himself just a bit. Though she wasn't sure, Mariela suspected Captain Dick's rugged honesty amused him.

"You're not selling them to the Aguinas family?"

"If we sell to them, the potions may never reach our forces. The quality and quantity of potions were already decreasing, but we've heard that inferior products such as so-called new medicine have been circulating recently. Yet, the injuries sustained by the army just keep increasing."

This time, he made a face of blatant disgust. Captain Dick didn't seem to think well of the Aguinas family. And the way he talked favorably about the Labyrinth Suppression Forces made her wonder if he was acquainted with anyone in them.

"I understand. Even if the prices go down, I won't mind. I'm just happy I can help out."

Potions healed injuries. She hated the thought of them being used as a tool to make a profit; she preferred they go directly to the user. Since the price of the low- and mid-grade potions would let her make more than enough money, she'd be happy if her potions reduced the harm to the army even a little.

"Is that so? You have my gratitude! Our group will be pleased, too."

Delighted, Captain Dick held out his hand for a handshake. He had a strong grip that hurt a little, but his large, thick palm was very warm. Mariela thought she understood why Lieutenant Malraux associated with a man as unsuited to business as he was.

"Right, then, let's celebrate!" he said as he began to get to his feet, but Lieutenant Malraux grabbed the back of his collar and sat him back down. This guy was quick. Dick choked as the collar constricted his neck.

"The contract is not yet finalized. Besides, celebration would undermine the confidentiality, would it not? Do you understand?" Lieutenant Malraux reprimanded the captain as he finalized the contract of sale with a swish of his pen. "Speaking of compensation, Miss Mariela, we will bear the costs of food, drink, and other such items during your stay here. Your stay has been extended by one week, and I have informed the owner as well, so please order whatever you would like. Oh, and we are to provide you with what you need in advance; what should we prepare?"

He was really a wining and dining type of fellow, wasn't he? She wondered if this offer included Sieg as well.

"This time I don't need anything in particular. Um, will those costs be covered for Sieg, too?" she asked, knowing it was the question of a commoner.

"Of course," Malraux replied with a smile. Just as Mariela thought, *What a generous man!* he added, "Ah, but, Captain Dick, please pay your own way. We do not need to incur any additional expenses."

He gave this reminder with a smile as well, and Captain Dick hung his head in dejection.

Mariela signed the finalized contract. A magic contract was executed by signing it with ink dribbled with blood. Captain Dick and Lieutenant Malraux signed their names in the space for the Black Iron Freight Corps.

They decided she would deliver the potions in this room at this same time two days from now.

Mariela and Sieg left the room and headed for the restaurant on the first floor. Captain Dick was about to go with them, but Lieutenant Malraux promptly seized him.

He seemed to be saying, "Where do you think you're going? Do that later." Seeing that the captain was probably about to get a talking-to, Mariela and Sieg quickly left them to it.

05

It was finally time for dinner. Sieg and Mariela chatted about what could be on today's menu as they went down to the restaurant.

The sun had just set, so it was a little early still for dinnertime. Just like yesterday, there were only a handful of guests here and there, none of whom belonged to the Black Iron Freight Corps.

Amber appeared and invited Mariela and Sieg to the counter. Since it was still early, she wore a stole over her red dress, concealing her overwhelming cleavage.

Today's menu offered beef stew made from some kind of bovine monster and meatballs with a vegetable demi-glace. When Mariela asked what kind of meatballs they were, Amber responded with a giggle.

"What kind of meat, indeed. I'm curious... Like the stew, it's not beef but some kind of cow monster."

Mariela ordered the beef stew, and Sieg ordered the meatballs. It wasn't as if she'd forced the mystery meat on him.

"Sieg, what will you pick? You can ask for whatever you like, you know," she'd said, and after thinking it over a little while, he had ordered the meatballs.

"You're a brave man, Sieg."

"It's meat, so...," he answered in a small voice. He seemed to have simply chosen a dish based on which one he thought had a lot of meat.

"Mister, your name is Sieg? You seem a lot better now. I'm glad. How 'bout it? A drink to celebrate your recovery."

Amber crossed her arms as she recommended a drink to Sieg. The act of crossing them lifted her own two meatballs, which bulged out of the stole. What a pair. The stole acted more like a diversion to needlessly draw the eye to her chest. You might say it was a trap. That stole was really putting in the work.

"No thank you." Sieg smoothly avoided Amber's temptation and looked to Mariela.

"Um, Sieg, it's okay. It's just one drink, y'know? I'll have one, too, so let's make a toast."

Although he'd recovered from his injuries, his physical strength hadn't completely returned. However, one drink wouldn't hurt, and she thought celebrating his recovery was a great idea.

"Lady Mariela, I am a slave. Truth be told, I'm not even allowed to...sit in chairs. Please, please...you needn't...concern yourself with me......" Sieg spoke haltingly, a slightly pained look on his face.

Come to think of it, Sieg stumbled over his words. Mariela figured maybe there had been a long period of time when he didn't speak.

I want to do this for him, one way or another...

She didn't want to act like a master; she wasn't that type of person. Being waited on bothered her. Sieg could speak only in broken sentences, was underweight, and had sustained a lot of injuries. Seeing him trying his utmost to serve her like this made her heart ache.

He's under a Contract of Servitude, though, so it's impossible for us to be totally like friends.

Gradually, they were becoming friendlier with each other, and she wanted him to be a trusted confidant, even if only a little bit. Mariela was unknowingly seeking a relationship like what she had with her master. That's why she liked the idea of a toast. Ignoring Sieg's hesitation, she asked Amber for an appropriately celebratory drink.

"The first toast for both of you, huh? Let's see here."

Amber picked out a number of bottles from the other side of the counter.

Erm. I dunno anything about these.

Her master used to drink, but Mariela had never had a drop of alcohol in her life.

"Sieg, which one would be good?"

She came to a realization only after tossing the question at him.

Crap. Maybe that was a stupid question. He went from a debt laborer to a penal laborer, so he probably doesn't know about alcohol brands or anything like that.

However, he calmly asked her, "Lady Mariela...do you...drink alcohol?"

"Huh? Um... I've never had any before..."

"If that's the case...either the Feliz or Mallo Moscato...might go down easily."

"Which one d'you like, Sieg?"

Sieg scrunched up his face before replying, "I suppose...the Feliz."

"Wow! You're pretty savvy 'bout those girly drinks, mister! Speakin' from past experiences, are ya?"

Mariela was relieved by Amber's good-natured jab. Sieg had shown a new side of himself. Just moments ago, she'd thought about how she wanted to become close friends with him, but now that she knew Sieg had a kinda cool side to him, she found her heart was pounding in her chest just a little. Shaking her head as she chastised herself, she ordered the Feliz. Amber opened the bottle and poured it into a glass.

The pale-pink liquor fizzed and bubbled in a pretty way.

"Oh, a toast? We'll join in, too! Hey, Malraux!"

Captain Dick came down the stairs to join them for the toast, forcefully dragging Lieutenant Malraux along with him. "I suppose I have no choice," Malraux replied with a wry smile and accepted a glass as well.

When all four of them had received a glass, three sets of eyes looked at Mariela. It seemed she would lead the toast.

"To Sieg's recovery! And to our assemblage!"

Following her lead, the other three responded "Cheers!" and clinked their glasses together.

Her first taste of alcohol was sweet and went down easy. It had a faint smell of wild strawberries. Immediately after the toast came their food piled high, apparently a celebratory gift from the owner.

Sieg gazed at his glass, then leisurely tipped some of the drink into his mouth. Rather than swallowing right away, he savored the taste, rolling it around on his tongue. Although he'd previously been shoveling food into his mouth yesterday and this morning, tonight he picked up a fork with his right hand, now that he could move it, and neatly ate bite by bite.

"Delicious...," he muttered simply. Sieg knew alcohol brands and table manners. Mariela wondered what kind of person he was. Surely it was the alcohol causing her heart to thump loudly and her cheeks to flush.

At any rate, I'm curious about him...

She stole a few glances at Sieg, who was seated next to her. He was cutting his meatballs into bite-size pieces before bringing them to his mouth and savoring them.

"What kinda meat's in those? Is it good?" Mariela couldn't stop herself from asking. This was definitely the alcohol's fault, too. Her master had mentioned how it could make people franker and more up-front.

Meanwhile, Captain Dick was saying things like "That stole doesn't suit you at all!" When he tried to tear it off Amber, she pinched the back of his hand. Maybe the alcohol was making him bolder, too? No, he was probably just under the influence of Ample Amber.

"Awww man, the party's already started! No faaair! We only just got done cleanin' the carriages!"

Lynx and the others had arrived. They were soiled with the

slaves' excrement and appeared to have been busy cleaning the iron carriages.

"Urgh, it's pitch-black...," murmured Lynx when he saw the evening's dinner specials.

I'm not gonna ask what he's imagining it is...

She took her eyes off Lynx, who seemed as if he was about to ask more questions, and glanced at Yuric and the others he had been cleaning with. Not just Yuric, but even Donnino and Franz, who looked as though they'd been repairing the iron carriages, had weary expressions on their faces.

"Maaan, I'm so hungry I can't even deciiide," said Lynx before ordering both dishes, just like yesterday. Incidentally, the meatballs were a combination of bovine monster meat and orc meat.

Mariela kept glancing at the meatballs, so finally Sieg offered her a bite. In return, she put a piece of the bovine monster meat from the stew onto his plate.

"This meatball tastes great! It's so juicy with the soup!"

"The meat from the stew...is also delicious. Very tender."

Lynx added his two cents to their mutual appreciation of the cooking: "Both are great—as long as there's a lot!"

Quantity over quality for Lynx. He couldn't appreciate any of the finer points of the food other than the facts that the stew's meat had been boiled until it was very tender and the beef didn't stink.

"What's a 'bovine monster' anyway? Maybe it was mystery meat after all," Mariela said with a laugh. They hadn't solved the case of the mysterious meat, but the fun party continued late into the night.

I think Captain Dick passed out sometime around then. He was wearing Amber's stole while Lieutenant Malraux was having a cheery conversation with the owner. Lynx and Yuric complained about cleaning the carriages as they gobbled down their food, and Donnino and Franz got all fired up talking about iron carriages. Even Sieg was smiling, so he must've been having fun, too. Yeah. That much I remember.

Mariela recalled last night's party. For some reason, she didn't remember going back to her room. Must've been one of those old folktales her master used to tell her about a basic liquor spell, *What Happened Last Night?*

Well, I did change clothes and sleep in my bed, so hey, I must be doing all right! Still, my head really hurts...

She seemed to have woken up very early. It was pitch-black outside the window, and everyone was probably asleep, since she didn't hear the usual nighttime hustle and bustle.

As she crafted a low-grade cure potion, Sieg woke up.

"Did I wake you? Do you need a cure potion, too, Sieg? It's not specifically for hangovers, but it's still kinda effective."

"No, I...didn't drink very much." Sieg looked perfectly well.

Mariela quickly finished the potion using a medicinal herb she'd bought in bulk, and she drank it. Even though this wasn't its intended purpose, the cure potion was effective at treating her hangover, as her headache dissolved away. However, now she felt the call of nature.

"I'm gonna use the toilet real quick."

She changed into her clothes, which had been neatly folded, and hurried out of the room.

When she'd finished her business and was climbing the stairs to return to her quarters, the door to Captain Dick's room opened without a sound, and Amber came out.

Amber looked back into the room and gazed at something,

probably the sleeping captain. Mariela couldn't see very well in the dim light from the small windows, but Amber's mouth was curved in a gentle smile with a look of deep affection. She wore that expression even though she treated him so coldly in front of the others. Was Captain Dick aware of her feelings?

Amber glanced back into the room for only a few seconds, but in that moment, Mariela felt as if time had stopped. For some reason, it was painful to witness, and Mariela felt her chest tighten.

Amber slowly and quietly closed the door so as not to wake Captain Dick, and then she noticed Mariela. With a smile, she murmured, "It's still early; you can sleep a little longer," as they passed each other, and then she descended the stairs.

Wha...? What's early, exactly...?

Mariela's heart was pounding.

By the time she returned to her room, Sieg was up. He had even changed clothes and made the beds.

"It's still early. You can sleep a little longer." Mariela tried out Amber's line.

"I was already up," he answered with a smile. *Huuuh? That was weird*, she thought in confusion, then prepared to take a bath, which she hadn't gotten to do yesterday. Sieg seemed to have taken one before going to sleep last night.

"I'll get you something to drink as well." Sieg, seeing Mariela getting ready for a bath, casually stood up from his chair. He had a gentlemanly, attentive way about him. Since he was going down there anyway, she told him to ask for some packed lunches and a trowel and hatchet.

Mariela took her bath in a big hurry so she wouldn't keep Sieg waiting.

He hadn't returned when she finished but was instead waiting outside in the corridor. Mariela wasn't used to being fussed over, so although he was probably just being considerate, she felt awkward.

After tomorrow's deal is done and I've got the money, I'm gonna rent a house somewhere, she thought as she sipped the tea Sieg had brought her. The two of them discussed their plans for the day.

"The owner said…he would leave the lunches…on the counter for us. He also said…you're free to use the tools…you asked for."

The owner had still been awake, and he had boxed up some breakfast and lunch for them. The trowel and hatchet were at the bottom of the storage closet for them to use whenever they liked.

"All right, let's head out around the time the yagu rental opens."

Sieg brought out the rucksack he'd prepared yesterday. It contained various materials from the hodgepodge box such as halite, magical gems, and herbs tucked into a burlap bag, as well as a wooden cup they'd borrowed from the room. Mariela carried some money, scraps of paper from the hodgepodge box, and a hand towel in her pouch. Once she crafted a monster-warding potion just to be safe, their preparations were complete.

The sky grew light. After collecting the lunch boxes and borrowing the trowel and hatchet, they set out.

Today, they would gather the materials to make potion vials.

CHAPTER 4
Days of Reminiscence

01

Mariela and Sieg headed north through town just after dawn broke.

The northern road bordered the business district on one side and the living quarters of those in farming and animal husbandry on the other. Near the northern gate was a yagu rental shop, the kind livestock farmers often ran as a second business. These places started lending out the creatures early in the morning.

"Pardon me, sir! I'd like to rent a strong yagu that can carry two people for one day, please."

"Never seen yer face before. This fella here's tough; he'll carry a beanpole and a li'l lady like yerself, no problem."

The man running the shop lent her a superb male yagu.

One day's rental, including a charge for animal feed, came out to one silver coin. Mariela also paid a separate security deposit of two large silver coins that would be returned to her when she brought the yagu back.

The creature took an immediate liking to her once she offered him some vegetables from her feed bag. Smart guy.

They practiced riding him on the premises. Mariela could manage just fine, but Sieg had a real knack for it. Maybe it came down to a difference in reflexes. The yagu had an even temperament and trotted with a light step. Due to the conditions of the deposit, Mariela could rent only one; but even if she'd rented two, she might not have been able to keep up with Sieg.

Mariela sat in front, and the two of them rode toward the north gate. The Labyrinth City had eight gates—the four in the north, south, east, and west were all so narrow that a single yagu could barely fit through. The gates were built this way to keep monsters out while still allowing city inhabitants to hunt or get to their fields or harvest nearby. Passing through these four gates was inconvenient, but because they weren't meant for trade, inspections finished quickly.

The sentinel stopped them, since they were unfamiliar faces, but when Mariela showed him the contents of her rucksack and told him they were going out gathering, he cautioned, "We're a long way from the Fell Forest, but there are still monsters out there, so be careful," before sending them on their way. He was a kind man.

After passing through the north gate, they steered the yagu slightly northwest. The northern side of the Labyrinth City was suitable for grazing with its small number of rivers and many shrubs. On the northwest side, a lot of rivers flowed down from the mountain range, and farmland extended far and wide. After traveling north along a river, they reached the forest. It was a normal one and much sparser throughout than the Fell Forest, but low-level monsters appeared once in a while, so Mariela and Sieg needed to be cautious.

But then, the pair had used a monster-warding potion, so they could operate safely here.

"Lady Mariela." Sieg glanced behind them.

"Ahhh, I knew it. He followed us after all."

She figured it was probably Lynx. They were on the verge of a major business deal, so it wouldn't be strange to have someone keeping an eye on her already.

I don't really want people to know where we're going today. Sorry, Lynx.

She stopped the yagu and pulled several scraps of paper out of her pouch. After feeding three of them to the animal, she passed the rest to Sieg. She had drawn them yesterday after her nap.

"These are charged with magic. Hold on to them until I say otherwise."

She urged the yagu onward again.

Their mount proceeded unhindered through the forest, as if the trees themselves were avoiding him. The three figures—Sieg, Mariela, and the yagu—began to fade, almost melting into the scenery as their presence quickly grew indistinguishable from the surrounding trees.

Swish, swish. They smoothly glided past the trees—or maybe the trees were gliding past them. Even Lynx, who typically had sharper eyes than a falcon, couldn't keep track of them. *Swish, swish.* All signs that the pair was passing through had already vanished. With another *swish*, the shadow of a tree completely concealed them, rendering the group invisible.

"Gaaah, I lost 'em. Seriously, though? Man, that Sieg is somethin' else. Wait, maybe it was Mariela who did it?"

Lynx's shadow emerged from the trees. As the Black Iron Freight Corps's scout, he was more than able to move through even the likes of the Fell Forest. He never thought he'd lose sight of Mariela's group here. He scratched his head.

"Lieutenant Malraux's gonna be mad at me, I bet. Ah well, I'm sure they'll come back safely. I lent Sieg my knife for just this kinda situation."

Lynx had been tailing them as an envoy, but there was nothing he could do about losing sight of them. They had the skill to give him the slip. He was a little worried that their weapons were no better than a trowel or a hatchet, but they'd probably be fine in this neck of the woods. He'd met Mariela wandering alone in the Fell Forest, and that was enough to tell him she had the ability to survive in her own way.

Lynx's shadow vanished with a *poof*, and he returned to the Labyrinth City.

After losing Lynx, Mariela and Sieg exited the forest, crossed several rivers, and rode for probably close to an hour. They followed a riverbank upstream and finally arrived at a waterfall.

"We should be good now. He's not following us anymore, right?"

Mariela had no reconnaissance ability, so it was really just a guess.

"Yes. It looks like we shook him off, but what are these?"

Sieg released the reins and held out the crumpled scraps of paper in his hand. His sweaty palms had dampened the paper and blurred the ink, but it was still apparent they'd been inscribed with some kinds of shapes.

"Ah, those are Magic Circles of Forest's Welcome, Obfuscation, and Delusion."

Forest's Welcome made it easy to move through the forest without getting tripped up by branches or brambles. *Obfuscation*, as the name implied, isolated your presence and magic power to make you disappear, and by using it in tandem with *Delusion*, you could evade most pursuers and monsters with ease. Even experienced hunters learned these sorts of techniques, so they couldn't really be classified as "skills."

Some beasts were especially immune no matter how many monster-warding potions you used. Even in the middle of town, there were bad people who would come after young ladies out all by their lonesome. Mariela had sewn several magic circles into her cloak to keep such riffraff at bay.

These magic circles were said to be the legacy of an ancient civilization, and even two hundred years ago, more than half of them had been forgotten. Although it was typical to choose the quality of the materials based on the effect, anyone could benefit from a magic circle just by drawing it with magical gem dust dissolved in ink, so it was convenient. However, if the drawing wasn't complete, it wouldn't activate, and one crooked line would keep it from working properly.

No matter how well someone could draw, at the end of the day, they were human. If it was crooked in any way, you wouldn't get the full effect. That said, even half the full effect was more than satisfactory, and copies of the originals themselves usually wouldn't activate. The original could be copied only by using *Transcription*, so you could compensate with other skills or magic like Mariela did. Depending on a person's training, some magic circles couldn't be inherited, and there was nothing to be done about that.

The original, perfect magic circles were recorded only in the Akashic records.

The few circles passed down by word of mouth that still existed were ones like those engraved on potion vials to prevent degradation or like Sieg's brand from the Contract of Servitude. But even those weren't perfect; that was why the effects of *Antidegradation* were delayed, and a Contract of Servitude showed results only when combined with contract skills. Subordination magic could be quite dangerous depending on the spell, but it was fully effective only if both parties participated—which was extremely fortuitous, in its own way.

On the other hand, the study of the shapes engraved in magic circles had continued since long ago, and people known as magical researchers had been creating a variety of magical tools from the results of such research.

"Magic circles... I heard their art had been lost."

Mariela and Sieg had tied up the yagu in an open area near the waterfall and were about to enjoy the breakfast that had been packed for them: two scrumptious-looking ham and vegetable baguette sandwiches.

"Well, see, my master was a high-level appraiser. I couldn't forget all these magic circles if I wanted to."

Mariela's master had been incredible—able not only to pull information from the Akashic records using a high-level Appraisal skill but also to use magic. Alchemic skills, too, of course.

Genius didn't even cover it; *superhuman* would be a better word. Conversely, the clumsier-than-average Mariela had a knack for getting herself into life-threatening situations. It went beyond common sense—or indeed, even the bounds of what could be accounted for by personality and behavior. She had never once experienced combat.

Considering her master's abilities, this wasn't the kind of person who lived in a cramped cottage in the Fell Forest and took on an apprentice like Mariela who had no skills besides alchemy. Or maybe that was just another eccentricity.

Mariela had even been forced to memorize magic circles on

a whim. "Your own stupidity might be the death of you, so I'm going to teach you something useful," her master had said, then called her over and placed a hand on her head. Young Mariela expected a pat, but then came the cry "**Imprint!**" and a magic circle was burned directly into her mind. It was only momentary, yet even now, she still remembered the incredible pain.

From that point on, Mariela was extremely wary of these "pats." Even then, there was one day her master ruffled her hair and praised her, beaming from ear to ear: "Ohhh, you did it, Mariela. Wonderful. So smart." The next instant: "You let your guard down! **Imprint!**" And that was how Mariela ended up being forced to learn so many magic circles. She had no doubt this was half for her master's own enjoyment; as she writhed on the floor screaming "GYAAAAH!!" her master pointed and roared with laughter.

Worst of all was the Magic Circle of Suspended Animation. It involved so many complicated processes that she thought it might just incinerate her brain. This time, her master provided an explanation for a change before casting *Imprint*, wearing a strange expression.

"By this point, you've been imprinted with so many magic circles that you've likely built up a tolerance. This one, however, will hurt a little more than the rest."

And so on and so forth. Mariela blinked in surprise and wondered if maybe the previous Imprints had all just been for kicks. Every magic circle she'd learned had proved valuable, and she was extremely grateful, but she'd always thought it had been more for entertainment purposes.

With a terse look, her master continued. "When you make

this magic circle, your training will be complete," to which Mariela obediently replied, "I understand."

She didn't want to remember the intense pain from the Imprint of the Magic Circle of Suspended Animation. It was so bad that it had knocked her out for around three days. When she finally came to, there were several potion vials scattered around the bed; she thought she was dying. "You overslept," her master said with puffy and bloodshot eyes; the task of nursing Mariela back to health had not allowed for sleep. Her master wasn't easy to read, but Mariela could tell. The pair had known each other for a long time.

Simply memorizing a magic circle wasn't enough to use it. It wouldn't activate unless drawn exactly like the original, so the next step was simply steady, repetitive practice. Mariela had no special talent, but you could say earnest perseverance was her forte. And yet, the Magic Circle of Suspended Animation was dreadful. Not only did its materials cost a lot of money, but it was large and complex. She continued to draw it in spare moments of her busy daily life, and finally, she completed two of them for her graduation assignment.

After inspecting the assigned magic circles, her master informed her, "You've graduated. Well done." Mariela was thirteen.

It was such an emotional moment that she had suddenly burst into tears. "Fank you sho mutch!" she had managed through sobs, her master comfortingly patting her as if she were a small child.

There, there. *Pat, pat. Ruffle, ruffle.*

"Carelessness is the greatest enemy! **Imprint!**"

"Eh?!"

02

"Damn you, Master..." All this reminiscing somehow made Mariela angry. She tore into her baguette. "That last Imprint was so intense that I was out cold for maybe a day, and when I woke up, I was alone."

Mariela's master had left a letter behind before disappearing. In it were a few scrawled notes, telling her the completed Magic Circle of Suspended Animation was payment for the last Imprint. *The cottage is yours now, a graduation present, so use it wisely. And don't forget about the magic circle in the cellar.*

"It's because of my master that I was able to survive the Stampede—actually, all the knowledge I've used to make it this far was because of my master. I should be thankful, but, like... how do I put it—I'm still kinda peeved."

Master may have been reckless, but I still have many happy memories of our time together. I was always incredibly grateful for that, and yet, all of a sudden Master just vanished. I even left that part of the bedroom untouched on the off chance we might suddenly be reunited one day.

"It's been two hundred years by now...," she muttered while gazing at the water's surface. Leaves from the trees gently fluttered down and were carried by the current through the rocky gaps in the riverbed. Just when it seemed as if several of the leaves would twirl their way through together, the water swept them downstream as if to wash them away. Only one leaf remained caught between the rocks, and even if it were swept up by the current now, it probably couldn't catch up with the others it had only just met moments ago. Mariela felt it was a metaphor for her own life, having been left behind in an era two hundred years past. She could never again see the people she'd met back then.

"I'm sure…you got through to your master." Sieg had a very gentle look on his face as he spoke.

"Yeah. I guess you're right. Gotta consider the source, after all."

She'd always wanted to convey her gratitude. Although she couldn't express it with words, there was no way someone as incredible as her master didn't know.

"Then, Lady Mariela, you're…an alchemist who survived… the Stampede."

"Yeah. It's a secret."

"Of course."

She particularly wanted to keep secret the part about how she slept for two hundred years after the lantern light consumed all the cellar's oxygen. That was embarrassing. As these thoughts crossed her mind, a new leaf drifted between the rocks she was gazing at. It rolled up with the single leaf that had been left behind, and together they were carried downstream.

"All right, we've finished breakfast, so let's get to work right away."

Mariela stood up with a *hup* and picked out some rocks in the vicinity. After watching her example, Sieg helped, too, and together they made a small stove. There was a notch in the top for inserting a vessel to be heated.

The stove was rather bulky for its size. She filled in the gaps among the stones with mud from the forest and dried it with

Dehydrate, then removed the crucible from the hodgepodge box. After leaning the crucible atop the stove at a slight tilt to face the front and surrounding it with more stones, she felt the whole thing began to look more like a kiln.

Between the two of them, the work took hardly any time at all. With the stove finished, Mariela had Sieg take the yagu to gather firewood.

Meanwhile, Mariela threw off her cloak, shoes, and pouch; took the burlap bags and the trowel; and headed for the top of the waterfall.

It was a large waterfall, about five Captain Dicks tall—and Captain Dick was a tall man. From a distance, it looked as if it had a single break, but it actually had two. A slightly open break was at the height where Captain Dick's hands would be if he raised them in a hearty cheer. Imagining the captain in such a pose made Mariela burst out laughing.

At the top of the waterfall was a mass of large boulders piled on top of one another.

"Oh, good, it's still there."

Between some large, apparently fallen boulders right next to the waterfall and the waterfall's rocky mountain was a narrow gap just barely wide enough for Mariela to squeeze through. Within, the space widened a bit, and the ground sloped upward. The innermost wall had protrusions at irregular intervals that served as footholds to climb to the waterfall's break.

Water droplets bounced off the break above and created a constant rain in the gap, and moss grew densely both on the walls and at her feet.

"Whoaaa! Jackpot! It's had two hundred years to spread, after all."

This faintly pink-tipped moss was called planada moss. It was a rare plant with an extremely slow growth rate that required clean water and minimal sunshine. Planada moss was said to reduce accumulated fatigue and restore a shortened life span. Although it sold for a lot of money, it was rarely seen on the market, hence why this place was a secret. Mariela would carefully safeguard the portion of the gathered moss she didn't end up using.

After collecting the moss within reach and putting it in a burlap bag, she pushed the bag out through the gap.

The rocks she'd cleared moss from were at the right height and arranged in such a way that she could climb them.

After climbing carefully so as not to slip, she emerged at one of the waterfall's breaks.

"Ooh, there's a ton over here, too!"

You wouldn't know it by looking from below, but the break had a wide space behind it, and at her feet were large piles of white sand—the ideal material for making potion vials.

Since the era of the Citadel City, this had been a place where Mariela could gather good-quality sand for potion vials. However, given that sand was a naturally occurring material, it contained some impurities. To refine the sand into glass for potion vials, these impurities could be sifted out with specialized devices or melted down by adding various sorts of auxiliary materials.

With alchemic skills, it was possible to create glass with even a simple stove like the one Mariela made, but the quality would only be as good as the materials used to make it.

This spot boasted the highest-quality sand, and when Mariela had first discovered it after coming here to gather planada moss, it was as if she'd stumbled onto a massive treasure trove. The discovery had her jumping with joy. She didn't know why, but out of all the kinds of rocks and sand that flowed down from the waterfall, this break was the only place that had the type of sand suitable for potion vials.

Not enough sand had accumulated here over the past two hundred years for it to be considered a quarry, but it was more than enough for Mariela's individual use.

Despite the slight distance from the waterfall, a large amount of water still sprayed into the sand piles. It was a bit cold for the season, and Mariela's hair and clothes were soaked in no time. Plus, the waterfall's spray came with the occasional pebble.

Ow, ow, another rock. Ugh. I need this for potion vials—just hang in there; grin and bear it.

The trowel crunched through the sand as she scooped it up and put it in a burlap sack.

After collecting about as much as she could carry down with her, she tied the bag shut and hefted it onto her back.

"Ugh... So heavy. I put in a bit too much."

"Lady Mariela."

With perfect timing, Sieg appeared. She wondered how he got through that tiny gap. No matter how thin he was, he had a fairly stocky build. That gap didn't seem like something he could squeeze through.

"Huh? You brought the yagu, too? How?"

She'd turned around to see Sieg riding the animal.

Apparently, when she'd dropped the bag of planada moss, he'd heard the sound from above and rode the yagu up the waterfall.

Incidentally, yagus loved cliffs. Mariela thought it was quite a sheer cliff and didn't have sufficient footholds, but the yagu was snorting happily and seemed as if it wanted to climb more.

She calmed the excited creature and had him carry the bag of sand down to the stove.

With Sieg and the bag in tow, the yagu kicked off the wall with a *clack* and descended the waterfall. The creature was amazing, but his handler, Sieg, was pretty amazing himself. The two of them shortly returned, and this time, Mariela rode down with them. The waterfall break itself was only as high as where Captain Dick's hands would be if he raised them in a hearty cheer, but adding the yagu's height to that made it a scary descent. Mariela let out a shriek as she clung to the animal, and when they dismounted, the yagu snorted in laughter.

Firewood had been piled up next to the stove and dried with magic. A fire was already going inside.

Why did Lady Mariela take the trowel and let herself get soaked doing all that hard labor when she has male help like me...?

"Whew, that felt good. I think I needed to move around." As Mariela talked, Sieg led her to the fire. Summer was already over, but she looked like a kid who couldn't get enough of splashing around in the water.

"I will...go gather the sand, so please...dry your clothes."

After spreading the sand on a flat rock near the stove, Sieg took the empty burlap bag and climbed back up to the sand piles once again.

"**Dehydrate**. And **Dehydrate**."

Mariela dried herself and the sand, then put her discarded cloak and shoes back on.

She took several materials out of the rucksack Sieg had left: trona crystals she'd bought from Ghark, a white powder from the hodgepodge box that had more than half solidified, and small metallic beads. Plus some powdered magical gems as well.

The white powder was lum stones that had been neglected for

a long time, causing them to react with particles in the air and render them useless in their current state.

"Form Transmutation Vessel, Pulverize, Ignite."

Mariela heated the powder to a temperature far hotter than boiling water but cooler than a candle's flame.

She then scraped down a proportionate amount of trona crystals for the lum stones and heated them in the same fashion.

Next came the sand.

"Form Transmutation Vessel, Pulverize, Drops of Life, Anchor, Coalesce."

After crushing the dried sand and infusing it with Drops of Life, she mixed it with the processed lum stones and trona crystals, as well as the magical gem dust. With that, the materials were ready.

The preparations were complete. She wouldn't be able to take a break after she started the next part, so although it was a bit early, she decided to have lunch.

Sieg returned not long after with two burlap bags filled to bursting with sand piled on the yagu. He had also brought more while she was preparing the materials, so in all there were just under five bags full. It was so much sand that she didn't have enough lum stones for it.

Lunch was orc meat cutlet sandwiches. The sauce had a good heap of mustard mixed in, giving it a delicious kick. Mariela was glad the weather was so nice; there was something utterly relaxing about eating a boxed lunch near the waterfall while listening to the chatter of birds. She wanted to take a long nap after finishing lunch, but she couldn't do that—there were vials to make through the evening.

She dried the sand Sieg had brought and finished processing it up to the mixing step. All the lum stones had been used; she wondered if she'd always been able to process such a large quantity.

"All that's left now is the tempering, so you can take it easy, Sieg."

Sieg still seemed to want to observe her and learn; he was watching from some distance away. The yagu should have merely been getting a drink of water, but he was watching Mariela get to work, too, for whatever reason.

She put one measure of the materials into the crucible through the slot in the stove. Since concentrated hot air would be pouring out of it, naturally she didn't insert them by hand, instead using *Form Transmutation Vessel*.

Though the firewood in the stove was burning with considerable heat, sand couldn't melt at this temperature. She needed to raise the temperature more, but with alchemic skills she could do so only by about the equivalent of a candle's heat, and that wouldn't be enough to melt the sand.

Next, she took out the metallic beads and added them to the fire.

"Spark."

She used alchemic skills to burn the beads by blowing oxygen from the air and magic power into them. Then, with a crackling sound, the beads began to glow in a variety of colors—first red, then orange, then green.

"Come forth, spirit of flames!"

She tossed the scraps of paper with magic circles written on them into the fire. Anyone with skills related to spirits, such as spirit magic or the ability to harness their power, can summon them with an incantation. Since Mariela had neither of these abilities, she summoned one by offering magic circles, flame, and *Spark*. Then again, she wouldn't be able to summon any impressive spirits with such paltry offerings.

The fire twisted and flickered before taking the form of a small lizard.

"A salamander? From a fire this small? That's a rare sight."

Salamanders were well-known fire spirits that by nature wouldn't inhabit a small fire like this. They formed covenants with prestigious dwarves and lived in large furnaces. And here Mariela would have been more than satisfied if she'd only managed to summon a wisp.

The spirit gobbled the Spark with a loud chomp.

"Spark."

Since the salamander seemed to be enjoying itself, she added more metallic beads and Spark, and the spirit swished its tail as it gobbled them all up.

"Say, Mr. Salamander. Think you could lend me some of your power?" Although the salamander didn't understand human speech, Mariela tried asking anyway because she worried her measly Sparks wouldn't convince the spirit to help her. In response, the fire burst with increased heat. It seemed the salamander was going to help.

The glass in the crucible rapidly began to melt.

"Form Transmutation Vessel, Retrieve, Refrigerate, Process Potion Vials, Refrigerate.

"Form Transmutation Vessel, Insert Ingredients, Stir.

"Spark."

After taking out the melted glass, she put in the next batch of ingredients and stirred them. As they melted, she formed the glass into potion vials.

I knew a salamander's power would be incredible. It must've put up a magical barrier to keep the heat from escaping, huh?

The barrier made her work a lot easier, but the salamander was melting the glass at a far quicker pace than a wisp would have, and Mariela barely had time to breathe.

The fire spirit seemed to consume a lot of fuel, as she frequently had to add more Spark. Without enough Spark, the thermal power decreased, which the salamander signaled by slapping its little tail up and down. The amount of magic power put into Spark was more important than the number of metallic beads, and the more power she put in, the more the salamander helped, fluttering its tail from side to side.

"We're running out of firewood!"

It was almost gone, but Sieg added more before she could get too worked up.

"Thanks, Sieg. That's a big help."

Even the salamander twirled around in joy.

After making a certain number of low-, mid-, and high-grade potion vials, Mariela would allow the remaining glass to cool in lumps the size of one vial each rather than finishing them. Not that she was too busy; she just wasn't up for the task of shaping them right now. Since shaping alone didn't require this much heat, she would be able to manage with alchemic skills alone, even though it would consume a bit of magic power. Plus, carrying that many vials would be a pain.

Insert Ingredients, Spark, Dissolve, Add Firewood, Retrieve, Spark, Insert Ingredients, Spark, Dissolve, Add Firewood, Retrieve, Spark, Insert Ingredients, Spark, Dissolve, Spark, Retrieve...

Before she knew it, she'd used all the ingredients.

The sun was still high, so it hadn't taken terribly long.

"Thank you, Mr. Salamander," she said, then infused the remaining metallic beads with plenty of magical energy and crafted a Spark.

The salamander tilted its head as if asking, "It's over already?" before swallowing the entire Spark in a single gulp.

"You're amazing! We finished in no time. You really helped me out."

If this area had been the domain of humans, Mariela might have been able to communicate directly with the salamander. She couldn't talk to the beast-like creature, but its behavior was extremely adorable. If possible, she hoped they'd make glass together again.

Ching.

The salamander spit something from its mouth with a *ptooey*. Then, just as when it appeared, the fire spirit made the flames twist and flicker and finally go out.

"...A ring?"

The spirit had spit out a simple ring that shone in all the colors of the rainbow—likely forged by solidifying the metallic beads with *Spark*. Mariela couldn't help but wonder exactly how the salamander had managed to get it so colorful, but such mysteries were typical of spirits. Perhaps if she wore the ring, the salamander would come to her aid again.

It fit perfectly on the middle finger of her right hand. The ring was quite lovely, and she wore it with much gratitude.

After the lined-up potion vials and glass lumps had completely hardened, they were cool to the touch, so Sieg packed them into burlap bags.

There were tons of them, enough to fill two bags to bursting. Altogether, they probably had somewhere over three hundred.

Something occurred to Mariela—her magical energy hadn't gone down very much, even though she'd used so much to infuse the Sparks. Though a salamander consumed a lot more than a wisp, she'd never made this much before. She felt as if her magical energy had increased a lot while she'd been sleeping. Maybe she should buy appraisal paper and check next time she had a chance.

The sun was still high, but their baggage had increased more than she could have imagined. Sieg and Mariela loaded the yagu with two burlap bags stuffed with glass and a bag of planada moss. No matter how strong the creature was, making him carry two people on top of all that would be cruel.

She decided to harvest more items while they took their time going back.

People didn't seem to come into this part of the forest; mushrooms, medicinal herbs, fruit, and more grew in abundance here. As she collected more and more on their way home, the herbs and materials tied together with vines formed a veritable mountain on the yagu's back, and the sun had begun to set by the time they reached the Labyrinth City.

Sieg and Mariela briefly parted near the Yagu Drawbridge Pavilion. After Sieg unloaded the baggage, he returned the yagu for her, while Mariela headed for Ghark's Herbal Supplies to pick up the items she'd ordered.

The street was bustling with adventurers returning from the Labyrinth. Ghark's shop was still open, and he handed over the medicinal herbs he'd gathered. Although he tried to conceal them with his sleeve, she noticed scratches on his arm. They may have been from gathering the herbs.

"Next time I'll bring some supereffective ointment for you. Thanks for the herbs!"

"I'll be expectin' yer ordinary medicine."

After their short exchange, she left the shop.

A group of what appeared to be adventurers had been drawn to a restaurant that gave off a delicious smell.

They probably had a healer among them, too. She hadn't noticed anyone with serious injuries, but she figured some must have had minor cuts and scrapes like Ghark's, while others, like ailing civilians, needed some "supereffective medicine" themselves.

I wonder if I should open an apothecary?

As she mulled these things over, Mariela returned to the Yagu Drawbridge Pavilion.

She'd gotten back to the Yagu Drawbridge Pavilion before Sieg. Since he'd already put the baggage in their room, he should be back soon after returning the yagu. As Mariela waited at the counter, one of the inn's shopgirls approached her.

"Say, sweetie, you're a chemist, right? Wouldja sell us some medicine?"

The lady was around the same age as Mariela, or perhaps a little older. Although not to the same extreme as Amber, she was voluptuous enough that Mariela couldn't even compare to her.

"There's gonna be a Labyrinth expedition soon, and we'll be getting a lot of business afterward. We wanna prepare ahead of time, but all the shops everywhere are low on stock."

In the busy season, the number of customers increased: adventurers riled up from battling monsters, spendthrifts who would get blackout drunk and become violent—and they were all armed with weapons. Dealing with such customers could easily escalate to the point that medical intervention became necessary. Although the inn's female staff always treated their guests with the utmost cheer, they weren't free to do as they pleased, so healing magic wasn't always an option. There weren't many clinics open in the middle of the night when adventurers were wallowing in their drinks. The inn should have had potions for times like these, but no one could get potions in the Labyrinth City.

Hence why the inn tried to stock medicine even though it was less effective than potions. However, before an expedition, apothecaries gave priority to adventurers needing salves, incense, and smoke balls, and as a result, they put the staff's medicine orders on the back burner.

"The owner here's a kind man, you see, and he'll provide the necessary funds. We'll pay you fairly, so won't you sell some to us?"

Mariela's feelings were indescribable. The only available medicine was low quality, and even then, the supply wasn't enough. And there were people like slaves who couldn't buy medicine themselves even if they needed it. Mariela knew all this, but it hadn't really hit home until just now.

"What's the matter?"

When Mariela gave no response, Amber appeared.

"Oh, sorry, Amber. Looks like I was askin' for a bit much."

"Honestly. And after Mr. Malraux asked us to take good care of her, too. Ela, I'm sorry she put you on the spot. Don't worry about it, okay?"

"No, I'm sorry, too. I'll make the medicine. Just tell me what you need."

"Really? That'd be great!"

"Thanks, Ela."

Mariela couldn't do much. She didn't understand anything about the present time or what had happened over the past two hundred years. Even so, Amber and the others were always so kind to her. Now they wanted medicine.

I'll make the best medicine possible without giving away that I can make potions.

Since there was work here, it seemed as if she'd be able to carve out a place to belong again.

"I'm back."

Sieg had returned. He held the deposit of two large silver coins out to Mariela. She took only one, leaving the other in his hand.

"Keep it. Use it for whatever you need. Oh, but I'll buy stuff like changes of clothes and everyday necessities separately. It won't be until the day after tomorrow, though, so just hang in there until then."

Sieg looked very uncomfortable. Of course he would. One large silver coin could buy him several things, but it wasn't an insignificant amount of money. Even though she told him to use it however he wanted, he couldn't just do so at a moment's notice.

This was Mariela's own self-satisfaction. She knew that. Even so, she wanted to give Sieg some kind of freedom.

"Keep it," she repeated, and she clasped his hand holding the coin.

When they finished dinner, Mariela left Sieg and ascended the stairs to their room. Since she was going to take a bath, she told him to wait a little while before coming up.

She felt kind of down; times like these called for a good soak. Since she still had magical energy to spare, she dissolved a generous amount of Drops of Life in the hot water before submerging herself, just like the other day.

When she got out of the bath, she dried her hair, then refilled the bathtub with fresh water.

Sieg hadn't returned yet, but she had an inkling as to why. When she opened the door, just as she'd thought, he was waiting out in the hall.

"…You can come in already."

"Okay."

He says that, but he'll probably just end up waiting out there again tomorrow, thought Mariela.

"You take a bath, too, Sieg. There's Drops of Life mixed in, and it'll be good for you. Make sure you get a nice, long soak." With that, Mariela shoved him into the bath, then quickly retrieved his clothes.

Laundry time! Sieg doesn't have a spare change of clothes anyway. And he was outside all day today and sweating. I gotta wash these!

Since she didn't know Sieg's size, she'd bought only one of each piece of clothing other than underwear. He'd been wearing his shirt and pants for two days. Mariela grabbed her own clothes that needed washing and dashed out to the backyard. She tossed the garments into the tub at the watering hole and used lifestyle magic to fill it with water. After scrubbing them with soap, she changed out the water to rinse them.

"Transmutation Vessel, Centrifuge: Super Weak."

After secretly using alchemy to evaporate the water, she rinsed the clothes again.

"Dehydrate."

She dried them with lifestyle magic. Lifestyle magic also had *Wash* and *Rinse* spells, but both needed a tub, and the one at the watering hole was a little small. Producing the invisible vessel already required the use of magical energy and used up more than lifestyle magic.

When she returned to the room with the finished laundry, Sieg peeked out of the bathroom.

"Here are your clothes. I washed 'em for you. I'll just put them over here."

She left them in a spot he could reach and returned to the bedroom. After Sieg changed into them and came out, he had an extremely apologetic look on his face.

"Um, I'm sorry..."

So her washing his underwear made him uncomfortable, as she figured. But it was more efficient to do everything together, and the idea of him washing hers made her more embarrassed than anything else. Going forward, she'd let both of them wash their own.

There's gonna be all sorts of issues cropping up with the two of us living together, she thought.

Before going to bed, she finished processing the materials she'd acquired that day.

First was removing the astringency from the apriore, a type of fruit encased in a tough outer shell. The insides were used as a base for mid-grade potions. However, apriore was incredibly astringent, and the more astringency left in it, the weaker its effects would be. There were other materials that could be used as a base for mid-grade potions, but apriore was the cheapest. Moreover, if you took about half a day to fully remove the astringency, it would be more effective than other materials, so Mariela always used it.

"Form Transmutation Vessel, Fragmentize, Wind Power Separation."

She crushed the apriore, removed the shell, and submerged it in hot water with a pinch of trona crystals. Since the apriore was fresh, it would turn out well if the astringency was removed overnight.

Next, the lund petioles. These were an expensive ingredient used for high-grade cure potions. At Ghark's Herbal Supplies, the amount for a single potion was sixty silver coins; outside the Labyrinth City, it would probably cost only one. Out of all the medicinal herbs she purchased in this batch, the lund petioles were the costliest, followed by the nigill buds for healing Sieg's leg. You could make only a single potion from one nigill bud, but one lund petiole would make twenty to twenty-five, so if you wanted a whole petiole, you'd be paying in large silver coins.

Lunds were plant-type monsters that inhabited poisonous swamps, and their petioles floated in the swamp water. A lund itself had low attack power, so instead it used swamp poison to catch approaching prey and drag it into the swamp for nutrients. The lund's epithelium was normally venomous because of the environment, but its petioles had neutralizing tissue that could counteract a variety of poisons. Thanks to this tissue, lunds could live in all kinds of poisonous swamps.

Because these swamps were poisonous to touch, she asked Ghark how in the world people captured lunds, and apparently, they were reeled in like fish. You would swing a rod from a safe spot, and when a lund latched on, you'd pull it in. If you rinsed off the exterior poison and soaked it in clean water, the neutralizing tissue from the lund itself would completely eradicate the remaining venom. It surprised Mariela to hear there was such a method.

Lund petioles were peeled, and then only the interior neutralizing tissue was frozen. Raising the temperature damaged it, so it was dried while kept at the low temperature.

"Form Transmutation Vessel, Control Temperature, Pulverize, Decompress."

By decompressing it at a low temperature, only the moisture sublimated, and the tissue dried little by little.

All that was left were the materials gathered today. She needed to wash the soil from the planada moss. Mariela decided to do that tomorrow in the backyard, and after processing the other materials collected in the forest, she was done for the day.

As Sieg was about to turn off the light, Mariela stopped him. "I'd like to keep the light on until I go to sleep," she said. Last night she fell asleep thanks to the alcohol, but a dark room would probably still bring back memories of the Stampede.

It had been a very busy day; she traveled a long distance and even after she got back, she was doing laundry and processing materials. She should have been quite tired, but for some reason, her eyelids just wouldn't stay shut.

"I had fun today," Mariela said to Sieg.

"Yes… It was…a beautiful spot," he replied as he sat in a chair. The long time spent as a slave had made him lose the feeling of "fun," and to be honest, he still couldn't remember what it felt like. However, Mariela seemed sad somehow, so he did his utmost to talk with her.

The yagu was fast. A ton of moss had grown. They'd gathered a lot of sand, and she'd made a lot of vials. She even saw a salamander for the first time. Mariela ran through the day's events one by one as if to confirm they weren't a dream but reality.

"Maybe I'll open an apothecary…"

"I think…it would be a good way…to hide that you're a Pact-Bearer, too."

"Sieg, let's open one…"

Before Sieg could reply, Mariela had fallen asleep. He couldn't even fathom how she must have felt when she woke up, the past two hundred years having become almost like a dream.

"I'll support you," he answered in a low voice, and he turned the light down just a little so as not to disturb her sleep.

04

The next morning, Mariela woke up at the usual time. The same time she used to wake up two hundred years ago.

"Good morning," Sieg said. He'd already changed his clothes. This was not the same as two hundred years ago.

Whoa, I slept like normal. What a relief...

She stretched and responded with her own "Good morning." Then she continued. "Today I'm gonna loaf around as much as I want! Then I'm gonna make as many potions as I can! And then—I'm openin' an apothecary!"

Mariela was in high spirits from the get-go. As soon as she finished breakfast, she would shut herself up in her room.

"Is there anything...I can help with...?" Sieg seemed restless without any work to do. He was fidgeting.

"Hmm. Nah, not really, so you go enjoy yourself!"

Just last night she'd invited him to open the apothecary with her, and now this morning she was full of beans and wanted to be left to her own devices. Perhaps confused by being told to "enjoy himself," Sieg started to say, "I'll do the laundry..." Understandable, considering he'd been expected to follow orders for who knows how long.

"No, I just did that, so nothing's dirty. Oh, I know! I haven't done anything with the planada moss I gathered yesterday. Could you do me a favor? Wash the soil off with well water rather than lifestyle magic. The roots contain nutrients as well, so do your best not to tear them off. And try not to wash away any of it, even the tiniest pieces. It's very valuable."

The moss truly was valuable, so she had figured she'd handle it herself. Instead, Mariela handed Sieg the bag of moss along with the appropriate tools, and he dutifully nodded before departing for the rear yard.

Mariela rolled up her sleeves, figuring she'd start with the low-grade potions.

She crafted monster-warding potions from daigis and bromo-minthra, low-grade heal potions from curique, and low-grade cure potions from jibkey leaves and tamamugy seeds. Making low-grade potions was easy, too. Apart from the tamamugy seeds, she had brought all these materials from her old house's herb garden in the Fell Forest. Tamamugy seeds could also be grown in gardens and even gleaned from riverbanks, but they were harvested in autumn, so it was still a little early in the season for them. With no other choice, she used the ones she'd bought at Ghark's Herbal Supplies.

The mid-grade items were next. The astringency was completely gone from the apriore she'd stocked up on yesterday, and everything seemed in good shape. Once she dried it and made it into powder, she dissolved Drops of Life into it and used alcohol for extraction. She also extracted the dried and powdered ogre dates with alcohol. After removing the residue, she soaked yurole flower buds until they changed color, then took them out. If they soaked for too long, they wouldn't turn out right, so she focused on them to make absolutely sure she didn't miss the timing. She extracted curique and calgoran in water mixed with Drops of Life. Mixing these three liquids together and condensing them produced mid-grade heal potions.

To make a mid-grade cure potion, you add jibkey leaves, tamamugy seeds, and fiorcus flower extract to those three liquids. However, the proportions and mixing process were different, so the end of the procedure wasn't the same.

"It's kinda annoying how long it takes to make a bunch of different potions at once. It'd be way easier if I could just make a whole bunch of the same kind."

Even as she talked to herself, her hands didn't stop.

Before she could make high-grade potions, she needed to engrave the vials.

She took lumine stones and magical gem dust out of the hodge-podge box and then creeper saplings and liquefied slime as well. She put just a fragment of a lumine stone and a little bit of liquefied slime into a vial coated with creeper mucus and shook it up. Adding magical gem dust turned it into ink for glass, but since this ink was dangerous, she made only the amount she needed. With the coated glass pen, she inscribed Magic Circles of Antidegradation on the vials.

Mariela cheerfully began to sing a little drawing song she made up on the spot. Not only was she incredibly off-key, she also cheated on some of the lyrics by singing "hum, hum, hum, hummm" here and there. It was rather silly that she'd forget the words to her own song, but there was no one around to point this out.

After a little time passed, the portion of glass covered in ink dissolved, and just the magical gem dust remained in the grooves. The final step was to use her alchemic skills to fill the magic circle engraving with the surrounding glass, and then it would be complete. Mariela grew more and more excited, crying out, "Done! Doooone! Aaaand doooone!" with every magic circle she drew.

"And nowww, for my final act!"

In the highest of spirits, she turned around and was about to pick up her next implement when she noticed Sieg standing in the doorway.

"How… H-h-h-how long have you been standing there?"

"Since around…'hum, hum, hum, hummm'…"

He'd caught her in the most embarrassing moment possible.

The planada moss had been very carefully washed. *That certainly must have taken him a long time*, she thought—and then she realized something.

Noon had long since passed.

"Sorry, Sieg, you're probably hungry, huh?"

She'd been so engrossed in potion-making that she'd forgotten about lunch. This sort of thing happened to Mariela all the time, but it must've been really hard on Sieg.

"I'm fine. I never…used to eat three meals a day…anyway."

What a sad thing to hear. She wanted him to eat to his heart's content from now on. When she looked at his face, she could see that even his cheeks were hollow.

"Huh? Did you shave?"

She hadn't bought a knife yet, so this morning Sieg's beard had grown a little, but now he'd come back all fresh-faced—literally and figuratively.

"Huh? Did something happen?"

"Yes. I met with Lynx… He said he would…lend me his short sword."

Ah, sorry, that wasn't very tactful. Also, thanks, Lynx.

Although she wanted to thank him, Lynx wasn't in the restaurant. Apparently, he'd come only to eat lunch and had then gone back to work.

Lunch was an omelet stuffed with fresh ham and tricolored paprika and a crisp baguette. Because the omelet had so much in

it, it was quite weighty. The saltiness of the fresh ham complemented the sweetness of the egg, and it was delicious.

After the somewhat late lunch, she still had high-grade
potions to make. There was nothing left for her to ask Sieg to do.
She remembered how fidgety and restless he had been this morning with no work.

"Sieg, I don't have any more tasks for you today. Besides, you
probably haven't fully recovered yet, so I'd like you to take it easy..."

"My body is...quite all right. I'm doing some training. If you
have any orders for me...I'll come straightaway."

*Whoa. And just this morning he was trying to wash clothes
that didn't need washing. Maybe something really did happen.*

It was a good change for sure, so after telling him "Don't overdo
it," Mariela returned to the room.

I must repay Lady Mariela for everything she's done for me...

Siegmund tightly gripped the short sword Lynx had lent him.

05

Siegmund was born in a remote village near the Fell Forest. His
father was a hunter, and his mother passed away back when he was
just a small child. Every once in a while, someone in his family
was born with an otherworldly eye known as a *Spirit Eye*. Those
who possessed it were blessed with sharp eyes and increased
long-range accuracy, as well as Spirit Sight. This additional benefit

allowed its user to see even the weakest of spirits if they so willed it. Although neither his father nor his grandfather had this sight, Siegmund possessed this power in his right eye.

The distance vision and long-range accuracy granted by a Spirit Eye was so incredible that Siegmund, just like those before him, could pinpoint his target's vitals, and he became a well-known master archer at a young age.

"I'm doing this so you don't grow up ashamed of your Spirit Eye."

Siegmund's father used his modest earnings to hire a teacher for his son's education. As a result, the adolescent Siegmund was educated in reading, writing, mathematics, and etiquette, a rarity in his village. This knowledge, combined with his Spirit Eye, made him arrogant.

He began to believe he was an exceptional human being worthy of the Spirit Eye.

Siegmund's father never realized his arrogance. Eventually, he was attacked and killed by a monster while out hunting. That may have been the beginning of his son's misfortunes.

It's a universal truth that young and talented men find empty, remote villages boring. After his father passed away, Siegmund left the village and became an adventurer in town. He formed a party with some of his peers, and together they defeated many monsters. For Siegmund with his Spirit Eye, the kind of monsters faced by elementary-level adventurers were hardly worthy opponents, and his party quickly rose in rank.

Practically every time he drew his bow, his fame, his income, and the number of women who flocked to him increased.

The idea that he was an exceptional man worthy of the Spirit Eye transformed into absolute confidence.

"And just who do you think got us to B Rank?"

Indeed, Siegmund was so powerful that not a single member of his group could refute him. There was no monster his arrows couldn't penetrate—until they reached B Rank.

The relationship between Siegmund and his party members was not that of equals but rather like a dictator and his servants. They were an odd bunch, not just in terms of relationships but also in their individual strengths.

Looking at their combat prowess, there was Siegmund, who might have been in reach of A Rank, and then there was the rest of the party, who were around C Rank. The difference in abilities was plain to see, and the more they battled, the stronger and more arrogant Siegmund became. His party members had long since run out of patience with such a domineering man.

A wyvern was a small flying dragon subspecies with a venomous tail. Typically, these monsters weren't a problem for B-Rank adventurers to handle. If the party's vanguard distracted it while Siegmund destroyed its flying membranes to reduce its mobility, it would be no different from a crawling lizard. They could easily defeat it if they kept their distance, and that was what Siegmund had planned.

"E-eeek...!"

With a power level no greater than C Rank, the party's shield shrank back and failed to keep the wyvern in check. Their teamwork was also in shambles, and people kept getting in the way of Siegmund's arrows. In the end, the wyvern chose to target the least-armored member—Siegmund.

The wyvern's armored hide was quite tough, and Siegmund's arrows couldn't bring down the approaching beast. He managed to kill it only when its mouth had opened wide to devour him and an arrow happened to pierce its jaw.

Siegmund didn't know if he counted himself lucky or not. The price he paid was the loss of his Spirit Eye.

Without his Spirit Eye, no one offered to help him. His party members, who'd received B Rank benefits thanks to him, all left.

His fame turned to infamy as his former comrades dragged his name through the mud, and now that he was out of work, the ladies who had once found company with him were nowhere to be found. Due to his previous indulgences, there was no way he had enough money anymore, so he took the small amount he got from selling wyvern parts and traveled to the imperial capital.

That was where he could get a potion that restored lost body parts.

He paid off an informant and finally found the alchemist said to be able to make a special-grade specialized potion to heal his lost eye. The advance payment was ten gold coins, something Siegmund couldn't provide even if he sold his bow, armor, and other possessions. However, if he could get back his Spirit Eye, that amount wasn't unattainable. He borrowed money to be able to make the payment.

Once the aged, white-bearded alchemist received his payment, he and his apprentices created the potion. The apprentices used complex, expensive-looking magical tools Siegmund had never seen before to perform various tasks. The alchemist issued instructions one by one, mixed together the finished medicines, and cast a spell to finalize the concoction.

Siegmund took the completed potion. With this, he could get his Spirit Eye back at last. *I'll be in debt for a good while, but hey, all I need is a little bit of patience. That's hardly an issue where I'm concerned.*

He drained the vial of every last drop.

*   *   *

His Spirit Eye didn't come back.

"You lied to me!"

Siegmund, shaking with anger and about to throw himself at the man, was restrained by a security guard. The aged alchemist looked at his missing right eye with curiosity.

"Was it by chance an otherworldly eye?" he asked. "A Spirit Eye, as its name implies, is an otherworldly eye bestowed by the spirits. It's impossible to heal it unless you use a potion created in the region to which those spirits belong. Didn't you know that?"

"I'm a B-Rank adventurer chosen by the Spirit Eye! You think I'm going to allow this?!" Siegmund screamed, but the old man merely mocked him.

"Oh-ho. How many B-Rank adventurers do you think are here in the imperial capital? No fewer than a hundred. Incidentally, there are three at S Rank and twelve at A Rank. Did you know? Including myself, there are only three alchemists in the capital who can make specialized potions and about ten who can make high-grade potions like these fellows. They match the number of S-Rank and A-Rank adventurers, respectively. So what can a person at B Rank possibly have to say?"

As Siegmund was dragged out of the room by a security guard with the same rank, the old alchemist added, "Someone with a rare gift like a Spirit Eye who rose no higher than B Rank is a fool."

Siegmund was born in a village on the edge of the Fell Forest. Ever since the Kingdom of Endalsia was destroyed two hundred years ago, no new Alchemist Pact-Bearers were created in that region.

His Spirit Eye would never return to normal.

Finally realizing this fact, he ended up a debt laborer as collateral for his previous indulgences in alcohol and women.

Siegmund was then purchased by a merchant who had amassed a fortune through inhumane means. A deviant with a cruel disposition, he took pleasure from tormenting conceited youths like Siegmund and forcing them to submit.

Not even half a year had passed before Siegmund's warped self-esteem had been completely beaten out of him. It was all he could do to cling to life through the harsh labor, incessant violence, humiliation, and starvation. If this period of his life ever came to an end, he could manage to survive. Eventually, something happened that heralded his days of misery would soon be over.

"I'm going to do business with the Labyrinth City."

Hearing rumors of the Black Iron Freight Corps, which had become famous over the past several years, the merchant's son began to talk about traveling through the Fell Forest. Ignoring his father's protests, he headed into the forest accompanied by his slaves, who were given neither sturdy carriages nor sufficient weapons.

Maybe being attacked by a flock of black wolves within the first few hours would have been lucky. With heavy steps, Siegmund walked at the back of the line. How could he hold his own against any monsters with one old short sword?

He felt as if something was calling him. When he lifted his head, he saw something glowing faintly.

A forest spirit...?

He'd heard about them from his father: Unlike monsters, forest spirits were fond of people and would even help them. When Siegmund was still a child, he could see so many that the forest seemed to be overflowing with them, but thinking about it now, it seemed as though he hadn't seen any in a long time.

The forest spirit appeared to be looking his way and beckoning to him. Instinctively, he left the line of slaves and stepped into the forest as the spirit called to him. Then it happened. A pack of black wolves attacked the merchant caravan.

With no combat training, the slaves had no hope of standing against the monsters. Their windpipes were torn from their throats before his eyes. The wolves destroyed the carriage and dragged out the merchant's son. Thanks to the heavy armor only he was wearing, he was able to ward off fatal wounds, but his arm and leg guards were crushed, and he was bleeding. He kicked and struggled and screamed, but he probably wouldn't last long.

Siegmund had to get out of there. He surveyed his surroundings. Because he'd left the line of slaves and followed the forest spirit, he'd escaped the black wolves' initial attack. The beasts were busy devouring the fallen slaves and the merchant's son, but the slaves had little meat on their bones. The wolves would soon finish their meal and find him.

The forest spirit gently lifted its arm and pointed. He looked where it had indicated and saw a raptor with only minor wounds tied to the carriage, unable to escape. He rushed over and cut off its yoke with his short sword, then mounted it. As he passed by the merchant's son, he hauled him up onto the raptor's back.

If Siegmund returned alone, his life would probably be forfeit. But if he saved the merchant's son... The only reason he saved the man was out of self-interest.

Robbed of their prey, the black wolves gave chase. Siegmund clung to the bareback raptor and spurred it toward the forest exit.

He swung his short sword to try to cut down the wolves that threw themselves at him, but he had no knowledge of how to wield a blade, and his raptor mount was unstable. Instead of landing any blows on the wolves, he was bitten.

He almost dropped the sword, but he managed to grab it with his left hand and stab it into the wolf gripping his right arm.

"AWOO!"

He shook one off, but several more still chased them. The raptor galloped on, foam dripping from its mouth. The strength was gone from Siegmund's right arm. He clung to the raptor with his entire body. When he looked up at the scenery rushing past, he saw a faint light veering to the right of the road.

It was as good a way as any, so he hastened the raptor after the spirit.

The black wolves were getting closer and closer, and one following from the left sank its teeth into his calf. When he shook it to get the wolf off, the flesh tore.

"Gaaah!"

He almost lost consciousness from the burning pain. Blood dripping from a wound would send the black wolves into a frenzy. He had no time to stop the bleeding with normal measures.

"Fire."

He burned his own leg. Normally, he was forbidden to freely use magic because he was supposed to use it all for the benefit of the merchant. The smell of burnt flesh and the intense pain turned his vision pure white.

The wolves leaped at them again. As he was resigning himself to his fate, the distance between him and the wolves suddenly widened.

A sacred tree?

He saw a young sapling budding in stark contrast to the rest of the forest.

Sacred trees were holy trees that warded off monsters; they were said to be the saplings of the World Tree that grew in some far-off place. They grew slower than other trees and withered if planted by human hands. No one knew exactly how they propagated, but even in places thick with miasma like the Fell Forest, they grew unseen by human eyes. Any traveler who rested at the base of a sacred tree would find temporary respite and wouldn't be attacked by monsters.

The black wolves surrounded the sapling from a distance and continued to pursue Siegmund and the merchant's son. A third time, the forest spirit emerged and indicated a new location. No doubt about it—the spirit was showing him how to escape. In a daze, Siegmund followed the spirit's directions and spurred the raptor on. The snarls of the approaching black wolves faded away. He had no idea how much time had passed.

The raptor carrying Siegmund and the merchant's son made it out of the Fell Forest.

Siegmund saved the merchant's son and somehow survived. However, the healer who had been summoned to treat the son used only the simplest healing magic on Siegmund, who was then tossed into the slave pen, which was even filthier than where they kept the livestock. Miasma from the black wolves' fangs had entered his body; although his skin had been healed, the injuries underneath had not, and they continued to throb painfully. Between the pain and a high fever, Siegmund found himself in a hazy, semiconscious daze.

By the time he came to his senses, he realized he was no longer in the merchant's slave pen. He was provided water and food—chilled millet, like livestock feed, but he would eat anything edible to stay alive. His body, weakened by high fever, couldn't tolerate food, and he vomited, then ate, then vomited again.

"What a shabby man." A well-dressed individual Siegmund didn't recognize was regarding him as one might look at trash.

"The healer had told me of an abused debt laborer, so I took you into my custody, but you're in even worse shape than a stray dog. I doubt you can even understand the words coming out of my mouth, but I have a duty to inform you. Listen up, you mutt. Your former master brought a claim against you. He said you failed to protect his son and allowed him to be injured, and that you ran away. Because of these crimes, you're now a penal laborer."

Siegmund's mind wasn't functioning due to the fever. He couldn't understand what the man was saying. Yet, his dulled mind did understand that although he was still alive, that didn't mean he'd been saved.

"If you don't want to die, then act *normal*."

Following the orders of someone appearing to be a slave trader, Siegmund somehow managed to stand.

A tall man was talking to the trader and buying all the slaves, including Siegmund, who wore nothing but a loincloth and had his hands bound in front of him. The men and women were then loaded into separate carriages covered in iron plates. He heard someone say, "It's the Black Iron Freight Corps. They're taking us to the Labyrinth City."

After leaving the imperial capital, the slaves were taken out once a day for the first four days. That was when they relieved themselves, washed off with water magic, and were given yagu milk in place of food. The yagu milk contained crushed beans and grains, and while it didn't taste good, it allowed Siegmund to regain a bit of his strength.

On the fifth day, they seemed to enter the Fell Forest. The iron carriages shook violently; monsters attacked day and night. The crew appeared to eliminate only the ones that got in their way. The carriages kept going without a break. Once a day, they stopped for a brief moment to make the slaves drink yagu milk from leather bags, but they weren't given time to relieve themselves. The floor of the iron carriage sloped like a drain board, and everyone relieved themselves on it. The violent shaking and the sour smell emanating from the slaves never ceased, and the shaking carriage flung up the filth that collected under the drain board onto their heads.

In the pitch-black carriage, the constant sound of monster cries and the jolts signifying battle were joined by monster fangs and claws tearing at the exterior. In the frightening and extremely uncomfortable environment, his injuries and high fever dimmed his consciousness. When he thought he was going to lose his mind, he recalled the figure of the forest spirit. Or rather, the pale light of an ambiguous shape. That light managed to preserve Siegmund's sanity but only just barely.

The cargo hold's door opened. "Get out," someone said, and they all disembarked from the carriage. They were standing for the first time in three days. A stone wall surrounded them, giving the impression of a prison.

They lined up single file and were splashed with water; then they were ordered to get washed. It wasn't much water, more to suppress the smell than remove the filth, but he was grateful even for that. Next, a man arrived to examine them. He poked Siegmund in the leg with a pole, and Siegmund fell forward from the sharp pain. When he looked at his left leg, the one that had been bitten and cauterized, he saw it had turned black and swollen to nearly twice its original size.

Siegmund had no strength to resist when a different man grabbed his hair and forced him to stand so that his wounds and scars could be poked and prodded with a pole as part of an examination. He was in so much pain now that he could no longer do anything but moan.

Perhaps the inspection was over, because after a little while, a tall man and a portly one began to talk.

Meat shield, mines, a plaything. The men were discussing how even those fates were too good for him.

I don't want to die... I don't want to die; I don't want to die; I don't want to die.

Siegmund trembled.

No matter the pain and suffering and horror I've been through, I'm still alive. I don't want to die. I want to live.

It was a lone girl who saved him from his fear, confusion, and darkest despair.

After they branded him with the symbol that designated him as the girl's property, he was loaded into the carriage again.

"We're here; get out."

The man who took Siegmund out of the carriage told him, "This belongs to your master," handed him a bundle of withered herbs, then indicated a watering hole and said, "Wash yourself there."

Siegmund headed there as he was told. It seemed he could draw clean well water. He gulped it down until his belly was swollen. Even if it had been dirty, he would have had to drink it while he could, because he didn't know how long it would be until he could have water again. He drew more into the tub and dumped it over his head. How many days had it been since he'd washed himself? His body was extremely cold, perhaps due to the fever, but the wounds on his leg and arm were hot, like burns. Siegmund washed himself quickly through the pain.

Hearing footsteps and voices, he peeked out from the shadow of the watering hole and saw the girl who'd become his new master. He hurriedly dried himself with his loincloth, picked up the bundle of withered herbs, and headed in her direction.

The merchant who'd been his previous master would get terribly angry if he was kept waiting and would have whipped him many times. Siegmund had washed himself as instructed and drunk water of his own accord, but the girl herself hadn't ordered him to do these things. He wondered if she might be angry, but she made no mention of it and instead told him to come with her.

He followed her into a building that looked like an inn. She led him straight to a room. Every time he took a step, pain shot through his left leg as if the flesh were being torn off. Maybe because of the fever, it was painful to breathe, and he was close to losing consciousness, but the pain in his leg brought him back to reality.

Still. I'm still useless. I can't let myself collapse. I have to appear fine so she'll think I'm useful. They said I was worth two large silver coins—you can't even buy a decent weapon at a price like that. Something so cheap isn't worth repairing if it breaks. You'd just throw it away.

Siegmund pushed through the pain, clinging to consciousness, and painstakingly donned the appearance of tranquility as he followed behind the girl.

When they entered the room, she told him to sit down, but his left leg was so swollen, he couldn't sit properly. The merchant probably would have said, "You can't even sit?" and lashed him, but this girl said nothing, simply waiting for him to have a seat however he could.

"My name is Mariela. Would it be okay if I call you Sieg? Under the Contract of Servitude, you have to follow my orders. Is that right?"

So his new master's name was Mariela.

"Yes. Please call me whatever name you like, Mistress. I will never forget the kindness you've shown in choosing someone unworthy like me. No matter what order you may give, I swear not to disobey. Please command me however you desire."

Just as his former master had ordered him to countless times, Siegmund spoke as politely as possible and touched his forehead to the floor.

"Dog." "Pig." "Trash." "Filth." No matter what he was called, his answer was always "Yes" followed by "Please call me whatever name you like."

Every time he was given a little bit of feed, worse than what livestock was given, he would say, over and over again, "Thank you for taking in a useless man with only one eye" and "I will never forget your kindness."

He would repeatedly reply, "No matter what order you may give, I swear not to disobey. Please command me however you desire," to orders with *gratitude* until he collapsed... No, even after collapsing.

He mustn't lift his head. With his forehead touching the floor, he mustn't move until his master left. Not unless he wanted to be whipped until he could no longer stand. He had learned this all too well under the merchant. However...

"Call me Mariela. Lift your head so I can get a good look at you."

...his new master told him to show her his face. Fearfully, he lifted his head. Hair clung to his face. She wouldn't be able to see it like that, so in a panic he brushed the hair upward.

His master lifted her hand, perhaps to strike him, and his body stiffened reflexively. Up to now, a hand raised toward him always meant him harm. However, this one moved slowly, truly slowly, and gently touched his face.

It's soft. And cool. It feels nice...

She touched the place where his Spirit Eye used to be and traced the scars that remained there.

Her hand felt the fever he still had and his aching right arm. When she asked what had attacked him, he told her black wolves. Come to think of it, this was the first time a master had touched his injuries and asked what caused them. After carefully looking at the unsightly, discolored, and swollen leg, she said, "First, I'm going to wash your wounds."

When Mariela, his master, poured the faintly glowing water she'd created on him, his fever and the pain from his aching wounds vanished—both in his arm and his leg. Siegmund could hardly believe such excruciating pain had simply disappeared. He'd seen the light emitting from this mysterious water before.

The girl was an Alchemist Pact-Bearer, even though such people in the Labyrinth City had supposedly died out.

The story of the Kingdom of Endalsia's destruction had been handed down from generation to generation, almost like a fairy tale. It was a tragic story of heroes who stood against the swarm of monsters approaching the kingdom at the height of its glory. It was said the monsters devoured both the heroes and the citizens, then turned on one another. Finally, the remaining monster consumed the spirits of the ley lines, and then the Labyrinth was born. The people who'd escaped from the kingdom gathered in Endalsia once more but were no longer able to hear the spirits' voices.

It had been about a hundred years since the last alchemists passed away, and none had materialized in this region—except for *her*.

It was just like the miracles you hear of in legends of old, Siegmund thought. And in that moment, to him, she was a miracle.

His body had been treated with contempt, like so much garbage, and yet she washed it with her own hands and gave him a potion. Then she gave him warm food and embraced him when he burst into tears from overwhelming emotion. He'd looked like an animal, and she cleaned him up and gave him human clothes. With her potions and her miracles, she healed his bitten leg and all the old wounds he'd accumulated.

He'd lost everything but, in turn, had gained an incredible master. A compassionate soul, a miracle made flesh and blood.

She ended up having to do the laundry because I'm a dunce. I should be the one doing chores like that. But she didn't get angry; she simply gave me a job. She said this is a valuable ingredient. I have to wash it with the utmost care.

"Heeey, Sieg. Haven't seen you since yesterday."

"L-Lord Lynx."

Lynx had appeared before Siegmund while he was washing the planada moss. Siegmund wondered when he'd gotten here, because he hadn't noticed him at all.

"Just 'Lynx' is fine. That 'lord' stuff doesn't suit me. More importantly, I see your leg's been healed. That's great!" Lynx's narrowed eyes suddenly opened wide. "And with a specialized potion."

"Wha—?!"

Lynx hadn't been present during the business dealing between Lady Mariela and the Black Iron Freight Corps. No one else should know the details of the transaction except for Captain Dick and Lieutenant Malraux. How did Lynx...?

"The heck're you doing, Sieg?" Lynx turned a sharp glare on

Siegmund, who was visibly flustered. "You spilled the beans, you fool. See how you were just washing that stuff, all laid-back and not a care in the world? I coulda easily run off with Mariela just now."

"Ah…" In a panic, Siegmund looked up at the corner room on the second floor and used detection magic to feel for her magical energy. She was fine. She was still there. He couldn't sense anything suspicious nearby.

"I could do it if I tried. You can fight, yeah?"

"I… I lost my eye, and my bow is…" Siegmund offered a faltering excuse. Lynx heaved a big sigh, then grabbed Siegmund by the collar and launched into a rant.

"The hell d'you think you are? You saw all the crazy stuff Mariela can do, and you still don't think she's that special? Your armor's full of chinks. She's got all those valuable items with her—d'you just lack any sorta sense of danger? You can't even see the crisis she's in, and here ya are, just slackin' off. Think she's some kinda goddess? The messiah who saved your miserable life? That was a onetime deal, so you oughta take a good look with that one eye of yours. She's just a regular ol' happy-go-lucky doofus of a woman. You're useless. I got all that info outta ya without breakin' a sweat. What wouldja do if her secret got leaked and she became a target? Think your savior's gonna rescue you again? Hell no! That's *your* job! So, what? Can't use a bow with just one eye? Dumbass. A bow don't do a guard no good. Just use a different weapon. You can move that right hand now, yeah? You oughta think about how valuable the stuff she used to treat you was."

With a thump, Lynx thrust his fist into Siegmund's chest. That fist gripped a short sword.

"I'm gonna lend this to ya. Don't tell me you can't use it; just practice till ya can. How many people in this town d'you think died 'cause they didn't have access to that kinda treatment?

Practice for them, too. Practice till you're pukin' up blood. Don't you dare take all this for granted!"

After forcing his short sword on Siegmund, Lynx disappeared through the rear entrance.

I... I almost...made a terrible mistake again...

He'd been trying to picture Mariela as a wonderful master, a miracle made flesh and blood—a *special* master. Or rather, perhaps he wanted to think he was a special person who'd met a special master. It's true that she possessed an exceptional power, but she was just an ordinary girl.

Siegmund had already paid a price for his stupidity, and yet, he hadn't learned from it at all.

But now I've realized it. Lynx set me straight.

He tightly gripped the short sword Lynx had thrust at him. This time, he mustn't make a mistake. It was no lie to say he wanted to protect Mariela—she'd given him everything.

Siegmund at last faced the day with newfound positivity.

CHAPTER 5
A Refuge for the Heart

01

"Dooone!"

Mariela stretched with a sigh. After lunch, she'd made high-grade heal potions and cure potions, several other potions and prototypes for her own use, and a stamp for sealing and engraving Magic Circles of Antidegradation. Because her work had been going so well, she'd even made stamps to label different types of potions, and she'd just finished affixing all the labels; Mariela had a bad habit of getting caught up in whatever she was doing. She'd filled all her time with crafting.

"A bottle for when you're tired! The new and improved version! A Yummy Potion!"

It was just a low-grade heal potion with sweetener added to it. She gulped it down.

"Bleh, *cough, cough*. Gross!"

She'd tried to make a sweet potion that would go down easily by mixing in a paste made from dried apricots and some sugary berries she'd picked in the forest yesterday. However, once the smooth, syrupy taste of the fruit juice passed, the bitter astringency of the medicinal herbs filled her mouth and stuck in her throat. The nasty flavor wasn't worth the potion's recovery benefits.

"Here you are." Sieg had returned unnoticed and offered her tea. It was delicious. Her "Yummy Potion" had been a failure, but next time would be a different story. She wasn't about to give up. As Mariela drank her tea sip by sip, Sieg stored the potions in a wine box he said the inn's owner had given him, and then he tidied up the materials and equipment.

Upon hearing that Lieutenant Malraux and the others had arrived, Sieg took the wine box with the potions and carried it to Malraux's room, where the two of them were waiting. Once he handed the box to them, they began to review its contents with a magical tool used for appraisal.

Since potions deteriorated over time, tools like this one were often sold in shops that carried potions. It wasn't a very expensive item; it was easy enough to have a rough understanding of a potion's type and level of deterioration.

"This is wonderful. It's as if they were just freshly made; they haven't deteriorated at all!" exclaimed Lieutenant Malraux in admiration.

Well, yes, I would hope so. I literally just finished making them.

After they were done checking the potions, Lieutenant Malraux brought out the payment and several documents on a tray.

"Here we have the payment for the mid-grade and lower potions, as well as their receipt, and a confirmation of receipt for the high-grade potions."

The payment came out to twelve gold coins and six large silver coins. To Mariela, it was an unbelievable amount of money. She signed the document where she was instructed to. This kind of document wasn't something Mariela could create. She didn't properly understand the workings of a business deal, so she would've been stumped had she been asked to draw one up. But since they'd told her not to worry about it, she was grateful she could presume upon their kindness.

"We will give you the payment for the high-grade potions after we have received it from the other party. Speaking of which, is the low price truly all right with you?" Lieutenant Malraux wanted to be sure.

She had already received so much for the mid- and low-grade potions. Depending on how or to whom the Corps sold them, they could probably make an absolute killing on the high-grade ones, the likes of which hadn't been on the market for ten years.

"As long as you continue to use them, I don't mind. Please let me know if you'd ever like to buy more."

It'd be no issue for Mariela at all even if they sold for the same price as the mid-grade potions. If they cost too much, she'd feel guilty about it. She would be grateful for her potions to be bought even at a slightly high price.

"More, you say? How many would you be able to give us?"

She almost answered "I'll just crank 'em out!" but instead she smiled and replied properly, "A lot." Actually, that reply was plenty stupid, too.

Making vials was a big pain, but potion materials were easy to get. She wanted to set up a workshop with shelves brimming with a wide variety of materials, like Ghark's Herbal Supplies, and focus fully on potion-making. She couldn't have a potion shop in the open, but with the funds she received today, she could open an apothecary with a workshop. Just imagining it made her tremble with excitement.

When Lieutenant Malraux asked what she intended to do now, she answered, "I want to open an apothecary."

"In that case, I think it would be a good idea to visit the Merchants Guild. If you register as a chemist, they will assist you in finding a shop and a place to live."

This was good to know. She'd go there tomorrow bright and early.

"Pleasure doing business with you," said Captain Dick. "Now let's have a toas—"

"We are going to deliver the potions."

"...Next time, then!"

The captain finally opened his mouth just to say that?

The stocky Captain Dick picked up the box with the potions and trudged after Lieutenant Malraux.

02

Before dinner, Mariela returned to her room to deposit the money: gold coins, and twelve of them, at that.

"Hey, Sieg—we can open up a shop with this!"

"Yes. As far as funds go, this is probably enough."

Mariela hid the gold coins in a box of medicinal herbs, then invited Sieg on a predinner stroll.

"I've been cooped up in the room all day, so my body's super-stiff."

They walked along a main road toward the heart of the town. The day was winding down, but it was too early to call it evening yet. Other groups lined the road as the two of them took their stroll: carriages making their final delivery of the day, housewives who just finished shopping for dinner, children rushing home carrying materials they'd gathered in the Labyrinth under their arms.

The pre-dusk ambience was the same as it had been two hundred years ago, and it filled Mariela with nostalgia. However, the townscape and the fashion reminded her that this place was unfamiliar.

"Is this style of clothing the latest trend in the imperial capital, too? ...Oh, just here? And they're *not* trendy?"

"Aren't the wheels on that carriage kinda small? ...Huh? They're the same size everywhere?

"Something smells good... Ah, so if you bring your own container, you can take the food home with you."

One by one, Mariela pointed out all the things that seemed out of place to her and bounced them off Sieg.

"Oh, that's glive. Looks like they make it into juice."

Glive fruit had a good balance of sweet and sour, and it reduced fatigue. At five copper coins per cup of juice, the price was a bit much, but it sold well to adventurers. The shops were probably opening for adventurers who would be returning from the Labyrinth at any moment. Mariela bought two cups of fresh glive juice at a stall near the Labyrinth, and the two of them passed through the Labyrinth's outer wall.

"There really is nothing left, huh?"

Where the royal castle of Endalsia had once stood, Mariela couldn't find even a fragment of anything she remembered. Of course, they were just things she'd glanced at from outside the outer wall, and she'd never gone into any of the buildings. This was the first time she'd been inside the castle walls, which now housed the entrance to the Labyrinth. The entrance was composed of huge stones that just looked like a single mass of rock so that it could be sealed at any time, and she didn't see anything else resembling a building. The spacious interior of the castle walls looked like a plaza, except for the monster-warding bromominthra growing there, and peddlers and luggage carriers called out to the adventurers returning home from the Labyrinth. Just like Mariela and Sieg, there were other people going out for a stroll, too.

The two of them moved to the edge of the road so as not to get in the way of the adventurers, found a good rock to sit on, and had a swig of the glive juice.

"I wonder what we look like to everyone else," Mariela muttered.

A group of adventurers had just emerged from the Labyrinth along with several slaves in tattered clothes and carrying a large amount of baggage.

The Labyrinth City was a mass of land blockaded by the rugged mountains and the Fell Forest—a veritable solitary island. Very few members of the general public passed through its streets. The Suppression Forces continued to subjugate monsters on a regular basis to prevent another stampede, and no small number of lives were lost each time.

Even slaves were encouraged to reproduce, and their resulting offspring were raised in an orphanage as ordinary citizens. However, without any support, most of them made a living as adventurers or knights when they reached adulthood. Whichever path they chose, they became essential members of the Suppression Forces and protected the people from stampedes.

In addition, the forces dispatched by the margrave, who had jurisdiction over the Labyrinth City, there was also a mandatory draft of experienced adventurers from the imperial capital's Adventurers Guild. However, even these two powers together weren't enough to keep both the Labyrinth and the Fell Forest in check.

Securing rations was also important, and they needed more than what could be grown within the castle walls alone, so the grain-producing regions ended up expanding beyond the castle walls where monsters appeared. Although sentinels performed regular patrols and culled the monsters, no ordinary citizen would dare do any farming in such a dangerous place.

To compensate for this shortage of labor, slaves were sent to the Labyrinth City from the Empire. If another stampede arose out of the Labyrinth or the Fell Forest, both the Empire and the surrounding countries would suffer heavy damage, so those neighboring countries were also proactive in providing penal laborers and lifelong slaves. The ratio of slaves to the rest of the population within the Labyrinth City was greater than that of any other town within the Empire, or rather, even those in the neighboring countries as well. However, because the mortality rate was so extremely high, many of the slaves—penal laborers and lifelong slaves, for example—had no human rights.

Of course, these enslaved people were unintelligent and of poor character, and the average civilian wanted nothing to do with them. Under the direction of successful management—professionals, or "Skill Users"—most slaves were employed in areas managed by the government, such as food production or the Suppression Forces, both of which were directly under the margrave, or in the mines.

A small fraction of well-behaved slaves were sold to civilians. However, even if they didn't go to professionals, they had to be supervised, so the majority were sold to businesses requiring many laborers, shops employing "nighttime company," or the mansions of aristocratic families who collected slaves as "entertainment." The small-to medium-size shops hired ordinary citizens who did business for them without needing supervision. Personally owning slaves was the privilege of experienced adventurers or the organized group of adventurers Mariela and Sieg saw just now, who brought them along as baggage carriers. It wasn't common.

No matter what, it was highly unprecedented for a young girl like Mariela to own a slave.

When she'd indirectly asked Amber, who knew about Sieg's circumstances, she'd replied, "It's rare enough for a girl from outside the Labyrinth City to come all this way, and Sieg's a pretty good-lookin' guy, no? A girl living with a man who waits on her hand and foot—I'd wonder what kind of relationship they had."

Mariela already harbored one secret—her ability to make potions. She needed to come up with a way to not stand out.

"I wonder if we look like siblings?"

"Siblings... I don't think we do."

"Urgh... Wh-what about something similar, like childhood friends? We're opening a shop, so you'll need to quit being so subservient and talk more normally."

"But...that's no good for a guard..."

Sieg didn't seem to approve of Mariela's idea. As someone who'd been a slave for a long time, not only was his master the absolute authority, but he owed Mariela his life; it was no exaggeration to say she held his life in her hands. Telling him to be "normal" didn't mean he would know what to do.

Watching Sieg sit in troubled silence, Mariela took another gulp of the glive juice.

"This is the first time I've had glive juice," she said, changing the subject.

"Because it's...a southern fruit. It was likely gathered...from the Labyrinth," Sieg responded. He seemed to imply that since glive grew in southern countries, it probably hadn't existed here two hundred years ago.

"Nope, they sold it here, too. For about the same price. I just couldn't buy any. If I had five copper coins, I'd spend it on five loaves of bread. I always wondered what it tasted like." Mariela gazed at Sieg as she continued. "There used to be a beautiful castle here, y'know. I only ever saw it from far away, but it sparkled. My master said it was 'cause the castle was blessed by the spirits. But now there's nothing left of it. There's no trace of the house I used to live in, either. I don't have a home to return to anymore."

She'd thought winter was finally over that day, cloudy though it was, but winter would soon arrive again. With two hundred years gone by and not a trace of Mariela's cottage left behind, this world was as alien to her as a foreign country.

"But Amber and the other ladies said they'd buy medicine from me. If I open a shop and work hard at it, I'm sure I'll be able to make a living here."

Sieg gave his all in listening to Mariela's story, to the thoughts she wanted to convey.

"Before, I could never even afford glive juice. Formalities just don't suit me. Like being called 'Lady,' for instance."

Ahhh, I see.

Suddenly, Sieg understood—why she purchased him, why she didn't dim the lights even at bedtime, why she kept talking about the most trivial things. And he understood the profound loneliness she felt in this world of two hundred years later. She wanted a place to belong. Not just a physical home per se but a refuge for her heart, a source of emotional support.

"I...understand. I'll...give it a try."

If that was his master's wish, it was his duty to comply.

Since Sieg was originally from a remote village near the Fell Forest, they decided Mariela would also be from the same village and that she had traveled to the imperial capital to become a Pact-Bearer.

"It is I, Mariela, the super-awesome gal who came all the way to the Labyrinth City to rescue my enslaved childhood best friend! Kinda makes me sound like I'm the heroine in some story, don't it? Like my adventure's only just begun and stuff! Not that I can fight, though."

The two of them returned to the Yagu Drawbridge Pavilion as they chatted. Mariela beamed, feeling they'd come up with a good backstory. Her smile was infectious, and Sieg managed one, too. But just then, he realized something:

If they'd had any other slaves for sale, she might have chosen someone else.

Even though he'd long since grown numb to abuse and insults, this mere thought pierced his heart with a dull pain.

03

"Good morning, Miss— *Ahem*, lovely weather we're having, Lady—er, lately, right, Mariela?"

"Pfaw, the heck was that?! Morning, Sieg."

Thus began the first day of Sieg's attempt at natural (?) speech.

They went down to the restaurant and placed their breakfast orders with Emily. Today, Emily's hair was in pigtails tied high on the back of her head. Maybe she'd done it herself, because her hair looked squished, and the two pigtails were slightly off-center. When Mariela fixed them for her, she said, "Thanks! I'll give you a big helping!"

Her father, the owner of the inn, stayed up until dawn when Amber and the others had finished their work, so Emily woke up early by herself and prepared breakfast for their customers.

"Sometimes the customers aren't so nice, so that's why Daddy stays awake until everyone's work is over. Thanks to him, everyone says they can relax! So I'm gonna do my best, too!"

Still can't quite tie your hair up right, though.

Emily hurried off to the kitchen.

Mariela admired how capable she was for a ten-year-old. The next moment, Lynx arrived with a bad case of bed head.

"Emily, get some for me, too! A big helping, pleeease!" he called to the kitchen before sitting by Mariela and Sieg. He scratched his stomach with a big yawn.

"Lynx, you're practically an adult, so act more your age."

"I was out late yesterday with the captain and the other guys."

Probably acting as an escort for transporting the potions.

As they ate breakfast, Mariela asked him what the Black Iron Freight Corps did while they were in the Labyrinth City.

Apparently, they usually had a day off after they arrived, and they would spend it repairing the carriages or resting. On the second and third day, they split into two groups: one to stock up on goods they would take to the imperial capital and one to negotiate on the goods they would transport next. On the fourth day—today—they would buy things like food and prepare to depart. Early tomorrow morning, they would set out for the imperial capital again.

It took three days to travel through the Fell Forest, and another four after that to reach the capital. They would spend four days there to rest and stock up, and then return to the Labyrinth City back through the forest. That meant they would return around sunset on the eighteenth day.

"Sounds rough. Come back safe, okay?"

"Yup. But y'know, this time we got a 'secret weapon,' so if we make good time, we could be back at sunset sixteen days from now," he said in a low voice so the people around them couldn't hear. When Mariela told him she intended to open an apothecary, he replied with a laugh, "I'll come visit when we get back. Just hang tight."

As Lynx got up to leave, he for some reason thumped Sieg on the chest with his fist. Sieg looked back at him and nodded.

Huh? What was that about? Is this like what Amber was saying about wondering what kind of relationship two people might have?

Mariela cocked her head to one side, deep in thought.

04

"More trouble with an unauthorized chemist?"

In the office of the chair of the Merchants Guild's Medicinal Herbs Division, Elmera Seele sighed. She was a woman in her early thirties wearing thin glasses, and the entirety of her brown hair, even the bangs, was gathered in a bun at the back of her head. She wore a long navy-blue dress that covered everything up to her neck, and though her legs peeked out slightly from the dress, they were hidden by boots. Her hands were also covered by gloves, so practically the only part of her that was exposed was her face.

The only makeup she wore was lipstick, and the subdued hues of her hair and dress left no sense of feminine grace about her.

Many people kept their distance due to the stubborn, superior aura she gave off, in addition to her promotion to chair of the Medicinal Herbs Division at a young age. Because she was the eldest daughter of the Seele family, a large business dealing in medicinal herbs, some people even said, "That's just the kind of position you'd expect for a woman with no chance of becoming a bride."

"I knew the exam was too hard, Miss Elmera. First, we ought to make it less difficult, and then the number of chemists will increase."

"What are you talking about, Leandro? There aren't even any potions in the Labyrinth City. What do you plan to do with more mediocre chemists? If we don't improve the quality of the medicine, the mortality rate will never go down. The general difficulty of the questions on the exam is such that an alchemist who can make mid-grade potions can pass it."

"When you say 'mid-grade potions,' they're the potion equivalent of a B-Rank adventurer, yes? Adventurers begin at the F Rank. Don't you think it's extreme to not allow anyone without B-Rank–equivalent knowledge to become a chemist? There are no Alchemist Pact-Bearers here, but there are those with alchemic skills. You know they can dry and crush herbs even at a low level. Wouldn't it be nice to let them become chemists so they can study and improve?"

"If they want to study, they can still do so without becoming a chemist. Our Medicinal Herbs Division has taken great pains to compile books, including *The Encyclopedia of Medicinal Herbs and Their Effects*, which can be read in the Merchants Guild library for free. We also periodically hold seminars for young people wishing to become chemists, and if they need work, they can apprentice at a guild-licensed shop where they can expand their knowledge of medicinal herbs."

"That book you're referring to—that tome with all the fine print and pages packed with information about herb characteristics and effects and extraction methods, yes? That would put a person right to sleep within minutes. By the way, my personal record is thirty seconds. No young person who just offhandedly thinks, *Hey, maybe I'll become a chemist!* would read a thing like that. They're not all as bright as you are, Miss Elmera. We ought to be a little more flexible when it comes to nurturing their talents."

The man called Leandro, who was in his late thirties, was Elmera's subordinate. Despite being older than his boss, neither he nor the other employees of the Medicinal Herbs Division had any complaints about her. They knew her abilities were the real deal.

Her meticulous appearance, as if she'd stepped out of a painting, and courteous behavior gave the impression she was difficult to approach, but if you got to know her, you would find her a friendly and sociable person. Although she was too serious in some respects, she freely gave her honest opinion and was always willing to lend an ear. Few bosses seemed to want to work hard with the rest of the team as she did.

"Nurture your own talents first, Leandro. Otherwise I'll never be able to retire, will I? And here I can't even be with my sweet children and see them grow up."

Although people gossiped that Elmera had "no chance of becoming a bride," she in fact had a husband and two sons. When she got married, she had wanted to retire from the Merchants Guild, but the entire department stopped her. They couldn't function properly without her, so they asked her to wait a little longer until her subordinates could manage on their own.

"Please don't say that, Miss Elmera. You know none of us could possibly replace you."

Leandro knew that a department that couldn't function without a particular person would be eliminated. The employees were developing their skills, so even in the unlikely event Elmera quit, the department could manage if it got about ten more employees.

However, it was quite rewarding and fascinating to work with Elmera, who was fighting to improve the medicinal situation in the Labyrinth City.

"In any case, we have to improve the quality of our chemists. Let's plan a seminar. Something easy, like 'How to Make Salves.' And you can teach it, Miss Elmera."

"Ughhh, I don't have time to play with children..."

Elmera suddenly hunched over. Normally, she always stood straight as a pin.

It was a pity for her to carry such a burden. Leandro would divide some of her work among the other employees. As he wondered what to do about the schedule, a knock came at the door to the office.

"We have someone who wants to register as a chemist. She wants to take the exam right away. I've come to get the question sheet."

"I will administer the exam. Take her to the first-floor conference room."

Elmera quickly got to her feet and gave instructions to the receptionist at her door, ready to get back to it.

Whoa, that was bad luck. Miss Elmera's enthusiasm will be running on empty right now.

She would need support. Leandro trailed after her.

"My name is Mariela. It's very nice to meet you."

Per Lieutenant Malraux's advice, Mariela had come to the Merchants Guild. She was surprised; the building was very large, and when she told the receptionist she wanted to register as a chemist, the lady had led her to what was apparently the Medicinal Herbs Division. It seemed she would need to take an exam before registering. It was the first time she'd taken one, but even if she failed, she could take it as many times as she wanted. They told her she could take it right away, so she might as well give it a shot.

After a short while, she was led to a room at the back of the building. Before long, a stern-looking woman and a wimpy-looking man entered.

"I'm Elmera Seele, the proctor of this exam."

"My name is Leandro Kaffa. Even if you don't pass, we have seminars, so please don't be too nervous."

There was a pen and ink ready on the desk, so Mariela thought she'd be writing on paper, but it seemed she would just have to answer Elmera's questions.

"Miss Elmera, this is…not an easier exam. This one's even worse," Leandro said with a troubled expression, but Elmera ignored him and began the first question.

"Tell me the processing method and effects of the apriore fruit."

"Once you peel off the shell, you remove the astringency with trona crystal powder dissolved in hot water. The amount of trona crystals needed is……"

The other questions involved the effects and processing methods of mundane medicinal herbs such as bendan flowers, jibkey leaves, tamamugy seeds, ogre dates, and yurole flower buds, all things Mariela was well acquainted with. When she readily answered them, the difficulty rose midway through to include questions about high-grade materials—how to extract lunamagia, how to remove the poison from arawne roots and leaves, and how to process the venom glands of parasitic leeches. However, Mariela didn't particularly mind and continued to answer.

It was fun to talk about things in her area of expertise. Elmera listened to her attentively, punctuating Mariela's answers with

"Mm-hmm" and "Uh-huh, uh-huh," which in turn caused Mariela to become further absorbed in her explanations.

"Marvelous...! I wonder who you studied under? No, there's no point in prying. You pass!"

Just like that, Mariela was now a chemist. It was so easy; was that it? The questions had extended to high-grade materials, but the details were all about the fundamentals.

"Um, would it be okay to sell medicine as a chemist? There's no limit on what kinds I can make based on my rank, is there?"

"No, as long as you're within the Labyrinth City, there are no restrictions. Is there a problem?"

"It's just that the questions were all really basic."

"My! Did you hear that, Leandro? There really are people who properly study after all!"

Elmera was elated. Leandro, who'd brought up the issue of difficulty in the first place, was in a tough spot.

This girl is just like Miss Elmera. She has no idea how difficult the questions really were.

If the chemist exam kept getting harder and harder like this, Leandro would have to pick up the slack. He'd come along with Elmera to provide support, but the number of people he needed to do that for seemed to have increased.

"Whew... Mariela, was it? You're quite informed for someone your age. It's rare for Pact-Bearers to come here from the imperial capital. I couldn't have answered those questions as well as you did," he said.

"What? If you're a Pact-Bearer from the imperial capital, does that mean you can make potions there?" asked Elmera.

"Pact-Bearers can view Libraries, right? So they merely rely on a Library for anything they can't memorize themselves."

A *Library* was an informational repository that allowed a person to record and view all sorts of information about things that could be created using alchemic skills, from processing transmutation materials to crafting potions. It was said that information was bound to ley lines, meaning a Pact-Bearer could not view it once they left the line's region. It was possible to connect to a Library after linking to a ley line with a Nexus, but even then, one could view information only from the same alchemic "school."

There was no exact definition as to what an alchemic school entailed, but Mariela understood it had something to do with close relations such as masters and their apprentices.

"But I can't view the next item in the Library if I don't have the entire thing memorized, right?" Mariela asked.

"That's not how Libraries are typically configured…"

Leandro looked positively dejected, unlike Elmera, who practically glowed as she said, "What a wonderful master you had!"

The Library could be "configured" by one's master to disclose information based on certain conditions. For example, a recipe for a potion might be revealed once you reached a level that allowed you to make it, or it might be revealed from the start even if you couldn't. Conversely, the master could configure things like dangerous recipes or recipes they wanted to monopolize so that only their successors could view them.

Sometimes a particular material had a large number of effects or tuning methods, and these were usually disclosed from the start.

Damn master. Stingy master. Evil master.

In Mariela's case, until she could create all the disclosed potions with just alchemic skills—no tools—she couldn't view the recipes for any new potions, nor could she see new information on materials until she perfectly memorized and processed the disclosed ones. Although she didn't pry, she guessed from Leandro's reaction that these prerequisites were quite harsh.

She had thought that was just the way things were, so she'd learned the information without minding too much. Now that she thought about it, though, she had started out able to view certain information unrelated to potions as much as she liked. Things like *101 Delicious Recipes You Can Make with Alchemic Skills*, *Essential Alchemic Products to Make Your Life Easier*, and *Alchemic Housework Techniques for the Busy Housewife*. Even as she'd wondered, *Who the heck registered these?* she'd looked through them all.

The *Delicious Recipes* were especially helpful. Since her master couldn't cook at all, it had been Mariela's job since childhood to prepare the ingredients her master brought in. Just as *Delicious Recipes* claimed, the dishes made with alchemy were delightful, and the two of them were both completely satisfied. Mariela got hooked on the food and didn't think it was at all strange that she could see only these kinds of recipes in the Library.

"Mariela, you want to open an apothecary in the Labyrinth City, correct? Where do you plan to establish it? If you're going to sell medicine to the shop in the Adventurers Guild, we can make an introduction."

"Um, I haven't decided on a place to live yet, so I came here to register and ask if you could refer me to a residence where I could open my shop."

Mariela got sidetracked when her master entered her thoughts. Elmera's question brought her back to reality along with her original purpose for coming here.

"Well! Leandro, take her to the Residential Affairs Division. Please be sure to show her some good properties. Don't forget to prepare her chemist license and resident registration. Mariela, when you've settled in, please feel free to bring some medicine. Ah yes, here's a congratulatory gift for passing the exam. *The Encyclopedia of Medicinal Herbs and Their Effects* is a collection of all the medicinal herbs identified within the Labyrinth City, though it might only contain information you already know."

Despite what her appearance would suggest, Elmera seemed to be a passionate person. Mariela felt very welcome.

The Encyclopedia of Medicinal Herbs and Their Effects was a thick, elegantly bound tome that looked far from cheap. Mariela had asked if it was all right for her to have such an expensive item, to which she was told, "It was transcribed by someone who had been reassigned to the Medicinal Herbs Division, so by all means!"

When she turned the pages, she found scattered tearstains here and there. "It's imbued with purification magic," Leandro had assured her, "so it's not dirty." Maybe the "tears" were actually drool instead.

The tome contained some herbs Mariela wasn't familiar with, but even for the ones she did know, it had harvesting information such as the strata and seasons in which they could be found in the Labyrinth, so it was very helpful. What an incredible encyclopedia. She was very grateful.

Mariela thanked Elmera as she left the room. Elmera showed her out with a smile that lit up her entire face.

After meeting up with Sieg in the hallway, Leandro started toward the Residential Affairs Division with the other two.

"You are something else...," Leandro said admiringly after they'd parted from Elmera.

I wonder why...?

Sieg looked elated.

I wonder why...? Mariela, the only one who didn't understand, tilted her head to the side.

05

Leandro led them to the Residential Affairs Division. The margrave entrusted this department with governmental tasks such as resident registration, residence management within the Labyrinth City, and mediation.

"Ah, Vice Chairman Leandro. I'm surprised to see you come all the way here."

The person in charge of residential services greeted Leandro.

This guy's a bigwig.

"Chairwoman Elmera has asked us to show some good properties to this young lady, Mariela."

Elmera's an even bigger wig. She seemed totally obsessed with herbs.

Mariela's thoughts were slightly rude. When asked if she had any particular housing requests, she replied, "Somewhere with a yard where I can grow herbs, plus space for a storefront."

"An herb garden...?" the housing official repeated, a concerned look on his face as he flipped through his categorized files on vacant properties.

"There are plenty of vacant storefronts, aren't there?" asked Leandro.

"Yes, but as far as those with an herb garden… All the housing with agricultural space is booked. Properties where one can safely grow food are popular. We have several available shops in good locations, but their yards are small and paved for carriages."

Leandro and the housing official put their foreheads together as they pored over the files.

"Um, I can plant an herb garden outside the Labyrinth City…"

When Mariela suggested this compromise, she was met with objections of "Absolutely not!" and "That's dangerous!" She watched the two of them hemming over this and that property as she sipped on tea one of the ladies from the Residential Affairs Division had prepared for her.

Oh, this tea's good. I wonder if they sell it in the Merchants Guild shop? I'll buy some before we go home.

"What about this?!" Leandro exclaimed as if he'd just found something. The housing official, on the other hand, looked positively morose.

"There's a tree growing right in the middle, which would make it hard to grow many herbs. It doesn't look like we have authorization to cut it down, either. Furthermore, the shop space was added to the building with a lot of cut corners and has deteriorated significantly."

"Ahhh, that one? Looks like a half-finished former mansion."

"Indeed. It's been remodeled by previous residents and from rezoning, so you might say it's a bit, ah, *unique*. The property is spacious enough, but the cost makes it hard to manage, and it's remained vacant."

Mariela peeked at the document out of curiosity. It showed a map, a rough sketch, and an overview of the property. The location was a little ways back from the northwestern district's north gate, close to the center of the Labyrinth City. Many ordinary citizens lived in the northwestern district, and its streets were lined with shops like the one where she'd bought clothes for herself and Sieg, as well as general stores. And since it was so close to the Labyrinth, adventurers probably frequented the area, too. It was a great location to open a storefront.

Hang on, isn't this the Spirit Sanctuary?

As the name suggested, the Spirit Sanctuary was a nature preserve teeming with spirits and an abundance of sacred trees. This was where Mariela's master had taken her when she connected to the ley line with a Nexus.

"Quit fooling around. If you make friends with the spirits and tell them your name, they'll guide you," her master had told her as she traipsed through the Sanctuary. Under the guidance of the spirits she'd befriended, Mariela was able to connect to the ley line with a Nexus. Although she'd gone to the trouble of making friends with the spirits and telling them they'd play together again, she never returned to the Sanctuary and thus never got to see them. Since she had missed her spirit friends so much, Mariela had convinced her master to tell her their location. There was no doubt about this place.

"I'd like to see that property, please."

Two hundred years had gone by, but she wanted to visit the Spirit Sanctuary again.

After thanking Leandro, she and the housing official headed for the location in question.

According to the official, the northwestern district had suffered the most severe damage from the Stampede and become almost barren as a result. Homes had been built when reconstruction first began. Apparently, this property was one of them and was originally a small mansion owned by aristocrats. The house's exterior was made of sturdy stone, and even after more than a hundred years, it still met the Labyrinth City construction standards.

When the aristocratic quarter in the southeast district was rebuilt during the reconstruction, this area's residents moved to more suitable dwellings over there. The remaining residences were sold to civilians, but the position of the outer wall was changed in accordance with the Labyrinth City town planning, shaving off about a third of the rear yard, and a garden was placed in front instead.

Residences in the Labyrinth City generally had no front yard, but even the ones that did had only a narrow space for lighting, and the rear yard took up a large amount of the acreage. The yards weren't meant to be scenic; rather, it was more logical for them to take up space in the back where they were out of sight and could serve for practical things like setting up a carriage storehouse or livestock shed, or raising crops.

Since this house had a roughly thirty-square-foot front yard in accordance with town planning, it felt half-finished from the point of view of a Labyrinth City inhabitant.

Furthermore, the area that used to be the kitchen had been demolished so as not to hinder the growth of the tree that was right next to the house. Normally, the tree would have been cut down, but the housing official consulted his files and explained that such permission hadn't been obtained, and the instructions were instead to alter the building accordingly.

The most recent residents of this property were apparently two families who ran the place as a restaurant. Where the demolished kitchen stood, they'd added a galley and dining room by laying a roof across the front garden between the house and the outer wall that ran along the main street. It was a building addition in the strictest sense, but only the galley had been properly built, whereas the storefront just had a tarp over it—perhaps due to budget constraints. The living room and terrace seating with the tarp across it made for a decent shop atmosphere, though.

"The terrace will be cold in the winter. Also, given the size of the plot, the rent is rather high."

Rent was three gold coins per year, which was one coin more than the typical rent for a storefront of a similar size and condition. The winter season brought fewer customers, too. The previous residents had moved, waiting for another store property to become available.

As the housing official went over the details, they arrived at the location.

"That's a sacred tree."

"A sacred tree."

Mariela and Sieg spoke in tandem. A single large tree towered above them slightly to the east of the plot's center. It was higher than the roof on the second floor, and they could see it just by looking up from the front entrance.

No wonder they didn't have permission to cut it down—sacred trees protected humans from monsters. By all rights, it should have been impossible to build a house next to it. It was said that a sacred tree will wither if you try to surround it and take it for yourself—"A sacred tree's spirits will transplant elsewhere," as the saying went.

Two hundred years ago, this spot housed the Spirit Sanctuary, but now it was unrecognizable. Had it really been abandoned? Judging from the tree's size, it must have grown from the seeds of the sacred trees that once inhabited the Sanctuary.

Mariela wondered where her spirit friends had gone. There

used to be so many of them, and now she couldn't find a single one; this lone tree was all that was left of its former glory.

She passed through the house and went straight for the tree. The soil around it was dry; it seemed as though nobody was taking care of it.

"Water."

She put more magical energy than usual into the water she poured over the base. The spirits who guided Mariela to the ley line had been delighted by her magic-infused water, so she was sure this sacred tree would like it, too.

Mariela gently touched the trunk.

"Hello. I'm Mariela. Would it be okay if I lived here?"

These trees were said to house spirits; she wondered if this one did, too. Not that she'd be able to communicate with it even if there was, though.

Slowly, gently, one of the leaves drifted down into her hand. It was flat, about the size of Mariela's palm, and it was a valuable potion ingredient. It looked as though it belonged to a deciduous type of tree, but sacred trees never lost their leaves, even in winter. Plucking one by force would cause it to wither and die immediately, so if you needed one, *it was essential to ask for it.*

I wonder if that means I can live here?

Following Mariela's lead, Sieg watered the tree as well. For some reason, he got about ten leaves in return.

Whoa, that's quite a warm welcome. Guess he's a popular guy, huh?

It seemed the sacred tree was just fine. The yard looked as if it had been scaled back at some point, but there was still plenty of room for an herb garden. In fact, bromominthra was growing with wild abandon over about sixty-five square feet of the garden's surface. She could make all the monster-warding potions she wanted.

Even if the land itself was relatively barren, medicinal herbs would grow without issue as long as the soil was rich with magical elements. Such was the case for the Labyrinth City, the monsters' territory.

The housing official led Mariela and Sieg on a tour of the interior. The Labyrinth City had architectural standards; in essence, buildings needed to be strong enough to withstand monsters if they stormed the town.

First, all plots of land had to be completely surrounded by a stone wall over one head tall. The wall's thickness had similar requirements—about the width of one person. The exterior likewise had to be dense as well, and all first-floor windows required iron bars to prevent monsters from getting in. Finally, all cellars had to be stocked with one week's worth of provisions in case of an emergency.

Although not specified in the construction standards, magic-absorbing daigis ivy crawled along the outer wall and the building to hide their presence from monsters by preventing the inhabitants' magical energy from leaking out. Instead of multicolored flowers, the brilliant reddish-purple leaves of the bromominthra herb had been planted in the flower beds to repel monsters.

To soften the heavy, prisonlike construction, the iron bars on the first-floor windows had been wrought into whimsical shapes such as ivy and flowers; a cloth of various colors had been draped like a tarp from the roof to the outer wall, from which a large banner hung in lieu of a proper signboard advertising the shop. *A spirited place like this, with its exotic townscape and decorative masonry, ain't too bad at all*, thought Mariela.

The building seemed plenty sturdy; it was said to be a former mansion, and it looked to be structurally sound. The first floor had a spacious living room, as well as a smaller room in the back about a third of its size—probably a parlor. A few tables and chairs from the restaurant had been left behind.

On the other side of the corridor was a lavatory, a bathroom, and a storeroom. The latter was against the wall that looked out onto the sacred tree, and since the wall was new, this must have been the former kitchen. The door to the rear entrance had also been installed far back to correspond with the new wall, and immediately upon entering, there was a staircase that led to both the second floor and the cellar. The cellar was divided into several rooms, which was entirely too much space for just two people.

The second floor had four rooms, plus one for storage. A small balcony had been built on the wall, which slanted to avoid the sacred tree. There was also a staircase that led up to the roof, where most people dried their laundry—hence the stairs.

Once they got a professional to check the plumbing, it looked as though the place would be ready for use with just a good cleaning. Depending on her budget, Mariela could even spiff up the place by changing the wallpaper or installing curtains and carpeting.

An addition had been constructed on the south side of the building where a thirty-foot-long yard had once stood between the main gate and the entryway; the previous residents used the building's exterior and the outer wall to build a galley and restaurant area. Having said that, the roof reached only far enough to cover the galley, while the restaurant had a tarp ceiling over the deck floor. Since the outer wall lacked windows, the tarp might have been intended as a source of light, but the passage of time had left it torn, allowing wind and rain to damage the deck floor. The interior had been painted a pale color—perhaps to emphasize that this area was, in fact, part of the interior—but much of it was peeling and looked downright shabby. All that remained of the former storefront was a built-in countertop against the building side of the wall.

If I'm gonna have a shop, this is it, but we'll have to do a lot of fixing up, thought Mariela as she toured the storefront portion.

"I assume it's okay to make repairs to the building. Could you recommend a carpenter?" she asked. The housing official looked slightly taken aback.

"Of course, as long as it complies with the building code. I will introduce you to someone familiar with the code," he explained. "However, given the state of the property, I daresay the repairs will be quite costly."

First, all land was under the dominion of the margrave and rented out. Rent was calculated based on the total size of the plot and the building, along with the corresponding section's unit price and levied in addition to taxes every year. Given the possibility of property damage from monster attacks, collecting annual rent provided proof that a resident was still living, and in the unlikely event a house was destroyed, it could be rebuilt by order of the margrave. Since all land was property of the margrave, there had yet to be an instance where a house was unable to be rebuilt because the landowner could not be identified.

"Rest assured that your leasing contract will be renewed so long as you abide by housing laws, and you will not be subject to any impromptu evictions. For further details, please refer to the

Residential Affairs regulations found within the Labyrinth City's special laws, etcetera, etcetera, blah, blah, blah..." The housing official began to blather on, so Mariela urged him to cut to the chase.

"In short, a residential leasing contract will be executed along with your resident registration, proof of existence, and tax collection, in addition to any emergency provisions."

There were two types of buildings—purchased and rented—and this one appeared to be the former. Mariela was apparently free to use any of the house's leftover items or remaining vegetation in the garden however she liked. It did, however, come with certain provisions, such as "the sacred tree may not be cut down."

"As far as the price of the property is concerned, given the severe deterioration of the addition along with the main building's depreciation from age, the total will come to three gold coins. The annual rent for the plot is also three gold coins. Since we're already about two-thirds through the year, rent for the remainder will be one gold coin. Any further particulars will be calculated for you once you return to the guild, but we will require four gold coins at the time of the leasing contract's execution, followed by an annual cost of three gold coins starting at the beginning of next year. Furthermore, the main building has no kitchen, and the one in the extension is in bad condition. It appears the repairs to the storefront will be quite expensive."

Indeed, this property was very complicated. It was too expensive for the average citizen, and even for someone with agricultural skills, the crop yield would be too low to make a profit. The size of the building itself was much too small for a wealthy merchant, and it was some distance from the aristocratic quarter, too.

"This place is fine. Please set up the contract."

However, for an alchemist, it was a mouthwatering property. To have a sacred tree in the garden was almost too good to be true. So long as Mariela was able to sell potions, paying the rent would be a breeze.

They returned to the Merchants Guild and drew up the contract the same day, and Mariela paid the four gold coins. After receiving the key and a copy of the contract, she was hit with the reality of having obtained the mansion of her dreams. She couldn't fully suppress a smirk.

"I will arrange for the carpenters. May we choose who will be starting the work right away? Since you were referred by Chairwoman Elmera, I'll be sure to send skilled carpenters. Please feel free to consult me personally about the repair plans and expenses. I will contact you on-site tomorrow afternoon."

The negotiations went off without a hitch. According to what the housing official told Mariela, she was allowed to move in today, but the property was normally cleaned and reorganized first. And carpenters were going to be arranged for as well. Apparently, luggage would get in the way of their work, and there was also the risk of it getting stolen.

Even so, she was thrilled. There were even four rooms on the second floor. Where should she set up her workshop? How should her storefront look? She had to check what furniture and other things she needed, too.

Back at the Merchants Guild shop, Mariela purchased some bread and a bottled drink. She remembered to buy the tea she'd had in the office as well and headed to the house with Sieg a second time. They ate lunch under the sacred tree and discussed what kind of remodeling they wanted to do.

06

"I'll line up shelves starting around here and put the worktable over here! That'll make a fine workshop, don'cha think?"

"Sounds...nice. What about a bedroom?"

"Next to the worktable! That way, when I'm tired, I can go straight to bed!"

"So...your bedroom...will be next to the workshop, then."

"Awww man, but going between rooms is such a pain!"

"Don't worry. I will...carry you."

"What, am I luggage now? What about your room, Sieg?"

"Next to yours...would be...fine..."

"Isn't the room right at the top of the stairs bigger, though?"

"That would make...a nice guest room. That seems...suitable, since you can fit two beds in it."

And so the two of them began to discuss how to allocate the rooms.

They decided on the second-floor ones right away. The large one farthest to the right would be the workshop, and the rooms to the west of it would be Mariela's bedroom, Sieg's bedroom, and the guest room.

On the other hand, they couldn't come up with a good plan for the living room and inner parlor on the first floor. The living room was twenty feet wide by forty-six feet deep when viewed from the door, and it had a fireplace on the end of the long edge. Mariela had heard that aristocrats would line up long, narrow tables in rooms like these and lounge about as they dined. However, it was just her and Sieg—they didn't need a living room this big.

That said, she thought the fireplace was great. When winter came, she wanted to get all warm and cozy and sit on the hearth drinking hot cocoa.

"But the fireplace wouldn't be able to warm a room this big, huh?"

"If we partition one section, it might work."

"What would we do with the sectioned part?"

"A guest room?"

"We've already got one on the second floor. Who would visit us anyway…?"

Neither of them could come up with a decent idea. The kitchen and shop were far beyond Mariela's scope; she'd lived in only a small cottage before, and no image came to mind. Sieg seemed to be in the same situation. They realized they needed to buy a lot of things, too, but there were so many that they didn't know where to start or where to put them.

"Let's talk with a carpenter."

From the very start, they were keen to delegate everything to a third party.

For the time being, they decided to go buy what they needed today and tomorrow and look at a variety of shops.

Sieg needed a change of clothes and a cloak, and Mariela had only one tunic and pair of pants. Her shoes and bag were falling apart, so she planned to buy new ones at Elba's Shoe Shop. That place had lots of things she needed, like knives she could use for harvesting and cooking, and sewing kits.

They took a look around, focusing on the stores near their

new home. In the middle of their browsing, they caught sight of a sign that read MERLE'S SPICES.

"Merle" must've been the name of the shop's poster girl. Mariela pictured a cute kid like Emily at the Yagu Drawbridge Pavilion as she peeked inside. It seemed to be a place offering spices and tea for sale. A large number of spices Mariela had never seen before lined the shelves.

"Whoaaa, that's not something you see every day!"

"Gosh, new faces. You two from outside the city?" An amiable and rotund middle-aged woman greeted them.

More than half of the items seemed to have been gathered in the Labyrinth. As with medicinal herbs, the Labyrinth had vegetation from all over the world due to the differing climate in each of its strata. Low-efficacy spices like these apparently grew in the earlier levels and were perfect for beginning adventurers to gather along with herbs for pocket change. Thanks to this, spices made the rounds in the markets of the Labyrinth City, and even the skewers in street stalls were sprinkled with salt and pepper for a delicious effect.

"The sugar's a little expensive..."

"It takes a lot of time to process sugar turnips. If you want it for cookin', this crude sugar I have here's perfect. I even put it in my tea, too."

Sugar turnips were a locally cultivated crop used to make sugar. Boiled turnip dregs were used for livestock feed, and crude sugar along with a small amount of regular sugar could be extracted from the broth. Because processing technology wasn't well-developed, this made only a small amount of refined sugar, and it was expensive. Crude sugar contained both sugar and impurities, and it was well-known as an inexpensive flavoring used by the masses for cooking and other purposes because of its distinct taste. Although sugar-refining technology seemed to have improved over two hundred years, much of what came from the turnips was still crude sugar.

Incidentally, sugar turnips were a favorite food of orcs, and during the harvest season, the creatures were drawn to them. Farmers set traps around their fields, of course, and even sentinels and adventurers would go orc hunting, too. A large volume of orc meat was distributed during the harvest season and benefited the Labyrinth City as food reserves during winter.

"Auntie, you eat too much of that sugar. I keep tellin' ya, you're gonna turn into an orc!" A young boy who appeared to work there teased the woman.

"Quiet, you. And call me Miss Merle here in the shop. Hey, go get me that delivery from a little while ago."

So the barrel-shaped woman was Merle. The passage of time had not been kind to her.

Mariela bought four pounds of the crude sugar and left the shop.

Before they returned to the Yagu Drawbridge Pavilion, they stopped by Ghark's Herbal Supplies; the shop was open, but nobody was inside. Surprised at his negligence, she called him loudly.

"Hellooo! Ol' Man Ghaaaark, are you in heeeere?"

"Sure aaam! In the back. C'mon round."

After calling him three times, she was summoned to the rear yard. When they arrived, they found an enormous bean pod hanging over a pot of boiling water. Five similar pods were piled up next to the pot.

"These are creeper seeds, aren't they?!"

"Aye, I got a big catch. There'll be an expedition to the Labyrinth soon, y'see. I picked 'em fer a group of adventurers."

Creepers were bloodsucking monster plants with vines, and creeper rubber, a high-quality material, was made from the viscous liquid inside those vines. Disposable rubber made from shoddy, cheap creeper saplings was widely distributed in the Labyrinth City.

Mature creepers bore seeds that were tightly packed in pods. Creeper seeds were both extremely effective in medicine and extremely nutritious. Not only were they an ingredient in Regen medicine, which raised a person's natural resilience and provided a continuous recovery effect, but they could be eaten as is, and a single seed provided a complete, nutritious meal.

However, it was much more difficult to subjugate a mature creeper enough to steal its seeds than it was to obtain its viscous liquid. For one thing, a seed-bearing creeper was intelligent—as far as a plant could be, anyway. To spread out and propagate, the seeds burst from their pods with a *bratatatat* like a flurry of sling stones. The parent creeper then used these like projectiles to shoot at its prey. Getting struck by one felt like being hit by a pebble, but since a single pod contained anywhere between one hundred and two hundred seeds, the rapid-fire assault was unbearable. Creepers used this barrage of seeds to lead prey into the clutches of their vines, paralyzing it with their poisonous thorns before finally sucking the victim's blood—a truly fiendish combo.

"How did you—?"

"Seed-bearin' creepers are intelligent, yeah? So alcohol works on 'em."

Apparently, you could pour alcohol mixed with sleeping medicine onto a creeper's roots and then cut off as many pods as you liked while it slept.

"So *that's* how you do it?"

Mariela had an epiphany. There were still so many things she had yet to learn. Had all her painstaking work gathering individual fallen seeds from creeper habitats been for naught?

"Yowww... This time I blundered a bit, though. Curse that infernal weed, drinkin' all my booze."

The area near the seam of the left arm of his armor had turned dark red with bruising—probably from being pelted with creeper seeds. She could see only a little bit through an opening in his clothes, but he'd definitely been hit in a few places.

"Oh no! We need to heal you, quick! Po— Medicine! Medicine!"

"No use gettin' worked up over a thing like this. It's only a bruise. I've got some medicine already, so don't worry. More importantly, I gotta finish dryin' these."

"What are you talking about?!" Mariela cried in a panic. "Treatment comes first! I'll do the drying!"

"Oh, izzat so?" came Ghark's reply. He caved to pressure with surprising ease. "I dry each pod in moist air so as not to damage the seeds. Keep an eye on the hot water so it doesn't run out." He went into his house.

As the old man had instructed, Mariela and Sieg watched the pot for a while.

This is sooo slow. The other pods will start to deteriorate while he's drying the first one. What a waste.

"Sieg, can you tell if anyone's watching us?"

"They're not. But—"

"Form Transmutation Vessel, Tune Humidity to Sixty Percent, Tune Temperature to Forty Degrees, Dehydrate."

Mariela used her alchemic skills on the five pods next to the pot faster than Sieg could say "—you shouldn't!" He stared at the pods that had been dried before his eyes, looking perturbed.

"*Sigh*... What are you doing...?"

"Hey, I didn't use any Drops of Life. Foreign alchemists can do this kinda stuff."

Since the other five pods were dry, she was getting ready to dry the one hanging above the pot, too, when Ghark returned. As he looked at the dried pods and the seeds inside them, which were also completely dry without a single one of them breaking, he grumbled, "What have ye done? I only left ye here fer a second—"

"I dried 'em for you!" Mariela replied, glossing over the details. As she laughed awkwardly, Ghark's clenched fist came down with a thud.

"Owwww...!"

Tears sprang to Mariela's eyes.

"Y'idiot. Don't do that sort of thing in public. There's more pain where that came from. Got that?" he threatened. "'Ey, you over there, keep an eye on this blockhead!"

Mariela hung her head dejectedly. "I-I'm sorry..."

She'd gotten carried away and gotten a scolding for her efforts. Sieg was probably shocked, too.

Feeling glum, Mariela was about to head home when Ghark shoved one of the dried pods at her.

"Here, this is yer payment. Take it. Er, that is... Well, ye helped me out. Come back anytime," he added curtly.

"I made Ghark angry," Mariela said to Sieg on their way home.

"I'm...angry, too. You were too careless."

"Yeah. I'm sorry. Thanks for worrying about me."

Even though Mariela had just been on the receiving end of a fist, her mood brightened. The many seeds inside the dried pod bounced around in time with her jaunty gait, jangling like a little bell.

07

"Excellent timing, Mariela."

Mariela was about to enter her room at the Yagu Drawbridge Pavilion when Lieutenant Malraux called out and stopped her. Come to think of it, his room was next to hers. Although he had his own home within the Labyrinth City, he always seemed to be here in his room. Maybe it was a stand-in for an office.

After taking a moment to deposit their baggage, she and Sieg headed for Malraux's suite. Captain Dick was sitting on the couch, as always.

"Sorry." The captain didn't usually say anything until the very end, but this time he spoke up immediately, and the first thing out of his mouth was an apology. Lieutenant Malraux also wore a contrite expression as he brought out a tray holding a document and a small mountain of gold coins. What in the world was this about?

"This is a copy of the receipt for the Labyrinth Suppression Forces."

Surprised, Mariela wondered if it was okay for her to look at something like that, but since it was offered to her, she picked it up and read it. The Black Iron Freight Corps had bought ten each of three kinds of mid-grade potions for themselves, and the details and the document indicated the number of the remaining ones. The bottom summed it all up: "Total cost of aforementioned items: seventy gold coins."

"It was due to the expedition's budget. We persisted in our negotiations, but this amount also came from the general's personal assets, and we were unable to acquire any further funds."

"It's because I was stupid enough to say we'd accept a discount."

She knew, or rather, had noticed Captain Dick was a careless person, but he seemed to be apologizing for the other party driving a hard bargain. All this after she'd made it a point to tell them she didn't mind if the potions sold for cheap.

"Um, so if you subtract the contracted price of the mid-grade-and-under potions, and with fifty-two gold coins for fifteen high-grade potions, that comes to about three gold coins each, yes?"

Captain Dick apologized again. "I'm so very sorry."

"I briefly thought we'd begun our negotiations with a clean slate, but they were firm in their conditions, and I had no choice but to accept their offer," Lieutenant Malraux explained. "I don't normally cave..." Even he was offering an earnest apology.

"I don't mind. Please lift your head."

As they heeded her request, Captain Dick's and Lieutenant Malraux's expressions seemed to be asking "Huh? Is it okay?" and "What do you mean?" respectively.

"The general even bought them with his own money, did he not? That's because expeditions need potions. Next time, I'll prepare even more."

In the Citadel City, the selling price of high-grade potions had been ten large silver coins—she got more than thirty times what they were worth before. The price was much more than enough, and if the potions were so desperately needed that someone was willing to dip into their own funds to pay for them, she would've been fine lowering the cost to the old selling price. Mariela was merely speaking what was on her mind.

"Mariela, are you being serious right now? Do you understand how valuable these potions are?"

Lieutenant Malraux had a dangerous glint in his eye. It may have been the first time she saw such an honest expression from him.

"Potions are consumable goods. Such a small dose shouldn't sell at a high price. If I need money, I can just sell a lot of them."

This was Mariela's policy. Her master had told her to "make a lot of potions," though she didn't understand the true motivation behind it. Such items had been commonplace two hundred years ago, and hers were driven down to such cheap prices that they were almost a loss. When she became independent, she made potions by herself in the Fell Forest and sold them all in the Citadel City every day. She was sustained many times by the expressions of gratitude after her potion had helped someone, rare though they were. "Make the potions for the money you need" was a matter of course for Mariela, and the fact that her potions helped people motivated her actions.

"Potions are assets. They can be left to one's offspring." Lieutenant Malraux's words were few but stern.

I do not know if she found them by chance or if she legitimately inherited them, but she seems to have a large number of potions. Even so, they are unmistakably limited and valuable items. I wouldn't call such idealistic claims of hers "noble;" there are no more Alchemist Pact-Bearers within the Labyrinth City.

Lieutenant Malraux was looking into Mariela's eyes as if searching for her true motives, but his misunderstanding wasn't communicated to her.

"Wouldn't it be better to leave behind more practical assets like a house or money?" Mariela replied, continuing the discussion on the wrong page.

Yeah, obviously. If something happened to me, Sieg would be

out on the streets. Even with the proceeds from those high-grade potions, he couldn't live in the house we just bought for more than ten years. Besides, I've only made a hundred potions so far. I can make and sell tens of thousands more.

Mariela's carefree attitude brought the conversation to a standstill.

Malraux looked unconvinced as he muttered, "She's a woman of few wants."

Mariela's share of the fifty-two gold coins came to thirty-one gold and two large silver coins. She took it and signed the document, and with that, the transaction was complete. She'd already heard from Lynx that morning, but the Black Iron Freight Corps would depart for the imperial capital early tomorrow, with plans to return in the evening sixteen days later.

Lieutenant Malraux was the one who'd reserved Mariela and Sieg's room for them, so she told him they'd found a place to live.

"Is that so? Then, when we return, we shall send Lynx as our messenger."

Although it would be sixteen days until their next business deal, Mariela would be busy with moving and renovating her new home. She probably wouldn't be able to mass-produce potions. Next time they met, she promised to provide as many potions as she could. Lieutenant Malraux put in a request for specialized high-grade potions as he glanced at Sieg.

Captain Dick had stayed quiet for the latter half of the business proceedings. He must have picked up on the mood, as he didn't suggest any toasts even after the talk was over.

Mariela and Sieg went down to the restaurant to find Lynx, Yuric, and the other Corps members eating. Today's menu appeared to be some sort of dark-fleshed fish, and she heard it could be requested as a steak or fried. Both seemed to be the same type of marinated fish and came with a salad.

Since they wanted to try both, Sieg ordered the steak and Mariela ordered the fried version. They were invited to the Corps's table and ate there. The steak didn't have a fishy odor, and it had so much fat that it didn't seem like fish at all. The sauce was light with its blend of citrus juices and pungent spices and didn't leave a greasy feeling afterward. The fried fish was covered in a sauce of coarsely chopped tomatoes and their juices. This coating trapped the fat within the fish, giving it a rich flavor.

Delicious as the food was, every one of the Black Iron Freight Corps ate in silence. Maybe they were focused on tomorrow, when they'd be entering the Fell Forest. Mariela didn't know for sure, but it was undoubtedly a dangerous trip. She savored her meal in a somber mood.

After the silent dinner, they were provided with tea.

"Mariela, Sieg, you both ate it all, huh?" Lynx suddenly spoke up. "What d'you think today's fish was?"

"Huh? Wasn't it freshwater fish? Although something with flesh this dark is pretty unusual."

"Saltwater…fish?"

"Aaand the answer iiiis, sahuagin!"

Mariela nearly spit out her drink.

Ack, I just snorted some of my tea!

She held her stinging nose and scowled at Lynx.

"You can't tell, right? Right? Ya just thought it tasted good and ate it up, didn'cha?"

"It's premium-grade fish, y'know? Made with regards from the owner," added Yuric.

"Aw man, I bet sahuagin's super-nutritious! Still, I never woulda thought you could actually eat it."

Sahuagin was a bipedal fish with a particularly foul-sounding cry that sounded something like *gyohhh*. Since they were built similarly to humans, Mariela never once thought about eating one, let alone even considered them edible in the first place.

But it was super-tasty, though. Super-tasty!

Mariela didn't actually say "Bleh," but her grimace was enough. Lynx and the others burst into satisfied, uproarious laughter.

"Ahhh, that was too funny. We're leavin' early tomorrow, so I'm gonna head on to bed. Later, Mariela. Catch ya next time."

Lynx took a good, hard look at Mariela before returning to his room.

08

Back in her own room at the inn, Mariela felt sad to be leaving the Corps members. As she put her luggage in order, she brought to mind the image of Lynx and the others unable to quell their infectious laughter.

"At first, I was a bit wary around them, but they're all good people, those guys in the Corps. They'll come back safe, won't they?"

"The Black Iron Freight Corps...is strong. They also have potions. They'll...be fine."

If Sieg, who'd been through the Fell Forest, was saying as

much, then they probably would be all right. Even so, she was a little worried. The five days she'd spent with Lynx and the crew had been really fun. After surviving the Stampede, Mariela had prospects for living in the Labyrinth City thanks to their meddling in one way or another.

They did a lot for me. I wonder if I can do something for them in return.

Mariela's hand brushed against a thick tome—*The Encyclopedia of Medicinal Herbs and Their Effects*. Come to think of it, she'd had a conversation about the Library today.

"Library Link."

Wondering if there was anything good in the information she had unrestricted access to, she connected to the Library for the first time in a long while.

101 Delicious Recipes You Can Make with Alchemic Skills, Essential Alchemic Products to Make Your Life Easier, Alchemic Housework Techniques for the Busy Housewife… She skimmed around there. *Alchemic Sweets.* Seeing this made her sad. She'd never been able to make sweets with such ample amounts of expensive sugar.

Oh right, I bought coarse sugar today.

Thinking maybe she could make them now, she began to read. The foreword was written in an extremely roundabout fashion, but it seemed to be a collection of recipes for making sweets with potion effects.

Whoa, what the heck? This is really neat! Ahhh, but the effects are about ten percent less than an actual potion. Hmm, this is dicey. But if these can help kids enjoy a bitter potion, maybe they're not such a bad thing after all.

Mariela had been working on improving the taste of potions and had failed to make a "Yummy Potion" many times. Her goal was to someday perfect one that had a good flavor without sacrificing efficacy and then register it in the Library.

She flipped through several recipes. They had names she didn't really understand, like "Regen Candy with Excellent Staying Power" and "Fight Until Dawn! Beast-Mode Berserker Chocolate," accompanied by even less understandable instructions.

"What's wrong?" Sieg asked, noticing the dubious expression on Mariela's face. When she told him about the recipes, he looked puzzled. "Are you going to make one?" They really did have strange names.

"Candy that stimulates continuous recovery of strength would be good for children weakened by disease, and this berserk-inducing chocolate could provide nutrition and really turn the tides for someone cornered by monsters. So they're wonderful ideas and all, but I dunno why they've got such strange explanations," said Mariela, and Sieg looked away awkwardly.

"Oh, there's this:

"'Peppy Beginnings Cookies—for the alchemist just starting out. Give these cookies under the pretense of a thank-you gift or as salutations. Supereffective even outside ley lines! You'll be sure to catch the recipient's eye once they're bursting with pep. With your preparations now complete, carefully reel in the thread to ensnare the prey in your web!'"

Thread? Was this recipe's author a spider or something? Not that there are any...nonhuman apprentices.

She didn't really understand the explanatory note, but she guessed from the ingredients and recipe that these cookies with creeper seeds kneaded into them used the maker's own magical power in place of Drops of Life to heighten the efficacy. The medicinal effect of creeper seeds reduced fatigue, not to mention the seeds themselves were also nutritious—consuming one was the equivalent of eating a full meal. They imparted a peculiar flavor if you ground them into a powder and blended them, but they were often crushed and combined with tea leaves for their aroma. Since the recipe didn't use Drops of Life, it would have only slightly more of an effect than regular sweets, but the effect wouldn't be lost even if they were removed from the area where the alchemist made their pact.

"Yeah, I'm gonna try to make these."

Mariela wanted to share them with Ghark and the ladies at the inn. And Sieg, too, of course. She would need the same number of creeper seeds as the number of people she wanted to feed and crush the seeds into powder. For the required tea leaves, she could use the ones she bought at the Merchants Guild. Then she needed flour, eggs, and butter. She could prepare sugar by separating out the coarse sugar from its impurities.

She went down to the restaurant to discuss with the owner whether he'd sell ingredients to her. He happily parted with them and even asked, "Do you want to use the kitchen?" but she politely turned him down. Although *Alchemic Sweets* used hardly any potion components, it was strangely fixated on alchemic skills, using them for every stage of the process instead of utensils or an oven.

Really, who in this world wrote this? What a weirdo. Well, whatever. Let's start the, uh…alchemy?

Feeling puzzled about the student author and their strange fixations, Mariela began the recipe.

"Form Transmutation Vessel. Control Temperature. Melt Butter. Mix Magic. Insert Sugar. Mix Magic. Control Temperature. Insert Eggs. Mix More Magic. Insert and Disperse Wheat, Seed Powder, and Tea Leaves. Mix

Magic. Mold. Control Pressure. Superheat. Preserve. Refrigerate."

She proceeded through each of the steps of the recipe with ease. The designated temperatures were loose, such as "about the temperature of boiling water" or "about room temperature," and whenever she added an ingredient, all she had to do was knead in magical power and mix them together. The sudden decrease in pressure midway through would cause the batter to bubble, and it seemed the cookies would turn out crisp. The recipe recommended making the cookies into a heart shape, but Mariela wasn't keen on the idea of such an inefficient shape, so she made all of them into squares.

Sieg had said he wanted to eat a heart-shaped one when she talked to him about the shape, so she made just one of them into a heart. It was a little difficult—the left and right sides weren't symmetrical, and it looked more like a daigis leaf. But the process was fun, so she tried to make another cookie into a raptor shape.

"A sahuagin?"

"No, Sieg, it's a raptor! Although... Yeah. It does look like a sahuagin. I'll give this one to Lynx."

She lined up all the cookies in the Transmutation Vessel and baked them in one batch. They turned light brown in the amount of time the recipe said they would. After refrigerating them, they were finished. When she took them out of the vessel, a pleasant buttery aroma wafted up from them.

"Let's each try one. Just a li'l taste test."

Sieg bit into the daigis-shaped—er, the heart-shaped one, and Mariela into a square one.

Crunch.

The buttery flavor spread through her mouth, and then a gentle scent of tea leaves reached her nose. The cookie had the peculiar taste of creeper seed, but coupling it with the tea leaves and eggs transformed it into a distinct flavor all its own.

"It's delicious."

"Wow, this is good!"

Sieg seemed to like it, too. Since he savored his bit by bit, she encouraged him to have one more, but he said he'd already had a meal and therefore had enough for today.

He's well-behaved. It's gotta be tough not to go for seconds.

She cut up some cloth she'd bought that day and wrapped the cookies in it, with the sahuagin-shaped one in a separate cloth so that it wouldn't break.

"I should go to bed so I can give these to the crew before they leave tomorrow morning. Wake me up if I oversleep, okay?"

Mariela was preparing to head to the bathroom before bed when Sieg stopped her. He pointed to the window, which overlooked the rear yard, and through it she saw the figures of two people.

It was Captain Dick and Amber.

Under the light of the moon, the pair embraced tightly. After gazing at each other for a little while, they reluctantly parted ways and returned to the inn.

Once she got back to the restaurant, Amber would probably greet customers as she always did, while Captain Dick would return to his room. Both of them disappeared from sight.

Mariela wouldn't be able to sleep tonight after all, and she wanted to pin the blame on the Peppy Beginnings Cookies.

Before dawn, Mariela chased after Lynx, who was boarding one of the iron carriages. After last night, she hadn't been able to sleep after all, but she could at least properly see him off.

"Mariela, it's still nighttime. Go back to sleep!" Lynx greeted her the same way he always did.

"I made these. They'll give you energy, so share them with everyone. Ah, this one's especially for you."

She handed over a bundle of cookies and the wrapped sahuagin-shaped one.

"No way, really? Wow, thanks! Can I open it?"

It was dark, so she couldn't see his expression, but he seemed delighted. He unwrapped the sahuagin cookie next.

"...The heck is this?"

"What d'you think?"

"A raptor?"

"The answer iiiis, a sahuagin!"

"SERIOUSLY?"

It actually is a raptor, though. Amazing that he guessed it right.

Lynx bit into the cookie with a light crunch.

"Oh, this's really good. Thanks much. I'll buy you a souvenir or somethin', 'kay?"

With that, the Black Iron Freight Corps departed for the imperial capital.

"They're gone."

After seeing off the Black Iron Freight Corps, Mariela and Sieg were now alone.

"It's still...early. You should go back to sleep."

In the dim light of the early morning, Mariela stood motionless as she stared after the iron carriages, and Sieg ushered her back to the room. Once she got into bed as he'd told her to, Sieg folded the covers all the way up to her neck.

"Sieg, you're not going to sleep?"

"I'm...fine."

Mariela seemed lonely, so Sieg hesitantly reached out and gently stroked her head.

"Good night, Mariela," he said, and he left the room.

After closing the door, he murmured, "I'll be by your side, no matter where that may be."

CHAPTER **6**
Labyrinth of Thoughts

01

"Good morning, Mariela."

Awakened by Sieg, Mariela opened her eyes.

"Would you like...some tea?"

When she got up, Sieg sat down on the edge of the bed and offered tea.

He'd gently woken her and offered her tea in bed. A soft smile lingered on his face.

What's going on here? It's like we're...

Mariela rubbed at her eyes, took the cup from him, and tilted her head to the side.

"Are we playing 'queen-and-her-butler' today?"

The corners of Sieg's mouth twitched upward. Oblivious, Mariela blew on her tea and took a sip. Sieg wasn't discouraged and continued talking.

"Is it good?"

"Yeah. Thank you."

"Starting tomorrow, I'll make it...every day."

"Mm, I appreciate it, but you don't have to." She turned down his offer gently.

"Drinking it together...makes it taste better," he replied, and Mariela looked up. For some reason, he averted his gaze. She had a feeling his face was slightly red.

*   *   *

Mariela knew she'd overslept, but it was about two hours later than her usual. Sieg hadn't had breakfast yet, either, so they went down to the restaurant together.

"Good mooorning! Breakfast is uni-corn soup today. It's my favorite!"

It was Emily the poster girl. Mariela tied her hair for her again, then gave her one of the wrapped cookies she'd made.

"Wow, a cookie!"

Emily tried to restrain herself, but hey, she was a ten-year-old kid. As soon as she opened the wrapping, her face lit up. Over-joyed, she gleefully stuffed it into her mouth at once.

"It's sooo good!"

"It's full of nutrients and energy, so it's best to eat them when you're tired," Mariela explained, then grabbed the young hand that was reaching for a second cookie.

Emily pouted. Her outstretched hand wavered for a moment before firmly tying the bundle back up.

"Daddy's having a tough time. He's real tired. So I'm gonna give these to him." She summoned the strength to resist her desire for more cookies and give them to her father instead. Her self-control was written all over her face.

Awwww, Emily! You're such a good giiiirl!

Mariela couldn't stand it.

"Your dad's share is over here, so it's fine for you to eat these," she said, and she handed Emily one more bundle.

Emily's face lit up as bright as the sun. It was a beautiful sight.

"I'm gonna go give these to Daddy! Thank you, Mari!"

Beaming from ear to ear, Emily took the bundle of cookies in both hands and ran off.

Mariela had wanted to see her reaction, so she'd secretly held back the owner's share on purpose. Mari was a meanie.

Amber and the other ladies were still asleep, so Mariela decided to give them their cookies when she came back later. She needed to make medicine for them, too. And there were some ingredients she wanted; since sahuagin had been on the menu last night, she figured she'd find what she was looking for.

After breakfast, she and Sieg headed for Ghark's herb shop. For once, Ghark was inside the building today.

"Mr. Ghark, I made these from the creeper seeds you gave me yesterday. I thought I'd share them with you."

"Y'really don't learn, do ye...?"

Ghark stared at Mariela in exasperation. She pretended not to care and pressed him further. "Come on, eat one. I dunno if it'll work on your bruise, but I think it'll restore your strength."

After Ghark chewed one of the cookies carefully, savoring it, he checked himself over, then went to the rear of the shop and brought back some kind of magical tool. He put Mariela's cookies on it and examined them.

"Um, you're supposed to eat those."

"So ye kneaded magical power into this to enhance the effect of the creeper seeds? Yer not plannin' on sellin' these, I hope."

Mariela's pout withered under a single glare from Ghark.

So mean. Here I was tryin' to be nice.

When she explained she was giving them out as thanks for people helping her, he checked who the recipients were going to be.

"Well, in that case, I s'pose it's fine. Listen, don't sell these.

Otherwise you'd end up makin' 'em till your magic reserves ran dry. Good grief, yer more of a handful than ye look, missy. Tch, have some self-restraint."

"If these are no good, then what kinda medicine should I sell?" Mariela asked despondently.

"What're ye plannin' to make…? Listen, if ye make any medicine, bring it to me before sellin' it. I'll test it for ye. 'Ey, sonny, make sure to bring 'er. No exceptions!"

"Understood." Sieg nodded meekly. At the very least, Mariela was grateful Ghark would check things for her before she sold them. She was a novice at medicine-making. Deciding to think of it in a positive light, she nodded in assent.

"Oh, right. Mr. Ghark, I wondered if you might sell something like ghost clams or snapping clams?"

"Didya even hear what I just said…?"

Ghark looked as if he was at his wit's end, and Mariela reassured him, "I'm not gonna sell them, so don't worry! Really, it's fine!" The old man's gaze was sharp. It looked as if his fist could come crashing down at any moment.

"Y'can get those kinds o' monster-based ingredients at the wholesale market next to the Adventurers Guild."

"D'you think I could get lynus wheat there, too? I'd also like to get some genea cream and salve tins."

"Finally, a good question. They deal with most materials that're obtained around 'ere, so they should have lynus wheat, too. And then, genea cream and salve tins? If ye just want a small amount, the Merchants Guild shop sells those. The Seele Company makes 'em, so if ye want a lot, ye'll need to go there. Tell 'em I sent ye, and they'll letcha have some."

Ghark was very helpful with all sorts of things.

"Thank you, Mr. Ghark! Next time I come, I'll bring medicine!" Mariela exclaimed while waving to him.

"Go to the library in the Merchants Guild and study before ye come back!" Ghark called back as he shooed her away with a wave of his hand. Mariela didn't miss how he picked up a cookie in his other hand and nonchalantly tossed it into his mouth.

Mariela and Sieg headed to the wholesale market Ghark told them about.

The Adventurers Guild was right outside the northeastern gateway in the wall surrounding the Labyrinth, and the wholesale market stood next to it facing the Labyrinth.

Adventurers would bring materials obtained in the Labyrinth to the Adventurers Guild or specialist shops. The wholesale market specialized in foodstuff ingredients, so they bought and butchered what the adventurers brought in; some items were also cured or processed before being sold.

Anything from vegetable and grain products from the Labyrinth City to meats from the animals hunted in the surrounding forest could be found in this market, making it something like the kitchen of the city.

Within the huge outer wall of the market, small- and medium-size shops crowded together. There were shops offering monster meat and seafood, regional meats, processed food like sausages and ham, dried goods, grains and vegetables, dairy products, and a variety of other ingredients.

It was around the time when adventurers were exploring in the Labyrinth, and the market was bustling with townspeople who'd come to buy ingredients. Some of the stalls sold cooked food, sending delicious aromas wafting through the air.

"Whoaaa, this is incredible!"

"Today's special is cockatrice! Take a gander at this leg meat! It's nice and tender just like yours, young lady! Look at the grease dripping down this skewer!"

"Aaapples, freshly picked aaapples! Delivered straaaight from the second level of the Labyrinth! And here we have pineapples, one slice for just two copper coins."

"Bargains aplenty! Today we're having a special on ground orc and minotaur meat!"

"How 'bout a freshly roasted orc sausage? The skin's crisp and bursting with flavor. We got hot dogs, too!"

Mariela enjoyed walking around listening to the vendors hawking their products. Her hands full of sliced pineapple, skewered meat, and a bundle of hot dogs, she made no attempt to mind her manners as she ate while strolling around the marketplace.

It took a very long time for them to finally reach their destination, a dried-goods dealer. Seafood must have been their specialty, as the shelves were packed with seaweed, scallops, and enough tiny sun-dried fish for an entire meal. She didn't see any big game like sahuagin, however. Though it would've worried her even if she did.

"Welcome. What can I do ya for?"

"Do you have any ghost clams or snapping clams?"

"Got snapping clams right here. They make a good soup base. How many you want?"

Sun-dried scallops the size of fists were stacked in a draining basket. Since there was no ocean in the Fell Forest, this was the first time Mariela had seen them.

One of these will let me do about ten practice runs.

This was the first time she'd handled this item, and therefore she didn't yet know its extraction method. After viewing information on handling a new material in her Library, Mariela had to either completely memorize it or forget it with *Reset* before she could view another one. Just by looking at this new material, it didn't seem as if its method would be very time-consuming. A hundred extractions would probably be all she needed to master the technique. She bought ten of the scallops for two silver coins.

Afterward, she went to a granary located all the way at the back of the market near the northern street. She asked if they had any lynus wheat.

"Lynus wheat's been selling real well this year. Sorry, but this is all I've got in stock. Next month's harvest should bring in more, so hold tight till then."

Lynus wheat was grown in the wetlands near the sandbanks of a river flowing through the grain-producing region of the Labyrinth City. It was highly nutritious and a good food for the sick. There were several other similar products, such as sap from old sugar maple trees; stumps called tuber roots that produced a sticky substance when rubbed; and genea cream, though that wasn't usually used for food.

Not only was lynus wheat high in nutrients, it was delicious, too. In other words, it was chock-full of Drops of Life, a blessing from Mother Earth that flowed through ley lines. All living things had trace amounts of it inside them; not just plants, animals, and humans but even monsters, too. The composition of each type of medicinal herb was different, with some containing a large amount of Drops of Life; the lynus wheat and genea cream Mariela was looking for were two such examples.

"Was there an epidemic?"

The shop had only about four pounds of lynus wheat in stock. It was enough for Mariela's purposes, but perhaps some kind of disaster had caused the supply to run low.

"Nah, the Aguinas family bought it all up."

Now there was a name Mariela wasn't expecting to hear. Two hundred years ago, the Aguinases were the top alchemists in the Kingdom of Endalsia. Now they controlled the distribution of potions in the Labyrinth City. Although they were a family of alchemists, she still wondered if a large number of people had fallen ill.

The granary worker didn't seem to know the details, so Mariela bought the four pounds of lynus wheat and left.

"Mariela, it's time."

She'd only just bought the scallops and wheat, but it was already time for lunch. They had arranged to meet with a carpenter about two hours from then. It wasn't like her to take her sweet time wandering around.

"Sieg, what are you going to do for lunch?"

"I'm going to…eat at the house."

Every time Mariela had bought some food that she ate on the spot, she'd bought some for Sieg as well. She thought he was going to eat it right then and there, but it turned out he'd stored it in the rucksack. There weren't any strange people in the market, but he was acting as her bodyguard just in case.

Sieg's got good manners. He doesn't stuff his face while he's walking around in public or anything like that.

Which was exactly what Mariela had so carelessly done without realizing.

02

The two of them left the wholesale market and headed for their new house. It was close to the exit on the northern street side of the market, and they got there in less than an hour. It really was in a good location. Around the time when Sieg finished his lunch, two people who appeared to be carpenters showed up just before the appointed time.

"Are you Mariela? I'm Gordon, the carpenter, and a dwarf, as y'can see."

"I'm Johan, the architect. Half dwarf, half human."

Between his short stature, stocky physique, and thick beard and brows, Gordon was the very image of a dwarf.

On the other hand, Johan had a small, sturdy frame, but he was taller than Gordon. He was clean-shaven, and he had fixed up not only his hair but his eyebrows, too, which gave him a stylish sort of look.

"Whaddaya mean, architect? Yer just a scrawny li'l punk of a carpenter who needs to brush up his skills some more."

"I think they'll be needing some guidance to build a proper, comfortable living space, don't you, Pops?"

Apparently, these two were father and son. Mariela wondered if they were going to have a fight right after making their acquaintance, but this seemed to be more like an introduction for them.

""So what kind of remodeling are you interested in?"" the pair asked in perfect unison. They were on the same wavelength.

She told them what she wanted: fix up the storefront and open an apothecary; repair all the furniture so that she and Sieg could move in; get their advice on the finer details; and first and foremost—show them the house. "Go ahead," she told the two dwarves, letting them through. Gordon began to check the main building and Johan the addition.

"There are no problems with this building here. The pipes haven't deteriorated at all. You can live here just fine, but the floor and walls are damaged. Depending on your budget, it'll need washing—nah, a cleaner—and after that, I'd recommend polishing the floor and stone walls. Johan, give 'em an estimate for all the furniture and upholstery they'll be needin'."

"As far as the magical tool in the galley is concerned, the magical gem is only cracked. It's still usable. There are no problems with the addition itself, but the roof needs repairing. Overall, there's so much grease and dirt on the wooden walls that it'd be better to refinish them. The storefront is in bad shape; the floor and pillars are rotting. If you want to set up a shop here, it'd be cheaper to just rebuild it. The counter and shelving only have surface damage, so they can probably be sanded down and restored. The problem is the lighting. Pops, give them an estimate for the construction work. Include the galley roof, too."

As Mariela and Sieg watched, dumbfounded, the craftsmen took turns creating a schedule for repairs.

In what felt like an instant, the father-son duo had agreed on the remodeling plan.

After cleaning up the living area, they would lightly grind

down and polish the wall and floor tiles to clean up the scratches and dents. Since materials were valuable in the vicinity of the Labyrinth City, laying down boards and tiles on the floor and putting up wallpaper seemed to be a luxury for the mansions of aristocrats.

Large furniture was often sold or left behind when residents moved out, and the furniture in this house was too old to merit paying transportation fees. Gordan and Johan offered to repair the wooden items that weren't rotting. They would craft any necessary furniture or minimally decorative items like shelves and desks and repair the deteriorating fixtures such as the loose hinges on the built-in shelves and the ill-fitting door.

According to the pair, the overly spacious living room on the first floor seemed to have been originally divided into two rooms, and the wall was probably demolished to make it into a guest room for the restaurant. The space would have better utility if they built a wall where the original had stood. The living room would catch customers' eyes with the proper furnishings, so they recommended buying nice-looking furniture for it.

The craftsmen informed Mariela and Sieg that once the current Labyrinth expedition ended, good-quality secondhand furniture would appear on the market within about two months. Yagu caravans would take two months round trip to transport materials obtained in the expedition before bringing back the finished goods from the imperial capital. Aristocrats would replace their current furnishings with the carpets and top-quality furniture parts manufactured outside the Labyrinth City, and the old furnishings would then become available for sale on the market.

The stench of oil that permeated the former galley would have to be cleaned by the proper Skill Users, after which the dwarves would polish the stones and refinish the wall paneling. Several of the roof tiles were broken, and they would replace those as well.

Since none of that would use much material, the estimate was one gold coin and seven large silver coins.

The storefront was the problematic part; repairing most of it would cost five gold coins, including a new roof to replace the tarp that had been set up to act as a makeshift cover. The outer wall would remain the same as before.

Given how high this wall was, even rebuilding the inner side would just block the view from the window. Getting less space for higher costs seemed to be the norm for remodeling in the Labyrinth City.

"It's a little less than seven gold coins altogether. Is there any part of the estimate that can be reduced?" Mariela asked. This would more than double the purchase price of the house, which had been three gold coins. Johan carefully explained the breakdown of expenses; he was genial about it and didn't have a pushy attitude.

Mariela also mentioned her concern about the shop lighting. The shelves behind the counter would store the medicine, so it would be optimal to keep them from being exposed to the light. However, if the outer wall was going to serve as the shop's wall, then the place wouldn't have even a single window. The gloominess would be stifling.

"Maybe if we got a large piece of plate glass," said Johan.

"What, and bring it in from outside the Labyrinth City? Fat chance o' that," replied Gordon.

I can make plate glass myself, though...

Mariela wanted windows. "If you did happen to have plate glass, what kind of storefront would you be able to make?" she asked, phrasing the question as if she was just checking for future reference.

"If we had a lot, we'd use it for half the ceiling," replied Johan. "Of course, since it would need to be sturdy, we'd cut the window frame into a square lattice shape and lay square-shaped glass diagonally, like this."

"That's a terrible idea. Typical architect. If it were me, I'd cut 'em into equilateral triangles to make it curved."

"What did you just say, Pops? ....That's brilliant!"

Mariela listened as the pair discussed the prospect of a glass ceiling with increasing excitement, tossing around ideas about what size the glass should be and what approximate thickness and about how many pieces.

"Could you give me two or three days on the shop part? I'd like a draft of the plan for the living area first. About how many days will it take?" she asked.

During that time, she'd prepare the plate glass. She'd need to come up with an authentic-sounding excuse for it, too. Including tonight, she and Sieg had five more days at the Yagu Drawbridge Pavilion, so she also wanted to know the move-in schedule.

"If you need it within five days, the living area will be ready in plenty of time. Now, hear me out, but wouldja consider using a group from the slums for the cleanin' work? The fee would be the same as if you had someone with cleaning skills do it. Of course, we'd be supervisin' to make sure they did a thorough job. It'll take a bit longer than normal, but would you let 'em do it?" asked Gordon.

The slums was probably the section in the southwest part of the Labyrinth City facing the Fell Forest where partially destroyed Endalsian buildings had been patched up. When she'd first arrived in the City, Lynx had told her the area wasn't particularly safe.

"Those who are unable to work as adventurers anymore due to injury or illness end up in the slums," Johan explained. "Plenty of 'em are honest folk. Would it be all right?"

"Is it possible…they would come back to steal things…in the future?" interjected Sieg, who'd left all the talking to Mariela up to now.

"We'll choose the workers ourselves. They'll only be day laborers, and we'll have them sign a magical contract stating that they will not use any acquired information for personal use," replied Johan.

Sieg was wary of hired slum residents taking advantage of their work to case the joint for a future theft.

I hadn't thought of that possibility… Even so, I'd want anyone to be hired under a magical contract.

"They ain't all bad guys. Won'tya give 'em a chance?" Gordon grasped his left wrist as he spoke. Mariela noticed a large scar on his left hand.

"Gordon, what's that on your hand?"

"It's from a long time ago, when I was an adventurer, see. I had to quit that line of work, but I managed to find success as a carpenter." The dwarf had probably been given a chance and wanted to pay it forward to the next generation.

"I understand. I look forward to seeing their work."

Sieg looked as if he wanted to say something. Even Mariela felt maybe she was being rash. But somehow, she thought that was what she should do. She remembered a certain person in the plaza of the Citadel City two hundred years ago; he gave her half his lunch one day when her stomach was rumbling with hunger while she was selling potions.

Maybe it wouldn't be such a bad idea for me to pay that kindness forward, Mariela wondered vaguely.

She paid one gold coin as a deposit. Tomorrow, work would begin after she signed the contract, so they told her they'd like to come in the morning. Apparently, she should also give them a duplicate key after signing the contract.

Gordon asked if she wanted to go choose the wood with them, but she declined, saying she'd leave it in their hands. She didn't know anything about wood quality, nor could she imagine what kind of finish it would need.

Her only stipulation was that it should have "a cozy feel."

Gordon and Johan nodded and replied, "Leave it to us."

03

There were still about four hours until dusk. Chairwoman Elmera of the Merchants Guild had said the Adventurers Guild shop sold medicine, so Mariela decided to stop by to do some market research.

She and Sieg headed to the Adventurers Guild near the Labyrinth's northeast gateway, the opposite direction of the wholesale market. If she was going to make plate glass, there were a few preparations she needed to make. Plus, she could finish up her shopping while she was at it.

The Adventurers Guild's kinda eerie somehow. I feel like as soon as I go in, some scary old guy is gonna threaten me: "This ain't a place for little ones!"

With thoughts like these at the forefront of her mind, Mariela timidly entered the guild. The lobby was bigger than the one in the Merchants Guild, and in it were several reception counters all lined up in a row. Large signs like ← MATERIALS TRADE-IN, ↑ REQUESTS DESK, BULLETIN BOARD ↓, and SHOP → hung here and there, along with helpful pictographs.

There were few people inside who looked like adventurers, probably because most hadn't yet returned from the Labyrinth. They were either seated at the edge of the lobby and jabbering away or reading the bulletin board. They took no notice of Mariela and Sieg.

Right as Mariela was feeling relieved that no one had bothered her, a man who looked to be a middle-aged adventurer approached.

"Somethin' the matter, miss? If it's requests you're lookin' for, come right this way!"

His bright-white teeth gleamed as he broke into a broad grin—along with his smooth bald pate.

Ohhh, right, they also do requests.

He might have thought she was a novice adventurer. How brazen. Obviously, Mariela was a client. "I came to see the shop," she said.

"In that case, it's just over there!" the man replied, pointing dramatically. He seemed to be nothing more than your typical busybody. She thanked him and headed for the shop.

For sale were weapons and armor for beginner adventurers, along with ropes, lanterns, portable rations, and various sundries. Medicine filled at least three of the shelves, and their types—Salves, Styptics, Oral Medicines, Etc.—were written above them along with helpful illustrations. It was actually quite a messy categorization system.

Even the salves came in many different types, she noticed. Apparently, they had been made by different people. Their ingredients weren't listed, but wouldn't the ingredients and effects be different based on who made them? Most of the salves and styptics must have been ointments, given the tins they were packed into.

The shop also sold oral medicines—antidotes, restoratives, antipyretics, and paregorics—as well as the usual everyday household medicines. They didn't appear to offer much in the way of liquid medicines like potions, but there were plenty of pills. Mariela checked the types and price ranges available.

"Can I help you find something?" a shop employee asked her. She was a beautiful, kind-looking young woman. The Adventurers Guild had a lot of attractive women, something Mariela had noticed just from glancing at the receptionists. Lots of adventurers were hot-blooded men; did the guild hire pretty ladies so that things would go more smoothly? On closer inspection, the male employees stayed on standby a certain distance away. They probably jumped in if any trouble occurred.

"Which of the salves is the most effective?"

"These ones here are our most popular products."

The item she recommended was elegantly packaged, and its price per unit was high for a salve. Mariela felt it was being marketed as "an expensive item that looks expensive." It cost fifty copper coins. Two hundred years ago, she could have bought ten low-grade heal potions in the Citadel City for the same price. Still, if you spread it thinly, you could probably cover the surface area of about ten palms, so maybe the price was reasonable after all.

She bought one and left the shop.

As they passed by the bulletin board, Sieg stared at one of the notices:

Information on Training Courses

The guild appeared to offer a seminar divided into courses: for instance, the materials and monsters found in the Labyrinth's lower strata; weapons training; beginner spells; and skills for explorers. Each course was designated an instructor who would teach their students one-on-one.

One large silver coin got you five half-day lessons that would be conducted every other day. For professional one-on-one guidance, it was a good deal.

"Would it be all right if...I took this course with the large silver coin...you gave me?" Sieg seemed to want to learn how to use a sword. "I can't use anything but...a bow. And even that..."

Sieg's right eye had been damaged and blinded, and Mariela couldn't heal it at present, either.

There was no "dominant eye" when you had only one eye to speak of. His aim would probably be out of whack, and he'd have a hard time gauging distance.

So she had no reason to stop Sieg if he wanted to learn a new way to fight.

Sieg went to the information desk to sign up, and Mariela followed him. He might not tell her if he needed something, and she wanted to hear about it.

At the desk, Sieg said he'd like to take the practical training, and the middle-aged man who'd shown them the way to the shop earlier called out to him.

"Ohhh, a new participant! I'm the instructor, Haage!"

The sunset light reflecting off his cranium was blinding. Apparently, the man with an easy-to-remember name, Haage, was an employee of the Adventurers Guild. Sieg asked when he could start the class.

"Sorry, but my slots are all filled up till the expedition starts. I'll have some openings in four days' time, though! All weapons will be provided, so you just come wearing clothes that're easy to move around in!" he answered with a broad smile that showed his white teeth.

"The Labyrinth Suppression Forces are the ones going on the expedition, right?"

Why would adventurers be taking lessons before an expedition?

"Because that's the perfect time to make a profit! They'll be delving deeper than usual, so there're lots of guys who want to train!"

The Labyrinth Suppression Forces aimed for the deepest part of the Labyrinth. Monsters gathered in the deepest part to ambush them, so fewer appeared in the shallow strata. While the Suppression Forces were in the Labyrinth, adventurers went deeper than usual because the risk of attack by a swarm was lower. Even people with no ability to fight hired adventurers and went down into the Labyrinth to collect materials.

Every once in a great while when too many humans gathered in one place, stronger than usual monsters would appear, so the Adventurers Guild dispatched seasoned adventurers to defeat them.

There were also plenty of chances to observe seasoned adventurers, so even rookie and low-class adventurers looked forward to it.

Apparently, during an expedition, the entire Labyrinth City would be buzzing with excitement like a festival.

"Four days from now, the Labyrinth Suppression Forces will have a morning parade on the northeastern main street on their way to the Labyrinth, so you can come for your lesson after watching!" Haage informed them with a big grin.

04

They reached the Merchants Guild just before dark and hurried to the shop.

The Merchants Guild shop had a collection of necessities for merchants and artisans. The chemist corner had the genea cream Mariela was looking for in two sizes: a "retail tin," which in actuality had about a five-cup volume, and an "ointment tin" packed with manufactured medicine. There was a much greater variety of medicine vials and paper for powdered medicine than Ghark had in his shop, and paper for vial labels was also for sale, so she bought several of each.

The shop also had a catalog listing items from mundane tools like mortars to instruments she'd never seen before. Pictures were shown along with explanations, and they introduced things like manual machines that compressed fine powder into tablets and rotating disk-shaped magical tools that made pills. It was the first time she'd seen tools like these. She could see how much technology had advanced, and she almost lost track of time gazing at it all.

No, no, she mustn't dawdle. The young man in the shop appeared to be closing up for the day, as he kept glancing in her direction.

Flustered, she hurried to the smithing section. The young man approached her as if he wanted her to hurry up and finish so he could close the shop, so she asked for eleven pounds of trona crystals, twenty-two pounds of lum stones, and seven pounds of metallic beads.

"Metallic beads? Those scatter during smelting and forging. We might have some in the back."

The young man briefly went to the rear of the shop to look for them. When he returned, he said, "These are old, but we were going to get rid of them anyway, so I can sell them to you for cheap."

She settled up the bill and left the Merchants Guild. She needed about 660 pounds of lum stones in all, so this wasn't nearly enough, but they should be available locally if everything went according to plan.

In any case, 4,409 pounds of glass would be needed to implement Gordon and Johan's glass ceiling. Twenty yagus would be required to carry such a large quantity. It wasn't even for an aristocrat's mansion, and she had no intention of making something so conspicuous. Mariela considered pretending she "happened across it" and handing over half or three-quarters of the plate glass.

For that large an amount, a small crucible like the one she'd used to make potion vials just wouldn't cut it.

Tomorrow, she'd head to her destination, and if things didn't go as she hoped, she'd have them just make several small windows.

When Mariela returned to the Yagu Drawbridge Pavilion, the sun had just set, so she handed Amber her cookies while the customers were still sparse. Amber looked as though she was in lower spirits than usual.

"These must be the cookies Emily was talking about. She said they gave her a lot of energy."

The cookies were popular with the ladies of the Yagu Drawbridge Pavilion and were gone in no time. Amber was also delighted, but the kind of energy she needed right now was different from what the cookies could restore, Mariela thought.

Hearing the excited clamor surrounding the cookies, Emily came running in a clatter of footsteps.

"Mari, Siggy, welcome back! Guess what? When Daddy ate a cookie, he felt sooo much better! We even went to the market together! He gave me a ride on his shoulders 'cause he said I'd get lost. I was up sooo high!"

Emily talked and talked, her cheeks flushed bright pink. She seemed thrilled that her father had spent time with her.

"Emily, time for a bath! And then it's off to bed!"

The inn's owner came out of the kitchen and urged Emily to return to her room.

"But I'm not sleepy yettt," Emily groaned with a pout.

"Mariela's gonna do your hair for you again tomorrow, right? What are you gonna do if you oversleep?" the owner gently admonished.

"Oh yeah! I'll get up nice and early tomorrow and get your breakfast ready. Do my hair again tomorrow, okay?" With that, Emily returned to her room. She was a reasonable child. Tomorrow, Mariela would braid her hair into cute little plaits.

"Hey, thanks for the cookies. Emily and I were able to spend more time together than usual," said the owner, and he brought out a tray with two kinds of dishes on it. It seemed to be a special meal that would let Mariela and Sieg enjoy everything on offer today at once. A gift of thanks from the owner.

They enjoyed it immensely and returned to their room before the evening hours.

05

"All right. Today, I'll be making 'general oil.' This process will be performed by me, Mariela, and my lovely assistant, Siegmund!"

"…I look forward to…working together?" Sieg replied.

Ooh, Sieg's on board.

The two of them had become quite good friends, much to Mariela's delight.

They sat down at the table across from each other and lined up the materials and implements:

A mortar and pestle, orc lard, and orc king lard. Orc king meat was both very delicious and very expensive, but the large amount of lard collected from the meat could be bought cheaply at a few coppers for a fist-size piece. She'd gotten the orc lard as a freebie. Both were fresh and still had some magical energy within.

Mariela put one fist-size piece of orc lard in her mortar and two fist-size pieces of orc king lard in Sieg's.

"All right, knead the lard, pleeease. Oh, but don't put any magical energy in it, okay?"

Knead, knead, knead, knead.

Knead-knead-knead-knead.

When the lard had been smoothed into a paste, they added water infused with Drops of Life little by little and kneaded it again.

"General oil" required whatever magical energy was remaining in the orc and orc king lard, so making it involved manual labor. No matter what, you couldn't use any skills or magic other than the necessary *Drops of Life*. If you did, your magical power would temporarily transfer to the material and erase the faint energy remaining in it.

Knead, knead, knead, knead, knead, knead, knead, knead.
Knead-knead-knead-knead-knead-knead-knead-knead.

"Hey, Sieg. You're from a village near the Fell Forest, right? I know you didn't use potions, but what about medicine? What kinds did they have?"

"There were…no potions in the village. The chemist…was an elderly lady…who made medicine."

Any small village would have at least several healing mages, and medical treatment was generally performed using magic. Apparently, salves and styptics were commonly used as first aid until one could get to a healing mage, and people didn't bother to use magic at all for minor injuries.

If a healing spell was cast on someone to treat an illness, the magic could even heal the disease itself, which was why regular medicine was the more common method of treatment. Healing mages were often loath to use this kind of magic on children in particular, since their lack of resilience could cause them to succumb and die even after being cured.

Since potions could be found in the imperial capital, low-rank heal potions were used there in place of medicine, Sieg explained.

"Where do they sell potions in the capital? For about how much?"

Mariela was grateful the conversation had turned to the imperial capital. It was where Sieg had been purchased, so it was hard for her to ask about it directly.

"Mid-grade and under potions...are sold even in general stores. You buy high-grade ones...at potion specialist shops."

Alchemists who could make high-grade-ranked potions and above ran potion specialist shops. Twelve alchemists in the imperial capital could make high-grade potions, but only three could make special-grade potions. As for the prices, Sieg explained as much as he knew in detail.

"Only twelve people can make high-grade potions?!"

"Were there more...two hundred years ago?" Sieg asked, and Mariela realized something.

Two hundred years ago, there were more people who possessed alchemic skills than there were bakers, but Mariela had no idea how many alchemists could make special-grade- or high-grade-ranked potions.

"Only specialist shops handled high-grade potions in the Citadel City, too. I dunno how many there were in the whole kingdom, but in the Citadel City, there were only three..."

After Mariela was able to make high-grade potions, she'd visited several shops to discuss whether they'd stock her potions. However, every shop turned her away and told her "Don't lie." Since many people possessed alchemic skills, she had believed it also meant many could make high-grade potions and she was chased away because the competition was so fierce. But it seemed she was wrong.

Oh crap, my hand stopped.

Her hand on the lard had fallen still. She added water infused with Drops of Life and resumed kneading. The fat part of the lard emulsified; it was now white and creamy, with bubbles starting to appear on its surface.

Knead, knead, knead, knead, knead, knead, knead, knead, knead, knead, knead, knead.

Knead-knead-knead-knead-knead-knead-knead-knead-knead-knead-knead-knead.

The prices of low-grade- and mid-grade-ranked potions weren't much different from their market prices in the Citadel City two hundred years ago. So they were abnormally expensive just in the Labyrinth City, after all.

"What do people from outside the City think of it?"

"I suppose it's a bit like…a rest stop or safe zone within the Labyrinth. People lump the Fell Forest and the Labyrinth together, and they think the City is safe enough to sleep in within a place like a Labyrinth where monsters roam. It's not considered…a permanent place to live. I was a B-Rank adventurer…and I planned to come here to reach A Rank."

She hadn't thought Sieg would tell her about his past.

He was a B-Rank adventurer…

Apparently, any adventurer could raise their rank by completing a designated number of requests of a difficulty determined by the rank in question. Rising from B Rank to A Rank required far more completed requests than previous ranks, most of which were concentrated in the Labyrinth City. It was more efficient to reach A Rank by accepting requests there.

Since the Labyrinth City was desperate for high-rank adventurers, it offered a service where those of A Rank who lived there would bring those of B Rank who wanted to go to the city. Incidentally, those who took advantage of this service would have to find their own way home, as they wouldn't be escorted.

The ability to get through the Fell Forest by oneself was an appropriate benchmark for A Rank.

If you were B Rank, you could go through the forest with an A Rank leading you. However, if you were C Rank or lower or had a lot of baggage, you had to travel without rest by armored carriage, like those the Black Iron Freight Corps had, to protect yourself from attacks.

There were only three ways for a B-Rank adventurer to leave the Labyrinth City. They could either attain A Rank and fight through the Fell Forest through sheer willpower, travel with a yagu caravan for a month through the mountains, or pay a private group like the Black Iron Freight Corps to carry them as cargo.

Sieg explained all this to Mariela as they continued kneading the lard.

Knead, knead, knead, knead, knead, knead, knead, knead, knead, knead, knead, knead, knead, knead, knead, knead.

Knead-knead-knead-knead-knead-knead-knead-knead-knead-knead-knead-knead-knead-knead-knead-knead.

The emulsification steadily continued, and it swelled and became fluffy like whipped cream.

"Yeah, this oughta be good."

Mariela ladled out two-thirds of the orc whipped cream off the top into a new mortar. The lower part contained impurities other than fat, so it couldn't be used. Then she scooped out about half of the orc whipped cream, put in the orc king whipped cream Sieg had kneaded, and handed the mortar with the mixture back to Sieg.

"Here, knead this."

Knead, knead, knead, knead, knead, knead, knead, knead, knead, knead, knead, knead, knead, knead, knead, knead.

Mariela added orc king whip to the stuff Sieg was kneading in his mortar little by little. The amount was tricky. If there was too little of the orc king whip, the effect was weakened; too much of it, though, and it would separate.

Knead, knead, knead, knead, knead, knead, knead, knead, knead, knead, knead, knead, knead, knead, knead, knead.

"That about does it, I think? Okay, now it's time to warm it."

After the orc whip had been evenly combined with the orc king whip at a ratio of about 1:2, she put each mortar in one large vessel filled with hot water and churned them slowly.

After a little while, the whip separated into oil and water. The orc and orc king oil mixed into a single layer. This fat was "general oil."

The recipe could be found in Mariela's library under *Essential Alchemic Products to Make Your Life Easier* and was meant for advanced students.

"General oil compleeete! Next, we'll use this oil to make orc leather maintenance cream!"

She put about three fists' worth of the genea cream she'd bought at the Merchants Guild shop into a separate mortar.

"Here, Sieg. Knead, knead."

Sieg made a face as if to ask, "More kneading?"

"You can do it, my lovely assistant."

Sieg didn't utter a word of complaint in response to Mariela's encouragement, and he took the genea cream. He kneaded and kneaded some more.

Knead, knead, knead, knead, knead, knead, knead, knead.

Man, it's real handy having an assistant. If I was kneading this all by myself, come tomorrow my arms would hurt so much I wouldn't even be able to lift them.

Genea cream was a vegetable oil that came from the seeds of genea fruit. It was solid at room temperature, but at body temperature, it would melt and permeate the skin. The cream enhanced the healing ability of the tissue it was applied to, as a natural material containing plenty of Drops of Life. It was used long before Mariela was born as a cream for dry skin and general moisturization, and it was also widely used as a base for salves and an ingredient in soap, among other things.

Genea seeds were relatively large for fruit seeds, and the fruit itself had only a thin layer of flesh, but it had high nutritional value and could be eaten. The flavor was harsh and distinctive, and it wasn't something you'd want to eat in large quantities. However, you could chop it or turn it into a paste, then put it on ham between slices of bread or mix it into a salad to provide a robust flavor. Incidentally, genea cream itself could also be eaten, but it didn't taste good, so it wasn't considered food.

Perhaps goblins enjoyed the distinct flavor of genea fruit, because they liked to eat it after it was ripe. Since genea trees grew in the shallow strata of the Labyrinth and Fell Forest, ordinary citizens could harvest the fruit as long as they were accompanied by an escort. The women who worked at the Seele Company before dawn went to the Labyrinth with an escort to pick the fruit and handle it all the way until it was processed into cream. Paintings on the labels of genea cream tins depicted them. The images were of women from middle age to old age, so perhaps it was a service to promote female employment.

The quality of the genea cream was good, and she didn't need to improve it with alchemy. She definitely wanted to use it after this, too, she thought as she added the newly completed general oil little by little to the genea cream Sieg was kneading.

Knead, knead, knead, knead, knead, knead, knead, knead.

Since she wasn't adding moisture to the genea cream, it gradually turned into a soft cream without becoming whipped. When the genea cream and general oil were uniformly mixed, the work was complete.

"Sieg, thanks for your hard work. We've made a cream for repairing orc leather! You can shine the orc leather clothes we bought yesterday with this, and the shoes and bags, too. It'll separate real fast, though, so you have to use it quickly."

Mariela put some of the cream on a piece of cloth, then spread it over the brand-new shoes, bags, and clothes used for gathering to polish them.

"What is this cream?" Sieg was surprised. The quality of the orc leather improved as he watched her apply the cream. It was flexible yet strong. Normal orc leather could barely withstand one hit from a goblin, but now it was entirely different.

"Now it's more like orc general leather!"

Typically, leather maintenance cream was mixed with fat from the same monster the leather was made from. Supplementing with fat from the same species resulted in some amount of tissue regeneration, allowing leather products to last longer.

Of course, simply spreading orc king fat on orc leather wouldn't strengthen it. Even though it was the same orc species, the rank was different, so it would have the same effect as applying genea cream alone, not even regenerating the tissue.

The maintenance cream Mariela made combined orc and orc king fat together with Drops of Life to give an orc king leather–like restorative effect to orc leather. Although it didn't bring it to the level of orc king leather, it did enhance it to the point it resembled mid-grade orc general leather.

Maintenance cream itself separated in about a minute and became useless, but while the strengthened leather might still look like it came from a regular orc, its performance was set at the level of the orc general class.

"If you polish orc leather goods with this stuff, they'll last a suuuperlong time," Mariela cheerfully explained.

An orc's greatest defense was its thick fat, and their leather itself was a cheap material.

Even the quality of orc general leather products made them something that only E-Rank adventurers might use, so the material was inferior to minotaur products, let alone wyvern ones.

"No, isn't this...rather significant? If you could strengthen wyvern leather to mid-grade dragon leather—"

"Ah, that won't work. This stuff's limited to orcs. The recipe said something like 'The essence of orc resides in its meat and fat!' Looks like it's only possible 'cause it's orc."

Mariela had also tried this with other materials before, but none of them had worked very well.

Incidentally, the true value of general oil manifested in orc meat.

"And get this! If you cook orc meat with general oil, it'll taste like orc king meat!" Mariela looked even smugger than she had the whole day. "Not orc general but orc *king*!" she repeated, really driving the point home.

This orc leather maintenance cream was a practical use of general oil.

General oil was recorded in *Essential Alchemic Products to Make Your Life Easier*, and when Mariela became able to make high-grade potions, this hidden recipe had inconspicuously been added.

Per the recipe's notes: "For my unfortunate juniors who can make high-grade potions but can't purchase orc king meat. (*The sale of this item is strictly prohibited. Please treat as a banned substance.)"

The first time Mariela ate orc meat cooked with general oil, it was so delicious that it brought tears to her eyes. So delicious that she even forgot the pain in her arms from kneading the lard. She was profoundly grateful to whoever had developed the recipe.

Sieg had cried when he ate the risotto, so Mariela assumed he'd want to sink his teeth into orc king meat, too. However, despite her diligent explanation, he merely narrowed his eyes suspiciously.

"There are a lot of things I'd like to say, but... Mariela, have you ever eaten orc king meat? Other than what this oil was used on."

"Nope."

"Wouldn't this make the meat taste like orc general? It's called general oil, right?"

"!!!"

Certainly, the recipe had said it was "for my unfortunate juniors who can't purchase orc king meat," but nowhere did it say it would actually turn into orc king meat.

"...Well, it's not as if a general-class oil can't make quality orc leather products." Sieg polished their orc leather items one by one as he spoke, paying special attention to hems and joints that wore out quickly. Mariela followed his example as she polished, too.

Around the time they finished polishing everything, the general oil and maintenance cream separated almost instantly and became useless.

Even though it wasn't orc king flavoring, it had made an incredibly tasty meat. If she'd had time, she would've wanted to put it on some meat, too.

As Mariela cleaned up the fat in disappointment, Sieg

mentioned, "Next time, we'll have real orc king meat. You can afford it now, right?"

"That's true. The Corps paid a lot for my potions, after all. I could even buy orc king meat myself...right? Wait... Huh? So I can even buy orc general or orc king leather goods? I didn't need to make any general oil?"

"......You probably could have. You didn't buy the orc leather on purpose to conceal your fortune, did you...?" Sieg asked as if he was speaking to a pitiful little child.

Mariela flopped onto the bed with groans of "Uuugggh" and "Aaaghhh" in a strange voice.

"I kneaded and kneaded and I didn't need to do any of iiiit..."

"Well, it probably wasn't for nothing. Cheap orc leather won't attract as much attention," Sieg said, trying to comfort her.

He's right; it wasn't totally pointless. And, Sieg, you're talking normally now.

They talked a lot while they were knead-knead-knead-knead-kneading, and Sieg's speech wasn't faltering anymore. Although he'd spoken in broken sentences before, he'd started talking fluidly before she realized it.

"Siiieg, could you please clean up for poor little meee?"

"I guess I have no choice. You can take a bath now, too, if you like."

He was even conversing more naturally. All that kneading really hadn't been for nothing after all.

Sieg was the one who did most of it, though.

Mariela put on her now-polished and sparkling shoes and headed to the bathroom.

06

Early the next morning, the two of them headed for their new house. Gordon and Johan were already waiting in front of the entryway. When Mariela apologized for making them wait, they responded simultaneously: "Gotta get the amateur started early." "Gotta get the old-timer started early." Then, also simultaneously: ""What'd you just say?!""

Incredibly, they managed to smoothly transition into business talk.

They handed over the construction contract and the contract of employment for the slum residents, and Mariela and Sieg checked the contents. Apparently, the contract for the shop portion would come once they'd hammered out more concrete plans.

They were simpler than the one she'd signed with the Black Iron Freight Corps, but they were proper magical contracts with writing like "Any confidential information obtained in the course of executing this contract will be hereby protected."

"Isn't this a bit over-the-top?" Mariela couldn't help asking.

"Naturally," the elder dwarf replied. "Besides, that's a sacred tree, right? I know this from many years of experience: Wherever you've got a thing like that growin', stuff tends to happen. For better or for worse. With this in place, should anything of the sort occur, we'll be protected, too, as long as we don't leak any secrets."

I get it now. Mariela was impressed. The magical contract was properly executed, not just to protect her and Sieg if information like the house layout was leaked but also to prevent Gordon and Johan from being threatened to hand over information.

They confirmed there were no problems with the contracts and signed the construction one. The father-son duo said they'd start work as soon as they got the key. Mariela could pay the remainder of the money owed after the work was completed.

"As for the plans for the shop, we ask that you please have it all together within two or three days," Johan requested.

"Understood," Mariela replied before leaving the house with Sieg.

Now was the time to focus on the glass she needed to build a lovely shop.

That's why today she'd worn the newly polished orc leather clothes for gathering materials and also brought packed lunches.

She and Sieg went to the yagu rental they'd visited three days ago and requested two yagus. They lent her the one she'd used last time and a slightly meeker one. Groups of yagus had a clear hierarchy, and those lower in the pecking order followed behind the higher ones. Traveling in single file was one of the behaviors that made them easy to use for crossing mountains.

Mariela climbed onto the meek yagu and spurred it into motion, but...

"Whoa, hey, too fast, too faaast! I'm gonna faaall!"

...Mariela's yagu ran after Sieg's, which was galloping along in high spirits. She was desperately clinging to the animal to keep from falling, never mind riding it properly.

In the end, the two of them rode on Sieg's yagu like last time and loaded their baggage onto the other one.

"All this after going to the trouble of borrowing two!" It was hard to swallow for Mariela, who was miffed, but since they could travel faster this way, she just had to accept it.

Unlike three days ago, Mariela, Sieg, and the two yagus headed downstream from the river where they'd gathered sand.

Neatly cultivated fields spread through the grain-producing region along the river where the sowing of wheat seeds was mostly finished. The employed serfs may have left for fields farther away where planting was still ongoing, or they were preparing for the Labyrinth expedition. The area was deserted.

Tamamugy grew wild on the banks of the river and would be ready to harvest in another week. Tamamugy was a material used in mid-grade and lower cure potions. Last time, she had bought it at Ghark's herb shop, but she wanted to gather it herself if possible. Since this area was a grain-producing region, she'd asked Ghark earlier if it was okay for her to gather it. As she thought about these things atop the yagu, they reached the end of the grain-producing region. A palisade had been erected here, and the monster-warding plants daigis and bromominthra were planted as well.

This was the end of the breadbasket region that humanity had cleared and reclaimed. The Fell Forest lay beyond the stakes. An extensive amount of palisade had been erected from the grain-producing region to the Fell Forest and stretched on endlessly along the border between the two. Its vastness reflected the people's fear of the forest, and despite using a monster-warding potion, Mariela felt a little scared.

The Fell Forest was even more vast than Mariela remembered. Although she knew this place was a cleared and reclaimed part of the forest, she felt like the trees were closing in on her.

Just to be safe, she used another monster-warding potion before she and Sieg rode into the Fell Forest.

They advanced along the river; it widened as they went farther downstream, but the amount of water decreased, resulting in distinct terrain with a large quantity of sand and small water currents. The soil around here was sandy even down deep, and the river flowed into an underground water vein. As the two of them traveled even farther downstream, the river went completely underground and disappeared.

River sand carried by water currents was deposited around here, turning the place into a high-quality sandpit.

Bit by bit, traces of stone buildings came into view.

This was today's destination. Two hundred years ago, there had been rows of glassmaking studios here.

Mariela and Sieg peeked into the remaining workshops that hadn't crumbled. The yagus also followed, naturally. Maybe they thought Sieg was their boss.

Only a single wall remained of the first one.

Around half of the second building remained, but creepers grew thick on the inside. Not just on the floor but on the walls, too. Maybe there wasn't enough nourishment to go around, as they were all just saplings, but they wriggled along the walls in an extremely revolting way. She decided she didn't want to look there.

They looked at a third and fourth one, but all of them were like this, so there were no remaining buildings with facilities she could use. This place had a lot of creepers because it was near a watering hole. Fortunately, the only kind growing were saplings, and thanks to their orc leather boots, Mariela and Sieg didn't have to worry about getting stabbed by poison needles. In fact, the creatures were so weak, you could almost kill them just by stepping on them.

Sieg went first and stomped them flat, and Mariela followed. The two yagus on either side of her also stepped lightly and trampled the creepers that tried to coil around their legs. Although the animals were simple herbivores, they were very reliable.

Leaving the river and going farther back into the ruins of the ateliers, they only rarely saw abandoned buildings. Thinking it was useless after all, Mariela was about to turn back when she spotted familiar plants.

Daigis and bromominthra.

It used to be an alchemist's workshop. It had no ceiling, and half of the walls had collapsed, but the daigis vines crawling along them and the bromominthra hidden by the trees protected the ruined building.

Maybe here, thought Mariela with high hopes. The moment she peeked inside, Sieg yanked her back.

Bratatatatat.

Stones pelted the place Mariela had been a moment ago. When she got a second look, they weren't stones but seeds she'd seen before.

"Whoaaa, a grown-up creeper."

And a seed-bearing one, at that. It was the intelligent, troublesome type.

Although the daigis and bromominthra had kept creepers from growing en masse, one had miraculously grown very large.

As far as she could tell from her quick glance inside, something resembling a furnace was in the back, and the place looked like a good spot for making glass.

"What should we do?" Sieg asked. Even though their equipment had been strengthened to the level of orc general leather, it was still leather, so the creeper's stonelike seeds would be too much for it.

Come to think of it, Old Man Ghark said seed-bearing creepers could get drunk.

"I wanna look for something that smells sweet, like in a tree hollow. There might be some in there, since it's autumn."

"Monkey Booze?"

"That'd be good, too, but Monkey Lure would be better."

Monkey Booze was a type of fermented liquid derived from the fruits hidden by monkeys or small animals in the cavities of trees. Finding this auspicious liquor was quite difficult. Monkey Lure was another type of alcohol that accumulated in tree hollows, but this type was fermented with tree sap and was poisonous.

Because Monkey Lure was always found in autumn, it was thought to lure prey with the sweet smell of alcohol and kill it with poison to provide nourishment for the tree in winter.

Mariela and Sieg didn't have time now to go buy alcohol and come back tomorrow; it would be a waste of a day. The two of them began to search their surroundings.

"I wish I had the Searching skill."

Sieg could use detection magic to follow familiar sources of magical energy, but he had no skills that allowed him to examine his surroundings for items. During his time as an adventurer, he'd only ever ordered his cohorts to bring him their spoils for him to kill; he'd never done any actual searching himself. The only weapon he could use was a bow, and he was much weaker than he used to be. Even a B-Rank adventurer could defeat a monster like a mature creeper with ease, but now he was of no use at all and extremely irritated with himself because of it.

My father was a hunter; how did he search for prey?

One of Sieg's childhood memories crossed his mind: One time, when he'd come down with a fever, his father had brought him some honey. And when Sieg asked his father how he'd found it, he clearly recalled him saying, "I asked the spirits. 'Please tell me if there's any honey nearby. My son, Sieg, is sick with a fever and a sore throat.'"

After his fever had gone down, Sieg had tried telling the spirits he wanted honey, too, but nothing happened.

"You see, spirits like it when a person says they want to do something for the sake of someone else. But you have to see that desire through your own merit."

That's no help at all, the young Sieg had thought. Come to think of it, that was around the time when the spirits had disappeared from his sight. Sieg had become so selfish, they'd gone and abandoned him. It was only now that he realized how the spirits must have loathed him.

Forest spirits, hear my plea. Mariela wants Monkey Lure. Please would you lend us your power?

Sieg caught himself mentally imploring the spirits and snorted at himself. He was praying to them even though he didn't necessarily believe what his father had said; even though he and the spirits ought to speak different languages. He couldn't even take down a creeper, and his amateurish sword skills were hardly enough to protect Mariela. On top of all that, was he going to leave even the responsibility of searching to someone else?

Mariela was putting forth her every effort to locate some

Monkey Lure. If Sieg had time to pray, he should be searching, too. His nose worked just fine, and he still had one eye left.

Sieg inhaled the scents of the forest and checked the trees one by one as he went farther in. Of course, to avoid monsters, he couldn't let his guard down. He didn't want to endanger Mariela. He wanted to grant her wish.

Just then, a gentle breeze wafted a sweet scent his way.

"! Mariela, over here."

When he followed the direction of the smell, he found a single tree releasing a fragrance.

"Sieg, you found it! Way to go!"

Mariela rushed over in great delight. She industriously stuffed the Monkey Lure into a disposable rubber bag made from creeper sapling.

"I'll take some mushrooms, too, while I'm at it."

She picked and refined some poisonous-looking fungi growing in the vicinity before adding them to the Monkey Lure.

"Mariela, what are those mushrooms for?" Sieg asked, implying she was doing something weird again.

"These're a poisonous type that'll make you get really dizzy and pass out if you eat 'em. Just a single one will have you out for three days straight, and pairing it with alcohol will get you drunk instantly. This place is incredible; it's full of stuff that'll put you away for good."

Mariela divided her special sleeping potion containing Monkey Lure into several rubber bags. She made all the bags into a size that could be carried in one hand.

The preparations were complete. They returned to where the seed-bearing creeper was to begin their process of subduing it.

The strategy was simple: They merely had to hit the monster

with a rubber bag containing the Monkey Lure and break it open. The creeper would suck up the substance off the ground, and when it lost consciousness, Sieg would approach and take it down. Mariela and the two yagus would be in charge of retreat. On the small chance Sieg was caught by the creeper, they would yank the rope tied around his waist and flee.

Actually, it wasn't exactly a foolproof strategy. Especially the retreating part. Would the yagus and the creeper end up playing tug-of-war with Sieg in the middle?

Sieg apparently had no interest in being captured; after he handed the end of the rope to Mariela, he got behind one of the walls that was still standing and threw a ball of Monkey Lure through one of the gaps.

He threw the ball, then dodged the incoming seeds and threw another in quick succession.

Thanks to his excellent agility, Sieg wasn't getting hit at all. Plus, he was landing everything very close to the creeper. Mariela cheered him on while oohing in admiration, and the two yagus munched on fallen creeper seeds out of harm's way.

Come to think of it, it'll be lunchtime soon. I wonder what we've got packed today.

As Mariela fell into a daydream, the creeper started acting intoxicated. Sieg threw the remaining bags of the Monkey Lure at it just to be on the safe side. Once he saw that the creeper wasn't reacting, Sieg took his small sword in one hand and approached the monster.

The yank-and-retreat squad remained at the ready. Mariela and the yagus watched Sieg attentively through a gap in the wall.

First, he cut off the pods packed with seeds and then severed the poison needle–bearing appendages at their base. The creeper must have been completely out, because it didn't even twitch.

After chopping off every last appendage, Sieg cut off the creature's central stalk. It was about as thick as a human neck. A large bud-like thing about the size of a person's head was attached to the tip.

The creeper's leaves trembled in fear. It no longer had its limbs or seed-filled pods with which to attack.

The remaining leaves turned brown and withered before their eyes. They'd managed to safely bring down the creeper. Mariela was really glad no one had gotten hurt.

"Yes! Great job, Sieg! That was awesome!" she shouted with joy. She and the yagus ran over to him.

Sieg laughed in apparent embarrassment and said, "I'm glad it went well."

They ate lunch to celebrate their victory, and Sieg thought it tasted even more delicious than usual.

After their lunch break, the first thing was to process the creeper materials. While Mariela dried the pods, Sieg burned and tied up the cut ends of the appendages so the viscous liquid wouldn't spill out. The yagus had eaten the scattered creeper seeds, so that issue was taken care of. The head-size bud contained magical gems roughly the size of fists, and the two of them were able to collect a bunch.

The former alchemist's workshop still had what looked like a prototype furnace for melting glass. The refractory had peeled off, but there were piles of clay nearby that had been used to make it, as well as a shed full of materials for making glass: sand, the main component, and lum stones and trona crystals, the subcomponents. There was also broken pieces of glass that had deteriorated to a pure-white color. Combining all of it with what Mariela bought at the Merchants Guild yesterday would provide her with enough materials.

The sand, lum stones, and trona crystals had deteriorated from prolonged exposure to the elements, but heating them all up would restore them to their original state. Mariela dried the sand and heated the subcomponents to return them to usable form, then took the furnace's crumbled refractory and varnished, dried, and molded it like clay.

The preparations were in order.

She threw firewood into the furnace, infused metallic beads with magical power, and created a Spark.

"Come forth, Salamander, spirit of flames!"

The ring on her right middle finger emitted a flash of light as she chanted; it was the one given to her by the salamander she'd summoned when crafting potion vials.

The fire twisted and flickered and took the form of a small lizard.

It was the same salamander. It really did come back.

"Mr. Salamander, lend me your power. I'd like to get things real fired up today."

The spirit turned to check out the furnace it had been called to, then chomped down on the Spark Mariela had created.

The fire burst with heat all at once.

With this much thermal power, she could make everything in one go. For every hundred portions of sand, she used fifteen lum stones and a fifth of a trona crystal. After mixing in the deteriorated glass fragments, she used her alchemic skills to put it all in the furnace.

She gave the salamander ample Spark whenever it slapped its little tail up and down to ask for more. Perhaps the spirit's power even had an effect on melted items, as the melted glass slowly formed a vortex and changed into a uniform liquid. All that remained was to harden it, but this was the most difficult part.

The only recipes involving glass-crafting were for potion vials, and she had just a smattering of knowledge of how to make plate glass. Because this glass was highly viscous, it was handled differently than the kind for potion vials that you blow and inflate. The furnace was the only equipment left in the workshop—there wasn't even so much as a device to salvage glass—so she'd have to come up with some other way of using her alchemic skills.

"Thank you, Mr. Salamander. I'd like just a little more help, but first, here's a li'l token of my gratitude."

Mariela fed the salamander lots of Sparks and turned her attention to the furnace's aperture. Although the spirit couldn't comprehend human language, it seemed to understand what she wanted to do. It gulped down the Sparks, then looked at her quizzically.

"Form Transmutation Vessel, Control Pressure: Vacuum."

She made a vessel about as thick as her forefinger and as long as her arm, then placed it on the surface of the melted glass and removed the air from it. With a *shwp*, it sucked up the glass.

Whoa, the Transmutation Vessel broke.

The high temperature was too much. In a fluster, she made two more vessels in the shape of rollers just as long as the previous one, then rolled the glass between them.

The rollers spun just about as quickly as the first vessels had broken. They would break from end to end, but since they were rotating right before breaking, the glass was getting pulled upward. She would then repair the broken Transmutation Vessels before they came into contact with glass again.

While the lifted glass was still soft, she cut it into uniform pieces, and Sieg stacked the finished plates in the shed. The drawn glass rapidly cooled and hardened, starting from one end— probably the salamander's doing. Mariela didn't have enough time to do that much; without the spirit's help, the plate glass would have hardened while it was still wavy and elongated.

This is touuugh...

Mariela couldn't even speak. There was no comparing the drain on her magical reserves between this occasion and the last. It was as if the magic were flowing freely out of a gaping hole in her body. The speed at which she had to regenerate the Transmutation Vessel rollers was just too fast. The glass had to be drawn quickly. Quickly, quickly—before she ran out of magic.

Somehow, she was able to pull all the glass out of the furnace before collapsing unconscious on the spot.

07

"Someone call a healing mage! Mariela is... Mariela is...!"

Siegmund rushed to the Yagu Drawbridge Pavilion carrying Mariela. She was clammy and unconscious.

One of the guests who appeared to be a healing mage saw how distraught Sieg was and examined Mariela for him.

"Ahhh, she simply ran out of magical energy. There's no need to worry so much; she'll wake up tomorrow morning."

Sieg breathed a sigh of relief. The inn's owner urged him to put her to bed, and while one of the lady staff changed Mariela's clothes, Sieg went to return the rented yagus.

When he arrived back at the Yagu Drawbridge Pavilion, the owner asked him what he wanted for dinner.

To leave my master's side for a mere meal would just...

Siegmund hesitated to take a seat, but the owner told him, "Eating's part of your job, too," and offered him some food. He cleaned his plate in silence, then returned to the room.

Mariela was sleeping peacefully in her bed.

Sieg quietly pulled up a chair and sat by her side. Seeing her like this made her look even younger than she was.

That skill of hers was incredible.

He recalled how Mariela had crafted the glass. She pulled it again and again out of the blinding white-hot furnace, cut it, cooled it before his very eyes, and passed it his way. Things kept speeding up, and he felt as if he was witnessing one of the most magnificent uses of magical expertise.

What a tremendous amount of magical reserves, Siegmund had thought, trembling in awe.

And yet—after the final piece of glass had been lifted out, Mariela suddenly collapsed where she stood.

He thought she'd stopped breathing. His heart pounded a mile a minute, and his stomach clenched and spasmed. When he scrambled over to her and lifted her up, her face was white as a sheet, but she was still breathing.

Holding Mariela in his arms, he urged the yagus on at full speed.

His hand holding the reins trembled. Breathing was difficult, as if his worry were crushing him. It felt as if his insides were full of rocks.

If I don't hurry, if I don't get Mariela to a healing mage quickly, I'll...I'll—!

"I'll be in a real fix if my master dies."

Siegmund covered his face with both hands.

That's exactly what I thought back there...

That *he* would be in trouble if Mariela died.

I'm grateful to Mariela. I owe her a great debt. She saved me from suffering a fate worse than death itself. She treated me as a human being, giving me three meals a day, clean clothes, new shoes, a warm bed, a daily bath, greetings every morning and night, casual conversation, everything. Everything. Not long ago, I had none of that...

Sieg lifted his face and saw two hands he could move freely and without pain. No more than a week had passed since this ability—something so normal for most—had come back to him.

I've already started taking all of it for granted.

Of course, he understood in his head. He was a penal laborer, and he would have been unlikely to find a master other than Mariela who would give him this kind of life.

Mariela was likely the only alchemist in the Labyrinth City. Even setting aside her rarity, her alchemic prowess was certain. Siegmund believed she was on the same level as the alchemists in the imperial capital. All that aside, however, Mariela herself was just an incredibly ordinary, unremarkable girl and a bit sillier than others her age.

He remembered what Lynx had said to him back at the inn's

rear yard: "She's just a regular ol' happy-go-lucky doofus of a woman."

I thought so, too. So I wanted to protect her—I resolved to protect her, to cherish her, to look after her... I believed I'd be there for her when Lynx wasn't. He was right. Other than being an alchemist, she's just a regular country bumpkin. I even thought she'd only kept me around for her own convenience, that if I had a kind enough smile, if I pampered her like royalty, surely I'd fall into her good graces. All the women I've known up to now have been like that. Mariela is precious to me—she saved my life; no other woman can even compare. She's wonderful, the only one I need. I felt that from the bottom of my heart. But surely I felt that way because Mariela is...irreplaceable, the perfect master, isn't she? I want to be special to her; that's no lie. I want a place in her life. Truly. I don't want to lose everything all over again—her smile, our daily greetings, the meals we enjoy together, her warmth, her kindness, this stable livelihood...

Siegmund recalled the week they'd spent together. He recalled her smiling happily and sometimes sadly. Her hands sticking out from under the sheets were so small, yet they'd given him everything. He couldn't forget how tenderly those hands had touched his face that first time. Her compassion, seemingly free of charge, was vividly seared into his heart even now, when he'd grown accustomed to being given everything. Even so...

Ahhh, what a selfish human being I am.

Siegmund had realized it deep down, and he balled his hands into tight fists.

I thought I was acting for Mariela's sake. How could I have thought that?

He hadn't been aware of his own feelings. He'd deceived even himself, and he felt a stitch tighten in his chest.

It was all for myself, wasn't it…?

Indeed, Siegmund had been observing his new master ever since she'd healed him—her personality, her likes and dislikes. He didn't talk unless asked a question, nor did he say anything beyond what was necessary. The idea that it was better to stay silent than to risk offense had sunk deeply into his consciousness from his long tenure as a slave.

He was actually against hiring people from the slums to work on the house. He didn't know what kind of trouble that could invite. But he hadn't said so. Mariela was a kind, gentle soul who'd bought him when he was on the brink of death.

If stopping them from getting hired would make Mariela think I'm coldhearted, then it'd be better to do as she wishes. If by chance something does end up happening, then all I need to do is protect her as best I can. Then she'd surely be grateful toward me.

He hadn't pointed out the problems such selfish thoughts might cause.

Not that he was fully aware of these ugly thoughts, these ugly feelings. They were almost entirely unconscious, because he'd deceived himself into thinking he was doing it all for *his master's sake*—for *Mariela's* sake.

He took the handkerchief out of his pocket. The name Sieg was embroidered at the edge in small letters. Mariela had given this handkerchief to him the day they met. He had been so happy and grateful, he had never parted with it, so she'd said, "I'll mark it so you don't mix it up with the others," and stitched it on for him.

The clothes he was wearing now, the shoes, the underwear, even his body—none of these belonged to him, and yet, he felt as if he'd received something to call his own; it made him so very happy.

There were no ulterior motives in Mariela's kindness.

He gently stroked the sleeping girl's head.

"Mm... Masterrr... Food..."

She often talked in her sleep like this.

He was certain she was lonely. Her master had assumed responsibility for raising her when Mariela was very young and was something like a foster parent. Whenever she talked about her master, no matter what kind of story it was, she always spoke with such deep affection. She said she'd become independent in her teens and had been living alone in the Fell Forest ever since.

When the Stampede broke out in the forest, I bet she escaped alone, activated the magic circle alone, and awoke all by herself two hundred years into the future. I don't understand what suspended animation is, but if it's like a very long sleep, then it's no wonder she's still afraid of the great disaster that destroyed a kingdom in one night. She must have been so ill at ease to wake up in a completely different world all alone without a single familiar face. Even when she purchased me, she could have been thinking of any number of ways to make use of me: as a source of information, a guard, a laborer. But it seems it was her own loneliness that brought her to extend a help-ing hand to me, as a child might pick up a stray dog on the side of the road. She wants a place where she belongs. I'm sure that's what was on her mind that evening at the entrance to the Labyrinth.

That's how normal a girl Mariela seemed to be.

Siegmund gazed at Mariela sleeping in the bed.

They said people who got kidnapped would sometimes fall in love with their captors, that someone who thought highly of the ones who held their life in their hands had a greater chance of survival.

Without a doubt, Mariela holds my life in her hands...

They also said injured or sick people treated by a healing mage would occasionally become attached to them.

There's no mistaking it was Mariela who saved me from dying...

Siegmund understood he harbored strong emotions toward her.

My feelings for Mariela...

No matter how much he ruminated, his thoughts kept going in circles, and he couldn't arrive at an answer.

What should I do from here on out?

Regardless of whom he was doing all this for, his desire to protect her was true. He understood in his head that providing counsel was necessary for that.

But I want her to like me; I don't want her to think badly of me. I don't want to voice any dissent.

And above all else...

I never want Mariela to know about these foolish feelings...

...he felt a tremendous surge of fear at the idea of Mariela learning what was going on in the depths of his heart.

Siegmund remained in the labyrinth of his thoughts as the night went on, until dawn broke at last.

"Sieg, good, uh, mornin'?"

Mariela awoke after a good, long sleep, looking completely refreshed.

She was surprised to see Sieg sitting in a chair at her bedside.

"Good morning, Mariela..."

He looked absolutely beat, his greeting utterly listless. Confused, Mariela wondered what was wrong.

Ahhh, that's right. I ran out of magic and collapsed yesterday.

She'd probably made him worry. And upon closer inspection, wasn't that his favorite handkerchief he was gripping so tightly?

Mariela got up and sat on the edge of the bed so she could look at him face-to-face.

Sieg's gaze was downcast and wouldn't meet Mariela's eyes as she peered at him.

"I'm sorry, Sieg. I made you worry."

"Yes..."

"Must've been quite a shock, huh? I should've told you I might run out of magic."

"Yes..."

"And here you'd be in dire straits again if something happened to me. I'm so sorry I worried you, really I am."

Sieg suddenly shivered and looked at her.

"Mariela... I..."

Sieg's mouth gulped repeatedly for air.

Did Mariela know—? Had she noticed? He was so utterly afraid of her finding out.

"I... I've been buttering you up. I don't want to go back to the way I was before. I don't want to lose everything. It's all for my own sake, even though you...you were the one who saved me—"

"Yeah. I know. It's okay, Sieg. I still love you no matter what you're like, so don't worry about it."

There was nothing romantic about Mariela's "I love you." Even Siegmund knew that much.

His tears spilled out in large drops, and Mariela stroked his head to comfort him.

That day, Sieg finally understood—even a puny, good-for-nothing coward like him, someone unable to comprehend his own thoughts and feelings, would be just fine right here, by Mariela's side.

Beneath the Sunlight's Canopy

01

Hundreds of soldiers marched along the main road toward the Labyrinth.

They were clad not in splendid, showy regalia but in shoddy armor cobbled together from magical metal and monster hide. Some wielded long-handled weapons like halberds or spears, but the only thing they all had in common was that each soldier wore a jet-black cloak. Every single one marched in perfect order.

These were the Labyrinth Suppression Forces, the strongest army in the Labyrinth City. They had tackled the lowest strata of the Labyrinth countless times and lived to tell the tale.

Many adventurers and citizens had gathered along the main road to see them, and it really was like a festival.

The cheering grew louder.

"It's the Gold Lion General!"

"Generaaal!"

A heroic-looking man with a thick mane of golden hair reminiscent of a lion rode atop a magnificent horse and responded to the people's cheers.

"With the general at the helm, one soldier is as good as ten men!"

"The man himself is incredibly strong, too."

"He's the mightiest general in history. It's about time for the Labyrinth monsters to reap what they've sown."

The enthusiastic fanfare continued until the expeditionary force disappeared into the Labyrinth.

Their two-week-long Labyrinth campaign had begun.

"Your right side's open!"

"What're you doing standing still?! You ain't using a bow here!"

"You're swingin' that thing way too slowly!"

Every time Haage called out to urge him on, Sieg was sent tumbling to the ground. He was getting clobbered, to say the least.

After watching the parade go by, Mariela and Sieg had headed to the Adventurers Guild. Today was the start of Sieg's training there. Mariela had come along as well to observe.

After verifying Sieg's aptitude with appraisal paper, Haage discussed with Sieg their combat objectives and settled on the one-handed sword combat style. After spending most of the first day's lesson strictly on practice swings, they were now having a sparring match.

Sieg had been agile enough to avoid a barrage of creeper seeds, but he couldn't even begin to compare to Haage. Every time Sieg slashed at him, Haage took advantage of the opening to rap him with the tip of the staff he used in place of a sword. Even though the hits didn't look very strong, Sieg always lost his balance and tumbled to the ground.

The ol' baldy Haage's really givin' it to him…

Mariela mentally narrated the fight as if she knew what was going on, but truthfully, she had no idea even as she watched. Although Sieg seemed to have long since reached his limit and was unsteady on his feet, he got back up every single time he was knocked down, eager for more. Somehow, she could tell he would

be fine. Mariela's gaze shifted down to the book she'd brought with her, *The Encyclopedia of Medicinal Herbs and Their Effects*.

Mariela thought Sieg seemed a little different ever since the day after she'd exhausted herself making glass.

When she'd woken up, he was whimpering a little for some reason, so she'd tried something a teacher at the orphanage had taught her: "If a child looks sad and says things you don't really understand, just hold them tight and tell them, 'I know; it's okay; I love you.'" It had worked beautifully.

Sieg had said stuff like "I've been buttering you up" and "for my own sake," but Mariela felt that was only natural. It wasn't as if he'd been particularly bothering her. He'd even searched so eagerly for the Monkey Lure, so if "for Sieg's sake" and "for Mariela's sake" happened to line up, wasn't that enough?

After she'd woken up, Sieg transported the glass she'd made to their new home and given them an excuse: "A creeper was guarding it. Some merchants must have left it behind."

The day after she ran out of magic, Sieg asked her to rest at the inn, so she'd passed the time making medicines and potions. She showed up at the new house the day after Sieg brought the glass there. For some reason, the dwarf population there had increased by one by the time she'd arrived.

Two dwarves and the half dwarf were having a heated discussion in the storefront area, surrounded by glass and scattered sheets of blueprints. All three of them had bags under their eyes as if they hadn't slept.

"Good morning…?"

"Name's Ludan. I'm a glassmaker from the same engineering firm as these guys. I've also joined in to work on the design."

As Ludan explained, glass this big was never used as is in the Labyrinth City, since people assumed monsters might swarm in from the Fell Forest or the Labyrinth. It would be cut into smaller parts and used in metal window frames. Even if some of it broke, someone with glasswork skills could fix it, and items made from repaired glass were used in ordinary people's houses in creative ways. Therefore, generally speaking, the quantity of the glass itself wasn't unusual.

"I'm just itchin' to get goin' on this project."

"We'll keep it reasonable."

"Wouldja let us do it?"

The three dwarves were bursting with enthusiasm, and Mariela decided to have them do the work under the condition they "keep things inconspicuous."

They settled the contract, and she paid the remaining money for the residence and the fee for the storefront. Including the advance payment, the total came out to seven gold coins. The leftover amount had been rounded up compared with the initial estimate, but considering the added window frames, it was cheap. She heard the three people they'd brought from the slums worked surprisingly hard, so they were appointed to work on the storefront, too.

"I'd like to meet those three."

At Sieg's request, Mariela decided they'd introduce themselves to all the workers.

The three people from the slums were young adventurers who had to take time off from adventuring due to injury, and although they were a bit thin, they didn't seem especially poor. You wouldn't know they were from the slums unless you were told.

"We choose people who should be able to get out of the slums when they recover enough to earn even a minimal livelihood. Since we're also working, it's difficult to hire people who've put down roots in the slums, as you might imagine," Johan explained. He said as long as the expedition was going on, the injured adventurers could gather materials in the shallow strata of the Labyrinth even if they hadn't fully recovered, and with this work, they wouldn't have to part with their weapons or borrow money. Sieg listened intently.

Mariela asked the three about their injuries, then told them about the medicine she'd just made yesterday and handed them a few samples. It was ordinary medicine created by referencing "How to Make Medicine: Beginner's Edition" at the back of *The Encyclopedia of Medicinal Herbs and Their Effects*, and it had also received Ghark's authorization. Since the samples weren't in potion form, their wounds wouldn't be healed immediately, but if they used it every day, they would probably recover faster.

The workers happily received the samples. "Once we're adventuring again, we'll come buy some more from you," they told her.

When she saw the joy on their faces, Mariela regretted not being able to give them potions.

She bought more ingredients and returned to the Yagu Drawbridge Pavilion, crafting more medicine to pass the time, but she couldn't help wondering if she could be of more help somehow.

02

"If your eye ain't doin' the trick, compensate with magic!"

"Your left arm's just hangin' there! You call that guarding?!"

"Too slow, too slow!"

Haage bellowed as he used his staff to strike Siegmund's openings. Although they were by no means strong blows, they would have probably been fatal if Haage had been using a real sword; Sieg fell to the ground with each strike as if he'd just dropped dead. He would fall, get up, and then fall again.

I'm used to pain. After I became a slave, I was forced to my feet even when I was too exhausted to stand. It's seared into my very flesh.

His muscles, his flesh, his bones all cried out in silent agony, yet Siegmund got himself up time and time again.

Haage's blows were quick, heavy, and precise. Every time Sieg tumbled to the ground, his body learned little by little the correct way to move. He truly felt he'd found a good instructor.

He reached for his practice sword to learn as much as possible in their limited time together. Training continued until he could no longer lift even a single finger.

"One thing I'll say is—ya got guts!" Haage said to his immobile trainee. "Aren'tcha ashamed to fall down in front of the young lady?"

Mari...ela......

The lack of oxygen made him dizzy. He couldn't even move his head, let alone look over at Mariela.

"Don't worry! She's so absorbed in her book that she ain't even watchin'!"

Bam! Haage gave a snappy thumbs-up. Siegmund hated that huge grin.

Just like that, Siegmund slipped out of consciousness.

"We're done for the day, young lady! There's a watering station in the back, so when he wakes up, he can wash up before going home!"

Apparently, Sieg's training had wrapped up while she was reading her encyclopedia.

Having given Sieg a thorough trouncing, Haage grinned widely, his pearly whites on full display as he returned to the Adventurers Guild's armory. The sunlight reflecting off the back of his head was dazzling.

"Sieg, wake up." He didn't respond when Mariela called his name.

All I did was run outta magic, and he made such a big fuss, keeping me cooped up in bed the whole day, and now look at him—he trained so hard he passed out. Geez!

Mariela rummaged around in her bag and produced a vial containing thirty green pills. This was a high-grade, health-restoring magic medicine called Regen, something she'd made during her forced convalescence at the inn.

As a deep-healing medicine, it would even restore a life span shortened by harsh conditions if you continued to take it regularly for about a month. It was a convenient pill believed to increase muscle strength in a short period of time when taken while training. Sieg, who'd seen plenty of hard days his lifetime, needed this medicine, and she was giving him three vials over one month.

Even regular potions could reduce fatigue from training, but since they'd just restore the body to its pretraining condition, it was pointless. In that respect, the Regen medicine increased the body's healing capacity, allowing the results of training to show at the highest efficiency.

The ingredients were snapping clams from the wholesale market, sacred tree leaves, creeper sapling, and planada moss. The moss was a rare potion ingredient that didn't appear on the market much, but she'd gathered a lot when she was crafting vials by the river. The processing method for the new material, snapping clams, was easy, and she was able to memorize it quickly. Once she got used to making the Regen medicine, it wasn't hard.

On first glance, the small grains that shone through the dark-green pills looked delicious, but they were in fact extremely bitter. The acrid taste, possibly the result of boiling down slime and creeper, filled your mouth with an unripe flavor that lingered, so the pills were coated with a thin layer of gelatin.

"Hup!" She took a pill from the vial and stripped off a bit of the gelatin with her fingernail, then tossed it into Sieg's mouth.

"*Cough*, ugh..."

"Ooh, he woke up."

That's Regen for ya. Its effects are spot-on!

Mariela spent the five days after she woke from her fainting episode buying and preparing a bunch of miscellaneous items to use at the new house, making medicine to sell at her shop, and observing Sieg's training.

Even outside his lessons, Sieg seemed to practice early in the morning while Mariela shut herself in the room making medicine. His gaunt cheeks gradually filled out, perhaps a result of the Regen.

They left the Yagu Drawbridge Pavilion and moved into their new home on the appointed day, but sometimes they'd stop in for an early dinner to see Emily. The inn swelled with adventurers as the evening went on, and Amber and the other ladies were very busy. They thanked Mariela when she gave them the medicine they'd asked for, saying it was a big help, and told her they'd come to buy more once her shop was open for business.

The ladies offered to introduce Mariela's apothecary to their adventurer customers, so she handed out lots of salve samples and flyers on which she'd written the opening date and a map. She'd have to find some way to thank them after she opened her shop.

Mariela and Sieg went to the wholesale market for lunch almost every day. All the materials the adventurers brought back were likely in circulation by now, because there were more items and heavier foot traffic than usual.

They found and purchased the necessary ingredients for medicine and potions, and before long, the shelves covering the walls of Mariela's workshop were lined with vials and bags of processed materials.

"I'd like to hurry and get these shelves filled up. The shop will be finished by tomorrow. I also need to set up all the products and get ready for opening day. So, so busy."

The prospect of her new life had Mariela's heart aflutter.

03

"The shop's renovations are complete."

The dwarven trio of Gordon, Johan, and Ludan greeted Mariela and Sieg with huge smiles. The front entrance to the shop had been out of service during the renovations, so neither of them had seen the interior. They could have peeked in through the windows or the rooftop, but they chose not to so that they could look forward to seeing the finished job.

At last, they entered the completed shop through the front entrance.

"Oooh, it's so bright!" Mariela was so surprised, she could muster only a limited vocabulary. The ceiling had been fitted with several glass windows.

They weren't that large on their own, but glass of different sizes had been embedded to imitate lovely tree branches and leaves, and the shadows of the grid on the floor created the impression of standing under the shade of a tree.

"Is this...a sacred tree?"

"Exactly right. Since there's one planted next to the house 'n' all," said Ludan, the glassmaker. "The branches don't reach this far, but this way you feel like it's protectin' ya."

"Not only that," added Johan, the architect, "these windows may look normal, but they actually have a three-dimensional structure. They're designed so that light will always shine in while the sun is out. And the skylight's been crafted to make sure the shop is well lit."

She didn't understand how it worked, but it was kind of incredible. Mariela stared up at the skylights with her mouth agape. The windows were a little bigger than what you'd see in other shops, but they didn't seem out of place. Aside from where medicine was stored, it felt like a sunny spot outdoors. Moreover, it gave her a feeling of peace, as if she was literally under the sacred tree itself.

"And...what're these chairs and table for?"

Gordon, the last dwarf to speak up, was sitting at a table right in the middle of the patch of sun when he answered.

"This is where I like to come."

"That's, uh, not an answer."

As Mariela had requested, the shop's center had a counter fitted with shelves for employee use, and display racks had been installed in the back where customers could view products at their leisure. Apart from these, for some reason there was a table that seated six people right smack in the middle of the sunshine and counter seating near the wall by the entrance that sat five people each. The chairs appeared to be made of scrap material from the previous storefront, but they'd been shaped to fit in perfectly with the new shop. The place was almost like…

"…A café?" Mariela wondered.

Gordon, Johan, and Ludan had seated themselves in the sunshine.

"Ahhh, this spot is the best."

"I'm burstin' with creativity!"

"Real nice…"

The dwarven trio started to really unwind when Sieg served them tea.

According to the trio's explanation, they had inspected the finished glass ceiling's workmanship the day before Mariela and Sieg got there.

"Quality's good."

"Uh-huh. But the shop's too big and a li'l dreary."

"It would be a waste not to enjoy this sunny spot."

"We got some scrap wood here. Wanna make some chairs?"

Tap, tap, clang, clang.

"I want some tables, too, about this size."

Tap, tap, clang, clang.

"It's too rustic; these won't fit in."

Tap, tap, clang, clang, tap, tap, clang, clang.

"Well, there ya have it."

There I have what? Mariela thought, but it wasn't bad as a spot for injured or ill customers to relax. Since it was a free gift, she decided to accept it gratefully.

"Ohhh, Miss Mari, I see yer shop's finished." A fourth dwarf arrived—no, wait, it was just Ghark. "Oh? This's a real nice place." For some reason, he joined the circle of dwarves at the table. Though it didn't seem as if they were acquainted, he didn't look out of place at all. "Miss Mari, if ye can spare the lad, I'd like some tea, too."

Um, sure, there's some space to relax in here, but this is an apothecary, *not a café! No, no, it's all fine. Once we stock the shelves with medicine, it'll definitely feel more like an apothecary.*

"Mariela, what should we do about the shop's name?" asked Sieg, interrupting Mariela's thoughts.

He gazed at the old men as they enjoyed basking in the sun and drinking the tea he'd prepared. In the blink of an eye, the shop had caught the four old men, hook, line, and sinker.

"Hmm, how about 'Old Man Grab Bag'?"

In the end, they decided to call the shop "Sunlight's Canopy."

No one's gonna know what kind of place this is from the name alone—not that they'll know even when they come inside, but hey, that works just fine.

After enjoying the sunshine for a while, Ghark returned to his shop. He told her he'd take her gathering in the Labyrinth the night after tomorrow. Her first labyrinth. She was way too excited.

After Ghark went home, the three dwarves finally seemed to return to reality and showed Mariela and Sieg the shop and galley.

First was the kitchen next to the shop. Since it used to be a galley, it was the size you'd expect, and the new dining table there had room for two or three people to sit and eat. It was conveniently designed so that the door served as a partition whenever it was open, blocking the inside of the kitchen from the shop's view—a rather user-friendly design.

Or maybe more like a café-friendly design. I mean, that's basically what they were going for here, right?

What surprised her was the magical tool that could be ignited and its heat adjusted with mere buttons. When she asked where to put in the firewood, Sieg explained to the dwarves, "We're from a village out in the sticks. Mariela, this doesn't need firewood," and gave her a demonstration.

That was quick thinking with the three dwarves here. Never thought our "childhood friends" story would come in so handy.

Something caught painfully in Mariela's heart.

There were magical tools for water in the kitchen, bathroom, restroom, and washroom, and each room had a magical tool for ventilation and a vent installed in the ceiling. Mariela had thought the windows of houses in the Labyrinth City seemed small and gloomy, so she couldn't believe how convenient this all was.

When she asked Sieg about it later, he explained that magical tools generally handled tasks that used to be done with lifestyle magic. It was one of the policies implemented by successive generations of margraves to make up for labor shortages in the Labyrinth City, and since the city subsidized the tools, they were also installed in commoners' houses.

However, the tools consumed many times more magical power than lifestyle magic did, and even when people had access to them, they often ended up resorting to magic. In particular, magical implements that needed to be kept running for extended periods of time—such as for storage and ventilation—used magical gems, and the cost of those was nothing to sneeze at.

There were even tools for laundry, heating, and sweeping, but anything easily accomplished through human labor alone cost a lot of money. Such tools weren't included in Mariela and Sieg's new house. Factoring in maintenance costs, it would be cheaper to hire someone or buy a debt laborer to do housework.

Regardless, Mariela was shocked at the incredible progress in technology.

The quality of modern medicine might be lacking, but perhaps alternatives to potions would turn up sooner or later.

They'd been living there for two days, and Mariela understood the residential portion of the house now. The living room, which had been used to store raw materials before, was now spick-and-span. There was no carpeting or furniture apart from the chairs and tables left by the previous residents, but she wanted to gradually gather some. Also, apart from the beds that were repaired for them and the dressers, there was no furniture in Mariela's or Sieg's bedrooms. The bedding alone made for a rather dreary place, like a hotel room.

As Mariela was wondering what kind of furniture to put there, Gordon said, "Oh, I almost forgot," and took them to the cellar.

The cellar had three rooms linked sequentially, the first of which was where Sieg had put the materials from the creeper he'd felled, and they planned to use it as a storeroom. The second room was furnished with the amount of emergency rations and evacuation tools designated by the "Labyrinth City Special Laws Residential Affairs Regulations Something-or-Other," enough for two people.

The third room had a wooden box in it for some reason.

"A massive hole opened up in here, y'see. Looked like the sacred tree's roots reached the Aqueduct and caused the floor to collapse. I went down to check, and the roots do in fact go all the way to the Aqueduct. Boy, I'd heard about it in stories, but gettin' to see the thing in person is a rare opportunity. Oh, but this didn't affect the drainage, and the wall's still sturdy, as ye can see. Since we're right under the sacred tree, monsters probably won't come up, but I hear the Aqueduct's got lotsa slimes, so we put a box stuffed with daigis here just in case."

With that, Gordon went on home. That was extremely important information to be casually dropping at the very end of his explanation.

I wonder if this is why the place went unsold for so long?

The Aqueduct was a remnant of the era of the Kingdom of Endalsia. Even now, two hundred years later, it still functioned as a sewer system in the Labyrinth City. Each home was installed with drainage treatment tanks called slime tanks, which held domesticated slimes tailored specifically to treat sewage. The sewer system wasn't a source of infectious diseases because clean water flowed into it after being purified by the sewage treatment slimes.

However, wild slimes seemed to propagate in the underground Aqueduct.

A slime was an amorphous, mucus-like monster with no intelligence. It was a weak creature that could be killed by crushing its nucleus, and you could do so just by stepping on it as long as it hadn't grown significantly. Also, since it lacked an outer shell, it was extremely vulnerable to magic absorption and wouldn't come near daigis plants. You could prevent slimes from leaking out of the Aqueduct just by planting daigis around the pipes that connected to it.

Although slimes preferred corpses with magical power remaining in them, they could decompose some organic and even inorganic substances, so they were used to treat human excrement and kitchen waste. Wild slimes attacked by generating acidic liquid from the components they'd decomposed, but trained ones would spit out lumps of earth during the decomposition process. These clumps were collected regularly by dedicated contractors for use as fertilizer.

Slimes were very familiar monsters and closely entwined with everyday life, but...

"Doesn't feel all that great, being so connected to the Aqueduct while it's full of squirming, mucousy monsters, huh?"

Even without the sacred tree, they could use dried daigis to prevent slimes from invading, but just logically knowing that didn't keep it from feeling unpleasant. She imagined them wriggling and oozing their way through joints in the walls' masonry.

"Let's fill the joints with daigis fibers later. After that, we should make sure to water the sacred tree so it doesn't wither."

Sieg and Mariela nodded to each other, agreeing to keep the third room closed off for the time being.

They'd unexpectedly found a literal pitfall at the very end, but she was glad both the shop and the house had turned out fantastically.

Mariela bought some orc king meat and made it into steak for the two of them to celebrate with. It was so good that tears came to her eyes. Turns out meat cooked with general oil has the flavor of orc general, not orc king after all.

Ohhh maaan, orc king's so good! It's just waaay too good! It

might be a vile creature that likes to attack women, but now it's all just meat to me.

Full of emotion and her cheeks stuffed with meat, Mariela had a request for Sieg.

"Shiiieg, you gotta get really shtrong 'n' take bown lotsa orkings!"

"I'll take down as many as you want, so please either eat or cry or talk, not all three at the same time."

The shop was scheduled to open in one week. She needed to buy everyday supplies, craft the merchandise, and collect tamamugy and a variety of mushrooms outside the Labyrinth City. All sorts of things could be harvested in this season. Mariela wanted to return to the spot where her cottage used to be and transplant the surviving medicinal herbs. Ghark said he'd take her foraging in the Labyrinth the day after tomorrow. She wondered what they might find.

The two of them enjoyed silly conversation over their orc-king-meat dinner for a while. Afterward, she tried out the appraisal paper she'd bought at the Adventurers Guild shop. Mariela needed to see what kinds of effects that two-hundred-year-long sleep had on her.

An appraisal paper was a type of form with data written in thin magical ink. When activated with a drop of blood, the color of the ink for the corresponding item changed to indicate the condition of the subject.

The seven abilities that could be appraised were stamina, magical power, strength, intelligence, dexterity, agility, and luck, and each one was evaluated on a five-point scale. For example, if your stamina was a one, one of its white squares would change to black. If you'd broken through the upper limit, the final black square would change to red. It was quite a useful piece of paper.

Also included was a list of the various skills the user possessed—if you had aptitude in a skill, its name would change to black; if you simply possessed a skill, it would change to red. If you had skills or talents that weren't listed, the "Other" column would change color.

If you wanted to know something that couldn't be gleaned from appraisal paper, you would have to pay a lot of money to someone with the *Person Appraisal* skill. However, appraisal paper was sufficient as a guideline for occupation options or growth strategies.

Mariela's magical power exceeded the five-point scale. To a certain extent, stamina and magical power didn't change much once you stopped growing. An exception, where both attributes would rise even in an adult, would be when the person has hovered on the barrier between life and death.

Her increase in magical power was likely a result of being in a state of suspended animation for two hundred years. She'd been aware of this change ever since she awoke, but where it used to be at the fourth level out of five, it now exceeded the upper limit of the appraisal paper. She hadn't known the exact value, but when she'd run out of magic while making the plate glass, she'd gotten a general sense of it. What pleased her even more was her stamina; before, it hadn't even reached a one on the scale, but now, it had risen to a two. She went from a one-hit KO to a one-hit almost-KO. She couldn't help from cheering and striking a little pose, showing off her "muscles."

The other items on her chart hadn't changed, however. She

still had only one skill, Alchemy; her lifestyle magic abilities just barely broke even.

Sieg was surprised to see Mariela's magical power, but Mariela was even more surprised to see his appraisal paper. All the items on his were threes or fours. Although it was a five-point scale, that didn't mean a three was average. A one indicated an everyday level, and if something was a three, it meant you could get a job using that trait. Mariela's strength and agility were only ones, but since she was an alchemist, her intelligence and dexterity were threes. For some reason, her luck was a four, the only ability of hers that surpassed Sieg's.

Sieg has more intelligence, even though I'm an alchemist. What the heck?

Mariela secretly folded up her appraisal paper and tucked it away in the back of her bedroom dresser.

04

"Light the incense and don't let it go out."

With Ghark in the lead, he, Mariela, and Sieg entered the Labyrinth. Mariela was unable to fight, so she was in charge of burning the monster-warding incense. The incense was made from dried and powdered bromominthra, and though it wasn't as good as a monster-warding potion, it was enough to keep the weaker monsters at bay. The incense was also easy to make, and plenty of the bromominthra grew both within and outside the Labyrinth City, so more than half the population could make it themselves. During the expedition, when the Labyrinth was crowded with people, Mariela had even seen children from the orphanage near the entrance selling baskets full of incense they'd made themselves.

It was late at night when the monsters were most active, and although she didn't see any children, a steady stream of adventurers trickled in and out of the Labyrinth—probably unique to the expedition period.

Just two guards kept watch at the entrance, and other than children who tried to go in to play, no one was barred from entering. Apparently, the guards' main purpose was as a point of contact in times of emergency.

As Sieg explained, other labyrinths had entry fees, and you even had to forfeit a portion of any materials obtained inside as taxes when you exited. The Labyrinth City, on the other hand, levied taxes only on materials taken outside the city limits; there was no tax for using them within the City itself. Incidentally, imported goods weren't taxed, either, but because it was so difficult to travel to the City, there was a chronic shortage of foreign goods.

The inside of the Labyrinth emitted a dim glow despite the dark, moonless night. Scattered across the cave-like rock face were stones known as moonstones, which gave off just enough light to walk around. Nonetheless, the low visibility wasn't sufficient for fighting monsters or gathering herbs, so Ghark donned night-vision goggles while Mariela used Sieg's night-vision magic.

Ghark steadily descended into the Labyrinth, felling the

occasional monsters that appeared—ones with poor senses of smell, such as goblins, slimes, and wraiths—with his double ax. To Mariela's surprise, Sieg had been taking down the ones at the group's rear, so she took the chance to observe the Labyrinth, all the while adding more monster-warding incense to the burner in her hand.

The stairs between the Labyrinth's different strata were concentrated at the center, making it easy to move from one level to another. These stairs were said to appear when you defeated the boss located somewhere in each stratum.

Mariela gave a slight shudder as she imagined the Labyrinth's mysterious leader birthing its underlings, the stratum bosses, as it ate its way straight down into the Labyrinth's depths.

"It's just up ahead. I'm gonna use a sleep orb, so put on yer masks."

Per Ghark's instructions, Mariela and Sieg donned masks soaked with stimulants to keep them awake. Ghark then tossed a lit sleep orb through a gap between some rocks. The faintly glowing moonstones were arranged in such a way that at first glance, the gap appeared to be a joint between the rocks, but a closer look revealed it was big enough for adults to pass through. Only the entrance was narrow; inside was a passage the same size as all the others in the Labyrinth.

Mariela followed Ghark into the chamber and was startled by what she found.

It's full of snakes...

They were small for monsters, but snakes with arms were lying asleep all over the place.

"There are a lot more of 'em than before. I'll cull 'em a little," Ghark said, then began to make quick work of the monsters as he went deeper in. He crushed the small ones' heads with his foot and chopped off the heads of the larger ones with his ax. Not long after they died, the majority of monsters in the Labyrinth would then start to fade and dim before their corpses eventually dissolved into thin air.

It was said this happened because their magical power hadn't manifested physically yet.

If a monster lived a long time, its magical power condensed into gems and manifested inside its body. When they were defeated, those gems could be collected as materials.

The snakes here were still young and weak, so most of them disappeared without leaving anything behind, but every so often, the larger ones left their fangs or magical gems the size of the tip of a fingernail. A bag full of the fangs sells for quite cheap, but they make effective painkillers. Ghark defeated the snakes along their route, while Mariela picked up the magical gems and fangs. Sieg cut down the more conspicuous snakes while acting as her bodyguard.

The winding, S-shaped snake passage looked like a dead end from the entrance, but once they turned the first corner, Mariela saw a hazy glow shining through the exit.

Maybe the snakes hated this light, because their numbers dwindled as the group got closer to it.

A bright, open chamber lay at the end of the snake passage. The space was narrow enough that it would take less than ten seconds to walk from one end to the other, and the ceiling was practically sky-high. Many moonstones shone on the walls and ceiling in an underground, starry nightscape.

The entire floor was covered in knee-high grass, much of which had buds emitting a gentle light.

Thousand-night flowers. These bloomed only once every one thousand days.

The buds spread so far across the chamber that it looked as if a full moon were shining down on them.

"Any minute now."

As if they'd been waiting for Ghark's cue, the thousand-night flowers burst into bloom.

The buds snapped open with a popping sound, scattering beads of light into the air.

Pop, pop, pop.

One by one, the beads spilled out of the blooming flowers and slowly fluttered up to the ceiling in fairy-tale-like beauty.

"So...pretty."

"They'll wilt if we don't hurry up and pick 'em," Ghark told Mariela as she gazed spellbound at the lights.

The buds had no effect, and the flowers themselves quickly wilted after blooming. It was a shame to not be able to enjoy such a magnificent spectacle, but these flowers were a valuable resource that could be obtained only once every one thousand days. Ghark, Mariela, and Sieg picked off the petals and put them in bags.

They must have picked about half of them. Many still remained, but Ghark beckoned her and Sieg to hurry and get out. The moment they reached the snake passage—

Plink, plink, plink, plink.

—a mass of pebbles rained down on the chamber they'd just exited.

"Ohhh, just in the nick o' time." Ghark laughed in amusement. The fluttering beads of light had been pollinated in midair and turned into seeds before falling back down to the ground. The seeds had a pointed shape to pierce the Labyrinth's tough ground, and if the trio had continued carelessly harvesting the flowers, they would've been turned into seedbeds.

"I only go in that chamber when the thousand-night flowers bloom. It's just a nest o' snakes otherwise."

The snakes in the passage must've run away from the hail of seeds, thought Mariela. *That's labyrinth plants for you—gorgeous but freaky.*

Mariela and Sieg tried to give Ghark half of the thousand-night flowers they'd collected, but he turned them down: "What ye pick is yours to keep."

Whoa, nice!

"Make me another cuppa tea next time I visit yer shop."

Ghark wouldn't take the fangs or magical gems from the snakes, either. He gave Mariela and Sieg a wave before returning to his shop. "We're not a caféééé!" Mariela hollered after him as she waved back.

05

At last, the opening day for Sunlight's Canopy arrived.

Many different items had been arranged in the display cases, from commonplace medicines such as salves and pills to soaps in both powdered and liquid form for use in laundry, dishwashing, or bathing; miscellaneous goods like cosmetics; monster-warding and insecticide incense; and consumables such as smoke bombs and sleep orbs to be used while exploring the Labyrinth. Mariela didn't know how much she'd be able to sell, but just in case, she had a bunch more stockpiled in the living room.

She'd also purchased various herbal teas at Merle's Spices to help her customers relax. She had plenty of cups, too—not that she was running a café here.

Sieg hung up a banner outside advertising the shop as an apothecary and put out a signboard showing they were open for business. A new one-handed sword hung at his waist.

It was a gift from Mariela on his fifth and final day of training.

Mariela felt Sieg had worked very hard. He'd studied under Haage every other day, exchanging blows until he could no longer stand. At first, Sieg had barely landed so much as a scratch on his instructor, but by the end, he'd even managed to beat him in a sparring match. His formerly emaciated body had developed muscles, perhaps partly thanks to the Regen medicine; he seemed like an entirely different person from when they first met.

As she watched Sieg gain muscle and grow stockier, she secretly worried what would happen if he got super-beefy, whether he'd be too heavy for a yagu to carry anymore. However, Sieg's growth stopped at the perfect point.

When she talked to him about it later, he explained, "If I gain too much muscle, it'll slow me down. My physique now is more suited to my fighting style."

"I see. That makes sense," she'd replied as she sewed the buttons of Sieg's pants back where they originally were.

Since the only weapon Sieg had was the short sword Lynx lent him, Mariela got him set up with a one-handed sword for his final day of practical training.

When the fifth day of training came to an end, Sieg bowed deeply to Haage and expressed his thanks. Haage dispensed some advice before telling him, "Ya got serious guts, kid! You'll grow even more if you apply yourself! Seems the young lady has a graduation present for you! Be sure to use it to keep her safe!" With that, the training was complete.

"Sieg, good job with your class. I got you this in honor of how hard you worked. Take it."

Mariela gave Sieg the one-handed sword she'd secretly prepared for him.

"Mariela...is this mythril? You're giving something this nice to me...? It fits perfectly in my hand, like it was specially made. A sword you chose for me. I'll cherish it. Thank you so much."

Deeply moved, Sieg reverentially received the weapon from Mariela. He gazed at its blade, then knelt on the ground and held it out to her.

"My sword is yours."

It was like a scene in a legend. Sieg swore fealty with the sword Mariela chose for him in his hand—his cheeks red with exaltation, his blue eye moist with resolve.

I can't... I can't tell him I had Haage choose the sword!

Instead, she gave a vague laugh and went with the act.

The sword was a good one—at least, from what Haage told her anyway—but it seemed like the kind of thing even B-Rank adventurers didn't own. On Sieg's third day of training, after he'd passed out like normal, Mariela had consulted with the instructor.

If something were to happen to Mariela, how could Sieg, a slave, make a living? Was there anything she could leave him?

Haage knew about Sieg from his appraisal paper at the beginning of their training, so she was right to ask him. Although Sieg's attitude and sweaty appearance didn't make it obvious, based on what Haage had seen in his training up to now, Sieg didn't seem to be an ordinary individual.

Haage didn't flash his trademark blinding grin but quietly looked to Mariela and the unconscious Sieg, then closed his eyes for a little while.

"Slaves with combat ability are priceless in the Labyrinth City! If you're gonna leave him something, a weapon would do the trick. A slave and his own familiar weapon are treated as a set. His manners ain't bad, either, so I doubt he'd be parted from it!" Then, as always, he beamed from ear to ear.

When Mariela said she didn't know what kind of weapon would be best, Haage mentioned he had some ideas. She showed him ten gold coins, about half of what she owned.

"...Don't make things hard for Sieg, now. That kinda money ain't something to be wavin' around all willy-nilly, young lady!" he exclaimed in shock. Still, he promised to find Sieg a weapon he could use for a long time. Haage was a kind man, just as she'd thought.

The sword Sieg held was made of mythril. His appraisal paper had shown he boasted a variety of talents in weapons and magic. His innate skill was with a bow, but with further combat experience, he could probably pick up some swordsmanship skills as well. However, since he had only one eye and was mostly going to act as an escort for Mariela, who couldn't fight, Haage had apparently trained Sieg with a focus on strengthening his body in tandem with wielding magic.

"Mythril's a good conductor of magical energy, so it suits Sieg's fighting style. And after it channels his magical energy just once, it won't channel anyone else's. It'll be a weapon special for him."

The mythril blade given to Sieg was a high-caliber specimen that came recommended by Haage, who also introduced Mariela to a master blacksmith who could repair it. He left nothing to be desired.

Behind Sieg, who stood overwhelmed by the mythril sword, Haage gave a snappy thumbs-up before departing, his broad grin positively radiant.

He's a guy who dazzles in many ways, not just with his smile.

It was a stark contrast to Sieg, who was holding his sword aloft with deep emotion.

"Okay, let's get back to Sunlight's Canopy."

"Yes, let's."

Mariela and Sieg returned to the home where they now belonged.

When Haage returned to the Adventurers Guild, a guild staff member approached him.

"You're in a really good mood, huh?"

"Sure am. It's been a while since I last had a student with a backbone. The first time I saw him, though, I thought, *Man, what a chump! How'd he end up in such bad shape with all that talent?* But he really sank his teeth into it even after I gave him a proper trouncing. Must be that young lady's doing."

"Well. Training the rookies is good and everything, but don't you think we're picking up too much of your slack?"

"You guys can manage, right? Rookie training and military enhancement—those're what's most important."

"We've certainly received our fair share of 'proper trouncing'

from you, too. However, Guildmaster, we've received a call for reinforcements from the Labyrinth Suppression Forces."

Haage's eyebrows twitched. A call for reinforcements from the Labyrinth Suppression Forces? From the Labyrinth City's mightiest? Inconceivable.

"I'll go right away. You folks oughta get ready, too. Ask Lightning Empress Elsee to look after things in my stead.

"This is gonna be a royal pain," muttered the guildmaster of the Adventurers Guild, Haage the Limit Breaker.

06

Sieg returned to Sunlight's Canopy after putting up the signboard for opening day. He flung the doors open to see they were decorated with flowers to celebrate the renovations. Amber had brought the bouquets and said, "The Black Iron Freight Corps asked me to bring this one when the shop opened. The other one is from us ladies." One of the bouquets featured flaxen flowers tied with a greenish-blue ribbon the same color as Lynx's clothes. It felt as if Lynx himself was right there with them.

The Corps had met Mariela, the sole survivor of the Stampede, in the Fell Forest and taken her to the Labyrinth City. Instead of just leaving the poor girl all on her lonesome, they somehow let themselves get tangled up in her affairs. Right about now, they were probably traveling through the Fell Forest on their way back to the Labyrinth City from the imperial capital. Even now, in their absence, their meddling and concern for Mariela still filled her heart with joy.

Several adventurers arrived at the shop thanks to the flyers and samples Amber and the ladies at the Yagu Drawbridge Pavilion had handed out. The salve samples had worked well, and the new customers were buying medicine, incense, smoke bombs, and other sundries. And it wasn't just Amber who came by; Ghark, the dwarf trio, and even Emily all showed up in turn to Sunlight's Canopy to relax under the patch of sun and do some shopping. Not even a month had passed since Mariela had come to the Labyrinth City, and yet, there were already so many people who cared about her.

Sunlight's Canopy was neither a roaring success nor exceptionally busy, but it had turned into a quiet, calming shop that was never without customers.

Sieg stood beside Mariela, who was all smiles at seeing what a wonderful shop it had become. Everyone they knew was gathered under the dappled sunlight. Lynx and the others would return soon, too.

No trace remained of her life two hundred years ago, but in this town, in Sunlight's Canopy, she'd managed to carve out a new place where she belonged.

"Mariela, I brought these sweets to celebrate the new shop. How about we share them with all these folks?"

"Wow, thank you, Merle! I'll go make some tea."

The spice shop proprietress had come bearing a large basket stuffed with confections. The shop was much livelier now; those who were offered tea sat in open seats and began chatting or even helped make the tea despite being customers. Sunlight's Canopy

was originally intended as an apothecary, but now on opening day, it was anyone's guess as to what kind of shop this was.

"I want some tea, too, miss!" a customer teased.

"This ain't a café!" Mariela responded with a laugh.

For the first time since she had awakened, the cold loneliness of having nowhere to turn disappeared, and warmth filled her instead.

"Congratulations on the shop, Mariela," Sieg said with a slight smile when their eyes happened to meet. He always stayed close by her side. Even though he'd once completely forgotten how it felt to enjoy things, his smile was as natural as could be. Mariela smiled back, similarly brimming with joy.

"Thanks, Sieg. I can't wait to see what the future holds for us!"

Mariela—the alchemist, the survivor—would build a life for herself here in this town. Even if it wasn't guaranteed to be a quiet one.

Appendix

Mariela ♀ Age: **16**

A young lady alchemist. She fortunately survived the Stampede but spent the following two hundred years asleep. Thanks to her master's teachings, she's an extremely skilled alchemist for someone her age; however, having spent most of her life as a commoner, and because of her carefree, happy-go-lucky disposition, she's unaware of her own prowess. The Labyrinth City may be a relatively small place, but it's plenty big for Mariela, who used to live in a tiny cottage in the Fell Forest. Her new life here, surrounded by kind people, fills her with hope.

Siegmund

♂ Age: 25

Born with a powerful ability known as the Spirit Eye, Siegmund had a lack of self-discipline that led to his eventual enslavement. Mariela saved him from the brink of death, and he's now settled into the role of something like both her guard and guardian. Siegmund is a sensitive soul with a good head on his shoulders and a tendency to worry a lot. However, with the help of Lynx's scolding and some comforting from Mariela, he's come back into his own and is making an effort to look at things in a more positive light. His feelings toward Mariela are complicated, hovering somewhere between deep affection and respect, but alas, he has yet to say anything to her about it.

Lynx

♂ Age: **17**

A young man who serves as a scout for the Black Iron Freight Corps. A sociable person who quickly makes friends with Mariela, though he can be a bit nosy. Perhaps out of concern for the blithe young woman, he gave Sieg a pep talk and even lent him his short sword. Lynx admires Captain Dick and tells Mariela he wants to be as tall as the captain—although Lynx is fully grown by now. A glutton who eats enough for two people, yet his height and weight never change.

Dick ♂ Age: 28

Captain of the Black Iron Freight Corps; a large-built man who wields a spear. Mariela thinks he's useless because he's either standing silently behind Lieutenant Malraux, getting drunk, or conspicuously fondling a cushion, but with the might of the Black Iron Freight Corps behind him, he's one of the most influential people in the Labyrinth City. He makes quick work of any monsters that get in his way, but Amber always makes even quicker work of *him* over at the Yagu Drawbridge Pavilion.

Malraux

♂ Age: **27**

The lieutenant of the Black Iron Freight Corps and the only married member. He's the brainy type—the polar opposite of Dick—and has both manners and good sense in spades. Perhaps a little thickheaded, as he hasn't realized Mariela is an alchemist. Malraux may seem calculating from his speech and conduct, but given the ways in which he's acted out of concern or interest in spite of profit—for instance, allying with Dick or allocating Sieg to Mariela—deep down, he may not be so different from the captain after all.

Ghark
⚥ Age: 70

The elderly owner of a medicinal herbs shop in the Labyrinth City. People may call him "old man," but his mind and body are still plenty active; Ghark goes into the Labyrinth himself to gather materials for his shop. Has a wealth of knowledge about collecting medicinal herbs and looks out for Mariela in one way or another, whether it's teaching her methods for gathering herbs or taking her to valuable harvesting sites. Perhaps because they share the same stubborn pride in their work, he gets on quite well with the dwarves, and he often drinks tea with them now that Sunlight's Canopy is open for business.

Master* Mariela's
Alchemy Recipes

Low-Grade Edition

* Unofficial title

Monster–Warding Potion

Be sure to bring some when adventuring or exploring!

A low-grade potion with an odor that will drive monsters away.
Works like magic on doggy types! Odorless to humans, so even
ladies can use it worry-free!

【Ingredients】 Daigis: A type of creepy, twisting ivy plant. Absorbs
magical energy. Grows anywhere.

Bromominthra: A purplish-red plant that emits an odor
monsters hate. Planted outside the outer wall along with
daigis.

【Quantity】 Daigis: 1 handful
(per potion) Bromominthra: 1 handful

Low–Grade Heal Potion

For scratches, gashes, and even dry skin.

Heals injuries that would normally do so on their own.
Drinking it works fine, but since it's a low-potency, low-grade
potion, applying it directly to the injury is more effective!

【Ingredients】 Curique: Grows wild everywhere. Easy to locate because
of its distinctively uneven leaves, which can also be
crumpled and rubbed onto very minor injuries and the
like. Young leaves and stems have a greater effect.

【Quantity】 Curique: 1 handful
(per potion)

Low-Grade Cure Potion

Stop stomachaches! Works for numbness and dizziness, too.

This'll heal just fine on its own—such thoughts can prove fatal! Cures minor maladies from upset stomach to monster venom.

【Ingredients】 Jibkey leaves: A medicinal herb that grows in the shade. Distinct for its reddish leaf tips and stems. Oxidization reduces its antibacterial properties, so drying it at a low temperature heightens its effects.

Tamamugy seeds: Grow in wetlands. In autumn, they bear ears filled with fruits the size of the tip of a pinkie finger. Their effects are heightened when taken with jibkey leaves.

【Quantity】 Jibkey leaves: 1 handful
(per potion) Tamamugy seeds: 10 (approx.)

How to Create Potions

1. *Dehydrate* the herbs and *Pulverize* into small pieces.

2. Dissolve Drops of Life into water.

3. Put the crushed herbs in the water mixed with Drops of Life, stir, and use *Extract Essence*.
Shake!
Shake!
Shake!

4. Use *Separate Dregs* to filter and remove the powdered herbs.

KYU (SQUEAK)

5. Once you use *Condense* to reduce it to about half volume, use *Anchor Essence* to complete the potion!

! *A Word of Advice*

Generally speaking, you should *Dehydrate* medicinal herbs before you *Pulverize* them.

You can mix them with *Extract Essence*, but shaking is faster.

If you don't properly *Condense* the herbs, the potion will have a weaker effect and odor.

Don't forget to use *Enclose* after putting the potion in the vial, or else it'll quickly evaporate!

Limit Breaker's Time

Kept ya waiting! This is the start of my story! There are several key words for Volume 2 hidden throughout the Life of Haage. It's a marvelous system where the words in bold are hints of the next book. That's what *Limit Breaker's Time's* all about!

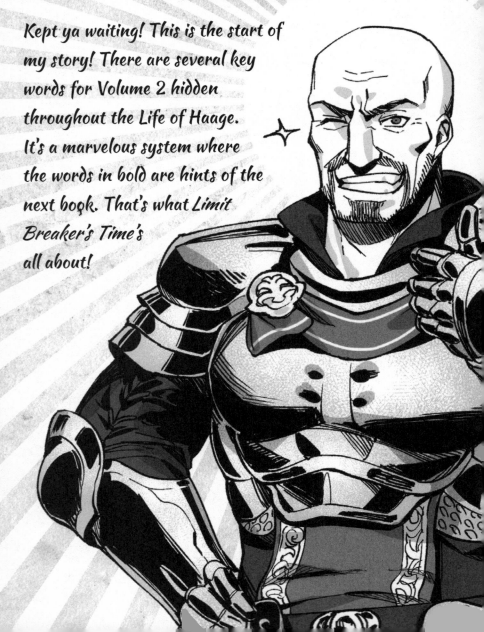

The slums are full of slimes, and the tables are overflowing with orc meat. The Labyrinth Suppression Forces finally reach the sea to exact revenge, and the alchemist's tale now awakens from a two-hundred-year-long sleep...

Haage was heartily gobbling up the packed lunch his beloved wife had prepared for him when one of his subordinates spoke up.

"All your lunches recently have been orc meat sandwiches, haven't they, Guildmaster?"

"Dey're filled wif lof from m'wife!"

"Urgh, how gross. Guildmaster, please swallow before you talk!"

After closing his mouth at his subordinate's behest, Haage gave a snappy thumbs-up. Why was it still so sweltering in here even after he'd closed his mouth? The number of lights in the room hadn't changed, and yet, the area around Haage's head was extremely bright. Staring at the guildmaster, the subordinate brushed himself off to get rid of the bits of chewed food, and then his eyes fell on the paper the lunch box had been wrapped in.

"Hmm? Isn't that paper about the *Orc Festival*? Speaking of, all the paper your lunches have been wrapped in recently is—"

Limit Breaker's Time!!

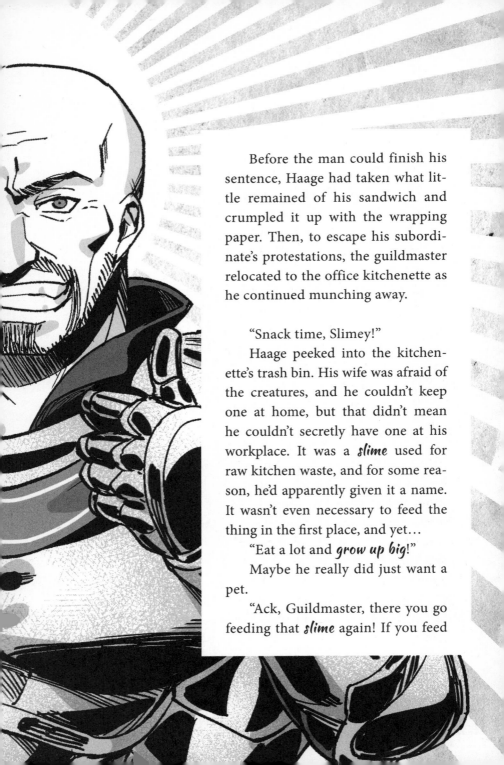

Before the man could finish his sentence, Haage had taken what little remained of his sandwich and crumpled it up with the wrapping paper. Then, to escape his subordinate's protestations, the guildmaster relocated to the office kitchenette as he continued munching away.

"Snack time, Slimey!"

Haage peeked into the kitchenette's trash bin. His wife was afraid of the creatures, and he couldn't keep one at home, but that didn't mean he couldn't secretly have one at his workplace. It was a *slime* used for raw kitchen waste, and for some reason, he'd apparently given it a name. It wasn't even necessary to feed the thing in the first place, and yet...

"Eat a lot and *grow up big*!"

Maybe he really did just want a pet.

"Ack, Guildmaster, there you go feeding that *slime* again! If you feed it too much, it'll *overflow*, and then what will you do?!"

Was there nowhere for Haage, the guildmaster of the Adventurers Guild, to catch his breath? He turned his back on the subordinate chewing him out and headed for the reception desk.

"Here's the latest delivery."

"Thank you very much, as always."

A beautiful young lady was talking to the shop clerk. Apparently, she was a chemist who'd come to deliver some items.

She was a skilled *chemist*, but he couldn't help wondering how things might be different if the city had potions. She seemed to be supplying some *new medicine* that was *red and black* to the Labyrinth Suppression Forces. *What kind of product* could it possibly be? Would using it *help capture the Labyrinth*? Haage never stopped hoping the people of the Labyrinth City would continue their *peaceful lives*.

"Eh, what will be, will be!"

Nobody paid any attention to the loitering Haage the Limit Breaker, the A-Rank adventurer-turned-guildmaster. It didn't mean he wasn't utilizing some secret skill. Averting his eyes from the adventurers who happened to be in the vicinity, he flashed his teeth in a wide grin, gave a thumbs-up, and returned to his own room.

Perhaps to finish some work.

Limit Breaker's Time!!

AFTERWORD

First of all, I'd like to thank everyone who has read this far into Volume 1 of *The Alchemist Who Survived Now Dreams of a Quiet City Life.*

It's now autumn, and the leaves on the trees are changing colors. Oddly enough, this season, when Volume 1 was released, is also the season when Mariela woke up from her long sleep.

It's a season for enjoying persimmons, chestnuts, potatoes, and a new rice harvest, but the colorful leaves scattering to the ground as they fall also create a sense of loneliness and melancholy. Perhaps it's nature's way of urging us to prepare for the coming winter.

Mariela awoke in such a season. Apart from her abilities, there's nothing to support a girl her age in the Labyrinth City. Even if she wants to go home, she has no choice but to live here. I think the loneliness of autumn resembles her thoughts and feelings. When you get caught up in daily life, you don't often take the time to look at the changing sky and foliage. But you've gone to the trouble of reading this far, so why not do so as you wander through autumn in the Labyrinth City?

Mariela may seem like a lucky "you can do it if you try" kind of girl, but in reality, even if she tries, even if she works hard, it's rare that things go her way. Similarly, I never thought in a million years my own work would be published. I am truly, eternally grateful for everyone who's supported me ever since I decided I wanted to be a novelist. It's thanks to your kind thoughts and identifying any errors within the text that I've been able to continue my writing.

To ox, who spruced up this book with such gorgeous illustrations expressing the essence of Mariela; Kawana, who designed Mariela's lifestyle; my editor Shimizu, who so meticulously arranged everything; and everyone at Kadokawa, thank you so much for all you've done.

Autumn will pass us by, and winter will arrive at last. The wind blowing through the Labyrinth City will carry with it the truths from two hundred years ago, and the snow will then similarly pile up over everything it exposes. I look forward to sharing these scenes with all of you in Volume 2.

Usata Nonohara

I ALWAYS USE ILLU- MINATION MAGIC, SO I FORGOT...

LIGHTING A FIRE IN A LOCKED ROOM WOULD JUST DEPLETE ALL THE OXYGEN.

OH...

...UNTIL THE DOOR TO THE ENTRANCE ROTTED AWAY...

EVEN WHEN THE STAMPEDE WAS OVER, I JUST KEPT ON SLEEPING...

JUST... JUST HOW LONG WAS I ASLEEP—!?

も さっ

MOSA (OVERGROWN)

WHY'S THE ENTIRE GROUND COVERED IN IT—!?

HERE'S A MEDICINAL HERB I GREW IN MY GARDEN...

SFX: PUCHI (SNAP)

HMM?

THE LANTERN'S... FLAME?

DID THE MAGIC CIRCLE OF SUSPENDED ANIMATION FAIL?

THE LANTERN WAS FAINT, BUT I SWEAR I TRIPLE-CHECKED EVERYTHING.

HMM...

HUP!

SAFE TO SAY THERE'S NO TRACE LEFT OF MY COTTAGE.

MUST'VE BEEN SWALLOWED UP BY THE STAMPEDE.

...AND THERE WAS THE STAMPEDE...

MONSTERS CAME FLOODING IN FROM THE FELL FOREST...

I... SURVIVED, HUH?

GOKU
(GULP)

GOKU

POU
(GLOW)

DROPS
OF LIFE.

......

PHEW
...

OH
YEAH...

KOFF!

KOFF!

HYUU (WHOOSH)

VENTI-LATE.

UGH...

PAKI (CRACK)

KOKI (CREAK)

DOKUN
(BADMP?)

DOKUN